FIREWALKER

Josephine Angelini is a Massachusetts native
and the youngest of eight siblings. A real live
farmer's daughter, Josie graduated from New
York University's Tisch School of the Arts in
Theatre, with a focus on the classics. She now
lives in Los Angeles with her screenwriter
husband . . . and she can still drive a tractor.

Books by Josephine Angelini

The Starcrossed trilogy
Starcrossed
Dreamless
Goddess

Trial by Fire
Firewalker

Chat to Josephine Angelini and find out
about her other books here:

facebook.com/josephineangelini

twitter.com/josieangelini

mykindabook.com/josephineangelini

WITCHES DO NOT DIE QUIETLY

JOSEPHINE FIRE-WALKER ANGELINI

MACMILLAN

First published in the US 2015 by Feiwel and Friends

First published in the UK 2015 by Macmillan Children's Books
an imprint of Pan Macmillan
20 New Wharf Road, London N1 9RR
Associated companies throughout the world
www.panmacmillan.com

ISBN 978-1-4472-6085-1

1 3 5 7 9 8 6 4 2

A CIP catalogue record for this book is available from
the British Library.

Book design by Eileen Savage
Printed and bound by CPI Group (UK) Ltd, Croydon CR0 4YY

For Pia

CHAPTER

1

LILY LAY FLOATING ON A RAFT OF PAIN. TERROR KEPT HER clinging to it. If she slipped off the side, she knew she'd drown in the smothering darkness that swelled like an ocean under the sparking surface of life. She wanted to let go, but fear wouldn't let her. When the pain became too much to bear, she hoped that at least the fear would end so she could allow herself to slip weightlessly into the hushed waters of death.

But the fear didn't end. And Lily knew she couldn't let go. She was a witch. Witches don't die quietly in the cold, muffled silence of water. Witches die screaming in the roaring mouths of fire.

"Open your eyes," Rowan pleaded desperately. Wading her way back to the sound of his voice, Lily forced herself to do as he said. She saw his soot-smeared face, smiling down on hers. "There you are," he whispered.

She tried to smile back at him, but her skin was tight and raw and her face wouldn't move. All she could taste was blood.

"Do you recognize this place?" he asked, looking around anxiously. "I've never seen anything like it." He tilted her up in his arms so she could glance around.

It was nighttime. Lily felt pavement under her hand and realized they were lying in the middle of the road. She heard a jingling sound when she moved. The shackles and chains from the pyre were still bound to her wrists, the weight of them dragging down her arms. She focused her eyes and looked up the street. It was snowing. The streetlamps were few and far between. Woods surrounded them, but not the impossibly dense, old woods of Rowan's world. These were young woods. Her woods.

The winding road and rolling hills were familiar. Lily knew this place. They were two towns away from Salem in Wenham, Massachusetts. She hadn't realized her pyre had been that far from the walls of Salem. The battlefield in the other Salem must have been enormous, and she had filled it with blood.

"I think we're on Topsfield Road," Lily croaked. "There's a farm up ahead."

"A farm?" Rowan said, squinting his eyes as he tried to peer through the trees. There was a flash of light and Rowan's head snapped around.

"Headlights," Lily rasped, her voice failing. "We have to get out of the road."

"You're badly burned," Rowan began hesitantly.

"Have to. We'll get hit."

Rowan reluctantly starting gathering her up in his arms, but Lily screamed before he could pick her up. It felt like he was tearing off her skin.

The raft of pain rose up again, lifting Lily up and out of herself. The headlights grew closer, blinding her. Tires squealed. Car doors slammed. As she drifted away from it all on her raft, she heard a familiar voice.

"Go help him, Juliet," the voice commanded. "Careful! She's burnt to a cinder."

"Mom?" Lily whispered, and then gave herself to the wet darkness.

Juliet stared at the charred girl lying in the middle of the road, momentarily unable to accept that she was looking at her little sister. The skinny girl was burned and bloody all over, but her raspy voice was unmistakable. It was Lily.

A frantic young man clutched her to his chest. Juliet had never seen anyone quite like him before. His hands and forearms were burned as well, but the rest of his leather-clad body was drenched in blood. Juliet got the sickening feeling that the blood was not his own. He was carrying two gore-tipped short swords strapped across his back and his sooty hands looked as if they knew how to use them. At his waist was what seemed to be a whole kit of silver knives arrayed from his belt and strapped down the side of his right thigh. He looked like an utter savage.

"Go, Juliet!" Samantha ordered.

Her mother's voice, strangely calm and in control for the first time in ages, was what snapped Juliet out of her shock. She strode forward and knelt down next to the stranger and saw a flash of silver around her sister's wrists.

"Why is Lily wearing chains?" she asked accusingly, her voice pitched low to keep it from shaking. When she lifted her eyes to meet the strangers', her gaze was caught by something at his throat. It was a large jewel that seemed to throb with dark light—if there was such a thing as dark light, Juliet thought. She blinked her eyes and looked away, both disturbed and drawn to the odd jewel at the same time.

"Samantha, do you know me?" the savage asked. Juliet stiffened in fear. Who was this guy?

"How do you know my mother's name?" she asked, certain

that it hadn't been said in his presence.

"Yes, I know you, Rowan," Samantha answered, waving an impatient hand in Juliet's direction to keep her quiet. "What do we need to do?"

"We need to get her by a fire so I can start to heal her," Rowan said. He started to lift Lily, and she moaned in pain.

"What? We need to call 911 and get an ambulance," Juliet yelled. She reached out a hand to restrain Rowan from moving her. "You're hurting her!"

"I know that," he shouted back, his expression desperate. "But we have to move her. I can't heal her here."

"Mom!" Juliet screamed. "For all we know, he *did* this to her."

"No, he didn't. Listen to him, Juliet. He's the only one who can help her now," Samantha said sternly.

Juliet searched for any sign in her mother's eyes that she had lost it, but all she saw was cold, hard sanity—something Juliet hadn't seen in her mother in a long time.

Samantha knew exactly what was going on, even if Juliet didn't, and it was Samantha who had said she knew where to find Lily and she'd forced Juliet to take her to this stretch of road in the middle of the night. Juliet had no idea how her mother could know where to find Lily after three months of her being missing, but right now there were more pressing matters, like saving Lily's life. And at the moment that seemed doubtful. Juliet had candy-striped in hospitals and trained as an EMT. She was going to med school at Boston University and she'd seen enough to know when someone was dying. Although Juliet said under her breath that they should be taking Lily to an emergency room, she knew it would make no difference at this point. Her little sister was going to die whether they got her to an ICU or not.

Rowan kept Lily on his lap in the backseat of the car while Juliet drove as quickly as she dared through the falling snow. She gripped the wheel as if she were trying to wring it dry in order to keep her hands from shaking. Her sister, missing and thought to be dead, was back. And she was dying in the backseat of Juliet's car.

Juliet's eyes kept bouncing up to the rearview mirror as she drove. She watched this Rowan character cradling Lily in his lap, trying to soothe her. He spoke to her gently to keep her conscious, saying anything that popped into his head—outrageous things, like how Lily wouldn't dare leave him alone. How he needed her. How lost he would be without her. But Juliet's suspicion was not as easily quenched as her mother's. Lily had been kidnapped three months ago, and Rowan must have had some part in it, no matter how tenderly he seemed to hold her and speak to her.

Lily was delirious by the time they got her home, humming and whispering to herself in a singsong way as if she were soothing a child. Rowan carried her inside and laid her in front of the fireplace.

"Fill a cauldron with water and bring it to me," he ordered as he unstrapped his weapons and started laying his knives out on the floor around Lily. Juliet stared at him, rooted to the spot. "Move, Juliet," he barked.

Spurred into action, Juliet began opening up cabinets even though she was quite sure they were fresh out of cauldrons. She ended up grabbing her mom's biggest copper-bottomed stockpot and filling it while Rowan listed more things he needed to Samantha. It was mostly herbs. Juliet hauled the pot of water into the living room where Rowan had a small fire going in the fireplace. He glanced at the pot dubiously.

"It's all we have," Juliet said with a defensive shrug.

"Then it'll have to do. Put it on the fire and open all the windows," he directed, scowling, as he stripped off his blood-soaked shirt.

"This is insane," Juliet said, but did as he instructed. As she pushed open the last window, Juliet saw an eerie pulse of light swell inside the room like an expanding bubble and turned to face the source of the light. Her skin tingled as it passed over her, membrane-like, and all sound in the room was muffled as if someone had stuffed cotton in her ears. At the center of the bubble was Rowan's odd amulet. Juliet looked down and saw three jewels like Rowan's winking at her sister's throat.

"She's so weak," Rowan whispered. He knelt down beside Lily and began cutting away what was left of her clothes. "Samantha, burn the sage and walk around the room counterclockwise," he said. "Juliet, start rubbing this salve on some of the lesser blisters. See if it helps."

Rowan took a tiny glass jar of greenish salve out of a pouch on his belt and put it into Juliet's hands. She started dabbing the stuff hopelessly on her sister's skin.

"This isn't going to—" she began, and stopped. She sat back on her heels. "Impossible," she breathed. Where Juliet had put the salve, Lily's blisters had shrunk away to nothing. Before her eyes, the broken skin was healed. Juliet looked up at Rowan, her mouth hanging open.

"It won't do anything for the really bad burns, but it will soothe some of the pain," he explained.

"How did you—?"

"Magic," Rowan answered automatically. "We need to make a tent. Lily's lungs are scalded raw and they're filling with blood. She'll drown if we don't stop it. Do you have large sheets and a way to prop them over her?"

"Yes," Juliet replied, and stumbled out of the room to the linen closet, dumbfounded by what she had just seen. No medicine worked that fast. Burned skin did not heal in a few seconds—if it ever really healed at all.

Juliet returned with the sheets, and saw Rowan leaning over Lily.

Tendrils of reddish-purple light emanated from the dark jewel at his throat and danced across Lily's face. One of the tendrils snaked down Lily's throat, and she gasped and sputtered. Rowan turned her head to the side and blood oozed out of Lily's mouth. Juliet took a step forward to stop him. When he looked up at her his face was pale and strained with effort and his eyes were so frantic that Juliet checked herself.

"Hold that sheet over us. Keep the steam in," he said weakly.

Juliet's arms shook with fear, and the hair on her arms stood up at an uncanny frisson when she came near Rowan's strange bubble of dark light. She threw the sheet over the three of them, including an edge of the now-steaming pot as she wrestled with herself. Juliet was a rational, sensible woman. She knew there was no such thing as magic—except she also *knew*, on some deep level, that what she was witnessing had no other explanation.

"Magic," Juliet muttered, half out of her wits with anxiety and disbelief.

"Yes," Rowan replied. "I've got to ease the blood out of her lungs before I mend the damaged tissue, but if I do it too quickly I could choke her." He suddenly leaned forward, tilting his ear close to Lily's mouth. "What? What are you saying?" Rowan whispered to Lily.

"Water, water everywhere . . . ," she replied, and then her eyes relaxed, half open and half closed, and her body went slack.

"Lily? Lily!" Juliet gasped, her voice quickly rising in panic.

"She's not dead," Rowan said. "She's spirit walking. We can't reach her now."

Juliet saw Lily's lips moving slightly. "Who is she talking to?"

"I don't know," Rowan replied. "Whoever it is, I hope they give her some comfort." He sat up and took a shuddering breath, his fierce gaze meeting Juliet's. "Now we really get to work. I know you don't

7

have a weak stomach, so I'm going to count on you, Juliet. This won't be easy or pretty."

"Don't worry about me," Juliet replied. He looked at her like he knew her. It puzzled Juliet because something in her whispered that she *did* know this young man, even though she'd never laid eyes on him before. "Just tell me what to do."

Lily saw her sister and her mother. She saw Rowan. She saw her home. All of the things she loved were inches away from her, but they drifted by like hawks soaring on an updraft. They kept falling away from her until all she saw was mist.

She was floating on a misty ocean. Across from her was herself. Lily and Lillian sat across from each other in identical poses—their legs drawn up close, chins resting on their knees, arms wrapped around their shins. Lily spoke first, and Lillian answered. Mindspeak was all they needed here on the raft.

"Water, water, everywhere,
And all the boards did shrink;
Water, water, everywhere,
Nor any drop to drink."
That's quite fitting, Lily. I'm so thirsty.
Are you burned, too, Lillian?
Of course. You and I are in the same boat—or raft, as you imagine it. The pyre gives more than it takes, but it always seems to take more than you can bear.
Where are we?
I call it the Mist. It's neither here nor there, neither living nor dead. Can you remember the rest of that poem, Lily?
No. I read it before I had a willstone. My memory wasn't perfect then like it is now—unfortunately, because I wish I could forget this. I know I won't, though. I remember every second of my life now that I have a willstone.

I've had a willstone since I was six and haven't forgotten anything since. There are things I would give anything to forget. But I can't.

I saw Rowan reading an old math textbook once. Tristan told me Rowan had to relearn nearly everything because he smashed his first willstone and those memories were no longer stored for him. I wonder how many memories Rowan entrusted to his first willstone that are lost to him now.

He's lucky, actually. I remember every second he and I spent together and it kills me.

I don't want to pity you, Lillian.

Then don't. All I'm asking is for you to let me show you some of my memories. We're both unconscious and barely alive. There's no easier time to communicate across the worlds than now. I thought you might like to know more about me. And maybe I want one person to understand me in case I die.

Okay, Lillian, but only because I need someone, too. Pain is lonely, isn't it?

It is, Lily. It really is. But fear is even lonelier.

Show me your fear then, Lillian, and let's be lonely together.

Lily was no longer on the raft. Nor was she herself. In joining Lillian's memory she became Lillian. She wasn't simply recalling what had happened to Lillian, she was reliving it. The first thing she felt was terror . . .

. . . The air is wrong. It's choking me and burning the back of my throat. Ash is floating fat as snowflakes. Did I even worldjump?

I had Captain Leto's men build my pyre far from the walls of Salem. In the world I am trying to get to there is no need for the wall anymore, and from my spirit walks with the shaman I have seen this other Salem is substantially different from the one I live in. I've learned that when I worldjump I end up in the exact location I left—only in a different universe—and if I were to worldjump from the top of the wall or from the fireplace in my rooms at the Citadel, I might appear inside a piece of furniture or forty feet in the air. The only safe place to worldjump is from the ground, and even then it's still dangerous.

You never really know what dangers await when you cross the worldfoam.

Leto had been reluctant to set my pyre so far outside of Salem. He worried about the Woven, but what I couldn't tell him is that where I was going, there would be no Woven in the woods to fear. I didn't want to promise too much in case the shaman was wrong. Leto and his soldiers are from Walltop. From their vantage, they've seen more of the evils of the Woven than have any other citizens of the Thirteen Cities and have more reason to want them eradicated. More reason to fear them.

I sit up. There's no flame under me. That means I'm not on the pyre anymore. I look around. There's nothing but charred ground and blasted trees as far as I can see into the murky distance. The air isn't just acrid. On the elemental level it roils with huge particles. Damaging ones. They tear through my cells, wreaking havoc.

I'm in the wrong world. One of the cinder worlds. I knew it would be dangerous to worldjump without a lighthouse, but I did it anyway. Rowan says I never listen to anyone, but what choice did I have?

I don't have time to panic. I stand up and run to the trees. I need to build another pyre to fuel a worldjump and get myself out of this dead place. When my hand touches the trunk of the first tree, the bark crumbles in my hand and falls through my fingers like the dried-out walls of an old sand castle. The next tree is the same. And the next. What caused this? The huge particles I see on the elemental level, destroying the life-helix? If so, what caused *them*? It's almost as if the surface of the sun had reached across the void of space and grazed this planet, scouring it of life.

I scan the horizon for Salem. I see the walls, but they aren't the right shape. There must be something wrong with my vision. I squint, trying to understand what I see before me. The walls are not in the process of being pulled down because they are no longer needed, like I saw on the world that got rid of the Woven. Here, the wall is just a useless tumble of rocks and judging from the angle of the stones, it looks as if they'd been blown down by a fearsome wind. No greentowers soar behind the walls nor can I see the spires of the Citadel. I look at where they should be, but they're simply *not there*. I stagger closer, unable to take my eyes off the ruin that was my city. It's nothing but rubble and ash. No hurricane, no matter how great, could have done this and there's no explosion I know of big enough to cause such total destruction.

Except—no, it can't be. Who would be insane enough to use elemental energy—the energy of the stars—as a weapon? But the shards of elements, crashing through all organic life in this world, are huge cell killers. They are the product of this kind of energy, and no other. You can't see the elemental shards in a spirit walk, but now I understand. That's what makes a cinder world. That's what destroys what life remains on those worlds after the initial firestorm has cooled I never understood until I came and saw the cause with my witch's eyes.

I have to find unburned wood or I will be stuck here until I die of thirst. Or worse. I could be found by someone ruthless enough to survive in this place for however long it's been since the holocaust. The longer it's been, the more animalistic the people here will have become. I've seen things on my spirit walks, even though the shaman told me not to dwell on the cinder worlds or wonder what caused them. I've seen what the survivors do to one another in the years of never-ending winter that follow the great burning.

Enough.

Stop crying.

Pull yourself together and find fuel for your pyre, Lillian . . .

Lily felt herself being evicted from Lillian's memory, despite wanting to see more. Whatever happened next, Lillian either didn't want to share with Lily or didn't want to relive herself. Lily looked across the raft at Lillian.

What happened, Lillian? How did you find enough fuel in that cinder world to build a pyre?

The answer to that is what made me who I am now. You think I'm a monster, but I think if you could see what made me who I am, you'd agree that my choices, as ruthless as they seem, are justified. The only question is, are you sure you really want to understand me?

Curiosity dug at Lily, but so did distrust. There was a reason Lillian had only showed her a fragment of a memory, and a half-truth could be more manipulative than any lie. Lily knew this, but she still couldn't say no outright because to understand Lillian's story would be to understand something huge inside herself. They were, after all, the same.

I honestly don't know, Lillian.

Juliet turned her head to the side, gagging.

"Easy," Rowan said in his low, steady voice. He reached out to brace Juliet by her elbow and stopped. His hands were covered in the charred skin he had just peeled off Lily. "Do you need to go outside and get some air?" he asked kindly. Not that there was any difference between the outside air and the air inside the living room at this point. Rowan had insisted they keep all the windows open and it was colder than a meat locker in there.

"No," Juliet said, shaking it off. "I got this."

Rowan narrowed his eyes for a moment, weighing Juliet's resolve, and must have seen more strength in her than she was feeling because he nodded once and bent his head over Lily.

The jewel at his throat throbbed with that eerie dark light and he went back to his task. He directed a tendril of light under a small patch of necrotic skin and even though his burned hands were bandaged, he used the *light* to ease Lily's skin away with a precision that no scalpel could ever match. She barely even bled.

It had been a full day since they'd brought Lily back home, and Juliet had seen Rowan do amazing things. Things Juliet could not explain in a rational way. All she knew was that these things Rowan was doing were keeping Lily alive.

"Spray the tincture here," he directed.

Juliet misted Lily's exposed muscle and sinew with the combination antibiotic and analgesic potion they had made that morning in Samantha's second-best copper-bottomed pot.

"Good," Rowan mumbled as Juliet sprayed the proper amount of tincture, and then stood back to survey the gruesome landscape of Lily's body. He went to the fire, over which hung Samantha's best copper-bottomed pot, and deftly lifted out a strip of something that looked like a thin film of gauze about three inches square with the flat of one of his silver knives. This was not the first time Rowan had done this kind of surgery, of that Juliet was quite certain.

"Is that really Lily's skin?" Juliet asked. She was fascinated now, rather than disgusted. She watched his stone's mercurial light dance around the edges of the skin graft as he eased it down over Lily's raw bones with infinite care.

"Yes," Rowan mumbled, finally answering Juliet's question after a long pause. "It's not hard to grow from a culture—not even in inferior conditions." Rowan paused to shoot Samantha's pots a resentful glare. The cast-iron cauldron he insisted on hadn't arrived yet, and Juliet had endured a full five minutes of his swearing before they went ahead and began the skin-growing ritual in one of Samantha's "inferior" pots a few hours ago. "But skin patches are hard to align," he continued, still focused on his task, "every border cell must link to its neighbor seamlessly, or it will leave a scar." He leaned back again to inspect his work and smiled.

"Will this?" Juliet asked anxiously, looking at his injured hands. "Scar, I mean."

Rowan shot Juliet a cocky look as if to express how beneath him the notion was, even with his hands burned and bandaged. She almost laughed. He had a way about him that inspired confidence despite the desperate situation they were in, but before Juliet gave over to a moment of levity she stopped herself.

She didn't know what to feel about Rowan. She was starting to trust him, but how could she trust someone with such an outlandish story about where Lily had been for the past three months? He claimed that Lily had been in a parallel universe, and that she had been burned in a battle against an evil witch. Juliet looked down at her sister's three strange stones—willstones as Rowan called them—and grew even more confused. They winked and roiled with a light that looked almost alive. Seeing them and the eerie way they sparkled even in the dark told Juliet that something otherworldly had happened to her sister. And Rowan was undoubtedly using magic to save Lily's life when not even the best medical attention in the world could have done so, whether Juliet wanted to believe it or not.

But what Juliet really needed to know had nothing to do with magic or willstones. She needed to know whether or not Rowan had any part in what had happened to Lily. But little things he said, and the way he seemed to feel so responsible for Lily, made Juliet suspect that Rowan had had a hand in burning Lily.

Rowan and Juliet worked straight on through the night, with Rowan peeling off and replacing Lily's skin in three-inch squares, and Juliet spraying and dabbing and keeping everything Rowan needed within his reach. By dawn Juliet could hardly see straight.

"You should sleep," Rowan said as he stood, appraising the last patch of newly applied skin.

"So should you," Juliet said through a yawn.

"I'm still breathing for her," Rowan said, fingering the stone at the base of his throat. She watched the light in his willstone subtly rising and falling in tandem with the rise and fall of Lily's chest. She didn't know how he was doing it, but Juliet could see that somehow Rowan was putting air in her lungs, and drawing it out again in a long, steady rhythm.

"Are you sure?" she asked. She hadn't seen Rowan eat or sleep since he'd gotten here.

"Yes. Rest, Juliet." He sank onto the floor next to Lily, never once taking his gaze from her. Juliet didn't know what was holding him together, but she was too tired to try to argue with him about who needed to rest more.

"Wake me if you have to," she said, too tired to think about it anymore. She pulled a quilt over her against the freezing cold and collapsed onto the couch.

She shut her eyes and, unfortunately, it seemed as if only seconds had passed before she felt Rowan shaking her arm.

"I need your help," he said. Juliet sat up, still dragging her brain out of sleep. Rowan looked terrible. His eyes were sunken and his cheeks were tinged with green. "We need to wrap her before your mother comes downstairs," he said.

Juliet followed him back to Lily's body and understood. The patchwork of new skin was livid and swollen. Lily looked like some hellish ghoul straight out of a slasher movie. They went to work wrapping Lily up mummy-style before Samantha could see her like that. While they worked, Juliet heard the phone ring and heard her mother answer the call upstairs. Samantha's tone became increasingly agitated as the conversation dragged on. A few moments later, she joined them in the living room as Rowan hurriedly passed at least one layer of gauze over Lily's injuries.

"That was your father," Samantha said. She was pacing and wringing her hands. "We have to tell him."

"Tell him what?" Juliet asked carefully.

"About your sister. That she's back. The nosy FBI agent won't leave him alone. She really thinks your father might be involved with Lily's disappearance."

"Mom, we can't," Juliet replied incredulously. She gestured to the living room. There were basins of bloody water and buckets of discarded skin on the floor. "We can't let anyone see this."

"He's worried about her, Juliet, and I feel awful letting him think she's still missing. Maybe dead." Samantha gave her daughter one of those disturbingly sane looks. "You don't know what it is to be a parent. He loves you girls, even though he's not the fathering type."

Juliet shot Rowan a look, and saw that he was as against involving their father as she was.

"That's understandable, Samantha," Rowan said equitably. "But right now our main concern has to be Lily, not James. If he knows she's alive he'll want to see her and she's too weak to be exposed to another person and risk infection."

Juliet shook herself and stifled her question. No one had told Rowan her father's first name, and she already knew that if she asked him, Rowan would say that he knew James from this parallel world he claimed to come from.

"You're right, Rowan. Of course you're right," Samantha said. She reached out and put her hand on Rowan's shoulder, taking comfort. "I'm so glad you're here."

The phone rang again. "That's probably that FBI agent," Samantha said. The hassled look on her face started to cloud with confusion as she went to answer it. She was losing it.

"Mom can't handle this," Juliet said under her breath.

"I know," Rowan replied. He looked just as worried about

Samantha as Juliet was. There was true concern on his face, and it irritated Juliet.

"Who are you, really?" she asked, her chin tilted down and her eyes narrowed in distrust.

Rowan sighed. "I don't blame you for not believing me." He smiled suddenly, as if remembering something bittersweet. "When I first saw Lily I couldn't believe it either, and she has a double in my world, another version of her named Lillian. I've known Lillian my whole life, and I could sense that Lily wasn't her, but I just couldn't accept it. Not for a long time. So I don't blame you for not believing me. Actually I consider myself lucky that you're helping me instead of turning me over to your city guards."

He sounded so genuine. Juliet wanted to believe him, but how could she? Samantha believed him without question, but Samantha's illness was tailor-made to believe in parallel worlds. In fact, Samantha seemed to *live* in a parallel world most of the time.

"I'm trying to understand all this in a rational way," Juliet said, spreading her arms wide to include the silver knives, the salt and vinegar, and the strange symbols Rowan had painted on a square of black silk. "I've seen magic work, and I'm trying to make sense of it, but I can't shake the feeling that you're involved. Rowan—were you the one who burned my sister?"

Rowan looked down, a pained expression on his face. "I was a part of it, yes. I shackled her to the pyre. But, Juliet—you don't understand."

Juliet backed away from him and he grabbed her arm, stopping her. She hadn't feared Rowan until this moment, but now that she did she couldn't help but notice how strong he was and how quickly he could move. She straightened her back to look up in his eyes.

"What was it? Some kind of Satan worshipping?" she asked breathlessly. Surprisingly, he laughed and let go of her arm immediately.

"Magic has nothing to do with any of that nonsense. It's about power, and fire is how your sister gains power. I burned Lily because she asked me to," he said simply.

Juliet stared at him, trying to find a lie in his eyes, but she couldn't. "I don't know what to believe, Rowan." She suddenly smiled, all the tension and fear gone, and shook her head. "Sometimes it feels like I know you."

"There's a version of you who does," he said, and went back to Lily's side, leaving her to mull over the disturbing notion that there were other Juliets out there somewhere.

Lily smelled snow and cedar smoke. She heard logs popping in a fire. She opened her eyes. She was lying on the floor in her living room, back in Salem, Massachusetts. All the windows were open and a fire was going in the hearth. Rowan sat beside a huge cast-iron cauldron that was suspended over the flames. The soot and blood that had covered him had been washed away—soot and blood from the battle against Lillian, Lily remembered. Lily hoped that her army had fled and that Alaric, Tristan, and Caleb had gotten safely away with the scientists.

She took a deep breath in and let a deep breath out. Steam billowed from between her lips. The room was sub-zero. Rowan's head spun around at the sound, and he scooted across the floor toward her when he saw that she was awake. She reached out to him and saw that her hands and arms were wound in bandages. A square of black silk was stretched out beneath her and strange symbols, drawn in salt, surrounded her. Silver knives were arrayed around her in a pattern—their lustrous blades flashing brightly in the firelight.

No, don't move! Your skin is too fragile, Rowan said in mindspeak.

He was wearing a thick wool sweater against the cold. Peeking out from the bottom of the sleeves and above the cowl neck were bandages. Lily could see the thin pink color of watery blood starting to seep through the wrappings on his hands.

You're hurt . . .

I'm getting better. So are you. Rest now, Lily.

Lily let her eyes close and kept them closed. Maybe a second, maybe forever passed as she floated on her raft of pain. She heard arguments swirling above her like a cloud. People danced in and out of her fever dreams. More often than not, she felt Lillian joining her on the raft—but only when Rowan left her side. Lily could feel Lillian waiting for Rowan to go and then she'd move closer to Lily through the Mist, asking for shelter on her raft. Lily let her come. She needed someone there with her in the dark.

Time passed. The pain started to itch around the edges. Lily heard her father's voice. Demanding. Impatient. She heard her mother's voice. Pleading. Desperate.

"James, I told you because I believe you have the right to know that your daughter is alive," Samantha was saying in a shaky voice, "but I only let you come and see her on the condition that you allow me to care for her as I see fit."

"You *let* me come and see her?" James sputtered. "Have you lost your mind completely? I may not be around much, but I still own this house and I have every right to see my daughter—who's been *missing* for three months—whether I agree to your psychotic conditions or not!" He made a strangled sound in the back of his throat as he paced around Lily's prone body. "I've been *questioned* by the police and the FBI since she disappeared, Samantha. We all have. If she dies on our living room floor because I didn't make you take her to a hospital, we're going to be charged with her death. You understand that, don't you?"

"Stop fighting," Lily said. Her voice was weak, and the effort to speak left her lightheaded. She heard Rowan in her head.

I'm sorry, Lily. Your mother thought it was cruel to keep your father in the dark, but he wants to take you to a hospital and I can't let him. They have no idea how to heal you. Your mother understands, but your father is difficult.

"You're taking her to the hospital this instant, and I'm calling Special Agent Simms tonight. I'm not going to jail because you're insane, Samantha," James said with finality. "And *you*, Juliet. How could you—"

Let me handle him, Rowan.

Lily sat up in one lurching motion and looked directly at her father. He was red-faced and the lines on his forehead were etched deep from anger. As soon as he noticed her, his words died in the back of his throat. Lily had never initiated mindspeak with him before, but she knew it was possible because, despite their many differences, he was still her father.

Dad. You're meddling in things you don't understand. Stop pretending you're in charge here. Do as you're told or get out.

His red face blanched and his jaw dropped. "Did you hear that?" he asked Juliet.

"She didn't. That was just for you, Dad," Lily replied in a papery voice that broke twice before she could finish.

"Lie back, Lily," Rowan whispered urgently in her ear. "Your skin is splitting apart. You need to be still."

Lily refused and stayed staring at her father. Her left eye went cloudy and started stinging as blood oozed into it, but she didn't blink. Lily waited until she was sure her father's will had faltered before she continued.

"We're going to take care of this privately. Is that understood?" she whispered. Her father nodded slowly. He was terrified of her. "Good."

Lily allowed Rowan to ease her back down.

That was harsh, Lily.

Did it work?

Yeah. He's leaving.

His favorite trick.

Rowan's breath brushed over her collarbones as he gave a bitter laugh. The feel of him near her was soothing. Lily shut her eyes and climbed back onto her raft, the pain bearing her up and over the dark water. She looked across the raft and saw Lillian sitting opposite her.

My version of James wasn't much of a father, either.

Wasn't? Is he dead, Lillian?

No. He lives in Richmond. I pay him well to keep him there and out of politics.

He's not a bad person. Just—

Spineless.

Yeah. I wish he could have been something more than that.

We have high standards when it comes to men, Lily. Nothing less than Rowan will do for either of us.

You still love him.

Of course.

Then why did you hurt him so terribly, Lillian? Why did you hang Rowan's father?

Do you really want to know? In order for it to make any sense, I have to show you more of my story, and it isn't pretty. It's going to hurt you, Lily.

I want to know—even if I also know you're only showing me the bits and pieces that will justify what you have done.

I am showing you the truth as I experienced it so that you can understand why I've done what I have. You can't blame me for wanting to show my life to you in a way that I think will have the greatest impact. You're still the one who has to decide whether or not you agree with me.

All right, Lillian. Let me see the truth as you wish to show it to me.

You must promise me one thing first. That you hide everything I show you. Not to protect me——but to protect Rowan.

I'd never let anything or anyone hurt Rowan. Not even you or me. But you know that, don't you, Lillian?

Yes.

Then show me.

Promise you won't show Rowan what I show you.

That's a lot to ask. I'm not sure I can hide anything from him. I'm not sure I want to.

You've never hidden anything from him?

Once. When I went to the pyre to fight you, he asked me if I was doing it for him.

And you didn't tell him.

I couldn't let him know I was doing it for him or the guilt would have killed him.

That's all I ask of you now——and for exactly the same reason. Think about it and tell me when you're ready.

Juliet heard the knock at the door and left Rowan to fiddle with the computer for a moment on his own. She answered the door, already knowing who was standing on the other side of it and dreading the conversation that was to follow.

"Hi, Tristan," she said heavily.

"How long were you going to wait to tell me she was back, Juliet?" he asked.

"Look, Tristan——" Juliet began, but he cut her off.

"I have to find out from Agent Simms that she's been back a week? A *week*?" he stressed. Juliet had to look away. Poor Tristan had been through a lot since Lily disappeared——more than anyone, probably. "Where is she?" he asked.

Tristan was about to push his way into the house when Rowan appeared at Juliet's shoulder.

"Now's not a good time, Tristan," Rowan said.

"Who the hell are you?" Tristan asked, bewildered and offended that Rowan had used his name so casually. Like he knew him.

"My name is Rowan Fall. I'm here to help Lily manage her condition," he replied calmly.

"Really?" Tristan said. His tone was loaded with sarcasm and more than just a bit of loathing for Rowan.

Juliet could sympathize with Tristan. After James told the FBI that Lily was back, they'd had to come up with a cover story for where Lily had been and why no one could see her. The alibi was still a work in progress, but the one thing they stuck to was that Lily had been getting radical treatment for her allergies and wasn't fit to see anyone yet—not even Tristan or the FBI agent who had taken an alarmingly deep interest in Lily's case.

"Yes. Really," Rowan said, standing his ground. "She'll get in touch with you when she's ready."

Out of nowhere, Tristan took a swing at Rowan. Juliet half gasped, half screamed, but before either she or Tristan could process it, Rowan had blocked the punch and moved Tristan back and out of the doorway.

"That's not going to do anybody any good, Tristan," Rowan said. He wasn't even surprised. Again, Juliet wondered who this guy was and what his life had been like in this other world. He obviously knew how to handle himself in a fight.

Tristan stared at Rowan in disbelief, and then shook him off. "I have a right to see her," he snarled.

"Yeah, I know you do," Rowan replied, running a hand through his hair. "And when she's ready to talk to you, she'll get in touch."

Tristan backed away, still not sure of what to make of Rowan. His confusion and jealousy were apparent, and Juliet couldn't blame him. Rowan wasn't just good-looking, he was downright devastating, and he appeared to be keeping Lily all to himself. While Tristan had never shown real interest in Lily before, something had changed in him. Juliet supposed that there was nothing like losing a girl to show a guy how much he cares.

"Tell her to call me, Jules," Tristan said before getting in his car and driving off.

Rowan came back inside and shut the door. "That was messy," he said with a sigh. "Guess I should have expected it, though."

"You know him, don't you?" Juliet asked.

"Oh yeah," Rowan said, rolling his eyes. "He's one of my closest friends—more like a brother, really. He always takes everything too far."

"Yeah," Juliet said, half laughing. "Moderation was never his thing."

"No," Rowan agreed. He stood for a moment, watching Juliet.

She knew he was trying to decide if she believed him now or not, but he didn't ask. Good thing, too. Because Juliet didn't know what she believed anymore.

He went back to the kitchen and sat down in front of the computer, gesturing for Juliet to sit next to him. "Now tell me more about this Internet," he said. "Can you really get any information you want from it, simply by asking?"

"Pretty much," Juliet said, shaking herself and sitting next to him. He was a quick learner, but he knew nothing about computers yet and Juliet was tired of ordering rare herbs and random minerals for him online. Rowan was frighteningly intelligent, though, and something told Juliet that in a few days he'd be teaching her things about computers of which she'd never even dreamed.

"Sounds like magic," he replied, looking back at the screen.

CHAPTER
2

ROWAN SAT AT THE DESK IN LILY'S ROOM, READING something on her computer. He was wearing the same dark wool sweater he'd worn before and a pair of warm sweatpants. His black hair was pushed up all around his head in a dozen directions, only making him more beautiful. Lily couldn't decide if she wanted to stare at him a bit longer, or if she was so hungry for the sound of his voice that she wanted to burst the quiet bubble of concentration that surrounded him.

She thought about reaching out to him in mindspeak, but stopped herself. He couldn't know that she was in contact with Lillian, and she knew she wasn't strong enough yet to keep all thought of Lillian out of her head while she and Rowan were in rapport.

It wasn't the first time Lily had avoided mindspeak with Rowan in order to hide what she was thinking, but it was the first time she felt guilty about it. The thought stuck with her, stale and lingering like a rotten mouthful.

"What are you doing?" Lily asked in a voice that crackled with disuse.

Rowan turned in his chair to face Lily. "This is amazing," he said excitedly. "It's like your people were trying to make up for everything you lacked without willstones and magic." He laughed boyishly. "You don't need to remember things—your computer does it for you. And if you don't know something, all you have to do is look it up on the Internets. Genius."

"Internet. Not nets," Lily corrected gently. "Come here. It's too weird to see you in front of a computer."

"It's Juliet's fault," he said, grinning. "She taught me how to use it. Now I'm hooked." Rowan came over, sat on the edge of her bed, and immediately began checking her injuries. He lifted up the edge of one of her bandages. "This is much better," he mumbled, pleased with what he saw.

"How long have we been back?"

"Nine days."

"How is Juliet? How have you been getting along with her and my mom while I've been out?"

"It's odd," he said slowly. "Neither of them knows me, but I've known them most of my life. At least Samantha doesn't look at me like a complete stranger. She's used to seeing me in other worlds, I guess."

Rowan's face fell. Lily knew what he was thinking. The version of Samantha in his world had died not too long ago.

"It's disorienting," Lily said, recalling how strange it had been for her to meet the other Juliet, and the other Tristan. "Has Tristan come by? Does he know I'm back?" she asked as soon as the thought of him entered her mind.

"He came by once," Rowan said, frowning. "Drink this." He placed a straw between her lips and Lily sipped at the bittersweet brew.

"What happened?" she asked.

Rowan let out a frustrated sigh. "Well—you'd been gone for three months. Everyone here thought you'd been kidnapped, and when you finally did come back you were like this," he said, gesturing to Lily's extensive burns. "We're telling everyone that you were at a private clinic to get radical treatment for your allergies. That's how we're explaining away the burns. We're calling them swelling and redness from subcutaneous exposure therapy."

Lily nodded. "They tried that on me as a kid. I looked like a leaky tomato. But how are you explaining the fact that my mom didn't know where I was?"

"She *did,* though," Rowan said, stretching out next to her on the bed. Lily tried to snuggle against him but Rowan stopped her. "Be really careful when you move. No friction," he cautioned. "While you were gone, Samantha told everyone that she could see you, but she couldn't get to you. Everyone's chalking it up to your mother's condition. They believe that she sent you to get treatment, but got confused and panicked when you were gone."

Lily grimaced. "And everyone's buying that?"

"Almost everyone. Juliet is backing her up to all the neighbors and the police." Rowan shook his head. "Strange word. Police," he mused. "Anyway, the police and another group, the FBI, were involved from the beginning. It was big news that you disappeared the way you did."

"Yeah, I can imagine. A teenaged girl with life-threatening allergies disappears into thin air with none of her medication. Right after having a seizure at a party," Lily said, grimacing as she tried to picture it.

"There's one FBI agent who's been particularly tenacious. Special Agent Simms. She's the reason we had to tell everyone you were back. She was giving your father and Tristan a really hard time and we had to let her know you were alive so she'd leave them alone."

"Tristan?"

"Yeah," Rowan replied in a clipped voice. "He came by after the FBI told him you were back."

"And?"

"I wouldn't let him see you," Rowan said carefully. "He has a mechanic's talent in this world, too. I can feel the potential in him, and I knew if he laid eyes on you, he'd know we were lying. He was really upset when I told him that he'd have to wait."

"What happened?" Lily asked again, already imagining the worst. She suddenly yawned so hard her jaw cracked.

"Don't worry." Rowan smiled down at her, a cocky glint in his dark eyes. "I kept him from doing anything stupid. You should call him."

Lily yawned again and put her head down in Rowan's lap. He smelled like dryer sheets and wood smoke.

"You're going to have to meet with that FBI agent, too," Rowan added. "She's been putting a lot of pressure on your mother to see you."

"Okay." Lily didn't want to think about Tristan or Special Agent Simms. She wrapped an arm around Rowan's hips and let her eyes drift closed.

"Can you hear Tristan or Caleb in my world?" Rowan asked after a long silent spell. Lily stiffened.

"I don't know," she replied.

"Try," he urged. "I want to know if they're okay."

Lily concentrated and reached out to her other two mechanics in mindspeak, but heard only faint whispers that she couldn't decipher. She tried calling to the particular patterns of their willstones and felt something stronger there. Lily could distinctly make out the unique energies that were Tristan and Caleb much more clearly than she could make out their mindspeak. She was still connected to their

willstones and she could tell that they could sense her energy n̲.̲
It was comforting.

Lily widened her awareness to the thousands she had claimed before the battle. She could feel them. Her army. They were scattered, but their willstones were waiting for her return. They hungered for her strength. Lily shrank away from the enormity of that sensation and nuzzled herself deeper into Rowan's lap.

"They're both alive and healthy," Lily said gratefully. "They can hear me calling them, but it's a long way. I can *almost* hear them, though."

"Don't push. Try again when you're healthier."

"I can't believe how tired I am," Lily said apologetically.

"Growing a new layer of skin takes a lot of energy. It's best if you move as little as possible," he said, stroking her hair.

Through hazy eyes, Lily glanced at the mug of brew she'd just drunk, resting on her bedside table. "You drugged me, didn't you?" she asked wryly.

She heard a rumble deep in Rowan's chest as he laughed, but she couldn't stay awake long enough to yell at him.

By that night, Lily realized that she didn't need to float into the Mist anymore. She wasn't in pain, but she had questions for Lillian, and as usual, when Lily wanted Lillian even in the slightest way, Lillian knew. They met each other on the raft.

Lillian?

Yes, Lily?

Why can I hear you so clearly, but I can barely hear Tristan and Caleb?

We are the same, Lily. Our bond is much deeper than any other. That's why I know you are the only one who can ever understand why I outlawed science and why I enforce that law so brutally.

You said once that it all started with Rowan.

Actually, it started with Mom, but I could never blame anything on her. You understand, because your version of Samantha is just like mine was.

What happened?

I still need that promise, Lily.

I can't. I can't keep anything from him.

Do you love him?

What a small question. I'd die for him.

But would you kill for him?

I already have. I sent my army into battle for him.

Then tell yourself that you're doing this in order to understand me well enough that you don't make the same mistakes I did.

Very noble, but that isn't really my reason, and I can't claim that it is. I need to know because I need to know. You aren't my friend or my sister— you are me, aren't you, Lillian?

Finally—you accept it, Lily. Yes, we are the same person in different circumstances.

That's why I need to know why I would hunt people down and hang them. Why I would murder Rowan's father. Why, Lillian? Why would I do that?

Promise me that Rowan will never know.

Okay, Lillian. I promise.

This is the moment everything changed for me . . .

. . . Rowan gathers my curls up in his hands and twists them up behind my head. We're in my study, but both of us would rather be in bed. It's late and I'm tired, but there's still so much to do. My technical college is facing a challenge I hadn't anticipated. I was ready to fight the Council and my Coven for as long as it took until they accepted that my school would not only admit both citizens and Outlanders, but it would also offer full scholarships to those who couldn't afford it. What I wasn't expecting was that there would be such low Outlander enrollment.

"There's your neck," Rowan says, and runs his fingers down my nape. "I thought I'd lost it under that mane forever."

"I'm trying to work," I plead through a breathy laugh, already turning to jelly. I look up at him. "Why wouldn't *every* intelligent Outlander want to go to college for free?" I ask pathetically.

"Because the loss of a healthy, intelligent young person is a big blow to any tribe," Rowan says quietly, still running his fingers over my throat. "Everyone would try to talk that person out of it."

"But it means a better life," I say, still looking up at him with pleading eyes.

"For that person," Rowan replies. "But not for the rest of the tribe."

I sigh and drop my head, letting him run his fingers through my hair. He knows my argument—that an educated Outlander could return to his or her tribe and make it better. But he didn't go back to his tribe, and has no intention to. Why would anyone with a chance at a better life ever go back to fighting the Woven and living in poverty?

"Lady?" asks a tentative voice by the door. Rowan turns and we both look across my rooms. It's Gavin, a new page and a possible future mechanic of mine—if he can survive Rowan's exhausting training, that is.

"What is it?" I ask, noticing Gavin's drawn expression.

"It's your mother, Lady Samantha," Gavin says. "She's on the wall."

I'm standing before he can say any more. "What is she doing up there?" I ask calmly, trying not to scare Gavin.

"She's . . . balancing," the boy says timidly. "Right on the edge, like it's a game."

I'm running now. I feel chilled and ungrounded, as if all the weight had been stolen out of my body.

As we exit my keep, Rowan is in my thoughts, telling me he's with me and that we'll fix it together. He likes to fix things—needs to, actually—but I fear my mother's fractured mind is in too many pieces for anyone to mend.

"Where?" Rowan asks the page. Gavin points in a northerly direction toward the tip of the oval wall that surrounds the miles-long city. She couldn't be farther away from my southerly, east-side keep. Rowan's willstone glitters as he weaves a field of still air around him. Undistorted air is easier to see through, and his vision is sharpened. He sees his target and takes me up against his side. I feel the familiar tug of his willstone, urging me to give him strength.

For a moment I teeter on a precipice of my own, wanting to possess him. He's so open. I could take over his will, but I resist as I almost always have in the past. I gather my energy, change it into force, and pour it into his willstone. Pure power pumps in his veins and we share in the heady rush of my strength in his body. He leaps upward, the ground shrinks beneath us, and in seconds we have flown to the top of the colossal wall that surrounds the city of Salem. We alight on Walltop. I have read of a wall like this in China. It is rumored to be much longer, but not nearly as tall as this. I dream of going there one day, but I doubt I ever will. This whole continent has been cut off from the others for the same reason we built this wall. The Woven.

Walltop is like China in a way. It is a world apart with its own rules and customs—a world that exists two hundred feet above the city of Salem. Generations have served up here. They even have their own slang and a distinct accent. Technically, I am the absolute ruler of Walltop. The Council and the Coven don't have any say up here, and my word is law. But secretly I know that Walltop is run according to its own complicated set of rules that I don't fully grasp.

"The Lady of Salem," announces Leto, the ranking captain. A flurry of stiff backs and crisp salutes follows.

"Captain Leto," I say in greeting. I break off when I see my mother.

She's in her nightgown. It's frayed and soiled at the hem as if it'd been dragging through mud for hours. Her hair, a riot of flame-red curls like mine, is tangled and frizzy. Her bare feet tread the very edge of Walltop. They are so dirty I can barely see the blood from where she's torn a toenail. The only reason I know it's torn is from the crimson footprints in her wake. Her face is serene and a small smile softens the corners of her mouth, but her eyes blink and burn with an unhealthy light. A strange shame flowers hot pink in my cheeks. It isn't her nightgown or hair or bloody feet—it's the insanity in her eyes that I'm ashamed of.

"Mom," I whisper. There's something about seeing my mother behaving like this that turns me into a child. I am not the Lady of Salem right now. I am a scared little girl who is desperate to diffuse a powder keg inside a woman I have never understood. "Come back from the edge."

"You know, Lillian, all I have to do is squint my eyes and there's nothing here," she says, stamping her feet and holding her arms out wide. "No wall. It's like I'm walking on air."

Rowan slowly inches his way toward my mother. "What do you mean, Samantha?" he asks lightly. He sounds amused and curious, rather than worried.

"I mean that in other versions of this"—she waves her arms wildly to take in the city and the Woven Woods surrounding it—"there is no wall, and no forest full of monsters."

"Other versions of what?" Rowan asks. He is within arm's reach of my mother now. His hands are relaxed but ready at his sides.

"Other versions of the world," Samantha says, smiling at him. She's always adored Rowan. If I tried sneaking up on her this way she'd throw a fit. I've never been able to soothe her the way he can.

"They're all here, you know. Right here, right now, there are other lives being lived. Down there"—my mother points over the side of the wall at the ground hundreds of feet below, her eyes half closed—"there are houses. Children play in the grass."

I sigh with frustration. She's convinced her hallucinations are real.

"They *do*," my mother says, rounding on me defensively. "I can see them, Lillian."

"I've seen lots of things over the wall, Lady Samantha," Captain Leto says kindly. "Children playing wouldn't be the strangest thing, but it would probably be one of the nicest." The rest of the soldiers around us chuckle sadly. Walltop guards see plenty of evil and very little of the sweetness of children.

"When I was young, the holy men of my tribe used to talk about multiple worlds," Rowan says casually, as if he were having a completely sane conversation. "They told us that anything we could dream was true in some universe. They even told us that somewhere, each of us was a king."

"That would be one of your shamans, now wouldn't it, Lord Fall?" asks Leto, playing the same game Rowan is playing. Acting like this is normal.

"That's right," Rowan replies. His face lights up with a thought. "You should talk to a shaman, Samantha."

My mother laughs nervously and looks out over the edge. "You think so?"

"I do." Rowan nods emphatically, and the guards nod with him. Rowan holds his hand out to my mother. "My father knows the shaman of my tribe. I think you should meet him."

"A shaman at the Citadel?" my mother says, fluttering a dismissive hand in front of her face. "Is that even possible? I hear the shamans refuse to bond with willstones, and aren't allowed into the cities." She looks at me uncertainly.

"I can make it happen," I say. Anything to get her away from the edge—even if it means I agree to seeing one of those ridiculous shamans. Everyone knows it's the hallucinogenic mushrooms they eat that make them imagine other worlds, but at this point I'd agree to anything. "I'd like to meet him, too."

"You would?" my mother asks. She's confused now. She was about to take Rowan's hand, but she pulls it back. "It would be so embarrassing if anyone knew you had one of those shamans come to see you, Lillian."

"Who'd find out? This is Walltop, Lady. No one here would ever say a word," Captain Leto says seriously. "Now, why don't you come into the guardhouse and get closer to the fire?" he adds in a congenial way. "We've got some tea on, haven't we, Sergeant?"

"Oh, yes," another soldier replies immediately. "S'not great, but it's still tea. You must be icy cold, Lady Samantha."

"That's great," I enthuse. "We'll go have some tea in the guard-house and tomorrow Rowan will arrange a meeting with the shaman."

We all stare at my mother as she tries to make sense of what we've said. Her hand wavers over Rowan's outstretched palm.

"I am rather cold," she admits, and takes Rowan's hand.

He leads her down off the edge and my Walltop men sweep in and take over. They shower her with promises of too-strong tea and too-dry biscuits as they unobtrusively surround her with their burly bodies and form a jovial barrier between her and the edge. I'm near to tears, and Rowan knows it. It kills him to see me cry.

"It's alright," Rowan says, pulling me close to his side.

"Is it alright?" I ask, my voice shaky.

"I'll make it right. I swear it. We'll make her better," he promises . . .

. . . *That was the beginning of my journey down this path, Lily. I met the shaman and I shouldn't have. There was a reason witch magic and shaman magic were kept separate, although I didn't know it then. But I did it for Mom.*

Lily awoke to the homey smell of roasting turkey. She rolled over and felt a body next to hers.

"Be careful. Rowan will strangle me if you reinjure yourself," Juliet said. She stowed the book she was reading and slid down on top of the covers, laying her head on the pillow next to Lily's.

"Where is he?" Lily asked groggily.

"Making dinner. He's an amazing cook," Juliet said.

"I know." Lily grinned. "Wait till you see what he can brew up in a cauldron."

"Oh, I've seen plenty of that while he was healing you, although he had to settle for one of Mom's old stockpots until he ordered a real cauldron off the Internet." Juliet bit her lower lip as she thought about what to ask. "I've seen Rowan do a lot of strange things. Is he really from a parallel world like Mom said?"

"Mom's not crazy," Lily replied quietly. "There are countless other versions of the world. I've been to one of them. Mom sees all of them, all the time. That's why she seems crazy—because she doesn't always know which world her body is in when her mind is in so many."

Juliet's luminous brown eyes rounded with sadness. "We just pumped her full of drugs," she whispered.

"We were wrong."

The two sisters cuddled closer to each other, silently giving the other permission to forgive herself.

"And everything Rowan told us about witchcraft and willstones and mindspeak?" Juliet asked, still trying to absorb it all.

It's all true, Jules. Magic is real. He's what's called a mechanic and I'm a witch. This is mindspeak.

Juliet's eyes widened for a moment when she heard Lily's voice in her head, and then they darted down to the three faintly glowing willstones hanging from a chain around Lily's neck. "I guess I should be more surprised, but I'm not," Juliet said, a dreamy look stealing over her face. "I think we've always been able to read each other's minds a little."

I think we have.

"You gotta teach me how to do that," Juliet said, grinning.

"Deal," Lily agreed.

"So," Juliet said, her eyes narrowing teasingly, "are all the guys in this other world like Rowan? And if they are, can you get me one?"

"No, they are *not* all like Rowan," Lily replied, laughing.

"Damn." Juliet sighed and rolled over onto her back. "I guess I'll just have to keep imagining a gorgeous, intelligent badass who lives and breathes for me."

"Your guy's out there," Lily said. She gave Juliet a devilish smile. "But Rowan's mine."

"Apparently," Juliet replied dramatically. "He's hardly left your side at all. I had to force him to take yesterday and today off and just get out of the house. And no wonder." Her face suddenly pinched with worry. "We thought you were going to die. You were so badly burned we were sure there was no way anything could save you. But Rowan did it somehow."

Lily took her sister's hand. "I'm sorry I put you through that."

Juliet suddenly smiled and got out of bed. "Well! You're here now, you're safe, and you're going to stay that way," she said briskly, avoiding her feelings. "Are you hungry?"

"Starving," Lily said. "Do you think you can get me downstairs? I'm sick of being in bed."

"Your feet are the worst," she replied dubiously.

"Please, Jules. I'm going stir-crazy." Lily gave her sister a pitiful look.

"I guess if we go slow it'll be okay," Juliet said, relenting.

Juliet heaved Lily to her feet and they shuffled down the hallway together. Lily's feet stung so much she found herself laughing at the pain as they minced their way down the stairs.

"What do you think you're doing?" Rowan asked scathingly from the bottom of the stairs.

"I wanted to eat at the table," Lily said apologetically.

"You have zero common sense," Rowan said, stomping up the stairs. "I tell you to stay still, but do you stay still? No. Why? Because you never listen to me," he mumbled grouchily, having a full-on conversation with himself as he gathered her up and carried her the rest of the way down the stairs.

Lily knew better than to pick a fight. "I am a giant pain in the ass," she agreed.

"Is that you, Lillian?" Samantha asked expectantly as she wandered into the kitchen.

Lily felt Rowan's back stiffen. Lily's mom was the only person who called her by her full name. Lily had never really thought too much about it, but now that name had an entirely different meaning for her, as it did for Rowan.

"Hi, Ma," Lily said, smiling, as her mother came over to inspect her.

Rowan deposited Lily in a chair at the kitchen table and Samantha fluttered over her. She pushed Lily's hair back and scanned her face, her eyes threatening tears.

"Will she always have these scars?" Samantha asked.

Lily drew in a shocked breath. She hadn't seen herself yet and hadn't given any thought to how she might be permanently maimed from the pyre.

Oh my God, Rowan. Is my face scarred?

"The marks aren't scars. They're graft lines," Rowan said quickly, answering both Samantha's spoken question and Lily's mindspeak. "As long as Lily gives the new skin I grew her time to scaffold properly, it will heal evenly and there will be no scars."

You grew me skin?

You can't save tissue if the nerves are dead, Lily. You have to start over and grow new nerves.

That's kinda gross, you know.

Much better than being skinless. I'm extremely fond of your skin, you know, and I have a vested interest in seeing it on your body.

Rowan suddenly bent down and stole a kiss. Startled, Lily looked at her mom and sister. She'd never been intimate with anyone in front of her family before, and she didn't know how to feel about it. Samantha didn't even seem to register it, as if she'd seen Rowan kiss Lily thousands of times before. When Lily considered it, she decided Samantha probably had seen them kissing in other worlds. Juliet, however, stared at Lily wide-eyed and Lily just knew she was going to get teased the second she and Juliet were alone.

Does it make you uncomfortable when I kiss you in front of your family, Lily?

I don't know, Rowan. It's never happened to me before.

I'll kiss you in private, then.

Promises, promises.

I'm good at keeping promises.

"Do you want some help, Rowan?" Juliet asked, unknowingly interrupting Rowan and Lily's telepathic flirting.

"No, you just sit," he said with a warm smile, and began serving the turkey, mashed potatoes, squash, and green beans.

"Why are we having Christmas in January?" Lily asked, helping herself to only the vegetable part of Rowan's feast. She was still vegan,

39

and after letting Rowan cut her hair to avoid drinking squirrel blood, she fully intended to stay that way.

Lily ran a hand through her hair, checking the length. It had been short to begin with and more of it had burned off in the pyre. Lily wondered how much she had lost. She ran the strands through her fingers and found it to be longer than expected.

"Because you missed it," Samantha answered, smothering her mashed potatoes with gravy. Lily forced herself to stop touching her head and tried not to worry too much over her hair.

"And I like turkey," Rowan said. "Haven't had wild turkey in years," he added quietly.

"*Wild* turkey?" Lily asked.

"Yeah. I went hunting yesterday."

"Why?" Lily asked, confused. "There's a grocery store right up the street."

"It was Juliet's idea that I needed to relax. And hunting relaxes me," he replied with a shrug. "Took me forever to find this bird, too. Not many left out here. Had to walk through the woods to this little stead called *Hop-king-ton* to find one," he said, sitting down and tucking into his meal.

Juliet's jaw dropped. "Please don't tell me you went to the bird sanctuary out there? Right on the border of Hopkinton and Ashland?"

"What do you mean, bird *sanctuary*?" Rowan asked, alarmed. "Is turkey sacred in this world?"

Juliet shook her head, and Lily made a mental note to explain to Rowan later about endangered species and the shrinking wild— something he'd never encountered before.

"No, they aren't," Juliet said, and Rowan relaxed. "Go on with your story."

"It was a long hunt, but that small area was strangely plentiful," he continued. Juliet nodded resignedly. A bird sanctuary would seem strangely plentiful to a hunter like Rowan. "After I moved to Salem my dad and I would hunt turkey on the weekends and I grew to love the taste. We spent summers out west where I was born, though, on the Ocean of Grass. No turkey out there."

"What did you hunt when you were out west?" Juliet asked carefully, hoping it wasn't another protected animal.

"Buffalo, of course," Rowan answered. His face suddenly darkened. "When we weren't overrun by Woven. Western Woven are much smarter."

"So how far west did you get?" Lily asked, trying not to think of huge Woven chasing her across the open land of the Great Plains.

"Into the flatlands, past the *Misi-Ziibi,* but not much farther," Rowan answered.

Juliet and Lily exchanged a confused look. "Do you mean the Mississippi River?" Lily asked.

Rowan laughed out loud. "In Algonquin, *Misi-Ziibi* means 'Great River.' So it's like you're saying Great River-River. Forget it." He waved it off. "I'm not making fun of you. Your accent is actually kind of adorable, Lily," he said, taking her hand under the table and squeezing it. "My tribe spent a lot of time hunting on the edge of the Ocean of Grass, but no one's made it across to the far river, the *Pekistanoui,* since before the Woven Outbreak."

"I think the Pekistan-whatever-he-said has to be either the Missouri or the Colorado River," Juliet said in an aside to Lily.

"He means the Missouri," Samantha answered, and went back to her squash.

"Thanks, Ma," Juliet said with a quizzical smile. Lily shrugged. She had no idea how her mother knew that, either, but the sisters supposed they'd have to get used to their mother knowing random details about other worlds. Juliet turned to Rowan. "So the whole west is lost in your world because of the Woven?"

"It is," he replied. "And the farther west you go, the bigger and more intelligent the Woven get, and we call them by different names, too. Almost like they've earned titles. The two worst are the Pack and the Hive, although the Pride can be dangerous, too. But the Pride never leaves the mountains and you can usually slip past them."

"The Pack—is that like a wolf pack?" Juliet asked.

Rowan nodded. "The Pack is usually what stops Outlanders from going farther west than the Great River. And the Hive may as well be a brick wall. More like a legend, really—" He broke off, his brow furrowed.

"Hasn't anyone tried to study them and maybe find out how to get past them?" Lily asked.

"The Pack doesn't let you sit quietly and observe them, Lily. If they catch your scent, they *track* you. Then they come to kill you."

"What about the Hive, then? They're like bees, I'm guessing."

Rowan shrugged in a noncommittal way. "Sort of."

"Bees leave you alone if you leave them alone. I'm sure there's a way to study them quietly while they . . . gather nectar or whatever."

Rowan looked at her like she was insane. "Most people who encounter the Hive are never heard from again. There are two kinds that we know of—Workers and Warrior Sisters. I've seen a few of the Workers. They just look like large bees, but the Sisters are different. I think I saw one from a distance once, but I didn't stick around to study her, Lily. No one does. If you see any member of the Pack or the Hive, your best bet is to run."

"So, no one knows anything about them?"

"We know that the Pack and the Hive are more organized—but no one knows why, exactly. The theory is the Pack adapted so they can coordinate to hunt buffalo. The Hive is just . . ." He trailed off and swallowed hard. "You just run."

Lily could tell Rowan didn't want to talk about the Woven

anymore. She leaned closer to him with a warm smile to coax him out of his dark thoughts. "About that. You hunted bison on the Great Plains? On horseback?"

Rowan shrugged. "How else are you going to do it? Buffalo are fast."

God, that's so hot.

Right, Juliet? Wait—you just—

"You just did it!" Lily squealed out loud. "You figured out mind-speak!"

"I did! And you *heard* me, even though I didn't mean for you to," Juliet said, her exuberance dampening. "That's pretty terrifying. My thoughts are, like, out in the open now, aren't they?"

Rowan met Lily's eyes and grinned. "You'll get better at controlling it, Juliet," he said, eyes sparkling. "But there's always that chance a thought will sneak out when your guard is down. A clear conscience is your best defense when you share mind space with a witch."

Lily suddenly darted forward and kissed Rowan—partly because she wanted to, but mostly to distract him. If he looked hard enough, he'd easily see that her conscious was anything but clear.

So I can kiss you in front of your family, Lily?

We'll make it up as we go along, Rowan.

Lily looked down at her plate, her appetite gone, while the rest of her family chatted happily with one another. None of them had anything to hide, but she did. Rowan gave of himself entirely, but she had secrets. She had Lillian in the back of her mind and a burning need to know more about her, no matter how much it hurt Rowan. In that moment Lily realized that Rowan was a better person than she was. She had to make sure he never found that out.

That night, Lily tossed and turned. Guilt kept her awake—guilt and temptation. She thought of what she was already hiding from Rowan, and as midnight came and went and she felt Rowan fall into a deep dreamless sleep, she somehow convinced herself that one more secret wouldn't make that much of a difference.

Lillian? Did Rowan bring the shaman to the Citadel?

He did. And the shaman told my mother that she had a talent that not many women have. Women gifted with power are almost always crucibles, and the best crucibles become witches. But she was a farseer. She could see into other worlds, like the male shaman can, which is very rare. He told me that I had that ability, too, and that it would get stronger as I got older. He also told me that if I didn't learn to control it I would end up like my mother.

Terrifying.

It was, Lily. I was so scared of becoming like her I didn't tell anyone what he'd told me. I didn't want anyone to think I was sick-minded, you know?

Yes, I know, Lillian. Sometimes I look at Mom and I see so much about us that's similar. All I can do is hope that I don't turn out like her. I'm ashamed that I think that.

I was ashamed, too. Which is why I started training with the shaman in secret. I didn't even tell Rowan.

Show me another memory. I won't tell Rowan. I promise.

Okay, Lily . . .

. . . I'm running along the wall. My Walltop guards see me pass, but I have no fear that they will tell anyone on the Council or in my Coven about the meetings I've been having up here. Walltop guards would rather die than betray me. That's why I chose this place over any other spot in the city. My secrets are safe here.

I arrive at the guardhouse and duck inside. It is a Spartan place. A fire pit blazes in the center of the bare-brick room and a few sticks of unpadded furniture bend under the thick bodies of my guards.

"Is he here yet?" I ask the room at large.

The guards stand as one and chant, "My Lady," in perfect,

deep-toned unison. Again, I am struck by how archaic the customs are up here. A room full of huge, rough men and women and all of them avert their eyes like I'm some kind of goddess.

It unnerves me to be so revered, but the more time I spend up here the more I understand it. I've learned that every warrior on the wall is gifted. Not one of them has opted out of being claimed by me, as happens sometimes with the city guard, and unlike my city-level guards they are much more talented—talented enough to feel the true power of my willstone. Apart from my mechanics, only Walltop guards can appreciate the kind of strength I can give them, and only they crave the Gift as much as a mechanic would. They are better warriors for it, but never entirely whole people without it.

I can feel the tug of all their minds, and tonight I can't help but give in to their craving. The fire bends toward me. A witch wind moans around the flames as I gather heat. I change the heat into force and fill all of their willstones with a few drops of my strength. It's enough. I watch as every eye droops with euphoria. Every mouth parts. Every heart pounds. I can feel my strength welcomed into them like rain in the desert.

This is the danger I must avoid—the lust to fuel an army. I will always want to possess them and fill them with more than just this little jolt of power. I will be tempted to build a pyre and fill them with the Gift.

I am one of the few who can go to the pyre and live, and I will always want war because of this. The history books are clear about firewalkers—also known as warmonger witches depending on what book you read. I know the history of my rare kind, but still fight with myself. It feels too good to fuel an army to *not* want war. This is why I let so few of my claimed get close to me, and why I exclude all my mechanics except Rowan. I rein in my lust for violence. I will not allow myself to become a warmonger witch, like nearly every firewalker before me has been.

I think of Rowan and take enough strength from the thought of him to cut off the communion with my Walltop guards. Rowan is vessel enough for me.

Leto steps forward. "Thank you for that, Lady. Your guest is in my private quarters, as always," he says, his voice rough with gratitude. I tip my head in acknowledgment.

I show myself to Captain Leto's tiny quarters, and let myself into the sweltering heat of the shaman's makeshift sweat lodge. Inside there is only a desk, a fire, and a cot to furnish the room. On the cot sits the old shaman. He is tall and slender, and his limbs are long and gangly. His cinnamon-colored skin is wrinkled, but his hair is still coal black. He has streaks of red and yellow paint on his cheeks and eagle feathers braided into his long, silky hair in the old way. Rowan's hair would look like that, if he ever let it grow— which he won't do no matter how much I beg. He thinks it would make him look like a savage.

"Have you eaten today, girl?" the shaman asks, as he always does.

"No," I reply, ignoring the fact that he calls me "girl." Strangely, I'm not offended. From him it feels like an endearment. "No food, no water. As usual."

"Good." The shaman pats my knee in a grandfatherly way. "I want to talk with you before we spirit walk."

"Okay," I say tentatively. The shaman is not a chatty fellow, and he usually saves his speech for teaching. "About what?"

"The Woven," he replies, his eyes far away. The shaman straightens suddenly and looks me in the eye. "What would you do to get rid of them?"

I'm stunned. I stare back at the shaman and think of all the times Rowan has awakened next to me in bed, screaming. I think of how many times I've tried to drop into Rowan's nightmares to lead him to safety, only to find him on a never-ending plain, being chased by countless monsters. He's always a child in his nightmares about the Woven. And he never, ever escapes them.

"Anything," I whisper. "I'd do anything to get rid of the Woven."

He nods, like he thought I might say that. "On a spirit walk, I found a world that was like ours, except for one thing. The Woven have been eradicated."

"When? Where?" I say excitedly.

The shaman sighs and tilts his head back to stare at the ceiling. "When?" he asks ruefully. "Maybe too late. Where? In one of the hardest worlds to find, buried between millions of cinder worlds." He looks at me, and I'm shaken to see deep regret in his eyes. "It's a miracle place, folded between so much death and destruction I'd never have thought it could be possible."

I know what that means. It means only one universe out of thousands that were nearly exactly like it got it right. One slip, one wrong choice, and the path to a Woven-less world will end in destruction.

"But it's there," I say, my face bright with hope. "We can go there and find out how they got rid of the Woven, and bring the secret back here."

"We'd be *stealing* something from a world we aught not to have," he says gravely. "We'd be puttin' the Great Spirit out of balance."

"The Woven are what's out of balance," I say angrily. "They are a mistake that witches made, and that a witch should fix."

"It will be hard to get there. There are no versions of you, or any of your loved ones, alive in that world," he says, his eyes stern. "You'd have to jump without a lighthouse."

"How did you find your way there?" I ask, my voice small. It's treacherous to spirit walk without the lighthouse of love to guide you through the darkness between the worlds and I've never even considered trying to worldjump to a place where there was no other me, Juliet, Mom, or Rowan. I look at him, my brow furrowed. "Is there a version of you there?"

"There is," he says darkly.

"And do you love me?" I ask him, my voice quavering. It's an awkward thing to ask, but the shaman is not one of my claimed. He could only be my lighthouse if that other version of him loves me. I realize as I say it that I want him to love me.

"Not there," he says gently. "And *that* me is dying. When he goes I'll lose my lighthouse and we'll have no way to find that world again. I've watched that world for months, hoping to learn the solution to our problem by watching alone, but time's almost up. We can't wait anymore. I'd go myself but——"

"You're not a witch," I finish for him. "You can spirit walk, but only a witch can transmute a body into pure energy and make it worldjump."

"Could you send me?"

"You'd have to be one of my claimed so I could key into your energy, and you don't even have a willstone," I say, not bothering to keep the frustration out of my tone this time. His antiquated ways about willstones have always annoyed me, but until now I've respected his taboo about keeping witch magic and shamanism separate. Little good his respect for the old ways does us now. I sigh and try to be more respectful. "Even if I were to send you, I'd still have to know where I was going. It has to be me."

"Yes," he whispers. "But stealing from another world is an evil thing, Lillian. I question whether I should have told you 'bout this at all. I've already got an account of my evils to settle with the Great Spirit, and maybe I shouldn't be charging debts onto your soul, too."

"As far as I'm concerned, the only evil here is the Woven," I say.

48

He looks at me with a worried frown, like he sees a moral flaw in my statement, but he can't bring himself to argue against his own wishes. It's my turn to pat his knee. "It's okay. This decision isn't yours. It's mine. And if it's evil, then the evil is mine, too"—

Stop. I can't take this anymore, Lillian. You killed him. You sent the shaman to the oubliette to die. You actually had me fooled for a while. I was starting to see things your way, but there is no excuse for what you did to him. How could I have been so stupid?

Wait, Lily. There's still something you need to know about Chenoa and the shaman. The account he had to settle—

Chenoa? The Outlander scientist you were so desperate to kill, you sent out an army to mow down a defenseless tribe? Rowan's tribe! You say that you did everything for Rowan, but you went to war against him and his people. I must have been out of my mind to have listened to you for so long. Just shut up, Lillian. I don't want to hear you anymore.

You want to bury your head in the sand? Fine. But first ask yourself this. Would you have worldjumped into the unknown to find a way to get rid of the Woven—even if the shaman told you it was evil?

You know I would have. You're not the only one who's woken up next to Rowan while he's having a nightmare. I've felt his fear and I hate them for it. The Woven never should have been created in the first place.

Then is it so impossible to imagine that maybe all the choices I've made— evil as they may seem—are the same choices you would make if only you knew the rest of my story? Everything I've done has been to save as many lives as I can. To save Rowan's life.

Go away, Lillian.

CHAPTER
3

LILY COULD STILL SMELL ROWAN'S DELICIOUS CHRISTMAS-in-January dinner when she awoke with a start. She wiped her mind clean of Lillian, wanting to kick herself for being so naive and so weak. How could she have listened to her for so long?

Lily got out of bed, feeling a strange disquiet. A quick glance around her room proved she was alone. But something was wrong. She could feel it.

Rowan? Where are you?

Living room.

Lily padded downstairs on her tender feet and found Rowan on the couch. The couch was made up like a bed and he wore a pair of her dad's old pajamas pants. His face was lit by the blue glow of Lily's laptop, his eyes staring at the screen.

What's going on, Rowan?

He slid over in his makeshift bed and Lily sat next to him. On the screen was an ancient black-and-white photo of a pile of bison carcasses. He clicked on another link, and Lily saw a vast field scattered with countless dead bison.

At least when Outlanders die fighting the Woven, we get to go out bravely. There is no dignity in starving to death.

The bison slaughter was only one part of it, Rowan.

Lily took the laptop and typed in "Native Americans, smallpox" and let Rowan read. When he was finished, Lily typed in "Trail of Tears."

She sat next to him for the next hour as he browsed through one atrocity after another. They both read about how the different tribes were rounded up and forced on death marches across the continent to the reservations. They both learned the many different paths the Native Americans were forced to take, all of which were different legs of the journey known as the Trail of Tears. They stored those paths step by step in their perfect willstone enhanced memories. Finally, Rowan pushed the laptop aside.

I can't read anymore tonight, Lily.

Do you want me to go?

Of course not.

Rowan pulled Lily against his chest and leaned back against the pillows. He was quiet for a while, just holding her. "The route that went through Arkansas on the Trail of Tears? That's where my dad and I used to hunt. I was born somewhere around there."

"So, you're from Arkansas?" Lily asked, trying to get her head around it.

"I guess so," he said, shrugging. "We don't call it that in my world, of course. It's confusing because there are some things about our histories that are the same."

"I know," Lily said, sitting up. "And I think I've figured it out. Our worlds used to be one. Then the Salem Witch Trials happened and our worlds split. Everything in history before the trials is the same in both worlds, but after, it's all different."

"Our worlds split?" Rowan brushed her hair back. "Why do you think that happened?"

Lily smiled down at him. "It's always happening. Every choice we make is the splitting of one universe into two. In one universe, you go right, in another universe you go left. During the Witch Trials here, the witches were hanged."

"And in my world they were burned," Rowan said, catching on. "It was the burning that gave the witches incredible power—the ones who survived the pyre, that is."

"And they took over your world," Lily finished. "In my world, they died or ran away from Salem and hid."

Rowan looked at Lily admiringly. "How do you know all this?"

"Your shaman told me," Lily replied quietly, resting her head back down on his chest. "So, what tribe are you from, Rowan? You never told me. Cherokee? Choctaw?"

"Mostly Cherokee, but the tribes in my world have evolved. We're not 'Native Americans,' as you call them. We're Outlanders. We're the survivors of the Woven Outbreak and the throwaways from the cities, so we're mixed now. Outlanders are a bunch of different races all blended together and we speak whatever language mash-up we need to in order to get by," Rowan answered, stroking her hair. "My mom was white, you know, but she never spoke a word of English."

"You remember her?"

"No. But I was told she had blue eyes." He tilted his head and looked down into Lily's green ones. "And red hair."

"That explains it, then," Lily said, smiling up at him. "That's why you can't lay off the redheads."

Lily's smile dissolved. She thought of Lillian, and her claim that she became a murderer to save Rowan's people. Lily didn't know the whole story yet, but she did know that no one can lie in mind-speak. Lillian believed she'd saved lives by killing. That was *her* truth. After over an hour of reading about genocide and about how people like Buffalo Bill were seen as heroes in their day, Lily wasn't so sure what the words "murderer" and "hero" meant anymore. Would she kill a few to stop what had happened on the Trail of Tears? And if she wouldn't—if she wasn't willing to get her hands dirty in order to save thousands of innocent lives—would that make her a bigger monster than Lillian?

What's the matter, Lily?

I thought of Lillian.

Don't. Put her out of your mind entirely or you may accidentally reach out to her in mindspeak. You're here, you're safe, and you're going to stay that way.

Lily held her breath, waiting for Rowan to ask if Lillian had tried to contact her, but he didn't. He didn't even suspect Lily was hiding something from him. She tightened her arms around him and vowed then and there to never reach out to Lillian again, no matter how much she still craved answers.

As long as I'm with you, I don't really care where I am, Rowan.

She felt his arms tighten around her briefly before he let her go and got up. "I'll take you back to your room," he said quietly, and gathered her up in his arms.

"Can't we stay here?" Lily asked.

She met his eyes. The house was quiet. Everyone else was sleeping. Lily slid her hand over his shoulder, cupping the muscle in her palm, before she let her hand flare out and wander to his bare throat where his willstone softly glowed. She felt his pulse start thumping under her hand. He stood very still, and Lily could feel heat building in his body as he stared at her. He suddenly looked away.

"This isn't a good idea," he said, then started carrying her upstairs.

Lily caught a glimpse of her reflection in a dark window as Rowan carried her past it. A patchwork of angry red lines marred her white skin.

Rowan. My face—

Your face will be just as beautiful as it was before. I promise.

And how long will I be hideous?

Rowan put her in bed and pulled the covers over her. "Don't say that again. That has nothing to do with—" He broke off and lowered his voice. "I'm not sleeping separately because I don't want you, Lily. I'm sleeping separately because your skin is too fragile, and I need more than you can give me right now. I had a shock tonight, and I don't trust myself to just go to sleep if you're next to me." He stared down at her, waiting. "Are we okay?" he asked, his voice rough.

"Yeah, we're okay." She reached up and ran her fingertips over his bottom lip. "But you owe me."

Rowan laughed under his breath. "We'll tally up the bill between us later. So start thinking about how you're going to pay me back."

He gave her a small kiss before leaving her to wrestle with her conscience. She wanted to contact Lillian even though she'd sworn to herself she'd never do it again. She wanted to know *why*. Why did Lillian kill the shaman? She'd learned so much from him, and Lily could feel that Lillian loved the old man. Did she let him rot in the oubliette to prevent some greater evil?

Lily shut her eyes and hoped that after she dropped off it would be Lillian who would reach out for her in the Mist. That way, Lily wouldn't have to break her promise to herself. It was a tiny distinction, one that didn't really absolve her, but Lily was too curious to care. She wanted to know Lillian's story. She wanted to know what had happened on the cinder world.

Lily left her mind open and didn't have to wait long for Lillian to join her, with a memory ready to be shared.

. . . I am running, even though I barely have enough strength to walk. My foot catches on something and I plow headlong into the frozen leaf litter. The dead trees haven't borne leaves in many seasons, and those that cover the ground are rotten and won't burn. I see my forearms in front of me. They are covered in scabby sores, like the rest of the walking dead in this poisonous world.

I've been in this cinder world too long, and even though I can heal myself, I can no longer keep up with the rate at which my body is deteriorating. I must get out of here, or I will be past the point of saving soon. I stagger to my feet and force myself to run faster. I can hear their eager shouts and taunting whistles behind me.

They're coming. I can't outrun them. I need to hide. I look over my shoulder at just the wrong time. I crash into someone's chest, knocking myself to the ground and nearly knocking the breath from my own lungs.

"Got ya, pretty," the man murmurs, a leer pulling up against his ulcerous gums. "What's a little thing like you doing running 'round the woods anyway? Don't you know the Woven can get ya? They're just about the only things left alive, besides me."

I scramble away from him as he guffaws lewdly. He grabs my bare ankle and yanks me back toward him. Fine. He chose his own death, then. Bare skin on bare skin is all I need. I begin to drain the charge right from his nerves, feeding myself on his life. His eyes widen as he drops to his knees, the muscles of his face twitching and twisting his face into an agonized grimace. Being drained is probably the most painful death there is, but this thing is not a man anymore. The only people left in this world are murderers and rapists. They are scavengers, like the Woven. Only the most vicious of the vicious survived, and like the Woven the only real defense I have against them is to suck the life out of them when either attacks me.

"Witch?" he groans, confused and in excruciating pain. "But all the witches died in their cities."

He falls to the ground, convulsing. At least death comes relatively quickly this way.

"Not all," I say, kicking the stiff claw of his hand off my ankle. I scan his body quickly for anything I might need. Knife. Crossbow. Net. I take them all. I notice he has no willstone. This is the fourth one I've killed and none of them wore willstones. It's a puzzle I have yet to solve.

The deaths of men like this have helped keep me alive so far. There is no food left in this part of the world. To find food you'd have to live through a trek across the Woven Woods and far enough out into the interior of the continent to escape the fallout. A trip like that would be suicide. Either the Woven would get you, or starvation would. All the plants close to the cities have died in the never-ending winter. The surviving animals were made sterile or unable to produce healthy offspring by the blast and then, in a matter of months, were hunted until there were no more.

It didn't take long for this area of the world to run out of food, and getting to another area would mean somehow getting past an army of Woven—whose number seem to have grown, not fallen, since the holocaust. They have thrived in the ashes of this world, hemming in the few survivors of the blast until they all starve to death. The only living things I've been able to find on this side of the Woven Woods are the Woven and the scum who hunt me. I can live on the body energy of both with no need to eat, but water I cannot do without.

There is a large group of them gathered at what used to be a heavily walled ranch outside the city of Salem. Ranches like this are rare and existed only to raise luxury meats for the wealthy who could afford meat that was born and not grown in the Stacks. We used to send petty criminals and poor citizens who could not find work to these ranches. Work camps, we called them. As if calling indentured servitude *work* would make it better. I did this or helped at least. As

Lady of Salem and head of the Coven I had to cosign the papers for worker transport along with Danforth, who was head of the other branch of government, the Council.

I tried to change the law. I tried to get the men fair pay, but too many powerful people made too much money off the ranches. Eventually I gave in to the pressure, and now I'm paying for it. I justified sending them to the ranches by telling myself I was protecting society from criminals. Ironically, what I did ensured that criminals would be all that is left of humanity.

The ranches were built outside the city and their thick walls, originally meant to protect precious livestock from the Woven, were the only things for miles to survive the blast. This particular ranch I've been orbiting for weeks is all that is left for protection from the Woven and one of the only sources of water for miles. The scum who now run the ranch know I'm out here, hiding in the woods, taking my chances with the Woven. They send out gangs to search for me. I can survive their attacks, as I can the Woven, but only if they come at me in small numbers. Too many of either of them would overwhelm me. I wouldn't be able to kill them fast enough.

This is a game to them now. They don't seem to value the lives that I've taken in the slightest. They laugh when they find the bodies and talk about having more food to go around. Probably because they know that soon I'll need water again, no matter how tainted it is, and I'll come back to their well. They'll catch me eventually, and then they'll put me in the barn . . .

The barn, Lily. They did catch me, and then they put me in the barn.

Lily shook herself awake, instinctively severing her connection to Lillian to protect herself, but her body was still flooded with every drop of Lillian's intense fear. Lily ran her hands over the top of her covers, still not sure if she was feeling the crackle of burned-out leaves under her fingers or the soft nap of her duvet. She circled her hands again and again until the echo of Lillian's feelings ebbed away.

Lily! What happened?

Lily looked around her bedroom as if it were the first time she'd ever seen it. Lillian had been close to panic and Lily couldn't shake it off, not even to answer Rowan. The image of a white barn with peeling paint and a rusty chain binding the door shut crowded out any other thought. Something had happened in that barn—something that had changed Lillian.

"Lily," Rowan said. She looked up and saw him standing over her. "What happened?"

"Nightmare," Lily answered, and realized that she wasn't lying. Her spirit had strayed into the Mist, that empty nowhere-land that was somewhere between deep sleep and death. What she had witnessed there had been a nightmare for Lily, even if it was a memory for Lillian. "I was being chased."

Rowan sat on the edge of Lily's bed. "I have that nightmare all the time. The Woven come out of nowhere. I run, but I'm too slow."

Lily frowned. She'd had nightmares about the Woven, but this was worse somehow. Humans had chased Lillian, and humans can hurt another person in ways that animals can't. Rowan brushed the tears off her cheeks.

Do you want me to stay with you?

"Lily?" Juliet asked from the doorway. She was wearing mismatched flannel pajamas. The top half was decorated with clouds, but the bottoms had cows jumping over the moon. She was so disheveled and adorable that Lily smiled.

No, Rowan. I think I want my sister tonight.

Okay. Whatever you need.

"I had a nightmare. Will you stay with me, Jules?" Lily asked, ignoring the hurt look on Rowan's face. She couldn't spend the night with him. What if she shared another one of Lillian's memories and he picked up on it?

"Sure," Juliet replied, already crossing the room. Rowan lifted up the covers for Juliet and tucked the sisters in together.

"I'll be downstairs if you need me," he said before leaving them.

Lily settled in and put her head on her sisters' slim shoulder. *Did I wake Mom, Juliet?*

She's out like a light, Lily.

Drugged again.

No. Rowan gave her tart cherry juice, a bite of turkey, and then he put lavender under her pillow. No drugs. He said she didn't need them anymore.

Rowan's treating Mom?

Yeah. And she's doing really well, Lily. She's more aware now. Damn, I love mindspeak.

It makes some things easier.

And some things harder, I'm guessing.

Lily didn't need to answer.

Carrick killed the spider very slowly, pulling off one leg at a time. He knew, if no one else did, that the moments just before death were the only pure moments in life. That's why when he killed he tried to make it last. Dying was the most important thing a body could do besides being born, and in a way Carrick saw himself as a mother—a mother who pulled her babies back into her warm self rather than pushing them out into the cold world. The only difference between dying and being born was that babies don't remember their births. But if souls live on, Carrick was sure that any one of them would remember their deaths, especially if he had been their death-mother.

Carrick was good at making death memorable. It was the one skill he'd been trained for since he was a small boy. He'd learned how to hurt things from his father, Anoki, who was the bait man for their small tribe. It was Anoki's job to lay trails of wounded animals away from the group. The blood and the cries of distress from the wounded animals led the Woven away from the tribe, and kept people safe.

Anoki was very good at his job. The best. He could make one sheep squeal until dawn, as it dragged itself, wall-eyed with pain, in any direction Anoki chose. He knew just how to break a dove's wing so that it fluttered helplessly for hours inside the scrub, or hamstring a wolf so it howled for help, until the whole pack came to share in its death by the Woven. Anoki was a feared man—the tribe could hear the echoes of his handiwork all night long as one tortured animal after another screamed its way to death. He was an important man—he kept his tribe safe. He was a loathed man—because everyone knew he liked it.

Carrick's mother, Mary, couldn't have been more different. She was a gentle soul, full of laughs and flashing smiles. Fair skin, light red hair, and blue eyes, like a city woman's. She was the bride that Anoki demanded for his services to the tribe, but she was too valuable for him to ever keep. Everyone said Mary could have been a witch if she'd been raised in one of the cities.

Mary's freedom from Anoki was helped along by River Fall. Some say because River had grown heartsick from mending her broken bones and stitching together that smooth white skin of hers. He pleaded with the elders to release Mary from her bond with Anoki. If they did not, he warned, Anoki would eventually kill her. The elders agreed, and freed Mary. But Carrick was not part of the deal. If the tribe wanted to keep their bait man, Anoki had to be allowed to keep his son. And in tribal law, sons belong to the fathers, while daughters belong to the mothers.

Mary left Carrick behind. She took River Fall for her next husband, even though she could have had any man in the tribe. She had magic in her blood, and everyone wanted a child with magic. Carrick could still remember how Mary looked at River. How the two of them fawned over that squalling baby boy.

Rowan.

Rowan was loved from the moment he was born. And when Mary took fever and died, it only made River love Rowan even more. Carrick had no memory of love. But pain—*that* was something he understood. Suffering had more meaning to him than any kiss or any caress ever could.

Love left. But death was forever.

Carrick saw light flashing down at the end of the cell block. He was the only inmate on this level, and since being imprisoned by Lillian for his involvement in Lily's torture in the oubliette, he'd been kept mostly in the dark as punishment. Much better than what had happened to Gideon for conspiring against her. Lillian sent him into battle, and the fool got his head chopped off in the first few seconds of fighting. By Rowan, no less, Carrick had heard. The dark, the cold, and the thin rations didn't bother Carrick. In fact, he applauded the witch's attempt to discipline him. He stowed his half-dead spider carefully under the metal cup chained to the faucet in his cell, smiling. No one knew more about discipline than Carrick.

"On your feet," growled a guard.

Carrick stood, blinking against the torchlight in the man's hand. Next to the guard he made out the slim shape of a small woman. Tiny though she was, he could feel her strength coming at him in waves.

"My Lady of Salem," Carrick said, soaking her in. He'd gone weeks without feeling that level of power, and he'd craved Lily's willstones more than anything else since—more than food, water, or light. "It's a pleasure."

His eyes adjusted, and he saw Lillian looking at him through the bars of his cell. Carrick was very good at reading faces, even a face that was still healing from burns as hers was. Lillian kept her expression blank, but he could still see loathing behind her calm eyes. And something odd that he couldn't quite place. Her eyes were turned in on herself. She barely took him in at all.

"You have talent," she said dully. "A lot of talent."

"Runs in the family," he replied in his deep, quiet voice.

Lillian nodded, her eyes wandering away from him, like she barely cared that he had hurt another version of her and would have hurt her if it had been her willstone he'd held in his hand.

"Can you spirit walk?" Her eyes flicked back to his and narrowed in warning. "And don't lie to me."

"No," he replied, stunning himself with his own honesty. "But I was told by the shaman that I had the ability."

"What happened?"

"He refused to train me." Carrick tried to hold her detached and puzzling gaze, but he couldn't. He didn't understand her, and he didn't like that. Carrick was used to understanding what people wanted and gaining the advantage by manipulating their desires. With Lillian, he didn't have the foggiest idea what she intended.

"Can you feel Rowan?" she said, cocking her head to the side.

Carrick searched inside himself. "He's very far away. Farther than he's ever been before. But I don't think he's dead."

"Come closer," Lillian said. "Right up against the bars." Carrick did as she said. "Has any other witch claimed you?"

"No," Carrick replied, still confused. He caught a flash of resignation in her eyes, and understanding dawned on him in an instant. "It's not me you loathe. It's *you*."

"Get down on your knees."

"Yes, My Lady," Carrick said, sinking down in front of her.

CHAPTER

4

OVER THE NEXT TWO DAYS WHILE LILY'S SKIN WENT from a checkerboard of red patches to smooth, she kept her promise to herself. She didn't reach out to Lillian, even though she thought about it every time she was alone—which, thankfully, wasn't very often. Every time Rowan and Juliet left the house to shop for food or new clothes for Rowan, her mom seemed to appear, anxiously hovering nearby.

"It was a good thing that Rowan killed Gideon," Samantha said out of the blue. Lily had just taken her morning shower and was trying to untangle her wet hair. Hearing Gideon's name made her hands stiffen. Her mom took the comb, her hands unsteady, and went to work on a knot at the back of Lily's head.

"Did you see what he did to me in the oubliette?" Lily asked, her voice low. She sat down at the vanity table and looked at her mother in the mirror.

"Yes. He and Carrick tortured you," Samantha answered. She didn't meet Lily's eyes in the mirror, but instead focused on gently working one of Lily's knots free. "At least, I think it was the version of you that I raised. It's hard sometimes, you know. Hard to tell which of the millions of you is the one that *this me* raised."

"I can't say I know exactly what you mean—not in the way you do—but I do understand."

Tears welled up in her mother's eyes. She smiled through them bravely. "I've been called crazy for years, but do you know what crazy is? Crazy is being able to see what your daughter is going through, and not being able to do anything about it."

"Mom, you saved me. And Rowan. You were the only one who was clearheaded enough to guide us home. To do that, you'd have to be the least crazy person I've ever met."

Her mom nodded, but didn't look up. She kept untangling Lily's hair, smoothing each spiral curl between her fingers before moving patiently onto the next. Her mother had magic fingers when it came to Lily's riot of curls, which were now barely shoulder-length. A lot of her hair had burned away in the fire, but her hair grew unnaturally fast. No one fixed her troublesome mane like her mom did, and the familiar touch soothed them both.

"Gideon deserved to die," Samantha said serenely. "Maybe Carrick does, too." Her brow pinched. "The other Lillian claimed him, you know. The Lillian who stole you has claimed Carrick as her head mechanic. She's training him."

"Do you know why she chose Carrick?" Lily asked, her back stiffening.

"I'm sorry but I don't. I can see into the worlds of my children, but I can only see directly around them as it happens. Like watching a million movies at once," Samantha said, and smiled. Her smile fell and her tone went cold. "I don't share mindspeak."

"Can't or won't?" Lily asked gently.

"Won't. Unless it's to save your life, like when I guided you back home." Samantha finally met Lily's eyes in the mirror. "I would never burden any of you with what's in here," she said, touching her temple. "It's too much."

"Thank you," Lily said quietly, knowing she would never be as strong as her mother.

"I love you, too, dear," Samantha said, probably answering another version of Lily who had said "I love you" instead of "thank you" in a different universe. Samantha kissed Lily on the head and wandered out of the room.

Lily sat for a while, wondering if she should tell Rowan about Carrick. Bitterness swelled inside her. Lillian had nearly convinced her that she had Rowan's best interests at heart. But what possible reason could Lillian have for claiming Rowan's half brother, if not to hurt Rowan? It seemed like every time Lily started to understand Lillian, she learned some new unforgiveable thing about her and hated her all over again.

Carrick was Rowan's only remaining blood relative, and in families where magic was strong, close blood relatives could mindspeak without using willstones or without becoming stone kin by touching each other's stones. Lily still hadn't deciphered all the different ways in which touching willstones was viewed in Rowan's world because it meant different things depending on how much magic each person was capable of, but Lily did know that the lesser the magic, the more superficial the bond. In the nightclub, Lily had seen how some people in Rowan's world touched each other's stones for a weekend thrill. For them, becoming stone kin wasn't very serious. The sensations exchanged and the bond that was created was temporary.

That was something Lily couldn't imagine. Touching willstones was a different matter for her, as it was for all mechanics, crucibles, and witches. As a witch, when Lily touched someone's willstone, she claimed that person for life. The only way to break out of that commitment would be for that person to smash his or her stone—something as painful as cutting off a limb.

Allowing oneself to be claimed by a witch or to become stone kin with a mechanic where the bond was lifelong as well, was never something that people in Rowan's world took lightly, but it seemed Carrick knew little of what witches and mechanics were capable of. Carrick had spent his life Outland. He hadn't been around people with magic the way Rowan had. The way Lily figured it, Carrick must have had no idea that those with strong magic, like Rowan, could mindspeak with blood relatives without becoming stone kin. That ability was extremely rare, and not something that Carrick had ever encountered before.

Good thing for Lily, too. When Gideon kidnapped her, Rowan had found Lily by exploiting his blood bond with Carrick, and even though the two had never become stone kin, Rowan could see through his half-brother's eyes. He had spied on Carrick and found the oubliette without Carrick ever knowing that Rowan had piggybacked inside his mind. Could Carrick now do the same to Rowan? Lily stood very still, trying to think.

The doorbell rang, shaking Lily out of her worried thoughts. She heard her mother answer the door and an authoritative woman's voice drifting up the stairs. Right away, Lily didn't like the way this woman was talking to her mother. There was something pushy and condescending about her tone. Lily went downstairs, already in a fighting frame of mind. Samantha was standing in the doorway, blocking the entrance with her body.

"Ma? What's going on?" Lily called out as she came swiftly to her mother's side.

Samantha moved a bit to the side and revealed a tall, solid woman. Her brown hair was dyed a shade too dark and Lily could make out gray roots growing in at her temples. The woman narrowed her eyes at Lily, and the look on her face was almost triumphant. Like she'd just won something.

"She's not *that* sick, I see," the woman said mockingly to Samantha as she tried to push her way inside.

"Who are you?" Lily asked, striding forward. "Mom, it's okay. I got this." Lily put her hand on her mother's tense arm and stood next to her. Together they blocked the door, not allowing the woman to come inside.

"I'm Special Agent Simms, Lily, and I've been looking for you," the woman answered. Her eyes skipped over Lily's face, the hash marks of Rowan's skin graft more apparent now that Lily was standing in the light coming through the doorway. It was obvious now that Lily *was* sick, and that some kind of treatment had been done to her skin. The agent's eyes pinched around the corners as she weighed a new strategy in her head.

"I've been recovering," Lily said briskly.

"Yes. From radical subcutaneous exposure therapy," Simms said dubiously.

"Yeah," Lily said, pointing to the red marks on her face and arms. "It's been sort of hard on me, which is why I haven't been in touch with anyone. They say I'm supposed to limit my contact with foreign substances until I'm one hundred percent." Lily pursed her lips, passively implying that Simms was a foreign substance.

"I completely understand," Simms said, suddenly smiling. "You look like you've been through hell."

Something flickered in Simms's eyes—a combination of pity and genuine concern. She could tell that something bad had happened to Lily, and more than curiosity drove her. Lily realized that Simms was a good person, even if she did rub Lily the wrong way.

"I'm feeling much better, actually," Lily said honestly. "No more seizures."

"That's wonderful." Simms's fake smile flashed back on again and Lily's dislike for her rekindled. "I'm so glad to hear that you've made such a miraculous recovery, especially considering how worried we all were about you."

"Thank you for your concern," Lily said cautiously. She didn't know where Simms was going with this and she didn't trust her.

"So you'll be going back to school soon? I'm sure you're eager to graduate with your class," Simms said smoothly. Lily hadn't thought about going back to school, and the very notion seemed ludicrous to her. Simms watched Lily's calm expression falter and smiled a *gotcha* smile. "That's why you got the treatment at such an odd time of year, right? You couldn't wait for summer break because it was your lifelong dream to walk with your class on graduation day. Or so I've been told."

"Right," Lily answered confidently, trying to recover from her misstep.

"Right," Simms parroted. "Just like you didn't tell your friends you were going away for treatment because you wanted to surprise them."

Lily kept her mouth shut. She knew Simms didn't buy a word of any of this, but it didn't matter. There had been no crime. All Lily had to do was stop talking and Simms wouldn't have anything to go on, but as the staring contest stretched out Lily started to understand what she was dealing with. Simms wasn't going to give up until she got an explanation she could live with—and maybe even a culprit to arrest.

"Well. I'll let you get back to healing from your ordeal," Simms finally said. She turned to leave, and then swung back around as if something had just occurred to her. "Oh, Lily? What was the name of that miraculous clinic you went to? I can't seem to get a straight answer about that from anyone. I thought *you'd* be able to help me, considering you were there for three months."

Lily's mouth parted and her mind went blank. Samantha spoke up to fill the void a second too late.

"I told you it was a holistic healing center on a Native American reservation, which is why it didn't show up as a hospital on your search. The name is hard to pronounce. It's Native, you know," she said, her hands fluttering to her frizzy hair like startled birds. "I'll send the details to your e-mail address when I can."

"When you can," Simms repeated almost mockingly. She'd seen enough. "I'll be waiting. And I'll tell the superintendent of your school how excited you are to be coming back, Lily." She looked Lily up and down. "You're so happy you're practically speechless, aren't you?"

Simms left them, but Lily didn't shut the door or turn away until her car had disappeared around the corner.

"Come inside, Lillian," Samantha urged.

"Has that horrid woman been harassing you this whole time, Ma?" Lily asked angrily, following her inside. Her mother was shaking and her eyes skipped around like she couldn't settle her gaze on anything solid.

"She's been very persistent," Samantha said, trying to smile comfortingly, but only managing a wan grimace.

Juliet and Rowan came rushing in the side door, just back from their trip to the market.

"Was that the FBI agent I saw at the end of the block?" Juliet asked. She plunked down a bag of groceries, her eyes wide.

"Yeah," Lily replied. "Don't worry. She can't do anything to us."

"Except keep harassing everyone, like she's been doing. Which is bad enough," Rowan said, tipping his chin at Samantha.

Your mom can't handle this kind of scrutiny, Lily. She'll crack.

What should we do, Rowan? I can't make Simms go away.

"You need to get back to your normal life as soon as possible," Rowan said aloud. "Blend in. Don't give the agent any more reason to be suspicious."

Samantha had started wandering toward the garage door. She was twisting her hands together so tightly the skin on her knuckles was thin and white.

"It'll be okay, Mom," Juliet said, chasing after her and catching ahold of her elbow.

"I think I'd like to make a pot," Samantha said, her eyes wild.

Juliet and Lily shared a pained look. "Ma, you're out of clay. Why don't you let Juliet take you upstairs so you can lie down?" Lily said.

"I'll make you some tea, Samantha," Rowan said, already reaching for the kettle.

"Oh, that'd be lovely," Samantha said with a relieved look. "I love your teas."

"I'll bring it up to you as soon as it's ready," Rowan replied cheerfully.

Juliet brought Samantha to her room, leaving Lily and Rowan to speak in tense undertones.

"We need to come up with a name for that clinic," Lily said. "Simms wants to know exactly where I've been for three months."

"Juliet and I are working on a phony Web site. It's nearly done. Look, let me worry about that," Rowan replied. "You focus on settling back into your life."

Lily laughed mirthlessly. "Like that's ever going to be possible."

"It better be," Rowan said sharply. "Or what was the purpose of coming back here at all?"

"I didn't come back to fulfill a purpose. I came back because——"

"Because you were dying, and if you were to go back to my world it wouldn't take long before something else would be threatening your life," he said, cutting her off. "We're here so you can live a long and normal life. There's nothing for you to do, except move on and be happy. That's it. You need to put my world behind you and rejoin this one like a regular person or your family is going to suffer for it."

Lily was taken aback by his vehemence. She didn't know what to say, only that she felt hollow and cut off from him. The adventure was over, and Lily had to accept that.

"You should sit. The skin on your feet isn't completely healed yet," he said, softening his tone.

Her feet were hurting her. Lily took a seat at the table and gingerly lifted a foot to look at the bottom. Blood had seeped through her sock. The sight of blood reminded Lily of Carrick.

"Could you tell if Carrick was inside your mind, spying on us?" Lily blurted out, changing the subject.

"Of course I could," he said, coming to her. He saw the blood on her sock and pursed his lips, back in angry mode again. "You can't be running around yet, Lily. You have no calluses on your feet anymore."

"Just before Simms showed up, Mom told me that Lillian claimed Carrick. Lillian made him her head mechanic," Lily replied through her teeth. Now that she was sitting down her feet had started throbbing.

"Here, let me do it," Rowan said.

He left the room and came back with a leather pack very similar to the one he'd carried when they were hiding in the Woven Woods. Lily assumed that he'd made himself a new one. Inside were the silver knives he'd worn into battle the last night they were in his world and all kinds of small jars and vials of potions.

"Lean back," he said. He pulled Lily's feet into his lap and began applying one of his tingly skin creams. His face was dark with anger, but his tone was gentle. "I've been trained to recognize it if someone tries to sneak into my mind. The only time I'm vulnerable is when I'm asleep, but I never sleep without casting a ward of protection around myself, which would wake me as sure as a hand shaking me if someone tried to steal into my thoughts. Didn't I teach you that?"

"Yes," Lily admitted.

He had taught her how to manipulate the finely knit fields of energy that make up what seems to be empty space. Field magic—wards and glamours—had several different uses. Wards operated like a bubble of security around a small area, and glamours distorted light and air to slightly alter the way things appeared, sometimes making things disappear entirely in dim light. Both were low-energy magic and not very hard to do; Lily just hadn't remembered to cast a ward around herself when she was half dead. And since then, maybe she hadn't wanted to remember to do it. A ward would have kept Lillian from contacting her, and whether she liked it or not, Lily needed to understand what had made Lillian the way she was and why she had made the choices she did, or Lily knew she'd be damned to repeat them. It was more than just curiosity or a perverse desire to view Lillian's memories. Lillian *was* Lily, and if Lily ever wanted to understand herself she had to understand Lillian.

"Lily?" Rowan was staring at her, worried.

"Sorry. I freaked out," she said, lying automatically. "I started thinking about Carrick and I freaked out."

Will you show me what he did to you in the oubliette?

Lily recoiled at the thought. To show him would be to go through it again. "I can't." Her voice sounded robotic and strangely disconnected, even to her.

You don't have to hide anything from me.

"I can't," Lily repeated, her face blank.

"Okay," he said, looking down.

Rowan stood and left the room, his face sad. As soon as he was gone, Lily felt empty. She wanted to call him back, but she knew if she did she'd have to open that dark box in the corner of her mind and show him what had happened in the oubliette. She couldn't share that with him. It would change the way she felt about her. There was only one person Lily was certain wouldn't judge her. Lily momentarily dropped her guard, just to see if Lillian was there.

When I came back from the cinder world I shut Rowan out because I couldn't tell him what I'd done, or what had been done to me. You and I are the only ones who can really understand each other. Come back, Lily. You need me as much as I need you.

No, I don't. Go away, Lillian. I hate you.

As I hate myself — but look inside, Lily. You hate yourself, too.

"Keep stirring," Rowan said.

"But my arm's tired," Lily whined. She propped up her stirring arm with her other hand and sighed dramatically. "And the fireplace is so hot."

"I know," he said without a shred of pity. "Takes a lot of work to make that salve for your skin, doesn't it? Maybe from now on you'll remember that before you go running down the hallway when I tell you not to."

"Yeah, yeah," Lily groused. She peeked into the bubbling cauldron and wrinkled her nose at the heady fumes. "I don't think the punishment fits the crime." She looked up at Rowan and tried to coax a smile out of him. She knew he was still upset that she wouldn't share memories from the oubliette with him that morning, and she'd spent the rest of the day trying to thaw the frost between them.

"The punishment definitely fits the crime," he said, finally giving her that smile she was after. "Keep stirring. I'll go see how Samantha's doing with dinner."

"Uh-oh," Lily said, looking across the living room and into the kitchen. "You left her alone in there? With the stove on?"

"She can handle it," he replied calmly. A clank, a hiss, and a cuss came from the kitchen. "And that would be her handling it without an oven mitt. I'll be back." Rowan let his fingers trail across the sliver of exposed skin between Lily's T-shirt and the waistband of her jeans before darting off to rescue her befuddled mother.

Lily watched his lithe frame disappear into the kitchen and heard his deep voice rumbling under her mother's nervous tittering and leaned toward it. Wherever Rowan went was where Lily wanted to be.

"Keep stirring, lover girl," Juliet taunted from the sofa. She put down her magazine and tucked her bare feet under her.

"You don't get to fill in as taskmaster just because he's gone," Lily said, making a childish face at her sister, but picking up her stirring speed nonetheless.

What's going on with you two, Lily?

It's complicated, Jules.

I'll bet. Relationships are hard enough without adding the whole "he's from one world, I'm from another" thing. Literally, in your case.

You'd think mindspeak would make it easier, but it doesn't.

The house phone rang and Juliet reached over her shoulder to pick up the receiver on the coffee table.

"Proctor residence. Hello, Dr. Rosenthal," Juliet said, straightening her posture when she heard the voice of the superintendent of the Salem school system.

Lily tried to get closer to her sister and listen in on the conversation, but she was stuck at arm's length, stirring the cauldron.

"Yes, Lily's feeling much better," Juliet said, waving Lily away. "They say she's practically cured. Can you believe it? She's almost completely over her allergies." There was another long, agonizing pause. "Well, yes, I think she would be able to go back to school.

Oh, yes, of course. Everyone wants Lily to graduate on time. Yes. Yes, I know, she's always been at the top of her class and she shouldn't have any problem making up for lost time."

What the hell, Jules? I can't do that!

Yes you can. You have a photographic memory now. All you have to do is read and repeat on your exams. Now shut up so I can concentrate on Dr. Rosenthal.

"Yes, sir. But you know things are complicated at home for us," Juliet said sweetly into the phone. "Lily is still going through a lot of changes and we have a . . . a . . . ." Juliet looked up at Lily frantically.

What's the word when you have a counselor working with you on your lifestyle, Lily?

A life coach?

Bingo.

"A holistic life coach working with her and our mother for the next few months until they readjust," Juliet said smoothly. "Yes. Yes, of course we all want Lily to graduate. I'll talk it over with my parents and we'll call you tomorrow, Dr. Rosenthal. Yes. Thank you." Juliet hung up the phone and looked at Lily. "You're going back to school."

Lily knew this was coming, but it still rankled inside her. Why couldn't Simms just stay out of it?

"When?" Lily asked around the bitter lump in her throat.

Juliet shrugged. "He seemed to want you back in class by next week."

"She'll be ready," Rowan said, joining them.

"This is so ridiculous," Lily said, rolling her eyes. "Just the thought of having to sit in class and do homework is so—not okay."

"Come on, Lily, think about it. Even if Simms wasn't watching everything you do, what else are you going to do?" Juliet asked honestly. "Do you want to be a high school dropout? Maybe get a job as a checkout girl at the supermarket, if you're lucky?"

Lily bit her lower lip, chastened. "I guess not."

"Not that many want ads for witches in this world," Juliet said gently.

"And you are staying in this world," Rowan said. "I don't see what's so terrible about going back to school. This is a nice place, Lily, and all the dreams you had and the future you'd planned before can still happen for you."

Considering the way Rowan was raised, complaining about having to sit through class for a few more months did sound petty. Any Outlander would kill to live the way Lily did, and as she thought about it, she realized how much she had to be thankful for.

"I never stopped to think about what I wanted to do with my life," Lily said sheepishly. "I always thought I'd be too sick to get a full-time job or to join a radical save-the-whatever group. But I can do anything I want, can't I?"

"Yes," Rowan replied in a subdued tone. "And you can stop stirring now. Dinner is ready."

Lily gratefully abandoned her post by the cauldron and followed Rowan and Juliet into the kitchen, wondering again why Rowan seemed so distant.

His dinner ritual was new to both Lily and Juliet, who had become used to fending for themselves when their mother's condition worsened, yet Rowan's insistence that they eat at least one meal a day together was welcomed. Since Lily had come back two weeks ago, Juliet had been commuting to Boston during the day to attend her college classes but so far she hadn't missed one of Rowan's dinners. Juliet joked about free meals and bad dining-hall food, and Lily laughed along with her even though she knew that for both of them this was practically a miracle. Samantha had never been the most attentive mother and their father was more like a tourist who dropped in a few weeks a year than a parent. But with this dinner thing, Rowan had quietly pulled their family closer together. It was the first time either Juliet or Lily felt like she was part of a real family, rather than the unlucky crew member of a sinking ship.

Thank you, Rowan.

He didn't have to be told what Lily was thanking him for. Lily opened herself up to him so he could feel her gratitude and the sense of peace she felt sitting at a table with her loved ones. While continuing his conversation with Juliet about something gruesome she was doing to a cadaver in her anatomy class, Rowan reached under the table to take Lily's hand.

It's your family. I'm just borrowing it, Lily.

You're not borrowing. You're a part of it.

Rowan squeezed her hand reassuringly, but he didn't answer her in mindspeak. Something had been bothering him all day. Lily waited until after everyone had eaten their fill and gone to bed to bring it up again.

Rowan? Are you still awake?

Yes.

Lily went downstairs and found Rowan transferring the salve they had made from the cauldron into little pots. She joined him and silently began to help.

It came out very well, Lily. You're getting better at potions.

I still don't know what the heck I'm doing without you talking me through every step, though.

They finished up with the cauldron in silence. Lily could feel Rowan growing tenser with each second. When he finally had nothing else to distract him, she faced him with a determined look.

"What's the matter with you?" she asked, keeping her voice down so she didn't wake her mom.

"You're hiding something from me," he answered accusingly, his whisper coming out clipped and harsh.

"Yes, I am," she admitted. "Aren't I allowed to keep a few things to myself?"

"Not this." His dark eyes narrowed until they looked completely black. "I killed Gideon for imprisoning you in the oubliette. Now I need to know why I'm going to kill my brother. I need to know what Carrick did to you down there."

Lily held her breath, her mind racing. If she gave him this, he'd never suspect what she was really hiding. She couldn't believe she was willing to relive even one second of her torture in Purgatory Chasm in order to protect Lillian, but given the choice, she knew what her answer had to be.

"Only a little?" she whispered. "I don't think I can take any more than that."

Rowan nodded and stepped closer to her, his face softening.

Show me, Lily.

. . . The cold and dark go on forever. I shiver so spasmodically that my body aches. I think I must have been sleeping a moment ago, but something woke me. I sit up—panic giving me strength. It was the rope. The rope creaked. *He's coming.* I know it's Carrick. Gideon always announces himself, like I'm looking forward to seeing him or something. But Carrick sneaks down, like he knows what he's doing is wrong. I call out to him. He doesn't answer, but I know he's there. I start to bargain with him. I offer him things. Silly things. Important things. Anything. He ignores me. My words, my body, my promises mean nothing to him. All he wants is to hold my power in his hands. I'm crying, but I'm so dehydrated no tears fall. Just racking sobs that hurt more than proper crying would. Please, not that. Please. Don't touch my three little hearts. He hears me, I know he hears me because I'm screaming now. He picks up my willstones anyway. I hit the bars of my cell with my fists. I wail and shriek. I beg. God help me, I beg. The searing pain will end eventually, but the violation never will. Never. I hate you. I hate you. I hate me . . .

"Stop," Rowan whispered.

"Had enough?" Lily said cruelly, wiping at her streaming eyes. She wanted to punish him for making her go through that again, even though a tiny voice in the back of her head kept saying she deserved it. She felt disgusted, but not with Carrick. With herself. Lily pushed Rowan away from her, shoving hard against his chest.

"It's okay, Lily," Rowan said, capturing her wrists in his hands and drawing her against him. "It's not your fault."

Lily shook her head. "I don't believe that. Isn't that crazy?" She laughed, although it was anything but funny. "That's the worst part. I feel like it's my fault it happened to me. Like I should have fought harder. Or I should have killed myself."

"Don't say that," he said harshly. Rowan studied Lily for a long time. "Do you know what it means to be a survivor? It means that not only do you have to live through things, you have to live *with* them as well. The second part is much harder and sometimes it takes the rest of your life to learn how to do it. But at least you have the rest of your life, Lily. And that's what's important to me."

"Oh, I'm alive," she said ruefully. "Even if I am damaged."

"You'll heal," Rowan replied confidently.

"What if I don't?" Lily asked, genuinely afraid that she would never be the same again. "What if I stay a little bit broken forever?"

"You might," he said, lifting one shoulder like there was nothing anyone could do about it. "But I'd rather have you alive than perfect. If anyone says differently, then they don't really love you."

"And you do?" she asked, not sure why he would love her anymore.

Rowan answered by opening up one of his memories to her.

. . . She's climbing down from the tree, muttering to herself, taking forever and making so much noise I have no idea how they're not hearing this all the way in Salem. She kind of looks like an angry squirrel with all the red hair fluffing around her head and shoulders. Feisty little squirrel. She has to be the feistiest person in the world. I wonder what her world is like. I know it's nothing like this. Last night, when the Woven killed that man beneath this tree, the look on her face was pure shock. She didn't get hysterical, though. She was in shock all night, but she controlled it and found a way to work through it. This morning she told a joke to make me feel better. She's tough and funny and caring. Beautiful. And that *ass*. Don't look at her ass, you idiot. It's the same ass you've seen a million times, so just forget about it because the last thing you need is to start remembering what it feels like. She really isn't Lillian, is she? She sort of is Lillian, though, in all the best ways. No, that's wrong. I'm not looking for Lillian in Lily anymore, and I haven't since we've been on the run. It's strange, but I'm starting to wonder if it wasn't Lillian I loved. Maybe what I loved was the Lily in Lillian. Oh, shit. I think I love Lily . . .

"A feisty squirrel?" Lily asked, incredulous.

"Is that seriously all you got out of that memory?" Rowan threw up his hands and turned away. Lily caught him by the shoulders and pulled him back to her, hiding her blushing face by burying it in his chest.

"No," she replied.

She felt him relax against her, his arms easing her softer body against the solid angles of his. Very slowly, he pushed her hair back from her neck and brushed his lips across the skin just behind her ear. Barely touching her, Rowan swept his lips across her jaw to her mouth and kissed her so lightly it was like he was breathing her in. Lily leaned against him, trying to press closer, but he pulled away.

"Careful, don't press too hard against me," he whispered, a pained expression on his face. "And I really shouldn't be kissing your skin yet."

"Then don't," she replied. Lily looked up at him and smiled slowly as she slid her hands under the hem of his shirt. She ran the backs of her fingers across his belly. His breath skipped. She tugged at his shirt and raised a questioning eyebrow. "Off?"

Rowan pulled his shirt over his head, leaving his willstone glittering on his bare chest. He stood very still and let her touch him for as long as she wanted, but kept his own hands at his sides. She'd never had the chance to explore a man's body before. She watched, entranced, as his skin flushed and his muscles jumped under her fingers. Fascinated, she lowered her head to kiss all the places she'd touched and felt him shiver.

Do you want to know what this feels like to me, Lily?

Yes.

Rowan opened himself up to her and she eased her senses inside of his. It was like sinking into an ocean and letting her body float inside a mirror-topped world that spread around her, unfathomably large and unspeakably beautiful once she dipped her face below the surface. She felt her hands on his chest in two-way, both touching and being touched. She traced his skin, following his need as her own. Learning him.

Enough, Lily.

Rowan stilled her hands and stepped back.

Are you serious?

"Yes," he whispered through a laugh. "I don't want to rush. I don't want you to miss anything."

"You made love to Lillian." Her throat stung with the words.

Rowan was quiet for a moment before answering. "After a very long courtship." He tilted her chin up so she had to look at him. "Trust me. It's better this way."

Rowan brought her back to her room. One kiss was all he would give her before leaving her to stare at the ceiling, alone, and more than a little baffled.

Lily?

She didn't answer him. There was a knot in her throat, and she was scared that it was about to dissolve into silly tears.

Lily. I know you're awake and I know you're upset.

Wouldn't you be, Rowan? Wouldn't you be upset and confused if I wouldn't give myself to you?

Yes, I would be. So dream with me instead.

Lily wiped at a few escaped tears and sniffed. *What do you mean, dream with you?*

We stay in rapport as we fall asleep. We share our dreams. Would you like to do that with me?

Yes.

I'll show you the way.

CHAPTER
5

"THIS IS COMPLETELY HEALED," ROWAN SAID, INSPECTING the bottoms of Lily's feet. "That means you can go back to school whenever. Tomorrow, even."

"Good," Samantha said. A hand fluttered up absentmindedly to her hair as she looked at Rowan and grimaced. "Dr. Rosenthal is getting a bit testy with me for putting it off. And that woman called again."

"Simms? What did she say?" Lily asked, feeling a swell of protective anger.

"Oh, you know," Samantha replied. "I'm just glad you're going back tomorrow."

Lily tried to smile at her mother, but couldn't put her heart into it. She had gotten quite comfortable over the past week. Lillian had tried to reach out to her—usually when Lily was in a deep sleep and her spirit had strayed into the Mist. But on those rare occasions Lily had managed to quench her curiosity and push Lillian out of her mind. Lillian's attempts to contact her had become increasingly urgent, but Lily was determined not to give in to her own curiosity, and so far she'd been successful despite the mounting anger and desperation she'd sensed coming from Lillian.

Now that she had a clear conscience, the last few days had been some of the best in Lily's life. Every day she spent time with her mom, sister, and Rowan just relaxing and watching movies or reading books. Rowan was still struggling with culture shock and trying to learn as much of Lily's world as possible. Their worlds were so different that there was a lot to teach him.

In Rowan's world the Woven Outbreak had decimated the population of North America and had left just thirteen walled cities huddled against the eastern seaboard. Europe, Asia, Africa, Australia, and South America had abandoned North America to its fate in order to avoid any Woven contamination. Trade, immigration, and even communication had been banned between the Thirteen Cities and the rest of the world for two hundred years. In Rowan's world, North America was basically a plague zone that the other continents had decided to forget about.

Lily had still been unconscious at the time, but when Rowan learned that he could fly to Italy the next day if he wanted, or read any UK newspaper online with just a few clicks, he left the house to go look at the ocean for a few hours. When he came back, he sat down with Lily's laptop and began his self-education in what the world might have been if only the Woven hadn't been created. He liked this world, and Lily could see that he was adapting to it quickly. She started daydreaming about the future—about the two of them going to college and getting an apartment together, like regular folks. But even with his willstone-perfect memory, Rowan still had a long way to go before he could pass for a regular guy. He needed a crash course in pop culture.

Lily got a kick out of watching her favorite movies and TV shows with the excuse that they were "educational" for Rowan, although his response to certain movies wasn't what she'd expected. More than once, she'd found herself defending the awesomeness of *Star Wars* or *The Matrix* when Rowan shrugged derisively at both Luke Skywalker's and Neo's fighting skills.

"It looks fake," he'd said apologetically. "And there's nothing special about being able to run up walls or do back flips over an opponent. That's kid stuff for a mechanic who has even a halfway competent witch. And the way Skywalker handles his weapon"—he rolled his eyes—"twirling it around like a toy so it makes a cool noise. What an idiot."

"But Luke is in space. *You* can't fly through space in a spaceship," Lily had argued, deeply offended for Luke's sake.

"No. But I don't need to," he'd replied, pulling Lily close. "All I need is you and I can go anywhere."

"But it's not the same," Lily insisted weakly. He nuzzled her neck and the part of her that wanted to argue with him dissolved completely. "You're impossible," she sighed, before melting against him

"Anthony Bourdain is on," Rowan had said, grabbing the remote.

"Whatever you want," Lily sighed, relenting. He loved cooking shows and travel shows more than anything else, and if he found a show that combined the two he watched it obsessively. Lily couldn't say no, even if those shows made her want to eat the entire refrigerator.

If the days were fun, the nights were nothing short of spectacular—although still frustrating for both Lily and Rowan. He would only let her explore so far, and then he'd insist they separate. His dreams were getting increasingly vivid, however, and Lily suspected that it wouldn't be long before he realized that they had taken it slow for long enough.

Lily had even seen her father. That visit had been less than fun, but at least he'd stopped threatening to involve child services once he saw how improved Lily was. Even her dad had to admit that Rowan's doctoring was nothing short of miraculous, although he stubbornly refused to use the word "magic."

And now all that was about to change. Lily was going to go back to school and leave Rowan behind. Even the thought of being separated from him for eight hours a day was intolerable, but what bothered her more was that he seemed to want her to go.

"Check again," Lily pleaded. "The bottoms of my feet still feel a bit tender."

Rowan gave Lily a doubtful look.

Lily, you have to go back to school.

But you won't be there.

I'll be here, taking care of your mother.

"If your feet start to bother you, you'll just have to go to the nurse," Samantha said regretfully. Lily nodded her head in acceptance. She knew there was no putting Simms off forever. "And, you should call Tristan," her mother added. Samantha's eyes darted over to Rowan, and then away pointedly. "Have you two discussed how much you're going to tell him?"

Lily was momentarily stunned. She hadn't thought much about her Tristan since she'd been back, which she could hardly believe. But Rowan had thought about him. He wasn't surprised at all by this question.

"I've only met this version of Tristan once, but I can tell he's got just as much skill as a mechanic as the one in my world. He's going to sense the change in Lily." Rowan ran a frustrated hand through his hair. "He's going to be drawn to your willstones without knowing why."

"So what should we do? Tell him?" Lily tried to picture that conversation. She laughed out loud at the thought. "No way. The Tristan here is never going to believe it."

Rowan's face was grim. "You don't know what it's like to be a mechanic and be near a witch as powerful as you. He'll chase you."

Lily rolled her eyes. "He had no problem resisting my witchy magnetism for years. Just because I have willstones now won't make any difference."

"It will," Rowan said with quiet vehemence. "You shine now. Even the air around you tastes like magic, and anyone with a mechanic's potential will come running to you. It'll eat at him, Lily."

"He'll get over it," she said firmly.

"Why not tell him?" Samantha asked with a timid shrug. "He's always accepted you the way you are before. He'll accept this."

"Because I don't want to mess him up," Lily replied, realizing that she'd hit on at least part of what she was feeling. "Tristan wants to be a doctor in this world, and I don't want to tell him anything that'll make him choose a different life. I want him to be a huge success, and in this world that does *not* include believing in magic. Besides, it doesn't make any sense to tell him. I'm supposed to be reentering my life, right? What would I do with another mechanic? I'm not going to be witching it up on the weekends or anything."

Rowan didn't say anything more. Lily could feel several charged emotions spinning around in him at once, but there was one emotion that she couldn't quite place. It was a big feeling that hung like a gray curtain behind the sharp sparks of frustration and jealousy that took center stage in his heart. Lily thought it might be sorrow or loss. Whatever it was, it thumped through him like a slow, sad pulse— dull, but ever present.

What is that emotion, Rowan? I don't understand.

Do you trust me, Lily?

Completely.

Then tell Tristan the truth and let him choose what he wants to do with his own life. Don't make his choices for him.

Lily pulled herself out of rapport with Rowan so she could think for a moment. Everything that he had said made sense to her, and she knew that if she were in Tristan's place she would want to know her own potential, even if she was in a world where magic wasn't accepted. But still, Lily felt alarm bells going off in her head. She recalled Lillian's memory on Walltop, and the warning about wanting to fill an army with the Gift. She thought of the thousands she had claimed, waiting for her return back in Rowan's world, and the words "warmonger witch" echoed in her mind.

You know how to grow willstones, don't you, Rowan?

Yes.

And how to train other mechanics?

Of course.

So how many should I claim—just Tristan, or everyone in this world who is drawn to my willstones? Do I keep claiming until I have another army? I'm a new power source in this world, a power source that didn't develop here slowly over time with checks and balances. That frightens me, Rowan. But what frightens me more is how much I crave it. I want to claim the whole world, and that scares the daylights out of me.

That's why I trust you, Lily. Every witch wants to claim the whole world, but you respect the power you have enough to never misuse it.

Then respect that I don't think it's a good idea for me to use it at all. Even if it means that Tristan never understands his own potential. If I'm going to live in this world, I have to do it as a normal person.

Rowan nodded, but frowned deeply. He was troubled in a way that only perplexed Lily more with every exchange they had in mindspeak.

Rowan, please tell me why you're so upset. You never answered when I asked the first time. You just answered my question with another question.

"I get why you don't want to tell Tristan. I just hope you reconsider. That's all. Are you hungry?" he asked, pointedly changing the subject.

Lily's stomach growled. "Apparently," she replied laconically. "But since you're my mechanic I'm guessing you knew that before I did, didn't you?"

Rowan smiled, his eyes glinting as he turned and disappeared into the kitchen. It was an elfin look—totally adorable, but evasive. It felt like the deeper she burrowed into him, the farther Rowan's true self retreated from her. He was so solid in his choices but so slippery down inside. Lily wondered if that's what real love was—understanding someone so deeply you were able to feel their own confusion about who they were and what they really wanted.

"It'll be okay," Samantha said dreamily. "I've never seen a world where he doesn't love you, you know."

"I don't think love is our problem right now, Ma. But thanks for telling me that. It's pretty incredible."

"It is. Please don't forget it," Samantha stressed. Lily raised her head and studied her mother's serious face, wondering what she meant by that, but the moment of lucidity passed. Samantha's nervous hands fluttered up to her frizzy hair and her eyes unfocused. "Did I put the cat out?"

"We don't have a cat," Lily replied, her face falling. "We've never had a cat."

"Oh good! That would have been *terrible*." Samantha turned and left Lily to wonder if what her mother had said had any meaning, or if it was all intended for another Lily in a different world.

Lily! You must come back!
Go away, Lillian.

My world needs you. Please. I don't want to use violence, but I will if I have to.

Enough! I'm not coming back, Lillian, so whatever circumstances made you what you are have nothing to do with me anymore. I'm done listening to you. Accept it.

Lily pushed Lillian out of her thoughts and sat up in bed. Lillian was good at creeping into her mind when she was asleep or emotional. All Lily's ward did was alert her to Lillian's presence, but Lily still had to shut her out—which was getting harder. Lily knew that Rowan would probably have a solution to the problem, but telling him about it would be impossible without revealing that she and Lillian had been in touch since her first day back in this world. He'd feel so betrayed.

"What a mess," she whispered to herself. She wondered if she should take Lillian's warning about using force seriously. Lillian was a dangerous woman, there was no doubt about that, but how big of a threat could she be if she was in another universe?

Lily looked at the clock. It was four in the morning—too early to get up, but too late to try to go back to sleep. She rubbed her face and swung her legs out of bed, figuring sleep was going to be impossible now. And anyway, she had to be up for her first day back at school, which was enough to make anyone jittery. She yawned and reached out for Rowan, in case he happened to be awake.

What is it, Lily? You feel anxious.

Are you sleeping?

Half asleep. Come down to me. I want to wake up with you.

Lily went downstairs and saw Rowan buried in blankets on the couch, still breathing the deep, slow breaths of sleep. She climbed in with him and felt his stomach flutter as he woke.

"Wassamatter?" he murmured, pulling her against his chest.

"It's weird to go back to school," Lily said, giving Rowan half the truth.

"It's just for a few more months," he grumbled, and fell back to sleep.

He was right, of course. All she needed to do was graduate, and then she and Rowan could move out of town, maybe get a place of their own. Or they could go to college together. With the help of a little magic, Lily had no doubt they could forge a past for Rowan, complete with a social security number and school records. They could be anything they wanted in this world—all Lily had to do was survive high school.

They lay together as the sun came up. Rowan's dreams were scattered images. When Lily pieced them together she realized he was dreaming about his own schooling. Tristan was there, and Gideon. There was a lot of fire, smoke, salt, and silver. Cauldrons bubbled and strange dragon-like creatures flew down torch-lit passageways. They weren't happy dreams, nor were they nightmares. It was as if Rowan were picking up on Lily's anxiety and dreaming it out for her. Lily laughed silently to herself. He was even dreaming for her now. Lily didn't wake Rowan until she heard her mother stirring. A quick kiss, and Lily stole back upstairs to get ready for school.

Juliet dropped Lily off before heading into Boston and her college classes. Lily was halfway across the parking lot, trudging past piles of old half-melted snow that looked like Styrofoam, when she saw Tristan sitting in his car. A huge smile spread across her face. She hadn't realized how much she'd missed him until she saw him. The smile stayed plastered on her face as she hurried to him. He didn't smile back.

"So you wear dresses now?" Tristan snapped. "Anything else I should know, or is everything still a big secret?"

"Dresses keep me cool," she mumbled, embarrassed.

Lily looked down helplessly at one of the floaty confections she'd adopted since becoming a witch. Just a few months ago it took a grand occasion to make her trade in her habitual jeans and slogan-covered T-shirts for anything with a skirt. She'd changed, but she hadn't noticed how much until that moment. It wasn't knowing that she was a witch that made her feel like a freak, but the way Tristan was looking at her dress.

Lily realized that she was falling back into a pattern with Tristan, and that it was a pattern that no longer applied to her. She didn't live and die for his approval anymore, and she wasn't going to get into some stupid argument with him over how much she'd changed and whether or not he liked it.

"Hang on—this is insane," she said. "We're fighting about my freaking wardrobe. That's not *us*. We're going to start over." Lily forced a chipper tone. "Hi, Tristan! Nice to see you! I've really missed you."

"Oh, you did?" he retorted sarcastically. He got out of his car and faced Lily, his body stiff with anger. "Then why didn't you call me? Not one call in three months. Everyone thought you were *dead*, Lily!" He realized he was shouting. He backed away for a second to calm himself down and lowered his voice to finish what he had to say, but it didn't stay lowered for long. "And then when you did finally get back that asshole—Rowan—said that I couldn't see you. But you know what? That's not even the worst of it. The worst is that you got back, miraculously cured of your allergies, and you *still* didn't call me. I had to find out from the FBI!"

Lily didn't have any excuse for him. There was no explanation she could give him for what she'd done. The truth was, she'd been dodging Tristan because she didn't know how to face him.

"You're right," Lily said, looking up at him pleadingly. "And I'm sorry. I can't explain it, but I went through a lot, Tristan. And I *am* cured now, but it was long and hard and really painful. Please believe me when I say that I couldn't call, and then when I got back I just—I don't know." Lily sighed deeply and threw up her hands.

"You what? Go on, Lily," Tristan said, still demanding an explanation.

"I wussed out," she admitted. "I'd been through so much I didn't know how to talk to you anymore. What can I say? I suck."

"Yeah you do," he said quietly, his eyes dropping. "I thought you'd been kidnapped. I was going crazy thinking about what could be happening to you. What some psycho could—"

Tristan suddenly stopped and wrapped Lily in a tight hug. Lily knew that he wasn't the version of Tristan that she had claimed and that she couldn't mindspeak with him, experience his emotions, or view his memories from the past three months, but it didn't matter. Lily could feel how devastated he had been and imagine what he'd gone through. She knew him so well.

"I'm really sorry," she said, feeling terrible.

"You have no idea what I went through. I haven't forgiven you yet," he said, letting her go.

"I'm willing to work for it," Lily replied, smiling. They stayed staring at each other even though Lily could hear people gasping and whispering her name.

"Should I just go away?" asked an amused voice. Lily turned and noticed Breakfast, standing a foot away, waiting for either Tristan or Lily to realize he was there.

"Breakfast! How are you?" Lily exclaimed, hurling herself at him. She and Breakfast hadn't been close throughout high school, but the night before Lily disappeared, he'd helped Tristan save her life. He'd earned a special place in her heart for that.

"Alive. As are you, apparently," he answered, blushing ferociously.

"It's great to see you," Lily said, a big smile lighting up her face.

"Right back at ya," he replied heartily, before growing embarrassed again. He looked at Tristan, who was pointedly staring at Breakfast's hands, and hastily removed them from Lily's waist. "So, do you want to hear all the rumors about you now, or should I ration it out as the weeks go by?" he said with a devilish grin. "There's a great one about aliens."

"Ration it out, please," Lily replied, groaning.

For the rest of the day Lily felt like she was being examined like a bug under glass. And not just by her fellow students. She spent the morning trapped in the office with the superintendant, the principal, the guidance counselor, and the school nurse. Lily didn't know if she would have made it through without Rowan with her in mindspeak to keep her sane.

"But can you explain for us why you didn't tell any of your friends where you were for three months?" the principal asked again.

"I thought things were fine," Lily said, her eyes saucers of innocence. "I spoke to my mom three times a week, but she got a little confused when I left."

"She did say that she could hear you," the superintendant said reluctantly.

"My mother could hear me on the phone—she just couldn't understand why she couldn't see me. The whole concept of telephones escaped her there for a bit."

Worried looks were exchanged over Lily's head. "How is your mother?" the nurse asked. "Do you feel safe at home?"

"Of course." Lily tried not to sound too offended or defensive. She wasn't eighteen yet, and one call from any of them could land her in foster care. "My sister's been staying at home since I got back, and we have a holistic life coach working with me and my mother."

Everyone visibly relaxed at the mention of responsible Juliet, but the grilling didn't end.

"I'd really like to meet your life coach," the guidance counselor said. "You should have him come in so we can discuss what the school can do to help you get well."

You know what, Rowan? I think the pyre was more enjoyable than this.

Light yourself on fire, then. That should end the meeting in a hurry.

Lily tried not to laugh out loud and endured the rest of the questions about her treatment. She managed to put most of the lingering questions about her disappearance to rest, but she still didn't get out of the principal's office until lunch.

"Lily. Over here," Tristan called, waving her over. He was sitting at a table with Breakfast and a girl named Una Stone. Lily made her way over to them, ignoring the stares and whispers that shadowed her every move.

"This is nice," Lily said. "Strange. But nice. When did the three of you start hanging out together?"

Tristan was probably the most popular person at Salem High, and he usually spent lunch surrounded by fawning girls and jealous jock guys. Breakfast was well liked by everyone, but he was a giant geek. Lily barely knew Una, although she'd always admired her cool intelligence and had wanted to make friends with her. Una was the kind of girl who tended to wear a lot of black clothes and blood-red lipstick, and she had at least a dozen tattoos and even more piercings. Add skinny, redheaded, sheer-dress-in-January-wearing Lily and they made just about the weirdest group anyone had ever seen sitting at a lunch table.

"Right about the time you disappeared," Breakfast said, sliding out a chair for Lily.

"Breakfast and me were the last two to see you, besides your sister," Tristan said. He huffed in frustration. "And we went through a lot of crap with the police over that, you know."

"Sorry," Lily said for what felt like the thousandth time. She looked at Una. "How'd you get dragged into this?"

"I was his alibi," Una replied, tipping her chin at Breakfast. "I saw him after you took the ice bath."

"I was really upset by the whole near-death thing," Breakfast said, blushing and reaching for Una's hand under the table. "I needed consoling."

"Then I guess we got used to each other," Una finished, indulging the handholding for a moment, before reverting to her usual self-contained posture.

"Actually, they were the only ones who were willing to hang out with me anymore," Tristan said quietly.

"Why?" Lily asked.

"I was the last person with you, Lily. Everyone saw me carry you out of that party half dead and then Juliet heard us get into that fight," Tristan replied, frustrated, like Lily should have considered that. "I think even she was starting to wonder if I'd killed you."

"Oh my God," Lily gasped.

"Now she gets it." Tristan sat back, shaking his head at Lily. "The FBI started hassling me, you know."

"Simms," Lily said under her breath.

She looked around the cafeteria and noticed that the stares and whispers weren't entirely directed at her. She glared at a few fellow senior girls, who were casting suspicious eyes at Tristan, and made a mental note to ask Rowan if he had a brew that would give them a raging case of acne. When she looked back at Tristan to apologize again, she realized that he was staring intently at her throat.

"What's that?" he said, reaching out for the willstones hidden beneath her collar.

"Just a necklace," Lily replied, hastily covering her willstones with a hand.

"May I see?" Una said, leaning forward with keen interest. Breakfast leaned forward, too, trying to peer through Lily's palm.

"Maybe some other time," Lily said lightly. "I'm a little superstitious about it."

They all forced themselves to look away. Lily knew what it meant, and why she had always been interested in Tristan, Breakfast, and Una. They all had some kind of magical talent that was drawing them to her—and maybe to each other, too.

"You promised me gossip, Breakfast," Lily said, changing the subject. "I want to hear all the nastiest tidbits first."

After lunch, the new group of friends didn't go their separate ways. Una and Breakfast walked Tristan and Lily to their next class, and then they all met up again a period later at Lily's locker. When school was over, the four of them loitered around Tristan's car in the parking lot. It was as if they didn't want to be separated from her, and it took Lily a moment to realize that they were expecting her to ask them all back to her house to hang out after school.

Lily made an excuse about her mom still being a little sensitive since she'd come back, and promised that she'd have them over soon to meet Rowan.

"So, who is he anyway?" Una asked, a feline smile pursing her cherry-red lips.

"He's my life coach," Lily said awkwardly.

"What does that mean?" asked Tristan, crossing his arms.

Lily looked down and tucked her hair behind her ear. "Um, he, like, helps me with my diet and managing my reactions—"

"I thought you didn't have reactions anymore," Tristan challenged.

Lily looked up, annoyed. "And he's helping my mom. Holistically. You know, using herbs and stuff."

"Cool," Breakfast said, sensing a fight building between Lily and

Tristan. He took Una by the elbow. "See you tomorrow?"

They said their good-byes and Tristan drove Lily home, still fuming a bit over Rowan. When he dropped her off, Tristan stayed in the driveway after Lily had gone inside.

Rowan came up behind Lily and looked over her shoulder through the curtains at Tristan, still sitting in his car. "He's not going to stop," Rowan said.

"It's just a few more months." Lily turned in his arms and smiled up at him. "And then you and I can go anywhere we want. We can drive cross-country. Or fly to Europe!"

Lily felt that huge, gray emotion well up inside Rowan again. She was about to ask him what was wrong, but he kissed her quickly and hugged her to his chest. "I would love to see the whole world with you," he said, his voice catching.

As Rowan held her, Lily felt his gaze drift back out the window. Tristan finally gave up and drove away.

For the next two days Lily managed to come up with an excuse every time Tristan, Breakfast, and Una hinted they wanted to come over to her house, but by Saturday, Lily's little entourage had had enough of her evasive behavior. They showed up on her doorstep with bagels and coffee at eight o'clock in the morning, and Rowan let them in with a huge smile.

You couldn't have lied and said I wasn't here, Rowan?

No. Now explain bagels. Do you dip them in the coffee?

You don't know bagels? Oy vey.

Rowan and Breakfast hit it off immediately, and strangely, over computers. Rowan had been fascinated by computers from the moment Juliet taught him how to use one, and he'd spent some of his study time teaching himself about telecommunications, computer processing, and coding. Breakfast couldn't believe he'd finally met someone who was as into code as he was, and for a while they seemed to be speaking a totally foreign language. Lily looked at Una, her eyes wide with surprise that Rowan and Breakfast would have so much in common.

"What can you do?" Una said. "He's a geek. But he's *my* geek."

Lily laughed. "Don't take this the wrong way or anything, but you two make kind of an odd couple."

"You think?" Una replied, smirking. "Believe me, it was a shock to me, too, but he grew on me. Like a fungus."

"But he's *your* fungus, right?"

"Right." Her smile suddenly fell. "It's still hard sometimes, though. We're such opposites."

"He's very affectionate," Lily said, following an instinct. "And I gather that you're not the hand-holding type."

"No," Una said emphatically. Her light expression suddenly darkened. "I usually don't like to be touched."

"Maybe that's why he's so good for you," Lily suggested quietly. She knew there had to be a story there, but she didn't push. Una wasn't a tea-and-sympathy kind of girl.

While Lily and Una were relaxing into each other's company, Lily could sense that Tristan was getting more annoyed as he watched Breakfast and Rowan's conversation.

"Wait a second," Tristan said, rudely interrupting Rowan. "I thought you were some holistic herbalist life coach, or whatever."

"I know a lot about herbs and how to use them," Rowan answered patiently.

"So what's all this about code?" Tristan continued. "Are you a computer programmer on the side?"

"No," Rowan said. His eyes narrowed slightly, but he kept his tone even. "I'm interested in computers, but I grew up learning how to handle special people like Lily."

"You grew up learning that, did you?" Tristan said sarcastically. He squared off in front of Rowan, obviously looking for a fight. "Where?"

"Well, I went to school for it, but more importantly I was born to do it." Rowan didn't blink. "So were you, Tristan."

Rowan, what the hell are you doing? Don't you dare tell Tristan he's a mechanic.

"Rowan's Native American," Lily interjected. "His tribe is really into herbs and stuff."

"Oh, that's so cool," Una said. "I've always been interested in herbs, too."

Rowan looked at Una carefully, like he was studying the air around her. "You've got the same talent Tristan and I have—which is unique, actually. Where I'm from you'd usually be like Lily, rather than like Tristan and me."

Rowan. Knock it off.

"What are you talking about?" Tristan said derisively. "You and I are nothing alike."

"Lily told me you wanted to be a doctor," Rowan said.

Tristan backed off completely, all the fight leaving him. He looked away. "Like that's going to happen now."

"What are you talking about, Tristan?" Lily asked.

"Forget it," he replied. "Breakfast, didn't you bring a movie?"

"Hang on," Lily said, standing and facing Tristan. "What are you talking about? You don't want to be a doctor anymore? When did you decide that?"

"It was decided for me," Tristan said quietly. "Not too many Ivy League schools accept guys who are being questioned for their girlfriend's mysterious disappearance, Lily." He laughed bitterly. "Especially not guys who have a record."

"You don't have a record."

"After I left you that morning I went to Scot's." Tristan sighed heavily. "I didn't hit him that hard, but his face opened up and he needed stiches. The neighbors called an ambulance and the cops."

"But you guys fight all the time," Lily said in a weak voice.

Scot had tried to get Lily drunk and take advantage of her the night before she disappeared, and the alcohol he slipped into her drink had given Lily a seizure. The next morning Tristan had promised to beat up Scot, but Lily didn't think Tristan would take it that far—at least not so far that Scot would end up in the hospital.

"You and Scot got into a huge fight freshman year and no one got arrested," she argued.

"We're not freshmen anymore, Lily," Tristan snapped. "I'm eighteen. Scot's parent's pressed charges. An assault-and-battery conviction goes on your college transcripts."

"I don't believe this," Lily said blankly.

"Your timing really sucked, you know that? Agent Simms wouldn't let me leave the state to go to any of my interviews. Can't leave the state when you're involved in an investigation. I tried to reschedule, but they all told me very politely that I seemed to be going through a lot of personal problems and that I should take some time to get the help I needed."

"But I'm back. It was a misunderstanding," Lily whispered. She felt like she'd been punched in the chest.

"They don't care." Tristan put his hands on his hips and sighed. "It really doesn't take much for an admissions board to say no to anybody. Having an arrest for a violent offense and an FBI agent breathing down your neck would be enough to spook any school, let alone the Ivy League."

"Tristan, I'm so—"

"Sorry. I know. You said that already."

He still has a future, Lily, if you tell him what he really is. Please, tell him. Tell all of them what they are.

"What about that movie, Breakfast?" Tristan said, deliberately changing the subject.

"Yeah," Breakfast said, grabbing his bag. "Comedy or horror?"

"Oh, for the love of Christmas, *comedy*," Una said emphatically, pushing Breakfast in front of her and into the living room.

Juliet showed up halfway through the film and eagerly jumped onto the couch next to Tristan.

"I love this movie," she said, grabbing herself a throw pillow and half a blanket.

They spent the entire day together, and luckily, Rowan stopped dropping hints about the rest of the group's hidden talents. Tristan even started to warm up to Rowan a bit, almost like he couldn't help it. Rowan certainly knew how to be charming.

You're good at this, Rowan.

Of course I am. I had years of practice as head mechanic to the witch, you know. The Salem Coven was expected to entertain often.

That's right—you were Lord Fall, weren't you? So strange to think of you as a lord.

Where did you hear that title?

Lily couldn't lie to him in mindspeak, so she shrugged her shoulders, playing dumb. Samantha saved Lily from a grilling by coming down the stairs. Rowan got up to check on her and offered to make everyone dinner.

"Thank you, dear. That would be lovely," Samantha said, smiling at Rowan like a son.

"Are you sure you don't want me to take you for a walk or something, Ma?" Lily asked nervously.

"Or I could take you," Juliet suggested.

Neither of them was comfortable having new people around their mother yet, especially since new people made it harder for Samantha to find herself in the blizzard of alternate universes that swirled in her head.

"We can all take a walk together after dinner," Breakfast said, his eyes narrowed knowingly at Lily. "Sit next to me, Mrs. Proctor."

Lily was surprised to find that Breakfast handled her mother well. He didn't even blink when Samantha mentioned a recent war with Canada.

"I think you meant to say Afghanistan, Mrs. Proctor," Breakfast corrected gently.

Samantha frowned deeply, resetting her worldview. "That's right. We're not at war with Canada here," she said, and changed the subject.

After dinner, while everyone was bundling up to take a walk, Lily sought out Breakfast and pulled him aside.

"Thank you," Lily said. "That was very thoughtful of you."

Breakfast smiled. "I have an uncle like your mom," he said quietly. "Not as serious, but sometimes it feels like he's in another world."

"Another world." Lily laughed weakly. "That's a pretty accurate way to put it."

"Anyway, you don't have to be embarrassed. It's nothing to be ashamed of."

Lily swallowed hard and nodded. "Thank you."

"Lily? It's really cold out. I think even you are going to need to dress warmly tonight," Rowan said, bringing her a jacket.

Did you hear Breakfast and me talking, Rowan?

The bit about his uncle. It means he has spirit walking in his blood. He could be a huge asset for your coven.

Lily frowned as she put her coat on. She tried to tell Rowan in mindspeak that she didn't want a coven, but she couldn't. Because it was a lie.

The well-fed group spilled out into the frigid night. Everyone shivered and laughed around their chattering teeth and frozen cheeks. It was so cold the snow crunched and squeaked underfoot. Lily went to Rowan and pressed against his side. After a moment he put his arm over her shoulder. He hadn't been affectionate with her all day, and Lily knew it had something to do with Tristan. She glanced over at him and saw him staring at them.

He loves you, Lily.

And I love you, Rowan. If he wants to stay friends with me, he'll have to accept that.

Don't push him away.

Lily looked at Rowan, confused. She knew Rowan wasn't the jealous type, and she appreciated that about him, but asking her to stay close to an ex-boyfriend seemed a bit much, even for him.

Rowan suddenly stopped dead, his body going rigid as he pushed Lily behind him.

"Everyone get back to the house," he yelled. Lily peered around Rowan's arm and saw a man's shape standing under a streetlight across the street.

"He found me," she whispered, panic buckling her knees. She didn't need to see his face to know who he was. She could recognize the hunched shoulders and cocked head of Carrick's crow-like silhouette anywhere—she'd seen it enough times looming over her in the dark oubliette.

Lily could hear Tristan and Breakfast asking what was wrong, but she couldn't make out exactly what they were saying over the ringing in her ears. Carrick took a step toward them.

Give me strength, Lily.

She felt the pull of Rowan's willstone, asking hers for power. Lily had no flame from which to gather energy, but she did have a belly full of food. She took the calories inside her body, changed them into force in her willstone, and poured as much of it as she could into Rowan. She saw a bright flash from his willstone, and then she saw Rowan charging after Carrick. Both of them were moving so quickly it almost looked as if they had disappeared.

"What the hell just happened?" Tristan shouted. Great trenches were dug in the snow, and deep tracks led into the darkness.

"Lily, are you okay?" Una said. Lily realized she'd collapsed, and Una and Juliet were trying to lift her off the ground. Una looked up at Tristan, Breakfast, and Samantha, standing over them. "Holy shit, did you see that?" she asked, breathless.

Juliet frowned, but said nothing.

"I saw it," Breakfast said. "They were glowing."

Tristan crouched down next to Lily, his face grim. "Where have you *really* been for the past three months?"

CHAPTER
6

THE MUG CLANKED AGAINST LILY'S TEETH. HER HANDS were shaking so badly she had to use both of them to steady her tea.

"What aren't you telling us?" Tristan demanded.

"I don't know what you're talking about," Juliet mumbled unconvincingly.

Rowan still wasn't back yet. Lily had tried calling to him in mindspeak, but he hadn't answered. She could feel him, though, so she knew he was alright. She could feel his rage and, behind that, his fear.

"Juliet, I've known you since I was five," Tristan replied. "And you have to be the worst liar I've ever met. What. Happened."

Juliet and Samantha shared a defeated look.

Should we just tell them, Lily?

Don't say a word, Juliet.

"Look, we all know that whatever it was, it wasn't normal," Breakfast said, barely keeping hysteria in check. "Rowan and Lily were *glowing*, and then Rowan frigging disappeared into thin air!"

"And so did that spooky guy standing across the street," Una added calmly.

"Something happened out there. We all know it. We *felt* something," Tristan said, looking at Lily. His eyes turned inward and he touched the base of his throat, almost like he was reaching for a willstone. "Just tell us the truth."

"And please don't say it has anything to do with aliens," Breakfast muttered.

"Stuart," Una said, using Breakfast's real name. "Not the time for a joke."

"It wasn't aliens," Rowan said. They all jumped and turned to see that he had silently joined them. His jacket was torn, there were scratches on his forearms and face, and his jeans were stiff and smeared with half-frozen sand.

Did you get him, Rowan?

I chased him for miles along the coast, then through a town, but he got away. He didn't come to fight me. He just wanted to let us both know that he was here.

He outran you?

Lillian must be fueling him. I don't know how much energy she can give him or how strong he is, but he was able to stay ahead of me. He couldn't have done that without a witch.

How did she do it? I can feel the willstones of my claimed back in your world calling to me. Asking for power. But fueling them across the worlds would be so hard.

Hard or not, she figured it out.

Breakfast turned to Una. "They're doing it again," he said.

"You guys talk with your eyes, you know," Una told Lily and Rowan.

"Not with our eyes," Rowan said. "It's called mindspeak. You call it telepathy in this world."

Rowan, don't!

"I have to, Lily," Rowan yelled. "Carrick is here for *you*—and if Lillian can send him, she can send others. You need a coven to protect you, and you need it now."

"He's right," Samantha said, breaking the tense silence. "She won't stop. Neither would you." Samantha went to Lily and kissed her on the forehead. "Good night, everyone. You're all welcome to stay," she said before shuffling upstairs to bed.

I'm scared, Rowan.

I know. You need to trust me, Lily.

"Did you just say 'coven'? As in, a *witches'* coven?" Una asked carefully.

"Yes," Rowan answered. He paused.

Lily sighed and nodded, reluctantly giving her consent. "Go ahead," she said.

"Lily is a witch. A very powerful one. When she went missing it was because she was taken to another world. That's where I'm from—a parallel world where witches and their mechanics, who are the vessels for the witches' power, run everything. All of you has the potential to be a mechanic like me. I'm going to give each of you a willstone like this," he said, pulling out his huge smoke-colored stone that pulsed with eerie light, "and train you to be vessels for Lily's power."

Tristan, Breakfast, and Una stared silently at Rowan's willstone, entranced. They could already feel what their minds were struggling to process.

"Your necklace," Tristan said, his voice rough. They all turned to Lily.

She opened the collar of her shirt and allowed her three willstones to shimmer with her strength. All three of her potential mechanics pulled in deep breaths and held them.

"Are you sure about this, Rowan?" Lily asked, already craving the stones they didn't yet wear.

"It's the only way," he replied sadly. He turned to Tristan, Breakfast, and Una. "You must decide for yourselves. No one can force you into this. Do you want to learn more?"

"What kind of power are we talking about here?" Tristan asked.

"What kind do you want?" Rowan replied, holding his gaze.

Tristan smiled slowly. "I'm listening."

Breakfast and Una shared a look. Una turned to Rowan. "You had me at *coven*," she said in her unflappable way. "Keep going."

"Breakfast?" Rowan turned to him. "This has to be your choice," he said firmly.

Breakfast nodded. "Just tell me I don't have to drink blood or worship a goat or anything like that," he said, grimacing.

"No. Breakfast—it's nothing like that," Lily said, shaking her head and trying not to laugh. "Magic isn't some creepy cult. It's more like science. Basically, my body is a crucible and it can transmute matter and energy. I can't create something out of nothing, but I can take energy from one source, like this heat," she said, reaching a hand toward the flames in the fireplace. Her willstones pulsed with light and a small witch wind moaned eerily through the room. "And I use the crystals of my willstones to alter the vibration of the heat's energy. Changing the vibration changes the fundamental nature of the energy without losing any of the power. So, right now I'm changing the heat of the fire directly into physical force. But I can't use this force myself. I need a vessel." She gave the force to Rowan. His willstone flared, his head tipped back, and his eyes hooded in pleasure. Tristan regarded Rowan's reaction intently, intrigued.

"Follow me," Rowan said, and led them all outside. "Watch

carefully." He grinned and then it seemed as if he'd disappeared. Everyone looked around, confused. "Up here," Rowan called. They followed his voice and found him halfway up a tree on the other side of the street. "I'll move more slowly," he called. They all watched him jump from the tree, to a rooftop, and then execute a graceful back flip before landing next to Lily.

"Damn," Breakfast groaned, almost like it hurt to see something so awesome.

"And that's just kid's stuff," Lily said. "Right, Rowan?"

"Right," he said, smiling at her.

"You can change any type of energy into any other?" Tristan asked, his excitement building.

"Yes. And I can alter matter—change it chemically, even without a mechanic," Lily said. "I can manipulate cells and DNA, heal wounds, and make medicines you've never even dreamed of. I can also change the way the light falls on my face." Lily cast a glamour and heard everyone gasp as they looked at a stranger's face instead of hers. She smiled and reverted back to her own face. "It's called a glamour. It's actually really easy, and it only works in dim light, but it certainly *looks* dramatic."

They went back inside, and Tristan turned to Rowan. "How does it feel when she gives you power?"

Rowan shared an understanding smile with Tristan, and for a moment Lily saw the two of them connecting as if this Tristan were the one that Rowan had known for years. "I can't think of many things that compare," Rowan replied.

"There's a downside, though," Lily warned. "In order for you to become my mechanics, I'll have to claim you. This is dangerous for you because it means I can possess you. I can control your thoughts, your speech, and even your movements if I choose. I can make you my puppet."

"But she's never done that to me," Rowan added quickly. "Lily is a very respectful witch."

A long silence stretched out as Tristan, Breakfast, and Una thought deeply.

Lily? Why don't you ask me to become one of your mechanics?

I'm sorry, Juliet, but you have no magic. I can claim you, but you wouldn't be a mechanic. I still want you on my side, though.

I'll always be on your side.

Lily could feel her sister's sadness and disappointment like an ache in her own chest, and tried to comfort her by letting her feel how much she loved her. Juliet smiled at Lily from across the room and nodded her head acceptingly.

It's alright, Lily. I'll make myself useful in other ways.

I'll hold you to that.

"You were all born for this, and you all know it," Rowan said, breaking the pensive silence. "Each of you has something inside you that you've never been able to shake. No matter how many women you go through"—he looked at Tristan—"or how many piercings or tattoos you get"—he looked at Una—"or how many jokes you tell to gain acceptance," he said, turning lastly to Breakfast. "You've all felt like there's been a hole in your life." He gestured to Lily and the three willstones that drew all of their eyes. "There's the answer."

Breakfast wiped a hand over his face and looked at Una. "Well?" he asked.

"I'm in," she replied immediately, her eyes never leaving Lily's willstones.

"Me too," Tristan said. He put his hands on his hips and sighed to himself. "Breakfast?"

"Yeah. Okay. I'm in, too."

"We don't have a lot of time," Rowan said. He left the room and came back with a neatly folded envelope of silk. He untied the string wrapping it, and revealed about fifteen ovals of lead-colored crystals in varying shapes and sizes.

"Rowan?" Lily said, surprised. "How did you get un-keyed will-stones?"

"I started growing them as soon we arrived here," he replied.

What? Why? Lily didn't even know how to formulate a question to ask him she was so stunned.

"I knew you'd need them," he replied unapologetically.

But we were supposed to blend in and be normal here. And I told you that I thought bringing magic to this world was wrong.

"A witch without a circle of mechanics to protect her is a dead witch, no matter what world she's in," he snapped, refusing to engage her in mindspeak. She felt that gray emotion drop like a curtain in his mind. He was avoiding contact to shut her out.

What are you hiding, Rowan?

He turned away. "Who wants to go first?" Rowan asked the three anxious candidates.

"Me," Breakfast insisted.

"It will be difficult," Rowan warned.

"That's why I want to go first," Breakfast replied, stepping forward. "I don't want to know *how* difficult and have any time to freak myself out."

Rowan coached Breakfast, Tristan, and Una through the pain of bonding with a willstone. Their ordeals weren't as intense as Lily's had been, but they still suffered the feeling of being invaded as the willstones attached themselves to their minds. To Lily, it had felt like an infection, as if a foreign thing were trying to claw its way inside her—and then, suddenly, her willstones were no longer foreign, but a new and beautiful part of her. Lily covered her three little hearts protectively and encouraged her friends as she watched Breakfast, Tristan, and Una sweat and shiver through the bonding ritual.

When it was over, Juliet brought extra blankets into the living room for everyone, but even though they were all exhausted from the bonding, the new mechanics found that they couldn't sleep.

"My teeth feel amazing," Una said, giggling. "I can't stop running my tongue over them."

"You sound *so* high right now," Breakfast teased, pulling Una close to him. She didn't shy away from his touch like she normally did when they were in public. Lily and Rowan exchanged knowing smiles. Touch was one of the senses most dramatically enhanced by a willstone.

"I think I can see through my hand," Tristan said dreamily. He was lying on his back on the floor, an arm raised above his face. He spread his fingers wide and peered at his skin. "Yeah, there are my metacarpals and phalanges. I can see my freaking *bones*. Unbelievable."

"I'll teach you how to look closer so you can see your cells. And then I'll teach you how to speed up the repair of them," Rowan said. "Mechanics need their witches for higher magic, but there are a lot of things you can do on your own. Healing on a small scale is one of them." Rowan looked at Lily and smiled. "Unless you're trying to heal a witch and she's blocking you."

Lily smiled back at Rowan, remembering how he'd tried to heal her broken ankle when they'd first met, and how she'd blocked him because she didn't trust him. She'd been terrified of Rowan and had to heal her ankle herself. That all seemed so long ago to her now, and even the memory of fearing Rowan was strange.

Tristan rolled over onto his stomach and faced Lily and Rowan. He had his willstone cupped in the palm of one of his hands. He opened his hand and showed the softly glowing smoke stone to Lily. She wanted to reach out and grab it. Knowing how tempted Lily would be, Rowan wrapped his arms around her in a hug that unobtrusively held her arms down.

"What happens when someone else touches it?" Tristan asked.

"If Lily were to touch it, and if you were to allow it, she'd claim you," Rowan answered in a low voice. "If I were to touch it, and you were to touch mine, we'd become stone kin. I wouldn't be able to possess you like Lily can—or you me—but we could share memories and mindspeak with each other. Even some of our energy and power. In order to function smoothly as Lily's mechanic's circle, it isn't necessary for us to become stone kin, but it might be a good idea."

"And how long does that last? Being stone kin?" Breakfast asked.

"As long as you have that stone, and I have this one," Rowan said, lightly touching the willstone around his neck. "But if one of us were to smash our willstone, the connection would be broken."

The three neophytes cringed at the thought of smashing their stones.

"That sounds awful," Breakfast said fearfully.

"Like gouging out an eye," Una added.

"For people with little or no magic it would be painful, but tolerable. Their connections to their willstones are weak, as are their abilities to use them. Their memories aren't perfect, like ours are, and most can barely share mindspeak, even with their stone kin. For them, touching stones is still intimate, but it's not as intense as it is for us. Our willstones are a part of our bodies and minds." Rowan's voice dropped. "I had to smash my first willstone. I wouldn't recommend it unless your life depends on it. So think before you share your stone with anyone. It's a vow people like us can't just walk away from."

Breakfast and Una looked at each other and their faces softened. They both reached out at the same time and gave each other their willstones, one hand taking as the other hand received in a mutual gesture of perfect trust. Their breathing stopped, their eyes widened and then closed. Lily leaned her back against Rowan's chest as they watched Breakfast and Una melt into each other.

So beautiful.

There's nothing like sharing that first moment together. I'm sorry ours was so rushed, Lily.

Really? I wouldn't change a thing.

Rowan tilted his head and looked down at Lily. He opened up his heart before he kissed her so she could feel his love as clearly as she could feel his lips.

Tristan's dying inside, Juliet told Lily in mindspeak.

Lily pulled away from Rowan and saw Tristan watching them. He held out his hand to Lily, offering her his willstone.

"Claim me," he said quietly.

Lily looked at Rowan. "It's his decision," Rowan said. "If he wants you to claim him, then I think you should."

"I'm going to see some of your memories, Tristan. It's unavoidable when a witch claims someone," Lily cautioned. "But I promise I won't pry."

"Wait—you see our memories? From childhood and stuff?" Una asked anxiously.

"Not necessarily from childhood," Rowan answered. "But it's common for a witch to see formative memories—either choices you've made in the past or a current issue you might be facing in your life. It really depends on the claimed."

Una bit her lower lip and looked away. Lily noticed that Breakfast took Una's hand in support, and knew there had to be a skeleton in Una's closet that maybe only Breakfast knew about.

Lily looked at Tristan and reminded herself to move very slowly.

"Ready?" she asked.

"Do it," he answered.

She reached forward and gently took Tristan's willstone

between her finger and thumb. He gasped.

Lily saw . . .

. . . Lily. I have to go by her house after Little League practice because I left my Hot Wheels in her room. I wish Lily played baseball. Then we could hang out all the time. I hope we're in the same classes next year. She's been sick a lot lately and everyone talks about her when they think I'm not listening. It's like they're scared of her or something since she had that seizure. I'm not scared of her. She's the only person who calms me down. I don't know why, but whenever she's not around I feel upset. Like something's missing.

. . . Miranda unbuckles my belt. I look out the windows of my car to make sure no one's around. Shit. There are tons of people still in the parking lot after practice. I really should stop her. Lily isn't technically my girlfriend, but we did make out yesterday. I wish I hadn't done that. I'm not ready for Lily. Miranda's hand finds what she's looking for and she smiles when I groan, like she's won something. What an idiot. It's Lily I love, not Miranda. Lily's the only person I've ever loved, and someday I'm going to marry her. But not today. Miranda's head lowers down to my lap. A few seconds of feeling whole. It's only ever just a few seconds, but it's better than nothing.

. . . Who the hell is this guy telling me I can't see Lily? After the crap I've gone through for her, and he's saying I can't come in? I tell him to get out of my way and he stops me. Damn, he moves fast. Wait—did I give him my name? How does he know my name is Tristan? There's something so familiar about this guy. Rowan Fall. I've never seen him before in my life and right now he's acting like he knows Lily better than I do. I should hit the bastard. How did he just block me? Wow. He's really strong. Like, *impossibly* strong. He says something about Lily having been through a lot. He's not lying. I can tell he really cares about her.

. . . Rowan and Lily. I'm staring at how their bodies mirror the other's movement, even when they aren't looking at each other. They lean toward each other without even knowing it. They're totally screwing. Oh my God, I lost her. I lost Lily twice. Once when I thought she was dead, and now because I know she loves him more than me. I can't believe how much this hurts.

I'm sorry I hurt you, Tristan.

I hurt you first. Do I have any chance at all?

Lily smiled sadly at him and shook her head. She released his willstone and leaned forward to kiss him on the cheek. Still deeply connected to Tristan, Lily felt an echo of her own lips touch her cheek. She also felt the regret that flooded Tristan as he realized how passionless, how sisterly, Lily's kiss was.

"Everyone should rest," Rowan said gently. "I have a lot to teach you in the morning."

I don't want to dream, Rowan. I'm scared Carrick will be there in the dark.

I wish I could promise that my dreams will be safer for you, Lily, but I don't think they will be tonight. The best I can do is promise that I won't leave your side or let the fire go out.

Lily stared at the flames in the fireplace, pulling the heat into her skin, as Rowan lay down and wrapped his arms comfortingly around her.

Lily awoke at dawn. She looked around the room at the cozy heaps of blankets and sleep-slackened limbs, listening to everyone breathe. The fire was banked low, but it still burned as Rowan had promised. She eased out of his arms and went to the window. The sky looked like lead, and the flat light seemed to drain hue from neutral tones and add intensity to bright ones, like a black-and-white film that had been painted over with splashes of color-saturated ink.

She could feel him out there. Carrick was somewhere close by, watching the house.

She felt Rowan wake up and heard him roll over to look at her. She turned to face him and for a moment saw herself as he saw her. She saw how she glowed ivory white and fire red in his mind. She was a thin thing, like a gleaming razor's edge—deadly, not delicate.

We should get started. Your new mechanics need a lot of work.

Rowan got up and went to Lily first. He ran his hands down her bare arms and rested his lips against the top of her forehead, just below her hairline. He took a moment to pull warmth and energy directly from her skin, rather than using willstones. It was an intimate gesture, and Lily sensed that it had special meaning between a witch and her mechanic. As he soaked in a bit of Lily's essence, she felt a bit of herself nestle deep inside his body. After only a few seconds he pulled away with a contented smile and went to the kitchen. Deliberately noisy clanks and slams soon followed, waking everyone else.

"You're a sadist," Una groaned loudly in Rowan's general direction. She and Breakfast untangled themselves from each other and sat up.

Lily? Are you still there?

I'm still here, Tristan.

For a second I wondered if I'd dreamed it.

Nope. You're still mine.

Tristan sat up and smiled at Lily, a wistful look on his face.

"Breakfast and I have been talking," Una said. She paused and wrinkled her nose. "Well, not actually *talking*. Mindspeaking? Anyway, we've decided that we want you to claim us, too, Lily." Una looked down, grimacing bashfully. "I feel like I just asked you to the frigging prom."

Lily laughed. "It is a big deal. Bigger than prom, even. But don't worry, Una. I've gotten really good at giving my claimed their space."

"And how many have you claimed?" Juliet asked, her expression troubled.

"Over ten thousand," Rowan answered. He'd silently joined the group from the kitchen, and everyone turned to face him. "Lily has an army in my world."

"Not by choice. It was a do-or-die situation, and out of that ten thousand only seven thousand survived the battle," Lily said solemnly. "I have a lot to tell you all about what happened while I was gone. The easiest way would be for me to show you some of my memories."

Una and Breakfast exchanged a look, obviously engaged in mind-speak.

"I want a willstone," Juliet said suddenly. "I want a willstone and I want you to claim me, Lily. I know I probably won't be much use to you—"

"You'll be very useful, Juliet," Rowan said firmly. "But why don't we eat first?"

Samantha joined them, declaring that she felt clearheaded enough to work on her old potter's wheel. While Samantha tried to get the feel of throwing clay again, Juliet bonded with a willstone and allowed herself to be claimed by Lily. Bonding was easy for Juliet because she would never connect with her willstone the way someone with magic would, but Rowan assured her that there were many things that she could still do with her willstone.

Juliet's memories were all familiar, even dear to Lily, and she decided to give back to her sister and share a few of her own memories. The two sisters suddenly burst out laughing over the time they decided to dig a swimming pool in the backyard.

"We got halfway to China before Dad got home from work and caught us!" Lily roared with laughter.

"Ooh, he was so mad," Juliet said, wiping at her streaming eyes.

"The backyard was trashed!" Lily had to put her hands on her knees she was laughing so hard. "And there's still a donut-shaped ditch back there."

"Good times," Juliet said, winding down. Everyone stared at them, perplexed. "You had to be there," she said.

The moment of levity seemed to lighten everyone else's mood. Breakfast grinned and said he wanted to be next, and understanding dawned on Lily.

You did that to put Breakfast and Una at ease didn't you, Juliet?

Juliet smiled and shrugged impishly, refusing to admit anything in mindspeak.

"Ready, Breakfast?" Lily asked, still smiling at her sister.

"Let's do this thing," he replied, pumped up, like he was about to jump out of an airplane.

Lily lightly touched his willstone and was swarmed with memories. They came so quickly that she could barely discern them, almost as if the floodgates had opened and Breakfast was completely spilling his guts. Lily could see how he had hid behind his class-clown persona his whole life, never letting anyone get to know him. But ironically, the only thing he'd ever wanted was to be understood and loved for who he was, not who he pretended to be. His parents paid little attention to him. They didn't care when he didn't come home or even notice. Breakfast had always wanted someone to notice him. He wanted to belong.

You will always belong now, Stuart. Tristan, Rowan, and Una are your family.

Why aren't you my family?

Because I'm your home.

Breakfast opened his eyes and grinned at Lily. She could feel the giddy playfulness of his nature like a burst of sweetness in her heart.

"That wasn't so bad," he said cheerfully, and stepped aside for Una.

Una stepped forward and swallowed hard, like her mouth was dry. Her hand shook as she gave Lily her willstone. Lily saw . . .

. . . My mom's gross new boyfriend. He waits for her to leave the room and then he slides closer to me. Too close. He puts his hand on my knee and pulls my legs apart. He says all he wants to do is look . . .

It's okay, Una. You don't have to show me any more—ever—if you don't want to. Is he still around?

No. They only dated for a few weeks and then he vanished.

We can find him if you want. We can find him and punish him. Wait until you see what you can do. Once Rowan is done training you, you'll never be a victim again.

Una looked up and smiled at Rowan. "When do we start training?"

"Now," Rowan answered. He cleared everything off the floor of the living room and put down a square of black silk. "Tristan. Put more wood on the fire."

Tristan did as he was told, while Rowan went to get his pack from the closet. Una turned the pack over in her hands, enjoying the detailing. Lily noticed that Rowan had added some beadwork since the last time she saw it.

"Lily. Sit in front of the fire. Everyone else sit around her in a semicircle, in the shape of a crescent moon," Rowan instructed.

He took the pack from Una and opened it, removing silver knives and laying them out in a pattern. Then he opened a pouch of salt and placed it close to Lily's right hand.

"Always offer your witch salt, and always keep salt on you." Rowan's eyes flicked up to Lily and he shared a flash memory of him cutting her hair in the woods. They shared a warm smile. "Don't run out of it."

He kept emptying the pack, naming the different elements and herbs as he placed them on the black silk—chalk, iron, phosphorus, feverfew, chamomile, hyssop, and poppy. He only had small samples of each element or herb, but he had many different kinds of them.

"You'll all start carrying a pack like this with you wherever you go. Even when you go into battle, you'll carry your silver knives on a special belt I'll make you," he told them. "From now on, you are a mechanic first and foremost. And a mechanic needs a kit."

The mechanics exchanged concerned looks at the mention of battle, which Rowan either missed or ignored.

"Everything here can be ordered online, and you'll know just by looking at a substance if it is potent. If it isn't, send it back. Una. Look at these two chamomile flowers and tell me which is more potent," Rowan said. Una inspected both and chose the one on the right. "Correct. Tristan? Find the most vital poppy seed." Tristan carefully plucked one of the impossibly small specks out from the tiny pile of hundreds of seeds. "Correct," Rowan said, smiling. "You will always select the best you have when making a potion before you offer it to your witch. Understood?" They all nodded. "The potions I will teach you one at a time. Today we're going to start with a basic one that mends cuts."

"What? Like, instantly mends a cut?" Breakfast asked disbelievingly.

Rowan took one of his silver knives and cut a long, shallow gash in the palm of his hand. While everyone gasped and moved toward him instinctively to help, Rowan calmly opened a small jar of salve with his uninjured hand and spread a faint green paste on the wound. He took a rag out of his pocket and wiped away the blood and salve. Underneath, the skin was perfect. It was as if he'd never been cut.

"Superficial wounds are very easy to heal. As long as there is no damage to tendons, nerve, or bone, the skin cells are designed to mend themselves an uncountable number of times," he said calmly.

The neophytes stared slack-jawed at Rowan. "We start with shallow cuts and move up from there. As a witch's mechanic, what you will be dealing with the most are burns." He looked at Lily. "And burns are a bitch."

"You are *such* a badass," Breakfast said, his timing priceless. Everyone laughed, releasing the tension.

"Let's get started," Rowan said. "Juliet? Fill the cauldron."

The rest of the afternoon was spent making salve. The new mechanics only needed to see Rowan do it once to memorize every step in the process and store that memory away in their willstones.

"This is cool and all, but what I want to know is when are we going to learn how to jump across rooftops?" Breakfast asked as he spooned salve out of the cauldron and into a small jar.

Rowan looked out the window, his expression severe. "As soon as the sun goes down," he answered.

Are you sure they're ready for that, Rowan?

Ready or not, we don't have any time to waste, Lily. Salve isn't going to protect you from my half brother.

At dusk, Rowan took them all down to the beach. The shore was cold, dark, and deserted. Right away Rowan placed the square of black silk on a rock and told Lily to sit. Then he had Tristan, Breakfast, Una, and Juliet start gathering driftwood for a bonfire.

"Pile it up in front of Lily," Rowan ordered.

"What I want to know is when does Lily get off her butt and do some chores?" Tristan said, panting, as he dragged a gnarly stump of bleached wood up the beach. "I feel like I've been stacking wood and stoking fires all damn day while she just sits there."

Rowan gave Tristan a disapproving look. "It's a mechanic's privilege to serve his witch. We get back the energy we spend on her a hundredfold."

Lily sniffed snootily at Tristan and made a show of getting

comfortable on her rock. He stifled a laugh and grumbled something that sounded like "insufferable," then went back to work. When the fire was high Lily stood up and faced it. All teasing and playfulness vanished from her demeanor. She held her hands toward the bonfire, sucking heat into her willstones, and a howling witch wind buffeted her on all sides, lifting her off the ground.

The awed faces of her new mechanics tilted up as Lily soared ten feet into the air, her arms thrown out wide, and her hair streaming straight up in the column of witch wind that shrieked around her suspended silhouette like it was full of demons.

Don't give them the full Gift, Lily. They aren't ready yet.

For a moment, Lily wavered. She felt the hungry baby willstones tugging at hers, begging to be fed. The Gift was the name for the level of power used in warrior magic, and in Rowan's world it was the test that separated the crucibles from the witches. Only a witch could give the Gift. Lily suspected the Gift not only fueled her vessels with god-like strength, but that it also filled them with a berserker fearlessness that sent them running, exultant, into battle. Receiving any level of energy from a witch was always a thrill, but the Gift was more than that. It made warfare transcendent, especially for the witch. The temptation to possess her vessels and Gift them—to send them leaping and screaming down the dark beach in chaotic rapture—was almost irresistible.

Don't do it, Lily.

She looked down at Rowan's face, which was looking knowingly up at hers. A spark of rebellion flared inside her. Who was he to tell her what to do? She was the witch. He was her mechanic. She would do as she pleased.

With no one to fight, they'll turn on one another, Lily. They don't know how to channel it like I do. Gift me alone if you need to feel it, but not them.

She wanted to tell Rowan that she didn't "need" anything, but she couldn't. He was right. She felt a craving for violence, and she hated it. More, she hated that Rowan had found her weakness and called her out on it. Lily fought to control herself and took deep breaths until she was calm enough to feed each of her mechanic's will-stones a moderate amount of power. It wasn't euphoric like the Gift, but she still reveled with them in the glorious sensation.

Great bubbles of laughter rose up in the air around her as the mechanics began to chase one another around the bonfire. They threw their arms up and hooted at the stars as they jumped ten, twenty, then thirty feet skyward, waving at Lily when they passed by her in midair.

As the fuel of the fire was consumed, the witch wind died down, and Lily sank to the ground. Her mechanics started whirling around the pit, throwing more driftwood on the flames, shouting and stomping their feet. They wanted more.

Lily. Control them so I can teach them how to fight.

She reached out to her mechanics and gathered the individual threads of their consciousness, uniting them. Like separate spokes on a wheel they were joined inside the circle of her mind, and could communicate with one another through her.

Listen to Rowan, she told them. *Do exactly as he says.*

"Tristan. Step forward," Rowan commanded. Tristan met him face to face. "Hit me."

Tristan looked over his shoulder at Lily, confusion widening his eyes.

"Do it," Lily said.

Tristan threw a punch, and Rowan easily deflected it. "Use the speed and strength Lily is giving you. Come on, Tristan. A witch's power isn't just for dancing around bonfires. It's for fighting. Stop squandering what she's given you."

Tristan circled in, angry at being scolded by Rowan. Rowan used that anger and directed Tristan's movement, correcting his stance and his balance. Lily heard Rowan feeding instructions to Tristan, Breakfast, Una, and Juliet through her mind. Every blindingly fast combination of punches and blocks was broken down and analyzed by Rowan at the speed of thought. It was a much more efficient way for him to teach the new mechanics than by speaking aloud. Through Lily, Rowan simply placed the fruits of his vast experience directly into their heads, and she finally understood why he was so coveted by every witch in Lillian's world—why witches and crucibles literally threw themselves at him in nightclubs, and why Nina and Esmeralda had been so jealous when they found out that he'd given himself to another witch. Rowan could tip the balance. With him to teach an army how to fight, any witch could conquer the world.

"Good," Rowan said after half an hour of sparring. "Una. Step forward."

Una faced Rowan with trepidation. "Not the face, okay? I've never done this before and you are scary good," she said.

"I've had a lot of practice," Rowan replied, smiling to put her at ease. "But we're not going to spar. The best strategy for your body type is to get in quick, go for an eye gouge or break a finger, and get out."

"I can do that," Una said easily.

"I know. You've got grit," Rowan replied. He looked at Breakfast and Juliet, both of whom had turned a little green at the mention of gouged-out eyes. "Everyone will have their own strategy. Tristan is a big guy, bigger than most, so a standup style is to his advantage. Una is little—but not squeamish. There's an ambush style my people use that I'll teach her." To illustrate what he meant, Rowan used Lily to pass on an image of a ninja-like fighter to everyone. They all saw a small, nimble person climb up someone's back to slit his throat and then jump down and crouch low to spin across the floor, slicing the

Achilles tendons of other enemies. "You strike first, strike to disable or maim, and then clear out. It's not pretty, but it is very effective."

"Got it," Una said, already crouching low like the fighter in Rowan's image.

They didn't exchange punches as Tristan and Rowan had—they grappled. Una's new style of fighting relied on her getting in close and zeroing in on fragile little bones or crucial nerves. Rowan taught her how to get right up against her opponents and knock them off balance while she took a joint and broke it, or shot in like a surgeon to skewer a vital artery. By the end of Una's grappling session, both Juliet and Breakfast looked like they were going to upchuck from all the gruesome images Rowan had conveyed to them.

"My girlfriend's an assassin," Breakfast said disbelievingly when Una brushed the sand off her clothes and sat down next to him. She kissed him loudly on the cheek. "I am so doomed," he said, grinning.

Juliet looked seasick. "I don't think I can do that," she said.

"I don't expect you to," Rowan replied, holding in a laugh. "For you and Breakfast, I'm going to focus more on self-defense, rather than attack. Which is incredibly useful for protecting Lily." Rowan's tone turned deadly serious. "And that's what this is all about. Protecting your witch. Never forget that without you, she's nearly defenseless, although a powerful witch will always have a few last-ditch tricks up her sleeve. I'll teach you those later, Lily," he said, tossing Lily a brief image of a witch throwing fireballs and forked tendrils of lightning from the palms of her hands. "But without a witch, a mechanic is as good as dead. Protecting your witch is more important than your individual life, because if she dies, *all* of her claimed are left without her strength. If you care about each other you must protect Lily first, and you must protect her to the last. Do you understand?"

They all nodded solemnly as the weight of this responsibility settled inside them.

"This is about that guy," Tristan said, his voice low and rough. "The one that you chased last night. Who is he?"

Rowan started to answer, but Lily stopped him. "No, Rowan. Let me." She took a deep breath and shared a memory of Carrick from the oubliette. For half a second she let all of them feel what she had felt when he touched her willstones, and then she cut off the sensation before any of them could scream.

"Son of a bitch!" Tristan spat.

"He should be torn apart," Una growled.

"Who is he?" Breakfast asked, his face stony.

"My half brother, Carrick," Rowan answered, looking down at the sand. "All I know of him is that he was raised by a vile man. Carrick knows just about everything there is to know about torture. And he's here for Lily." Rowan looked Tristan in the eye. "Can I count on you? Can I count on you to never leave her?"

Tristan nodded. Rowan looked at each of them in turn, waiting until they all nodded in silent agreement.

"Wait. There's something else you need to know. Carrick has a witch fueling him," Lily said. She turned to Rowan. "You know her better than I do."

"I'll explain through you," Rowan said quietly.

Rowan allowed everyone to view a few of his memories of Lillian. He showed them how she started out idealistic and progressive, then how she disappeared for three weeks and came back terribly sick and inexplicably changed. Finally, he showed how she started hunting scientists with a maniacal single-mindedness. He let them all see one moment of his father's body, dropping through the trapdoor on the gallows while Lillian stood no more than two steps away, before he abruptly ended the flow of images.

"We're fighting *you*?" Una asked disbelievingly.

"A version of me," Lily answered. "You need to understand that no matter how strong I may seem to you, our enemy is just as strong and she's had years more practice. She's mastered things that I'm still struggling to understand. She brought me to her world—something that had never been done before—and now she's sent Carrick here to bring me back to her."

"Why?" Tristan asked. "Why does she want you?"

"She wants Lily to replace her as the leader because she's sick. From the way she looked in Rowan's last memory, I'd say she was dying," Juliet answered. Everyone turned to her, surprised that she could guess this. Juliet smiled warmly at Lily. "You wouldn't trust any one but yourself to rule the world. So why would she?"

Lily stared at her sister, hurt.

Am I really like that, Juliet?

You tend to think you know better than everyone else, Lily. Please don't think I'm judging you. I know it's just the way you are.

"Come on," Rowan said, his eyes on Lily's troubled face. "It's late and you all have to be alert tomorrow."

He started shoveling sand onto the last embers of the fire.

Breakfast groaned as he hauled himself up to help. "I haven't done any of my homework. Maybe I'll skip school tomorrow."

"No," Rowan said firmly. "I need all of you to stay with Lily."

"Give me your homework, Breakfast. I'll do it for you," Tristan offered as they headed up the beach.

"Thanks, but I don't think that'd do me any good," Breakfast said despondently. "My teachers would know I cheated because of all the right answers."

As they walked back to Lily's house, she could hear Tristan and Rowan speaking quietly to each other at the back of the group.

"In that last memory—that was your father?" Tristan asked.

There was a long pause. "Yeah," Rowan replied.

"I was there. I saw my face in the crowd," Tristan said, shaken.

Rowan laughed under his breath. "You were there for me. In my world, you and I have been stone kin since we were kids. You're my best friend, Tristan."

"No, seriously," Tristan said disbelievingly.

"We fight all the time," Rowan said.

"Constantly," Lily chimed in, looking at them over her shoulder. "When I first got to Rowan's world, you two bickered for hours."

"Really?" Tristan said, cracking a smile. "About what?"

Rowan shrugged, like the answer was obvious. "What we always fight about. Her."

"Are we in your world?" Una asked. "Breakfast and me?"

"I don't know," Rowan answered. "But anything's possible."

CHAPTER
7

CARRICK GOT OFF THE TRAIN THEY CALLED THE T. HE WAS so used to trains running only underground that it unnerved him when, occasionally, a train would pop up from the safety of the tunnel system. Luckily, his stop was underground. Carrick made his way up the short staircase to the center of this tiny city of Boston. It was so easy to move around this world. No walls, no citizen checks, no Woven. Anyone could get on a train and go anywhere, even clear across the continent, at any time of the day or night. All one needed was money, which was unbelievably easy to steal here.

Without wards protecting the buildings, Carrick could walk up to nearly any property and let himself in without the tenants ever suspecting his presence. The "alarm systems" people used here were a joke. All Carrick had to do was cast a glamour over himself to blend seamlessly with the shadows, wait a while for a tenant to come home, and watch that tenant type in the entry code on the keypad. The same method applied to those bank machines. Watch a mark's fingers type, pickpocket his card, and off you went with his money. Even more ridiculous were the locks and keys they used on their apartment doors. A nudge from any willstone could knock the inner tumblers into place, opening the door in a moment.

Everyone here was so rich and stupid. This world was one big purse waiting to be robbed. Thieving had never been to Carrick's taste, but there was something gratifying about how naive the people were in this world. It had made the few days he'd spent here remarkably easy. Carrick had only had to trouble Lillian once, asking for power. And that was to escape Rowan.

His little brother was faster and stronger. He had years of experience being a mechanic on his side. Carrick escaped only because he'd led Rowan into a populated area. Carrick didn't care if he injured or killed innocent bystanders as he ran through traffic, but Rowan did. Next time he wasn't so sure Rowan would let him go, not even to save innocents. While Carrick learned more about his new skills as a mechanic he'd have to try a different tactic. Facing Rowan head-on would be suicide right now, especially since Rowan was swelling Lily's ranks with native recruits. Her growing circle of mechanics had some real talent among them, but Lily was vulnerable in other ways. People who cared about other people always were.

It wasn't a long walk from the station to Carrick's destination. Lillian had found where Carrick's target lived in this world. Carrick sometimes forgot James existed because he had so little to do with Lillian's life, although their estranged relationship was a constant source of gossip-fodder among the bored and vapid city folk back in his world. Apparently, this version of James had little to do with Lily's life as well.

Carrick let himself into the apartment building, nodded at the sorry excuse for a guard at the front desk, and took the elevator up to the correct floor. He paused at the door, savoring these last few seconds of knowing something that someone else didn't.

Carrick knew with utter certainty that the man in this apartment would be in agony in a few moments. The man, on the other hand, knew with utter certainty that he would be safe for the rest of the night. For just this one moment they were both right. Two possible universes coexisted inside one.

Carrick slid the bolt on the door aside with the faintest nudge from his willstone and let himself in. With that one choice, the two universes collapsed into one. The one that was filled with agony.

My father!

"Lily? What happened?" Rowan propped himself up on an elbow, his willstone flaring with mageclight. Lily's panicked face looked like a pale mask in the otherworldly glow. Rowan got up from his mattress on the floor and sat on the edge of her bed.

"He's in pain. My father's in pain," she said through panting breaths.

"Nightmare?" Rowan asked.

"No." Her brow wrinkled with doubt. "Maybe. I don't know."

"Check. Reach out to your father," Rowan urged.

Lily tried, but all she felt was numb darkness. "He's there, but out. Completely unconscious."

"Deep sleep?"

She looked at the clock. It wasn't even four a.m. yet. "That would make sense."

"It could have been *his* nightmare then," Rowan said comfortingly. "Deep sleep usually follows vivid dreams. If you don't wake up, that is."

Lily flopped back onto her pillows and sighed. "That's annoying." She reached up and touched the bare skin at the base of Rowan's throat, circling her finger slowly around his willstone. "I don't mind sharing your bad dreams, but my dad's? I don't want to accidentally stumble into any of his dreams—bad or good." A disturbing thought occurred to her. "Especially not a *really* good one. Ew."

"Block him out."

"Yeah. Maybe I'd better."

Rowan smiled down at her, and a thought occurred to him. "I don't have as many nightmares in this world."

"Because your subconscious knows there are no Woven here."

"Must be it," he agreed.

Lily pulled on Rowan's arms. "Lie down with me."

A pained look crossed his face. "You should sleep."

"Can't. I'm wide awake," she whispered, easing Rowan down on top of her.

He gave in with a lost expression, allowing himself to be pulled under the covers. The silence in the room filled up with the tense sound of their half-held breaths and the low, almost imperceptible hum of their shaking. Rowan pushed her nightshirt up over her head and laid his cool chest on her warm one. He slid a knee between her thighs, rocking his hips against her as he kissed her. Lily opened herself up and let Rowan feel what she felt.

"Wait, wait, wait," he whispered, suddenly turning his head aside, his eyes squeezed shut.

"Why?" Lily asked, smiling patiently up at him. "And this time, tell me the real reason."

He looked young and scared. Lily felt that huge gray emotion sweep through him again. "Because I can't stay in this world," he answered. "And I don't think I'd be strong enough to ever leave if I make love to you."

Lily shook her head, his words not sinking in. She sat up and fixed her nightshirt, pushing him back so she could see him clearly. "What are you talking about?"

"We left at the start of a *war*," he said, his voice wavering. "My friends, my people—they're fighting and dying. No matter how much I love you right now I know that if I stay here for you, I'll start to hate you. I'll hate you because I'll hate myself for not going back."

Lily stared at him, dumbfounded. "But—I can't go back there," she said.

"No. Not you. It's too dangerous there for you," Rowan said in a low voice. "Just me."

"I almost died the last time I went to the pyre," Lily said, unable to believe that he was asking her to risk her life for this.

Rowan rubbed his face. "Because you'd fought an entire battle before trying to worldjump. This time, you'd just be sending me. I know you can handle that. And if you do get burned, Tristan will be here to heal you. I'll teach him how."

Lily finally understood. She winced at the slippery, nauseous feeling in her stomach. It was as if she'd jumped a little too high and it was only now, at the top of the arc, that she realized how terribly hurt she was going to be when she crashed back down.

"That's why you wanted me to claim them so badly. And why you didn't want me to push Tristan away," Lily said. "You've known from the start you wanted to leave me."

His dark eyes narrowed in anger. "This has nothing to do with what I want."

Lily thought of catching Tristan in the bathroom with Miranda. How stupid she'd felt for not knowing, and how small that hurt was compared with this.

"I thought there was no way I could know anyone better than I know you. I can read your mind, and I still had no idea," Lily said, amazed. "It's impressive, actually. While I was planning our future you were planning how to get away from me."

"Lily," he said pleadingly. "Who would I be if I walked away from everything I've ever believed in and lived only for you?

Would I be someone worth loving?"

Lily leaned back. "You see, that's the thing, Rowan. Whether you stay here or go back, it won't change me. I'll always love you."

"Then let me go," he whispered. "Because I can't love myself if I stay."

Lily knew if she refused he'd have no recourse. She could keep him chained to her for the rest of his life, but even the thought was ridiculous. Rowan wasn't anyone's to keep. She remembered him telling Nina at the nightclub that he belonged to himself. She should have listened to him then.

"Okay," she said numbly. She knew she'd already lost him, anyway. "I'll send you back."

"I won't go until I've dealt with Carrick—or not until Tristan, Breakfast, and Una are trained," he assured her. He could feel Lily detaching and pulling away, and it worried him. "You know I'd never leave you defenseless, right?"

Lily breathed a sad laugh and got out of bed. She felt heavy and slow and too empty to cry. "Sure, Rowan," she said.

She left him sitting in her room, staring at the messy sheets. It was hours before dawn, but she knew there'd be no point in trying to sleep. More images of suffering swept through her mind. Pain. Begging. Blood. Carrick's face loomed over hers. Lily banished it all from her mind, unable to process anything else that morning. With an aching head and a blank heart she stepped into the shower to start her day.

"You were up early," Juliet said right before Lily stepped out the door to go to school.

"Sorry if I woke you," Lily replied, distracted. She waved at Tristan, trying to signal that he didn't need to get out of the car and walk her the twenty steps from the house. He was taking Rowan's admonishment to never leave her alone literally, and Lily wondered just how annoyed she was going to get with the constant supervision over the course of the day.

"I was already up. Guess neither of us slept well."

Lily noticed that Juliet was wringing her hands. "What's the matter?"

"It's nothing," Juliet said, forcing a smile. "Be careful, okay?"

"Let's go," Tristan called out impatiently. Lily shouldered her school bag and ran to his car. Something about what Juliet had said nagged at her. She stopped and looked back, about to ask Juliet in mindspeak why she hadn't slept well, and saw Rowan watching her from the living room window. As she jumped into Tristan's car, the only thought left in her head was that she wanted to get away from him as quickly as she could.

As soon as they pulled away from her house, Tristan started eyeing her cautiously. "I think I can *feel* you," he said, only partially freaked out. "And you feel terrible."

Something popped inside Lily, and huge, hot tears spilled down her face. "Rowan wants to leave me," she sobbed.

It had been such a long time since she'd had the luxury of being able to cry. For months she'd had to be strong no matter what she was feeling, and now that she was safe with her best friend it all came tumbling out of her in a hysterical rush.

Aided in her explanation by the images she passed to Tristan in mindspeak, Lily told Tristan everything, starting with the Outlanders, and the Woven. She recounted Lillian's persecution of teachers, scientists, and doctors, and Lillian's law that magic—which the Outlanders couldn't access or afford—be the one and only way. She told him about Alaric's rebel tribe, and how they had fought back to defend three scientists, and how that battle had ended with her and Rowan accidentally worldjumping.

"And now he wants to go back and fight for his people with Alaric, but I can't go with him," Lily said, hiccupping as they pulled into a parking space at Salem High.

"Why not?" Tristan asked, turning in his seat to face Lily.

"Because that's exactly what Lillian wants me to do," Lily shouted, like Tristan should know that. "And he'd never let me, anyway. I almost died, like, every five minutes I was there. You think Rowan would ever let me go back? Or that I'd *want* to? Horrible things happened to me there, Tristan. I can't go back. Ever."

Tristan reached out and pushed one of Lily's wild curls away from her damp cheek. "I guess you're stuck here with me, then," he said quietly.

"Oh, Tristan, it's such a mess," she said, fresh tears streaming down her face. "And the thing that's just killing me is that I had no clue he was planning to leave. I thought I knew everything about him, but I never even suspected—"

"I know," Tristan said, pulling her into a hug. "It's the secret that hurts the most."

"Yeah," Lily whispered. She thought of how she was hiding the contact she'd had with Lillian from Rowan, and gnawing guilt swallowed what was left of her tears.

They heard a tap on Tristan's window, and jumped apart. Una and Breakfast looked in the window as Tristan rolled it down.

"What's up?" Breakfast asked, eyeing Lily's tear-streaked face meaningfully.

"It wasn't me," Tristan replied.

"That's a first," Una said, smirking. She looked at Lily and her face pinched in sympathy. "What happened?"

"We're going to be late," Lily said, gathering her things. "Let's walk and talk."

As the day went on, Lily recounted the situation for Una and

Breakfast. She spent more time fleshing out the dire situation the Outlanders were in, how they didn't even have antibiotics to treat a fever, and the barbaric cruelty that Lillian exacted on anyone who even attempted to study science—even doctors who tried to heal sick children. The more Lily explained about Rowan's world, the more she painted herself into a corner. By lunch, she wasn't getting much sympathy from her mechanics.

"Lillian hanged Rowan's *father*," Una said delicately as she opened her vintage My Little Pony lunchbox. "That would make anyone a little revenge y."

"She's also slaughtering what's left of his tribe because they're trying to make a better life for themselves," Breakfast added, frowning down at his sandwich. "Damn, I'm not even from there, and I want to go fight."

"Aw," Una said, like she was looking at a fluffy bunny. "He's so cute when he wants to kill people."

Lily looked to Tristan for help. "I get where you're coming from, Lily, and it sucks that he kept it from you, but come on," he said, shrugging sheepishly. "Rowan's going back to fight alongside his stone kin—one of whom happens to be another version of me. How against that can I be?"

"So you all think I'm being selfish," Lily said, frustrated. Silence. "Thanks, guys. I feel so much better after our little talk."

"Lily," Una said through a laugh. "You have every right to feel hurt. Secrets destroy relationships." Una's face suddenly fell and she looked down at her hands. Lily saw a memory flash of a woman with Una's black hair and fair skin. Lily guessed from the feelings of anger, blame, and love she felt that the woman was Una's mother.

"But you all think he's doing the right thing," Lily said, finishing Una's thought for her. Her mechanics nodded in agreement. "And you're right," she said tiredly. "He is doing the right thing. I just wish he'd do the *wrong* thing in order to stay with me."

"No you don't," Tristan said bitterly. "When you lose respect for someone, Lily, you're done. You'd stop loving him."

Like you stopped loving me, he added in mindspeak.

Lily dropped her eyes and stared at her carrots. She'd gotten used to the Tristan in Rowan's world—the one who didn't know all of her faults and call her on them.

The day lurched on for Lily, in the most torturous way imaginable until last period when Lily felt Rowan's mind brushing against hers as she and Tristan walked to their last class.

Make sure they come home with you after school. They need to train.

I told them you were leaving. They think you're doing the right thing.

What about you?

I know you're doing the right thing. I don't have to like it, though.

"Lily!" someone called out urgently. Lily turned around and saw Scot making his way toward her through the crowd. She stopped and waited, surprised.

Who's that? Rowan asked in mindspeak.

A friend of Tristan's who put something in my drink and tried to jump me at a party the night before I disappeared.

He did what?

Easy. I can handle him.

Careful. He's got the potential to be a mechanic.

Huh. You're right.

He'll chase you.

I can handle him.

Lily shoved Rowan out of her mind before he could get too worked up.

"I told you to stay away from her," Tristan said angrily. Scot recoiled slightly, but gathered his courage. Lily noticed a red scar on

Scot's cheek that hadn't been there before she disappeared.

Lily put her hand on Tristan's arm. "It's okay, Tristan. I have a feeling he just wants to apologize." She turned to Scot and met his eyes. "Don't you, Scot?"

"Yeah," Scot said, swallowing hard. "I didn't know a little vodka would do that to you. I just wanted to——" He broke off suddenly, looking at Lily desperately.

"You wanted to get me drunk and take advantage of me," Lily said plainly. He grimaced like he was in pain, shifting from foot to foot. "Here's the thing, Scot. We're not going to be friends. We're not going to hang out. And if I ever hear even a whisper that you've tried that crap on some other girl, I'm going to come after you. Get it?"

Scot nodded slowly, his face frozen.

"Good." Lily turned and continued on to her class.

"I think you made him pee a little," Tristan said.

"He's lucky I didn't——" Lily stopped herself. Didn't what? Have him thrown in a dungeon? Hanged? Lily's insides chilled at how easily her thoughts had turned draconian. She remembered when she first met Alaric—how he'd made her meet his gaze and how he'd known without a doubt that she wasn't Lillian. He'd said there was no death in her eyes. Lily wondered what he would find inside them now. She looked at Tristan, laughed nervously, and pretended to brush it off. "I should have kicked Scot in the ding-ding."

Tristan smiled, relaxing a little, but the tense set of his mouth told her that he hadn't totally let it go, either.

"That's quite a scar he's got," Lily said quietly as they settled into their lab table.

"I hit him harder than I meant to," Tristan replied, his tone heavy with regret. "I was so angry, and not just because of what he did to you, but because you were right. I left you with him at that party so I could cheat on you. I wanted to blame him for what I did."

"Sorry I got you arrested." Lily smiled at him, thinking how much he'd grown up since she'd left.

"No, that's on me, not you." Tristan sighed. "His parents were right to press charges. I sent him to the hospital."

"So you've forgiven me?" she whispered as Mr. Carnello swept into the room to start class.

"Of course," Tristan whispered back. "I forgave you the second you got back, but I had to make you suffer a little."

After school Rowan allowed only a short homework break for the other mechanics before diving into their training, starting with teaching them about burns and how to heal them.

"What's the big deal with burns, anyway?" Una said, frazzled. Lily could tell that she'd been standing over the hot cauldron inhaling fumes for a bit too long.

"Lily, would you show them?" Rowan said.

Lily walked to the fireplace and stuck her hand in the flames. Una pushed Lily back reflexively.

"Are you crazy?" Una scolded angrily.

"It's okay, Una," Lily replied. "Look." She held up her hand to show that it was uninjured. "The best way for a witch to gather energy is for her to go into the flames."

"It's called firewalking," Rowan said, breaking the tense silence. "It's extremely dangerous and very few survive it. Even those who can survive it, like Lily, are often injured."

"But in order to generate enough energy to get Rowan back to his world, you'll have to burn me," Lily finished quietly.

It took a moment for someone to respond. Tristan crossed to Rowan and shoved him to the floor. "You bastard," he said, standing over Rowan.

"Tristan," Lily began, taking a step forward to intervene.

"No, Lily. I thought Rowan was doing this big noble thing by going home, but you didn't say anything about us having to burn you to get him there," Tristan shouted.

"Yeah, I have to agree with Tristan on this," Breakfast said hesitantly. "I mean—what do we do? Tie you to a stake?"

"Yes," Lily answered. Breakfast's smile dissolved. "It's pretty intense."

"Okay, time out," Una said, pulling on Tristan's arm until he moved back enough to allow Rowan to stand. "I'm sure Rowan would never do anything to endanger Lily's life, so why don't you tell us what level of damage we're talking about here. Bad-day-at-the-beach kind of burn, or meltdown-at-the-power-plant kind of burn?"

"She'll be okay if you three are properly trained," Rowan answered calmly. "Look, this isn't going to happen tomorrow. Lily still needs to *find* my world."

"Don't worry about that," Lily replied, looking away. She knew Lillian would guide her if she decided to worldjump. In fact, there was little chance Lily would be able to ignore Lillian once she entered the spirit world.

"How are you going to find Rowan's world?" Breakfast asked.

"It's called spirit walking. Your spirit leaves your body and you send it into parallel universes. It's a talent that runs in certain families," Lily answered, looking at Breakfast meaningfully. "My mom and your uncle do it all the time without even trying."

Breakfast put a hand to his head. "Oh, no way," he said slowly as understanding dawned on him. "My uncle's actually *in* another world?"

"His spirit is," Lily replied.

"Sweet," Breakfast said appreciatively.

Rowan regarded Breakfast through calculating eyes for a moment, and then looked out the window. "The sun's almost down," he said. "As soon as Juliet gets here we can go to the beach and get back to combat training." Something caught his eye. He went to the window and moved the curtain. "There's someone sitting in the car parked across the street."

Tristan was by Rowan's side in a moment. "That's Scot's car," he said. "I'll handle him."

Una's arm shot out and she stopped Tristan. "Breakfast. Why don't you go out and have a chat with dear old Scot?"

Breakfast hurried outside and crouched over the driver's-side window. After a few minutes, the car drove off and he returned with a troubled look on his face.

"What'd he say?" Lily asked.

"He really wanted to talk to you, Lily. He looked pretty strung out," Breakfast replied.

"He's not going to stop," Rowan said darkly. "The farther you push him away, the more desperate he'll become."

"Well, what can I do about it?" Lily asked, frustrated. "Let him sit with us at lunch?"

"Claim him," Rowan replied.

A short, surprised laugh burst out of her. "You're joking."

"I'm not."

"Do you have any idea what he tried to do to Lily?" Tristan asked angrily.

Rowan glared at Tristan, silencing him, and then looked at Lily. "Unclaimed, Scot's a wild card. Claimed, you can do whatever you want with him."

Lily stared at Rowan with her mouth open. "That's why *she* claimed Carrick," she whispered.

Rowan nodded slowly. "And Gideon before him," he added. "You have to start thinking tactically, Lily. Claiming isn't just about surrounding yourself with loving people who adore you. It's about keeping your enemies in check. You need to claim Scot as soon as possible. Today."

Lily's stomach turned at the thought of being inside Scot's mind. "I can't, Rowan."

Rowan backed off, but he looked at Tristan. Lily was miffed to see understanding pass between the two of them. Somehow, Rowan always seemed to end up with Tristan on his side.

Juliet arrived, shedding books and winter layers as she made her way from the garage to the living room. She paused when she sensed the tense atmosphere. "What'd I miss?" she asked.

While her mechanics explained the whole sordid mess with Scot to Juliet over dinner, Lily and Rowan stayed quiet. She could feel Rowan's mind constantly brushing against hers, asking for entry, until she snapped.

Stop it, Rowan. I don't want you in my head right now.

Show me what happened between you and Scot. I saw a fragment of that memory when you claimed me, but not the whole thing.

Why? You're leaving. I'm done sharing myself with you.

She felt the sting in Rowan's chest as keenly as he did. Worse, even. Lily realized that the problem with loving someone more than she loved herself was that when she hurt him, she was the one who was hurt the most.

When it was dark, the group went down to the beach and built a bonfire. They trained until dawn. Rowan barely let any of them sit for a moment to rest.

"Dude. We have school in the morning," Breakfast complained, panting.

"When you get to school, you can take energy from Lily," he replied unsympathetically. "With a witch to fuel you, you can go days without sleeping or eating."

"And what about me?" Lily asked.

Rowan wouldn't meet her eyes. "I have herbs that will keep you energized. You'll be fine."

You want them trained as soon as possible so you can leave as soon as possible, right?

He didn't answer her, but she could feel that sting in his chest again. Hurting him hurt her, but she couldn't seem to stop doing it.

When Rowan finally said they were finished for the night, Lily and Juliet trudged up from the beach alongside each other with the rest of the group several paces behind.

"I'm actually okay with the no sleeping thing," Juliet said, yawning. "Been having horrible nightmares, anyway."

Lily's skin pricked. "About what?" she asked in a low voice.

"Dad. He was getting—"

"Tortured," Lily finished for her. The sisters looked at each other, their faces mirroring the other's dread. They both broke into a run at the same time.

"Lily, wait," Rowan yelled.

They didn't stop. Lily and Juliet ran side by side, their fear entangled. "Please, no. Please make it have been a dream," the sisters chanted under their breath.

When they were still a block away, the sisters could see a police cruiser and an unmarked car parked outside their house. Their legs got rubbery and heavy as they stumbled across their front yard. They saw their mother standing at the door in a tatty old bathrobe, surrounded by officers and Agent Simms. Samantha's hair was a ball of angry red tangles and her eyes swam with confusion that bordered on hysteria.

"Girls!" she called out, the pitch of her voice sliding up to a shriek. "It's your father!"

Lily and Juliet stopped running at the same time. They knew instinctively that running wouldn't help anyway. Their father was already dead.

CHAPTER
8

THE POLICE WERE THERE FOR HOURS. TRISTAN AND Rowan got questioned first. Rowan, because he didn't have any form of identification he could give to the police, and Tristan, because the authorities had gotten accustomed to suspecting him of foul play where the Proctor family was concerned. Rowan handled the questions calmly. Tristan was defensive and confrontational, especially with Simms.

At some point, the police turned their attention to Lily. They told her that they knew about the bonfires on the beach. They'd also heard that odd things were happening down there. Strange, howling noises had been reported, and eerie, pulsing lights had been seen from a distance.

Lily could barely discern their muffled questions through the monotonous hum that had taken over her mind. She saw their lips moving, but it took time for her to string their words together. In her thoughts she played the "nightmare" she'd had about her dad over and over.

The beating he'd taken had been real. The blood. The begging. Carrick's face looming above—watching the pain he inflicted with such hungry interest. And she had ignored it. She could have found him, saved him, but she hadn't believed it could be real. She hadn't believed Lillian would ever go that far. Her father had never understood why he was being hurt, but Lily understood. *Now* she did, anyway.

"Miss Proctor? Lily?" an officer asked.

"She's in shock," someone else answered.

Lily realized they were talking about her and sat up straighter. "Bonfire," she repeated. She looked at the faces of the officers and realized that she was alone with them. They'd separated her from the rest of the group.

Rowan?

There you are! You fell so deeply into yourself I couldn't reach you. You really scared me. Don't give them any information, Lily.

I don't even understand what they're saying.

Good. Say that to them. Say you don't understand what's going on. Say we were on the beach for fun.

"I don't understand what's going on," Lily parroted numbly.

The officers exchanged looks. Simms sat down opposite Lily, and the look on her face was of real concern. "The nature of your father's death points to certain ritualistic practices," she said carefully.

"What does that mean?"

"Tell us about your friends Rowan and Tristan," Simms said, ignoring Lily's question.

Lily shook her head slowly. "Tell you *what* about them?"

"Well, for instance, who had the idea to start building bonfires?"

"I'm pretty sure kids have been building bonfires on the beach since there was a such thing as fire," Lily replied. "I don't know who suggested it first."

The officers exchanged more looks. "Have you ever heard of Wicca?"

Lily burst out laughing. "I'm sorry," she said, collecting herself. "This is *Salem*. Of course I've heard of it."

"Your father was beaten savagely by an unusually strong person and he was found with symbols cut into his skin," Simms said. Her tone turned on a dime when she saw Lily flinch. She looked at Lily with compassion. "You know your mother is very unstable."

"Where is she?" Lily asked urgently.

"Sleeping. Your sister, Juliet, gave her a sedative when she got, ah, confused," said one of the other officers gently. They pitied her. Lily could see it in their eyes.

"You know the sooner we catch whoever did this, the easier it will be on her," Simms continued. She always knew there was more to this story, and now she was determined to hear it. "I know you have relationships with these two boys, and that your group of friends got very close very quickly. You may feel loyalty to them, but think about your mother. Please, talk to me. Tell me what happened to you. You didn't go to some Native American holistic clinic, did you. Lily, there's a *cauldron* hanging in your fireplace. Tell me what Tristan and Rowan did to you."

"We go down to the beach to party. That's it."

Simms nodded, disappointed. "Did you know I was from Beverly? That's why I got your case—because I understand the area and know the people. I used to party on that beach. Same spot, too." She gave Lily a conspiratorial look, like they were buddies. "But in my day we used to go there to drink, smoke, hook up, and eat takeout. Every now and again someone would have weed. You know what the strange thing is about *your* bonfire?" Again, Simms's tone changed swiftly. "No empties, no cigarette butts. Not even a hint of marijuana. We couldn't even find a Taco Bell wrapper. Just footprints in the sand."

Lily kept her mouth shut and slid back into her own head.

Everything around her turned into static. Simms put a card in her hand, in case Lily "remembered" anything else. The police officers stood up, milled around, wandered in and out of the room, until finally one of them said something about being sorry for her loss, and they all left. Lily sat in her chair, not really seeing or hearing anything. She could feel her coven waiting for her in the living room. They were worried, sad, and stricken. She smelled the smoke from a fire being stoked in the fireplace.

Lillian. How could you? He was your father, too.

I've had to make a lot of tough decisions in my life. I've had to sacrifice my personal feelings many times. But I remember what I'm fighting for. Come back, Lily. Come back and no one else has to die.

Did you think killing my father would make me agree with you? Sympathize with you?

No. You'll always hate me for this. Just so you know, I didn't order Carrick to hurt him first, and he will be punished before the end. Hate me or not, you'll agree with me once you know the whole truth.

You better watch your back, Lillian. Carrick isn't the only one who's going to get punished for this.

Lily shoved Lillian out of her mind like she was slamming a door. She stood up and went into the living room. Juliet was crying on the sofa. Breakfast sat on one side of her, scared out of his mind, and Una sat on the other side, holding Juliet's hand. Tristan and Rowan were standing in front of the fire, waiting for Lily.

"What the *hell?*" Breakfast said, his voice shaking.

"They have no physical evidence any of us were involved," Una said in a level tone. "There's no way they can pin this on us. Period."

"They can make our lives miserable, though," Tristan said quietly. "And they can do it for as long as they want. Agent Simms made that clear."

Rowan shook his head and sighed. "Lillian didn't have Carrick kill Lily's father to get you all in trouble. She did it to send a message."

"What message?" Tristan asked.

Rowan's dark eyes met Lily's, inviting her to answer.

"Come back to my world and take my place, or I'll kill everyone around you," Lily said.

"Carrick will start with your parents," Rowan said. "Lily can't be everywhere at once, so when you all scatter to try to protect your families some of you will be separated from her power. He'll be able to pick you off one at a time."

"What do we do?" Breakfast asked. "My parents are dicks, but I still love them."

Anger raged in Lily until she had to fight to pull it back. She looked each of her mechanics in the eye in turn, ending back where she began, with Rowan. "I want Carrick dead."

Rowan nodded once, accepting her order. "He isn't far."

"You can feel him?" Tristan asked.

"Barely. And that's why I think I know where he is."

"Surrounded by granite," Lily guessed.

"Remember that turkey I cooked?" Rowan asked Lily. She nodded—confused, but going with it. "While I was hunting it I followed the Sudbury River and I found a long street cutting through the woods called Salem End Road. On it, there's this huge granite boulder marking the Danforth plantation site. I got curious—for obvious reasons—and looked it up online. There are caves in those woods. Granite ones."

"The Witch Caves, right?" Juliet said. "I've heard about that. There's a legend of the witches fleeing down Salem End Road to get away from the trials, and supposedly some of them hid in the caves for the winter."

"If I needed to hide from a witch who wanted me dead, that's where I'd go," Rowan said. "The more granite, the better."

"Why is granite so important?" Tristan asked.

"Granite is full of quartz crystal, and quartz vibrates at one rate, like clockwork," Lily said. "In order for my willstones to affect yours, I need to be able to manipulate matter and energy on the level where it's all just vibrating strings. I change the vibration in order to change the things themselves. But large amounts of quartz in between my willstones and yours block me. It's like drowning out a symphony by outshouting it with one monotonous note."

"It also blocks mindspeak between willstones," Rowan continued. "Only people who have a blood bond and don't need willstones to communicate can still hear each other, and even then, just barely."

"So we'd be cut off from Lily's power," Una said.

"We'll only have what we take with us into the caves. She won't be able to give us more. And we'll be unable to mindspeak if we separate," Rowan said. "But while he's in the caves, Carrick won't be able to get energy from Lillian, either. What he's counting on is that if he can take witchcraft out of the equation, he can beat all of us."

"Really?" Tristan said, insulted. He looked at Rowan. "I don't know about that."

Rowan smiled back at him. "He's a murderer, Tristan. I know you're a good fighter, but you've never killed a man. Are you sure you're up to this?"

"Don't worry about me," Tristan replied.

Rowan looked at Breakfast. "You're never to leave Lily's side. Understand?"

"Yeah," Breakfast said grimly.

"Una, I want you in the fight with Tristan and me," Rowan said.

"Wouldn't miss it," she said, her eyes narrowing.

"Juliet, you'll stay here with your mother," Rowan said. "There's a slim chance Carrick might circle back for her. You'll always be able to reach Lily in mindspeak because you're sisters. If there's a problem, she can get clear of the granite and give you some power to defend Samantha."

Juliet pursed her trembling lips and nodded resolutely.

"When do we go?" Una asked.

Rowan looked out the window. It was still early afternoon. "Tonight. Until then we should get some sleep."

The group broke up slowly. Una and Breakfast spent some time outside talking with Tristan. Lily hugged Juliet, checked on her mom, and dragged herself to the bathroom to wash off the sand and salt of the night before. When she got back to her room, Rowan was waiting in her bed. She closed the door behind her and went to him, already crying. He wrapped her up tightly in his arms.

"I'm so angry with you," she said into his neck.

"I know," he whispered.

"And I'm angry with my father for never being a father."

"I know."

"I feel like I can't really be sad about losing either of you because I'm so angry. It's like you both robbed me of any chance I had at getting over you, because even when I'm done being sad, I'm still going to be angry."

Rowan squeezed her to his chest and brushed her cheek with his fingers. "I know."

He didn't try to cheer her up or tell her that she was going to feel better in a few months—he just let her feel whatever she needed to feel until she was done. Lily cried herself out and fell asleep on Rowan's shoulder. When she woke up, he was staring at the ceiling.

"Did you sleep?" she asked.

"No," he replied.

Lily propped herself up on an elbow, her head miraculously clear. It struck her that Rowan was just as angry as she was, and even more sad about having to leave her. Her anger fell away when she really allowed herself to feel his sadness.

"I wanted to travel with you," he said, his voice breaking. He pulled Lily down until she was resting on his chest again. "I'd even started imagining what it would be like. We'd drive all the way to California and when we got out there, I'd take cooking classes to be a chef someday. We'd get a stupid dog, not because it could hunt or guard anything but because we love it. We'd live in a place with a swimming pool. There'd be no walled cities. No Woven. And we'd never be afraid again."

Lily could see the whole thing in Rowan's mind. She saw the rolling hills of Napa Valley, and the utterly useless mutt Rowan wanted running blissfully around their yard. She saw the turquoise pool and the wide-open spaces that he didn't have to constantly scan for danger. She could nearly smell the outdoor grill and hear their friends' laughter as the sun set on another perfectly golden California day. But mostly, Lily saw herself. She was happy, always happy, in his mind's eye.

"But every time I'd almost let myself believe in that fantasy," he continued, "I'd remember something."

"What?"

"While my life was perfect, every person who I owed that life to would be fighting and dying."

Lily saw the bright, sunny dream inside his mind's eye hollow out and bleed away and understood what the big, gray emotion she sensed in him was now. It was his dream dying.

"I could rescue them," she offered weakly, knowing it would never work. "I could get Tristan and Caleb and anyone else you wanted, and bring them all here."

Rowan sat up, smiling sadly at her. "You know I can't run from this," he said. "I was born for the world I was born into. Here, I can *feel* good. There, I can *do* good."

"Then I'm coming with you," Lily said. Rowan was shaking his head before she even finished the sentence.

"Absolutely not," he said.

"But, Rowan, if this is really about doing good, I'm the one who can do the *most* good there."

He rolled over, pinning her under him. "Look at me. You're never going back there, do you understand? I can take a lot of things, but not that."

"But——"

"No."

Something hurtful squirmed behind his eyes. Lily heard a whisper in his thoughts, a whisper he shied away from.

. . . thousands of braves back in my world. An army. With them she could do the most good—or the most evil.

"I don't mean that," he said, his brow furrowed with regret. "You didn't ask for any of this. You didn't want an army."

"It's okay, Rowan. I worry about that, too," Lily said softly. She laughed mirthlessly. "Look at what power did to Lillian."

"You're nothing like her," he said. "You don't think like her. You don't agree with her or what she's doing."

"No, I don't," Lily said, although they both knew the truth even if they didn't want to accept it. Lily had lived a different life from Lillian, learned different lessons, but they were still the same person down deep. Lily hoped that in her case nurture outweighed nature. "I'd fight her if I ever saw her again," Lily added bitterly, thinking of her father. Rowan relaxed and laid his forehead against hers.

"Good," he whispered.

They held each other for a while, both of them trying to get used to the idea that they wouldn't have many more opportunities to be together. When it was dark outside Rowan stood and peeled off his white T-shirt and jeans, exchanging them for his darkest clothes. Lily watched his bare skin sliding through the faint moonlight filtering through her bedroom window, already missing him so horribly she couldn't even cry.

"Wear all black," he reminded her, looking out the window. "And dress warm. It's snowing. I'll call Tristan, Una, and Breakfast."

They loaded up Tristan's car with backpacks, weapons, axes to cut firewood, and shovels to bury the embers when they were finished with the bonfire. They arrived at the Framingham-Ashland border before midnight. On one side of Salem End Road there were Colonial-style houses, some of them ancient looking but well maintained; on the other side of the dimly lit and winding road was nothing but forest. A crumbling stone wall, centuries old, rimmed the side of the street, preventing them from pulling the car over.

"No place to park," Tristan said. "And there's no parking lot or hiking trails through this woods. It's just rocks and trees in there."

They had to circle around the forest to the Ashland side. They drove up another dark, rambling road, aptly named Winter Street. The snow-blasted trees bent over the road from both sides, forming what looked like a tunnel of white ice. It seemed to snow even harder here. The wind kicked up flurries from the ground so that the air billowed with sparkling crystals.

"It's a dead end," Rowan said.

"Let's just leave the car here," Una said. She looked back up the street. "Wait a sec."

They all turned to see car lights coming up the street behind them. Tristan killed his engine. The car behind them seemed to slow down and stop. After a few moments the driver backed up and turned down a street to the right, the headlights finally disappearing.

They got out of the car, shouldered their gear, and sank silently into the woods. Rowan closed his eyes. "Follow me," he said, feeling his way toward Carrick.

They found something like a path, and crunched through the super-chilled snow for almost an hour. The brush was thick underfoot in places, and it gripped at them, dragging them back with spindly fingers.

"Stop," Rowan whispered. He pointed in front of them. In the moonlight, Lily could barely make out a rocky cliff through the trees. Close to the top, but still inside the cliff face, came the faint orange glow of a campfire.

"That's it," Tristan whispered. "I saw some pictures online. The Witch Caves are in the cliffs."

"Damn it," Rowan said under his breath. "He has the high ground." The fire suddenly went out. "And he knows we're here."

"How—" Tristan began.

"Because he's been waiting for us." Rowan shook his head impatiently. "Let's get a fire going."

"You're not going up there, are you? How can you defend yourselves from him if you're busy climbing?" Breakfast asked, whispering frantically. He looked at Una pleadingly. "Don't."

"Stuart," she said, smiling softly, "we either do this now, or we live in fear forever. I won't live in fear again. You know that."

Breakfast stared at Una, probably sharing a private exchange in mindspeak, before finally nodding.

"We have to hurry," Rowan said.

They gathered as much wood as they could and piled it in front of Lily. All the wood was wet, and it smoked ferociously when Rowan finally got it lit. "It could go out at any time," he warned Breakfast. "Watch it carefully."

Lily's mechanics stood around her, packs resting on the ground, knives sheathed at their belts, all of them anxiously awaiting her strength. She drew the heat of the fire into her willstones and a witch wind howled down the cliffs and through the trees. Power surged through Lily, lifting her feet off the ground as a shrieking column of witch wind formed around her. She rose up in the air, suspended as if she were floating in water. As she filled her mechanics' stones with pure force, one cold-blooded thought echoed through her mind.

Kill him.

Her three warriors went streaking to the cliffs like black lightning. Lily stayed connected with Rowan, Tristan, and Una as they climbed but she lost them one by one as each ducked into a different cave to seek out Carrick. They would have to check every crevice. It was Carrick's goal to pick them off one at a time, and it occurred to Lily that he probably didn't want to meet Rowan first. Carrick had far less experience as a mechanic and simply wasn't ready to face his half brother. Carrick would go for the weakest, but how would he know who was the weakest when he didn't know any of their potential abilities?

He wouldn't, she realized.

He'd let Rowan decide who was the least capable fighter—by waiting to see which one he left behind.

In a panic, Lily's eyes snapped open and she saw a hunched, crow-like shape appear between the slim trunks of a birch tree stand.

"Breakfast!" she shouted, but not in time. Carrick's willstone flared with Lillian's power, and in an instant he was on top of him. Carrick took Breakfast by the throat so that he couldn't even scream.

"Someone help!" Lily wailed. She saw a flicker of silver in one of Carrick's hands. She filled Breakfast's willstone with power and he wrenched an arm free, stopping the descending blade just inches from his eye.

"Holy shit!" a strange voice yelled. Lily saw a person stumble into the light of her bonfire. It was Scot.

"Scot, help him!" she pleaded desperately. He stared at her floating form, his jaw dropped in shock. "Now!" she commanded.

Scot managed to snap himself out of it and he tackled Carrick, knocking him off Breakfast. They rolled and twisted across the ground. Lily heard Scot scream. Breakfast righted himself, reared back, and hit Carrick with everything he had. Carrick tumbled away from Scot, who was gasping and gurgling in the snow. A pool of black blood fanned out around Scot's head. Carrick had cut his throat.

Lily! What's happening?

Rowan, it was a trap! Come quick!

Breakfast knelt next to Scot and pressed his palms against his neck as if he could hold back the tide of blood. As Scot clutched at Breakfast's arms, drowning in his own blood, Carrick scrambled to his feet and reached a hand into the collar of his overcoat.

"Lillian," he called, clutching his willstone. Lily saw a brilliant flash of magelight that haloed Carrick for a split second, and then he disappeared between the trees.

Rowan, Tristan, and Una arrived a moment too late. Rowan took a handful of steps down Carrick's escape path, and stopped.

"He's already too far," Rowan said through gritted teeth.

Tristan threw himself down next to Breakfast, tearing at the hem of his shirt.

"Tie it off," Tristan said, wrapping the rag around Scot's neck.

"Here," Una said, joining the circle around Scot's head. "My scarf."

"Everyone just stop!" Breakfast snapped. "Rowan, do something!"

"The cut is too deep to heal," Rowan said regretfully. "It's almost to the spine."

The frantic motion around Scot slowed and one by one they all sat back on their heels. Lily let go of the power loop, her witch wind died, and she dropped back down to earth.

"Let me see him," she insisted, running forward and sinking to her knees by Scot's side. The snow around him steamed with the heat of his spilled blood.

"He's dead," Tristan said, closing Scot's vacant eyes.

"I should have claimed him," Lily said. They'd been sitting in the snow for twenty minutes, the fire popping behind them, trying to come up with a plan.

"I should have known he was following us when we saw that car back up behind us on Winter Street," Tristan said.

"How?" Una asked, grimacing. "You're not Jason frigging Bourne."

"There's no point in trying to assign blame to anyone but the murderer," Rowan said. "Scot is dead because Carrick killed him. The end."

"What do we do?" Breakfast asked.

"We could bury him here. Hide the body," Una suggested weakly.

Tristan shook his head, laughing bitterly under his breath. "It doesn't matter if they find the body or not, Una. If he goes missing, who are the police going to think is responsible? Probably the last person who got into a huge fight with him, threatened to kill him, and then sent him to the hospital."

"They're going to suspect all of us, not just you, Tristan," Lily said, holding up a hand before Una could say something sarcastic. "They already *do* suspect us. Agent Simms isn't going to quit. Ever."

"Yeah," Breakfast said quietly. "They'll keep looking until they find his body and once they do, we're all screwed." He looked at Scot's corpse, which was covered with bits of their clothes, fingerprints, and who-knows-what DNA. "Even if we burn him, we'd probably leave something behind on accident."

"I'm not going to jail," Tristan said, his voice leaden.

"Me neither," Una agreed.

"I don't know if we can avoid it at this point," Breakfast said. "I mean, we might get an insanity plea to work if we all start babbling about magic and parallel universes."

"No," Lily said sharply. "No one in this world can know about magic." She conveyed one brief image of the battle she fought against Lillian. She showed them how—with her power in them—her army of Outlanders had fought with impossible strength, speed, and ferocity. "Can you imagine our jacked-up world with those kinds of soldiers in it?"

"It would be a bloodbath," Rowan said. "The Woven aren't the only reason my world is so sparsely populated. There was an era in our history when witches regularly sent out their armies to fight each other."

"Over what?" Breakfast asked.

Rowan gave a half smile. "You've felt what it's like to have a witch in you, but you haven't felt the Gift yet," he said in a deep voice. "When you do, you'll understand."

"We don't have to show them warrior magic. We can just show them medicine and kitchen magic," Breakfast said hopefully. "And it could be a *good* thing. Do you know how many burn victims would be saved because of what you taught us the other day, Rowan?"

"No. No magic in this world. The shaman was *very* clear about this when he taught me how to spirit walk," Lily said. "You can't steal advanced technology from one world and bring it to another without something terrible happening. It doesn't matter what your intentions are. Just think it through. It'd be like introducing the plague to a bunch of people who've never even had the sniffles. I won't be responsible for genocide just because I don't want to go to jail."

"So we can't tell the truth." Una looked at Lily, her cat-like eyes narrowed. "Our only hope is to run, but there's no place in *this* world we can hide. Not for long."

Rowan looked up from the ground and around at the group, the first to catch on to what Una was suggesting. "You can't leave Lily," he said fearfully.

"Hang on," Breakfast said, his brow furrowed. "Una, are you saying we should go with Rowan to his world?"

"Doesn't it make more sense than staying here?" she said, her excitement building.

"No. It doesn't," Breakfast said.

"Stuart, I just found out who I really am inside. For the first time in my life I feel like I understand where I fit. I'm not giving that up," she said, eyes blazing. "And anyway, we're mechanics. We *are* magic, so we don't belong in this world. We might even be a threat to it because eventually someone is going to find out about us."

"But if we go, we won't be able to do much magic without our witch," Tristan said.

"Then she should come," Una said.

"No," Rowan said sharply. "It's too dangerous."

"More dangerous than this?" Una argued, gesturing to Scot's dead body.

Rowan nodded sadly. "You have no idea."

"Tristan," Una implored. "Back me up."

"I'd go in a second," he said with a shrug. "My life here is over anyway."

Una looked at Lily hopefully, biting her lower lip.

"No," Rowan said.

"Yes," Lily countered quietly. She looked at Rowan. "It's never going to end unless I go back. And who'll be next? Juliet? My mom? Rowan—I can't run from Lillian any more than I can run from myself, and it was stupid of me to even try. I have to go back."

Rowan's face crumbled. Lily felt that unthinkable thing well up in him again.

Back to her army. What will I do . . . , he thought before shoving a new, dark idea away.

Rowan, if I use that army, it will be to fight Lillian. How could you ever think anything different of me?

I don't want you fighting at all! Your last battle against Lillian almost killed you

She sighed, frustrated. As soon as she decrypted one confusing part of Rowan's feelings it seemed another even more baffling emotion swooped in to take its place. She honestly didn't know what he wanted from her, probably because he didn't know himself.

"So, we're leaving," Breakfast said disbelievingly.

"I am," Una said, uncertainty creeping into her eyes. "But I can't force you to come with me."

"If you're going, I'm going," he growled. "I told you—you're never getting rid of me. Even if I have to follow you to another universe."

"Good." She smiled, suddenly shy, and took his hand.

Tristan stood. "I have paper and pens in my car. We should let Scot's family know where to find him. And we should all leave notes for our families." He looked at Lily, one corner of his mouth tilted up in a regretful smile. "It isn't right to just disappear on people."

They hiked back to Tristan's car in silence. Lily reached out to Juliet in mindspeak and shared what had happened and how they had come to the decision to worldjump. Juliet fought Lily leaving at first, but she stopped when Lily pointed out that their mother could be next.

I wish I could go with you, Lily.

No! It really is unbelievably dangerous there, Juliet. And anyway, you need to stay with Mom.

Aren't you at least going to come back and say good-bye, Lily?

I don't know if I can, Jules.

Lily looked up at the rest of the group. "Do you guys want to go home and say good-bye to your families in person?" she asked.

"We can't run the risk of being separated. Carrick wants you all to panic and scatter," Rowan objected gently. "If you split up to go to your homes, I guarantee Carrick will be waiting for one of you. It's what I'd do."

"And all of us going to each other's houses together would take too long," Una added. She looked down at her blood-soaked clothes. "We'd get caught for sure."

"Yeah, I wouldn't put it past Simms to come by my house at dawn. Or any one of our houses," Lily said.

"She likes to drop by and harass suspects," Tristan said bitterly. "She came to my house every day for a week straight after you disappeared, Lily."

"It's probably better if we just leave letters and go now," Una said, her voice rough. They all stopped and looked at one another, their faces saddened as the enormity of their decision sank in.

"Wow. This is it," Breakfast said, stunned.

"Yeah," Una said, nodding and looking blankly at the ground.

Lily reached out to Juliet and let her know of their decision to leave immediately. While the sisters discussed what Juliet should tell Simms, Una and Breakfast helped each other compose farewell letters for their families. Tristan insisted on being the one to write the letter for Scot's parents. He knew them best.

"What are you going to say to them?" Breakfast asked.

Tristan shrugged, at a loss. "I guess I'll tell them he died trying to save someone else. Maybe thinking he died a hero will help."

Breakfast gave Tristan a doubtful look, but he didn't object. What could any of them really say to their parents besides good-bye and I love you?

"Tristan," Rowan said, pulling Tristan aside. "Do you have chains or rope in your car?"

"No. I have bungee chords," he said, opening the trunk. "What do you need them for?"

Lily answered for Rowan. "You'll have to tie me down so I don't instinctively jump off the pyre when you burn me." A heavy pause followed. "There's no other way to worldjump, you guys," she said calmly. Something occurred to her, and the words were out of her mouth before she could recall where they'd come from. "I'm a witch. And witches burn."

They placed their good-bye letters in a neat row on the dashboard and left the car doors unlocked. Dawn was near. They were running out of time.

"The people in the house over there will report an abandoned car when they wake up," Tristan said, gesturing down the block. "We should go."

They hiked back through the woods and built Lily's pyre.

Juliet. I'm leaving now. Take care of Mom.

I will. Promise that you won't stay away forever.

Lily stared at the pile of logs in front of her, unable to answer her sister. She didn't know if she would ever be back.

"Let's do it," she said, nodding at Rowan.

She approached the unsteady heap of wood carefully. This pyre was much smaller than the one that had fueled her in battle and, thankfully, it lacked the intimidating stake jutting up from the center. Instead, Rowan had ordered that one long birch log be laid across the top. The pyre was still large, and Lily's legs were clumsy with fear as she climbed onto it.

Or was it excitement that was making her stumble? Now that she smelled the wood sap and saw the white, splintery guts of the split logs, she remembered the power of the pyre as sharply as she remembered the pain. It coiled in her like lust.

"You won't burn for long. Remember, you don't have to last through an entire battle this time. Just long enough to worldjump," Rowan said, helping Lily lie down on top of the long birch log. His hands shook and his eyes were wide. "If it's too much—"

"It won't be," Lily whispered. She guided his mouth to hers and kissed him. As he kissed her back he pushed her arms over her head and bound her wrists tightly to the birch log beneath her. When he pulled away he kept his eyes locked with hers. "Tristan. Tie her feet," he said.

Lily felt Tristan strapping down her ankles with the bungee cord while she and Rowan stared at each other. She could feel Rowan's need and fear mirroring her own. On the pyre they were always one.

Tristan and Rowan moved back and Una stepped forward, a makeshift torch blazing in her hand. She looked at Lily with a mix of fear and pride in her eyes while she touched the torch to the logs under Lily's body, setting them aflame.

The heat came on much faster this time. As soon as Lily smelled the smoke she felt the fire. In seconds she was screaming.

Lily! How can I help you?

You can't, Rowan. In fact, you have to go.

Lily pushed him out of her mind. She knew that having him there would only make her focus on this world, rather than allow her to spirit walk and find the world she was seeking. In order to do that, she needed Lillian—and Lillian was always easy for Lily to find when she was in pain. Lily still hated her for what she had done, and when she wasn't burning she knew she would remember that, but her hatred seemed to vanish when it was just the two of them, clinging to each other on the raft.

I'm here, Lily.

You've won, Lillian. I'm coming back.

This isn't a contest between us. You could have gone to your authorities and revealed your magic. You could have cleared your name and had the police hunt Carrick for you. But you didn't choose that. You chose to be known as a murderer in your world. You chose your world's safety over the safety of you and your coven—the good of the many over the good of the few, even if one of those few is you. You will be thought of as a murderer and a villain in your world. Like me.

I may be you, Lillian, but I don't make the same choices you do.

This choice proves otherwise. The reason I killed the shaman and the reason I hunt the three scientists is because they did exactly what you won't— what you're willing to leave your world in order to avoid doing.

What are you talking about?

Do you really think three Outlanders, no matter how intelligent, would have the ability to invent and to build nuclear devices out of thin air?

Explain.

In a moment, but you must worldjump now, Lily, or you'll die. Gather your mechanics and find me in the worldfoam. I will be your lighthouse.

A vibration too large and too complicated to ever store in her willstone buzzed through Lily's body like a swarm of bees. She called to the unique patterns in Rowan's, Tristan's, Breakfast's, and Una's stones as the heat and the pain of the pyre catapulted her up and out into nothing.

One shining light called to Lily. She followed it through the numbness between the worlds and found Lillian. Her mission completed, her physical body tired and charred, Lily's spirit gladly wandered into the Mist, where Lillian met her.

Let me show you what I meant about the shaman, Lily . . .

. . . I heave into the basin until I'm shaking.

"You should be in your bed, Lady, being tended to by Lord Fall," Captain Leto scolds. He steadies me as I lean back against the side of his cot and dabs at my sweat-streaked face.

"He isn't back from the Outlands yet," I rasp, shaking my head. And it's a good thing, too. If Rowan had been at the Citadel, rather than out looking for me when I returned from the cinder world two days ago, he would know everything that had happened to me. He would have seen what happened in the barn.

Never. He can't. I can't ever show him that, even if it means he never touches me again.

"You have other mechanics," Leto presses as he helps me off the floor and onto his cot. "Surely their care would be better than mine." He gestures helplessly around his spare quarters on Walltop. He has little more to offer than a fire and tea. I can hear the wind howling at his door.

"It doesn't matter now," I say. "There's a tipping point with this disease and I've already passed it. I spent too long being exposed to something that damaged too many of my cells. I can keep this sickness at bay for a long time, but there is no cure for me now, Leto. Sooner or later it will take me." I see genuine sadness in his eyes. I touch his arm and try to smile.

"Captain," a soldier calls from the other side of the door. "The shaman is here."

Leto leaves us, and the shaman joins me on the cot. He moves more slowly than he did just a month ago. He seems older. Tired.

"Shaman," I say, getting right to my point. "We must stop searching other worlds for a way to get rid of the Woven."

He studies my face, reading death there, and closes his eyes. "I'm sorry I got you into this, girl." I see his wiry hands grip his bony knees. "But we can't stop."

I'm confused. It takes me a moment to reassemble my thoughts.

"I'm not saying this because of what happened to me but"—I falter and pause, taken for a moment by the savagery that crawls through my thoughts—"but because that cinder world I was trapped on was not of their own making. The few people left there—if you could call them people—told me that their destruction came about because of something that didn't belong there. It was technology *stolen* from another world and it wound up being their destruction."

The shaman nods, but he won't look at me or reply.

"Do you understand what I'm saying?" I ask, unable to accept his indifference. "If we keep seeking a miracle solution for the Woven on other worlds, we could end up a cinder world like them. That's how it happens, and I think that's how it *always* happens on the cinder worlds. They start off thinking they're doing good—"

"I understand what you're saying, but it's too late," he says, cutting me off. "We must press on."

"No," I say, my brow furrowing with dismay. "I won't do it. And I forbid you from continuing this madness with another witch. I'll imprison you if I have to. I'll throw you in the deepest oubliette I can find—don't think I won't just because I care for you."

"I've never doubted your ferocity. Your will to do what's necessary. *Will* is what makes a great witch, and I believe you'll prove to be the greatest witch in history, Lillian," he says softly, finally meeting my eyes. I don't think he's ever used my given name before and it startles me, as does the look in his eyes. There is as much death in his face as I suspect there is in mine. "But it's too late. I've already stolen from other worlds."

I stare at him. The room seems to fall into a hole. "What did you steal?"

"Equations. Plans. Schemes for building devices and power plants. Everything I could see or read on a spirit walk and then copy down later on the subject of elemental energy," the shaman said in a dull voice. "It took decades. And it turns out it's much easier to build bombs with this kind of energy than it is to build a power plant, like I'd originally hoped." He swipes a weary hand across his face. "I started stealing to find another power source for the Outlanders so we could drag ourselves out of poverty. So we could have electricity and build cities of our own—anything to sever our dependence on the witches who treated us like we were less than human. I didn't mean for them to turn it into a bomb." He turns his eyes on me, pleading. "You believe me, don't you? I never meant for them to make bombs."

My hand shoots out and I slap him, trying to knock the words back into his mouth. It doesn't work, but I slap him again anyway. He takes my wrists in his hands, gently pushing my arms down.

"If that would help, I'd gladly let you beat me to death," he says.

"Who else knows?" I demand, my voice low and shaky. "Who have you told?"

"For years I've been giving all the numbers and drawings to a woman of my people who understands them. Her name is Chenoa Longshadow."

"Professor Longshadow?" I say, nearly shouting. "Head of the department of Fundamental Laws of Nature at *my college?*"

"She's been using your laboratories, your resources, and your students at the school to develop what I've stolen. She has two students in particular—acolytes, really."

"Who are they?" I ask, my lips twisting into a snarl.

"I don't know their names. Alaric keeps the particulars compartmentalized—even from us who are most involved. We each just know bits. All I know is that Chenoa has two students who're special. They know everything she knows, just in case something happens to her."

I'd never interfered with the science department at my college, and in fact, I'd never even met Chenoa. Never toured her labs. Never took the time to concern myself with anything except student enrollment. I thought it was my job to bring as many of the disenfranchised to my school as possible, and to fight for their right to an education before the Council and in the Coven. The actual schooling I left to the professors.

"I trusted them to teach," I say feebly.

"She did teach. She taught Outlanders to hate the Covens," he says. "And for the past two years she's been using your money and your laboratories to make and store parts of the bombs."

"But I was trying to help." My eyes dance around frantically, not really seeing anything. "How could they?"

"Did you really think one little school was going to erase centuries of injustice?" he asks, an eyebrow raised. "Too many Outlanders have watched their children starve to death or die in the mines or be torn apart by the Woven for too long. That kind of bone deep hatred doesn't just disappear because one witch builds a school."

I've never felt such a weight pressing down on me. I feel so sick I'd vomit again if there were anything left in me but bile.

"I won't let her," I whisper.

"How can anyone undo what's already been done?" The shaman shakes his head sadly. "The only way to stop the Outlanders now is to give them another way to get rid of the Woven. If we do that, I know Alaric will abandon elemental energy."

"Alaric Windrider? The sachem who has sworn to destroy me?" I say incredulously.

"He's not a madman," the shaman insists.

"But he can't use elemental energy against the Woven," I object, confused. "He'd have to bomb the whole continent. I understand this energy—every witch knows what powers the sun and the stars—and I tell you it causes more damage than the enemy you would use it against."

"He doesn't want to use the bombs against the Woven. He wants to use them against the Thirteen Cities."

"Why?" I whisper.

"What choice do we have? The Covens won't allow Outlanders to own property and build walled cities of our own. If we continue having to fight both the Woven and the laws of the cities, the Outlanders will die out. Our very existence is at stake, Lillian. What would you do if you were caught between hammer and anvil as we are? If we can't get rid of the Woven, Alaric will get rid of the cities."

"I can't make the Council and the other twelve Covens change the law!" I shout defensively. "I've tried! I only have so much power, shaman, and quite frankly too many people make too much money off the mines that the Outlanders work."

"The mines the Outlanders *die* in," the shaman corrects quietly. "You need us to be poor so you can get rich. Is it any wonder some of my people want to see every single one of the cities burn?"

"So what's stopping them?"

"The bombs aren't finished," the shaman admits. "We need to find a way to get rid of the Woven before those bombs are complete or Alaric will blow you to hell."

Seconds crawl by, each getting heavier than the last. I've never thought of time as having mass before, but it does. When time slows down it takes on so much weight that even one second could drag a star down into darkness.

"Are the bomb parts still in my school?" I ask calmly.

"I don't know. Maybe." He makes a frustrated sound. "You're focusing on the wrong thing. No one person knows where all the bomb parts are except Alaric. You gotta focus on finding the world that got rid of the Woven to end this."

"Getting rid of the Woven isn't going to stop Alaric and Chenoa now," I reply. "They'll just wait until after I deliver the Woven solution, and then they'll use their bombs. Not because it makes sense, but because they hate us. You said it yourself. They want to see the cities burn. I've seen what elemental energy does to cities. I've *lived* it, and I know there's only one way to keep the Outlanders from detonating your stolen poison."

"What are you talking about, girl?" the shaman asks fearfully. But he knows. He's not naive. "Look, there's no telling how many students, teachers, and science-minded folk Chenoa has shown a little bit of this and a little bit of that over the years. It could be hundreds of people."

I am dead inside already. I've let go, like a child letting go of a beautiful birthday balloon. It was only ever full of air, anyway. All that's left for me to do is clean up the mess.

I'll save as many as I can by killing the rest.

CHAPTER
9

LILY HAD A VAGUE SENSE THAT SHE WAS MOVING. SHE FELT a steady flow of air rushing over her singed skin and the occasional jolt of a misstep. She was having trouble catching her breath and, as she wiped away the cobwebs still connecting her mind to Lillian's memory, she realized she was having trouble breathing because she was slung over someone's shoulder.

"I think she's coming around," Breakfast whispered frantically.

Lily peeled her eyes open and saw a chaotic mix of upside-down limbs and woodland landscape bouncing around as if someone had thrown her in a dryer. She propped herself up against Rowan's back and saw Breakfast's panicked face huffing and puffing as he ran through the milky light of a snowy dawn.

The world righted itself as Rowan swung Lily around and looked in her eyes. "There you are," he said, relieved. He was still running and he suddenly ducked, careening to his knees as he clasped Lily painfully to his chest. "Everyone down," he ordered.

The little group huddled together against the rocky side of a cliff. The trees were bigger here, and the air crisper, but even with these differences Lily recognized this cliff. They were at the Witch Caves—they just weren't at the Witch Caves in Lily's world. It always stunned Lily how quickly a memory exchange could happen when the memory itself seemed to last ages. She felt like she had been inside Lillian's memory for at least half an hour, but only minutes had passed.

"Shh," Rowan breathed. His eyes went up to the treetops. Lily huddled close to his chest and looked at the faces of her coven, wild-eyed and bleached white with cold and terror. Rowan's head snapped around, and then Lily heard it—a hooting, bellowing sound echoed through the forest. "Woven," he whispered. "Simians."

Lily saw the trees shake. She heard the crack of brittle branches as the animal calls rose to a frenzied chorus. They were surrounded.

"Breakfast, get a fire going," Rowan said. There was no point in whispering now. "Lily, we need your strength. Can you handle this?"

"I'm okay," she lied. "Light the fire."

Rowan nodded once and looked at Tristan and Una. "Take off whatever clothes you don't want torn to shreds," he said, shucking off his jacket and shirt. Too confused and frightened to question him, Tristan and Una did as he said.

Breakfast led Lily back into the boulders strewn about the bottom of the cliff. He tucked her among the stones as deeply as he dared, trying to provide as much cover as he could without hemming Lily in with so much granite that it would block her connection to her mechanics. Tristan, Una, and Rowan took position between them and the Woven. Breakfast kicked the snow aside with the edge of his boot and gathered what leaves and twigs he could and put them in a pile. He cussed a blue streak as match after match fizzled in the icy tinder.

"Breakfast?" Tristan said uncertainly over his shoulder as he watched the shadows in the treetops loom nearer.

Breakfast's f-bombs rained down on the tinder with more fervor, and somewhere between the matches and his explosive language a spark managed to catch as a dark body dropped from the trees and swung on huge knuckles toward Lily's three warriors.

"Sweet *jeezus*," Tristan whispered, his mind struggling to come to grips with the monster in front of him.

Lily had never seen a simian Woven before, either. It looked mostly ape-like with its hulking shoulders, long arms, and short legs, but snake scales flashed between the clumps of longhaired fur and a forked tongue spilled out of its fanged mouth as it roared. Two more dark shapes thudded to the ground and barreled up behind their leader, hooting with excitement.

"Oh, please," Lily begged, staring at the tiny flame Breakfast was nurturing, wishing she could make it grow faster. It still wasn't large enough for her to harvest any strength from it.

The simian Woven roared again, and Rowan charged out, howling like a wild animal himself, to meet it. The Woven balked. Lily felt *intelligence* inside of it as it knuckled around Rowan in a circle, sizing up this smaller but fiercer opponent. Rowan didn't back down or show even a flash of fear, although Lily could feel how terrified he was. Four more Woven dropped from the trees and crashed forward through the snow and underbrush to flank Lily's pitifully outnumbered coven.

Tristan and Una managed to gather themselves after the initial shock of seeing their first Woven and charged forward, trying to mimic Rowan's battle cry as bravely as they could. Rowan never took his eyes off the leader.

"Stand back, Breakfast," Lily whispered. If the fire wasn't large enough by now, it would be too late anyway. Lily took a deep breath, pulling heat into her already-singed skin. A clap of air threw Lily skyward and kept her there, suspended in a pillar of moaning witch wind while she transmuted heat into force and fed it to her mechanics.

Their willstones gorged on the full power of the Gift. Breakfast rooted himself staunchly under Lily's dangling feet while Rowan, Tristan, and Una swept forward and attacked the Woven in a blur of flashing knives and bloodlust. A part of Lily went out with them. She could feel their bodies moving, leaping, and stretching as if she were wearing their physiques over hers like a cloak. She could feel her strength filling them up and spilling over into an ecstasy of rage. They slashed, tore, and crushed the Woven beneath them in seconds.

And right on the edge of her mind was that creeping temptation to take over her claimed completely—to possess every bit of them, even their dreams.

Rein it in, Lily. You must be strong and control it, or we'll turn on one another.

Lily's insides squirmed with guilt.

I will. I'm sorry, Rowan.

I understand—I really do. But you must not let it swallow you whole.

Lily released the loop of power and dropped into Breakfast's outstretched arms, limp as a rag doll. She was so tired and injured from the pyre that she could barely lift her head. Her mechanics gathered around the fire while Breakfast gently laid her on the ground. Tristan and Una were stark white under the livid streaks of blood painting their nearly naked bodies. They shook with shock over what they had faced, but more so over what they had done.

"Tristan. Una. Start gathering all the body parts and pile them away from the cliffs," Rowan said gently. "More Woven will come to scavenge the dead."

Tristan and Una blindly followed Rowan's order. Rowan turned to Breakfast. "Well done," he said. "It takes a strong man to resist and stay behind. Not many can do it."

"I'm a lover, not a fighter," Breakfast replied, a watery smile tilting his lips.

Rowan laughed under his breath while he rubbed his bloody hands in the snow to clean them. "Climb the cliff and scout out a cave for us to sleep in tonight. Light a fire when you get up there. Watch out for Woven along the way."

"Breakfast, wait," Lily said. She transmuted a little more energy for him to take with him on the climb. "Be safe." He gave her a shaky look, then vaulted up the icy cliff face.

Rowan took his cauldron from his pack and started scooping snow into it. He put the snow-filled cauldron on the fire and stared at it while he rubbed salve onto Lily's singed skin. Luckily this time she was not too badly burned.

"Are you hungry?" he asked, staring at the melting snow in the cauldron. "You need salt."

"Not yet," she whispered, every muscle relaxing under his hands. "Too tired."

"They did well."

"They're scared out of their minds."

He paused before responding, the fire popping and sending sparks and smoke up into the early morning light. "They should be."

When Tristan and Una returned, Rowan told them to drink from the cauldron first, and to use the rest of the water to wash before they put their outer clothes back on. Blood would attract scavengers. They silently obeyed him, relieved to have someone to take charge and tell them what to do. Lily could feel that they were on the edge of losing it, and the last thing they needed was too much time to stop and think. The group struck camp, climbed the cliff, and joined Breakfast in one of the Witch Caves. They piled into one big heap and fell into an exhausted sleep together.

When Lily awoke, she could hear urgent whispers. Tristan and

Una were sitting by the fire in the mouth of the cave, talking. Lily could feel that Rowan and Breakfast were not with them.

"They've been gone too long," Una said.

"Rowan knows what he's doing," Tristan replied. "He'll look out for Breakfast while they hunt. I guess we're all going to need to learn how to hunt and gather now."

"Yeah. This is our life now," she said, incredulous. Una sighed. "I still can't believe it. I can't believe what I did," she said.

"I know," Tristan replied in a leaden tone. "I tore one of them apart with my bare hands."

"Me too." Una pulled her knees against her chest, hugging herself tightly. "And it felt so good," she said, her voice small.

Tristan nodded. "If it had been a person in front of me I would have done the same." He groaned. "I've never felt anything like that. Never felt so"—he paused, searching for the right word—"*fulfilled*. And I hate this about myself, but I want more."

"I know, I'm disgusted with myself, but I crave it, too. All that power. Tristan, are we sick?" she asked tremulously.

"No, you're not sick," Lily said, sitting up. She stood and joined them by the fire. "The Gift is what it is. It's always a struggle not to give in to it."

"What's it like for you?" Tristan asked, a curious smile narrowing his blue eyes.

Lily swallowed. "I feel what all of you feel combined," she replied, leaving out that she also felt the temptation to possess every one of them.

"So what's it like fueling a whole army?" Una asked.

Lily thought about it, seeking the right way to put it. "Like being a mighty river, I guess. I could grind down mountains or wash whole cities out to sea. It's a lot to take in."

"If you're the river, are we the fish?" Tristan guessed, smiling.

Lily smiled back vaguely, not really agreeing or disagreeing. "You could show us, couldn't you? You could share your memory of it with us," he pressed.

Lily sensed Tristan's hunger. Restraint had never been his forte, and she was grateful that she was the one in control of her awesome power—not him. But, she wondered, how would she use that power if Rowan weren't there to remind her not to give in to it? She looked out the mouth of the cave and changed the subject. "They're almost here," she said, feeling Breakfast and Rowan before she could see them.

They came back in the late afternoon with a dead rabbit, and Rowan immediately began to teach them how to skin it.

"I know this is probably a dumb question, but why go hunting?" Una asked. "Why don't we just eat the Woven we already killed?"

"They're poisonous," Rowan answered. "Only Woven can eat other Woven."

"Seriously?" Lily asked, surprised. "How can that be? There are so many different breeds, you'd think some of them would be edible."

Rowan shrugged. "I don't know why they're poisonous – they just are. Believe me, plenty of starving Outlanders have wished it were otherwise, and have died because it isn't."

Lily looked away while Rowan pulled the rabbit's skin off in one brisk tug, like he was peeling a tube sock off a foot.

"It doesn't make sense. Gorilla meat isn't poisonous, and snake meat isn't poisonous, but Woven gorilla-snake meat is?" Something about it bothered Lily and she couldn't let it go. "Nature doesn't work like that," she said, frustrated.

"They're not from nature," Rowan replied, raising an eyebrow. "Remember, they were made by witches."

"They were made by witches to build cities and haul heavy loads, and basically play the role that machinery plays in my world. Why would they also be made to be poisonous? Why go through the trouble of engineering them to be poisonous for no good reason?" she argued. She accidentally glanced down at the skinned rabbit and covered her mouth, gagging.

Rowan stifled a laugh at her reaction and shrugged again. "I don't know, Lily. Maybe there *is* a reason. We just don't know what it is."

While the rest of them shared what little rabbit there was, Rowan gave Lily a few olives from a jar he had brought in one of the packs. The salt in the brine restored her more than the food.

"Feel better?" Rowan asked. Lily nodded. "Good. We should stay here one more night to rest and leave early tomorrow morning. Can you contact Caleb and Tristan?" Rowan glanced quickly at the Tristan to his right. "I mean, *my* Tristan. The one from this world."

"I'd have to leave the cave," Lily said.

"Tomorrow. I don't want you out there in the dark," Rowan said. "I tried reaching them to find out where Alaric is while Breakfast and I were hunting, but they were too far for me to reach them."

"You want to go straight to Alaric?"

"The sachem should know you're back before anyone else does." He gave her a wry smile. "You did claim several *thousand* of his braves. He's going to want to know where you are."

"I'll try in the morning," Lily said. She noticed that Tristan was frowning uncomfortably. "You okay?" she asked him.

"It's just weird," he replied. "The thought of meeting myself is just mind-blowing."

"Yeah," Lily agreed, looking down. "It changes everything."

The thought of Lillian chased through her mind. Although Lily wanted to avoid dealing with it, she knew that Lillian's latest memories had changed her.

Lily didn't see this struggle between Alaric and Lillian as a battle between good against evil anymore. Lillian hanged hundreds, but Alaric was prepared to nuke millions. Alaric hadn't actually perpetrated mass murder the way Lillian had, but he had considered it. There was no right answer anymore; no one Lily could follow without question, but she'd still have to choose between them soon. Now that she was back in this world, Alaric wouldn't simply allow her to keep his army of braves and not use them. Eventually, he would ask her to fuel them in the fight against Lillian and the Thirteen Cities. Lily wondered how many thousands more would die, and for what reason? To stop Lillian, who was only fighting to stop a potential nuclear war? Lily looked over the fire at Rowan, patiently showing the group how to make a rabbit snare, and didn't know what her answer to Alaric would be.

She couldn't even discuss it with Rowan. His answer would be automatic, and his feelings of betrayal understandable. It was one thing to talk hypothetically about how the good of the many outweighed the good of the few, and quite another when one of those few is someone beloved. When Rowan thought of Lillian, he thought of his father hanging on the gallows.

The sun set, sucking the light from the sky. Night was darker and deeper here than in Lily's world, and even stubborn Una had to give up on trying to make a snare when she couldn't see her own fingers anymore. Everyone was too exhausted and too rattled to want to stay up late anyway.

"I'll take first guard," Rowan said. "Who wants second?"

"I'll do it," Tristan offered. "Wake me when you get sleepy."

Lily curled up between Tristan and Una, sensing that Rowan had taken first guard because he was too anxious to sleep. Rowan was back in his deadly world with four people who had no survival skills, and Lily knew he felt that the enormous responsibility to keep them all alive was on him.

We'll be okay, Rowan. We'll find your tribe tomorrow and you won't have to worry so much about us.

I'll always be worried about you, Lily. It's my curse. I don't know if I'm going to end up dying tonight to protect you, or if I should strangle you now and save myself the trouble.

Lily stifled a laugh. She drove him crazy and she knew it. *I hope you're less grouchy when we find Caleb and Tristan.*

Having them at my back will make me less jumpy. I'll probably still be angry with you, though. He glanced over the fire at her and smiled regretfully. *What are you doing back in my world?*

Do you wish I wasn't here?

I want to say yes, but I can't. You're not safe. Everyone here wants a piece of you, but I guess I'm even more selfish than they are. I don't just want a piece, Lily. I want all of you. I want you with me wherever I go, even if that puts you in danger.

Wherever you are is where I'm safest and happiest, Rowan.

I haven't thought about being happy in a while.

Maybe you can start now. Maybe we both can. At least we're together.

When we find Tristan and Caleb, I'll consider it.

Rowan looked out the mouth of the cave, his eyes scanning the darkness.

Lily floated on top of her coven's dreams, bobbing gently as if she were sunbathing in a pool of their sleeping minds. She sensed another mind floating along like hers on top of the sleeping minds of her claimed. Lily joined her other self, only to find that she had wandered into the Mist and into another one of Lillian's memories. This time, Lillian didn't choose to share another memory of the shaman. Her story, and therefore her reasons to support killing all Outlander scientists, had more to it than rational arguments about saving the planet from Alaric and Chenoa's bombs. It also had gut-wrenching fear.

Before Lily could register the burned-out trees and the acrid air, she knew from the panic that enveloped her that Lillian had brought her back inside another memory of the cinder world . . .

. . . They're coming after me with nooses on poles. They've finally smartened up and realized that my touch will kill them. I don't know how many of them there are, and that's a problem. I scramble through the thick underbrush, my breath rasping in and out of my lungs in fear. I can't see. Not clearly. But I can hear them, and they're getting closer. I run. Their baying laughter seems to come from all around me.

"Come on, pretty! Where you going? We'll take good care of you," they taunt.

I turn from the direction of their voices, and hear the whipping sound of rope flying through the air before I feel the net tangle around me. They drove me into a trap, I realize. A sob bursts out of me as I fall onto my side. I try, but I don't have enough stored energy in my body to manifest either an electric current or a fireball. I haven't had salt in days.

"We got her!" one of them hollers.

I have a knife in my skirt, but that's not what I reach for. I know I'll never cut myself out of these thick, oiled ropes in time. I snake my hand up to the willstone at my throat. My last resort.

"Quick! Before she swallows it."

"I'm not touching her. Hand me the pole."

While they bicker I manage to rip my willstone off its chain and swallow it. It's huge and chokes me, but I get it down.

"Ah!" the first one growls, shoving the second one to the ground. "You were supposed to stop her."

I hear more voices and the sound of many feet, but I can barely turn my head and can't see more than five of them standing over me. They must have sent the whole gang after me. One of them in particular leans close. His face is scarred and he has the air of a leader about him.

"That stone won't stay in her forever," he says. A cruel glint lights his bulging red eyes. "And once we smash it, she'll be a helpless little zombie. We can do whatever we want to her."

I try not to show fear, but I fail. I shrink under his appraising look.

"She's still healthy. That's why I like the young ones," another says eagerly. I can see saliva wetting the inside of his scabby lips and have to turn my head before I gag.

"Get her up," the leader orders. "Use the poles to disarm her."

As they unwrap the net, the stink of sickness overwhelms everything, even their sour body odor. They'll all be dead in a few weeks or months at the latest—though much good it'll do me.

They have their noose poles ready as soon as the net slackens, but I make a desperate rush at them anyway. There are too many for me to drain, but I'm not going down quietly. I can't. A switch has gone off in my head, like the way a leg will kick if you hit the knee just so. Three of them lay hands on me, and I suck the life out of them with a snarl. I'm enjoying this.

I feel a noose tighten around my neck and the thrill of the fight ebbs away with my breath. I wonder when did I become this *thing* that I am now?

As white, blue, and black dots blur out the sight of their oozing, pockmarked faces, I hear the leader say, "Put her in the barn." . . .

Lily sat up, her scream echoing off the walls of the cave. Rowan sat up with her, trying to hold her. They were alone.

"Nightmare?" he asked.

Lily nodded, lying.

Rowan narrowed his eyes, picking up on the ragged edge of her thoughts. "About Lillian?" he asked.

"Yes," Lily admitted.

"What was she doing?" He pushed her hair back from her sweaty forehead, his face so open and trusting she had to look away.

"Killing people. Draining the energy right out their bodies."

Rowan nodded. "It's a gruesome death. But if anyone tries to take you—if you're ever cornered and have no choice—" he began.

"I know," she said, resting her forehead against his. She felt him go still, his body tensing.

"How do you know?"

"I was going to do it to Gideon or Carrick when they had me in the oubliette. I figured it out on my own, but I never got a chance to lay a hand on them," Lily said, reminding herself to keep her voice even.

Rowan sensed she was holding something back, something that might be about Lillian. It troubled him, but she was telling the truth about this, at least, and he could sense that. She felt him relax. He held her tightly, smoothing her hair, his heart sore from sharing what she'd been through.

"Where is everyone?" Lily asked.

"They'll be back soon," he said. "Do you want to try to reach Caleb and Tristan this morning?"

"Yes," she said, suddenly smiling. "I miss them."

"Me too." Rowan leaned back to really look at Lily. "Don't think about Lillian," he said, his forehead furrowed with worry. "We're back in her world now, and the more you think about her, the more you open yourself up to her influence. She's had a lot more practice manipulating minds than you have, and she knows how to do things you haven't even dreamed of."

"Like what?"

"Like making a mind mosaic, for starters." Lily raised an eyebrow in question. Rowan pushed a hand through his hair, thinking of how to explain. "When you've claimed hundreds of thousands of minds like she has, you can use the perspectives of your claimed to build a bird's-eye view of any particular moment. And as long as you don't try to control them or communicate with them, you can do it without your claimed even knowing. Only trained mechanics can tell you're looking through their eyes. Everyone else just believes they're thinking of their witch at that particular moment. It's really subtle."

"Apparently, because I don't get it," Lily said, feeling a little stupid.

"Come on," he said, standing up. "I need to get you out of the cave to show you."

They climbed down the cliff and stood facing each other. Lily saw Rowan shiver from the cold, and she offered him her wrist. He grasped her wrist lightly between his thumb and forefinger like he was feeling her pulse. Lily fed him some of her ever-fever.

"Thank you," he said, smiling with pleasure. She got the feeling he wanted to stand like this, warming himself with her heat for hours, but he forced himself to break away and concentrate. "I'm going to use something from your world to explain this, so you understand. Think of your claimed as thousands of different cameras all on the same movie set, filming the same scene but from different angles."

"Okay."

"Now gently reach out, barely brushing their minds, and look through the lenses."

Lily thought about Tristan, Breakfast, and Una and ever so softly *looked*. "Oh my God," she gasped, sticking out her arm and grabbing on to Rowan's jacket to balance herself. What she saw was a sweeping, panoramic 3-D view of one particular place in the woods. It was bobbing up and down as the three of them walked.

"Okay, stop," Rowan said, trying not to laugh. "You don't know how to integrate what you're seeing yet, and I don't want you to throw up."

Lily disentangled her mind and regained her balance. "That was freaky."

"So I've heard," he said, his eyes momentarily darkening as they usually did when he referenced Lillian.

"Can you do this with your stone kin?" Lily asked.

"No. Only witches have enough control over the minds of their claimed to make a mosaic. And you can make one for any moment in time. You can skip through the minds of your claimed at"—he waved a hand, making it up as he went along—"noon two weeks ago, and watch one person run through a crowd of them, like you're following alongside that running person. All you need is for that person to keep running past people you have claimed."

"I can spy on people who I *haven't* claimed by using my claimed like surveillance cameras?" she asked, starting to feel uncomfortable with this ability.

"Yes. Your claimed don't even have to be aware of the person running past. They don't need to actively remember an incident—it could be background noise to them—but as long as they were there at noon two weeks ago, an imprint of it is somewhere in their willstones, and you can find it."

"I can access memories people don't even know they have?"

"Yes."

"That's—" Lily broke off, stunned. "The word '*wrong*' doesn't seem to be strong enough in this instance."

"It's very useful," Rowan said with a shrug. "Say someone kidnapped a child in the Swallows at sometime between four and eight last Wednesday," he said, making up another hypothetical time and place. "You could find that child and see who took her by using the memories of your claimed who happened to be in the Swallows at that time. Even if they weren't aware that the girl was being kidnapped, if it occurred somewhere in their field of vision, you can filter it out and find it. Mind mosaics can save lives."

"But it's like being Big Brother," Lily sputtered, horrified. Rowan obviously didn't get the reference. "I'm not asking permission, and my claimed never know it happened. That violates their basic right to privacy," she explained. Lily couldn't understand how Rowan could be so accepting of this.

"Absolute privacy is one of the things you agree to give up when you let a witch claim you," he replied, a little confused by Lily's outburst. "Lily, you saw some of my most intimate memories when you claimed me. You knew this was how it worked."

"Yeah, but that was unavoidable. And claiming is a one-time thing."

"Most witches don't see it that way. If they want general information—not an entire specific memory, okay? We're just talking about snapshots in time. If a witch wants to see what a group of her claimed has seen, she usually just takes it from their minds."

"Well, in the world where I grew up that's totally wrong."

He stared at her for a while. The look he had on his face made him seem younger than usual.

"What?" Lily asked, half a smile tugging at her lips. "Why the goofy look?"

"You're just cute," he said, wrapping an arm around her neck and kissing the top of her head.

"A-hem," Breakfast said, fake-clearing his throat to interrupt. "Rowan? Did you send the three of us out to scout around so you could get some nookie?"

They had no idea Lily had used them like spy-cams while they were trekking through the woods. For a moment she felt bad. She only managed to let go of her guilt by promising herself she would never use that skill again.

"Actually, I'm teaching Lily something," Rowan said, moving away from her. He was blushing a little, which Lily found quite amusing.

"Uh-huh," Una said, crossing her arms and cocking an eyebrow. "I bet you got a lot to teach her, teacher-man."

"He is a fountain of knowledge," Lily said, grinning.

"He must be taking pointers from me," Breakfast said, brushing imaginary dust off his shoulder. Una gave Breakfast a skeptical look. "I'm just getting warmed up with you, numero Uno," he told her confidently. "I got mad skills coming your way."

"Okay, okay," Rowan said, smothering his grin and trying to get serious. "What did you three find?"

"There's a stream on the other side of the forest and a path," Tristan replied briskly. He was the only one who hadn't joined in on the laugh, and he seemed to be looking anywhere but at Lily.

"Good," Rowan said, all business now. "Lily? Can you feel Caleb and Tristan?"

Lily concentrated on them and made contact. She felt a spark of recognition and then relief from both of them. A dozen questions flooded her way—not clearly enough so that Lily could discern actual words, but she got the gist of what they wanted to know and answered back in kind. She sent images of Rowan standing next to her, and one of the outside of the walls of Salem so that they knew she was in the woods near the city.

"Yes. They're still really far," she mumbled to Rowan.

"Where?" he asked.

"Someplace warm. Warmer than here, anyway," Lily answered. "I see a huge wall. They're outside another city?" she queried uncertainly when the images ended.

"What color are the walls?" Rowan asked urgently. "The rock—what color is it?"

"Kind of a blue-gray," she said. "They're paler than the rocks in Salem, but I could still see quartz glinting in them."

"Virginia," he said. "They're outside Richmond."

Tristan, Una, and Breakfast shared worried looks.

"Can we make it that far on foot?" Una asked.

"No," Rowan replied. "But we won't have to." He looked at Lily. "Summon them. Have Caleb and the other Tristan start riding north with extra horses." Lily nodded and called to them, adding a feeling of urgency. She wanted them to hurry.

Breakfast raised his hand. "Ah, Rowan? You mentioned horses," he said through a nervous laugh. "I don't think I've ever seen a real horse, let alone ridden one."

"You'll learn," Rowan said confidently, and started back to the cliff. "Let's get our gear and head out," he called over his shoulder.

"Horses bite, don't they?" Breakfast whispered to Tristan.

"Constantly," Tristan replied, just to mess with him. He clapped Breakfast on the shoulder and then followed Rowan.

"You're such a comfort to me in these uncertain times," Breakfast called testily after Tristan.

They had their gear packed and the fire extinguished in minutes. Rowan led them south and pushed the pace all day. No one argued or complained. In the first few hours they passed what Rowan identified as Woven tracks several times, and no one wanted to linger even a moment to rest if it wasn't absolutely necessary. By dusk, they were all slumping with exhaustion. They came to a small copse of trees that offered a little protection from the wind.

"Alright. This is as good a spot as any," Rowan said, sliding the straps of his pack off his shoulders and dropping it to the snow.

"I thought you said we *weren't* going to walk to Richmond," Una joked.

"We're not," Rowan replied seriously. "We're going to Providence."

"Why?" Tristan asked.

"An underground train system links the Thirteen Cities," Rowan replied. "We'll ride it south while Caleb and the other Tristan come north. We're going to have to sneak on, though."

"Why can't we just take the train to Richmond?" Breakfast asked.

"You really hate horses, huh?" Tristan teased.

"Because I don't know if we'll be able to get a train at all," Rowan said, ignoring Tristan's banter. "But the train tunnels will give us shelter, which is better than this." He gestured angrily to the darkening woods. His tone made it obvious that he wasn't in the mood for playfulness. "And because my tribe will be camped *outside* Richmond. I don't know how far outside, so we'll need those horses to get to them."

Breakfast nodded, chastised. Una tapped him on the leg. "Let's get some firewood," she said quietly.

"No," Rowan said sharply. "No fires. And no one goes more then twenty paces away from camp, and even then, you don't go alone. Understood?"

Everyone stared silently at Rowan. He was usually so patient. None of them were used to seeing him stressed. Lily had only seen him this way once before—when they were hiding in the woods after Gideon's raid, and Rowan had run out of salt.

Go easier on them, Rowan.

I can't, Lily. We couldn't be camping in a worse spot if we tried, but we've got no good choices anymore.

How bad is it?

You let me worry about that. You need to rest.

"It's just for tonight," he said. Rowan took a deep breath and calmed himself. "We traveled about eighteen miles today. If we're lucky, we can push even harder tomorrow and be in Providence shortly after dark tomorrow night. *Then* we can all relax a little." His lips hinted at a smile. "But not much."

Rowan fed Lily a few more olives, anxiously checking her pulse after every mouthful, before nodding with a semi-satisfied look. "If anyone needs energy, take it from Lily," he said, screwing the lid of the half-eaten jar of olives back on with a furrowed brow.

They lay down on top of the snow and arranged themselves in a circular heap around Lily. Each of them grasped one of her wrists or a bare ankle in order to stream her heat directly into their bodies. Tristan insisted on being the first to keep watch. After much coaxing, Rowan finally positioned himself next to Lily. Lily was asleep in seconds, and only awoke because she felt intense fear.

Her eyes popped open and her muscles tensed before she knew what was going on. In the dark she was just able to make out the shapes of Tristan and Rowan crouching defensively between the sleeping group and the dark forest. A bit of darkness broke off from the rest, and moved toward her protectors. Lily heard a rasping, inhuman moan coming from the menacing shape, and knew it had to be a Woven. She kept her head down and stayed perfectly still as she watched.

"Me," Rowan called commandingly to the Woven. Despite his authoritative tone, Lily noticed that he kept his voice down, barely speaking above a whisper. "Look at me," he said again. The creature seemed to obey. "Tristan, work your way around and get to its tail."

Tristan moved out of the way, and Lily got a better view of it in the moonlight. It was one of the insectoid Woven that Lily had seen before, but like all Woven it seemed to have its own distinct physiognomy. Lily had yet to see two insect Woven that looked the same. This one's head was shaped like a beetle's with giant pincers for a mouth, but after the swarm of thin centipede legs that propped up its front section ended, a snake's tail coiled out behind it. It must have been over four feet tall and fifteen feet long.

"Pin it, while I go in," Rowan said calmly to Tristan.

Tristan threw himself down on the Woven's long tail. The Woven hissed and turned to attack Tristan, but Rowan was on it before those long pincers could snip Tristan in two. Rowan thrust his dagger up into the underside of the beetle-like head. No sound came out of it, but the little legs in front wiggled and flailed, at first quickly, and then slowly until they stopped. The creature slumped over onto its side as Rowan yanked his dagger out.

Tristan stood, panting, and looking down at the dead Woven. "Do we just leave it, or try to drag it away?"

"More will come if we leave it, but I think it's too heavy to drag anywhere," Rowan said quietly, crouching down and grabbing a handful of snow. "We should wake everyone and move the group instead." He looked up at Tristan and smiled while he cleaned his hands and his dagger with the snow. "You handled that quietly. That was smart."

"I didn't want any more of them to hear a struggle and come help their buddy," Tristan said shakily.

"You have good instincts."

Tristan smiled back, touched by the compliment. "I'm really trying to hate you, you know," he admitted candidly.

"Yeah, I know," Rowan replied, clenching his wet, frozen hands to warm them.

"I had her all to myself for years and I thought she'd stay mine no matter what I did." Tristan laughed bitterly. "I told myself that I needed to get all the other girls out of my system first because I wasn't ready for forever yet."

"Maybe you weren't," Rowan said kindly. "Most people aren't ready for forever when they're eighteen."

"But you were."

Rowan smiled to himself. "Ready or not, it was forever for me from the first time I saw her. I was seven, Tristan. Not everyone's built like that."

"But you're talking about the *other* one," Tristan said, confused. "The other Lillian."

"No," Rowan replied enigmatically. "It was always Lily." Lily heard Rowan stand and closed her eyes, pretending to sleep. "We should get them up and get moving," he said.

They woke the rest of the group quickly and quietly. Una was annoyed when she saw the dead Woven. "Why didn't you wake me?" she said, angry to have been left out. "I need the practice."

"Next one's yours," Rowan promised with an indulgent smile. "Now hurry. The scent of its blood has been on the breeze for a few minutes already."

They grabbed their gear and moved away from the dead Woven. Rowan's gaze kept lifting up to the treetops. He didn't like to travel when it was still dark out.

"It's nearly dawn," Breakfast said. "Maybe we should just push on rather than trying to find another campsite?"

Una nodded in agreement. Tristan and Rowan shared tired looks. Between keeping watch and fighting the Woven, neither of them had gotten more than a few minutes' rest, but they agreed to keep going. The group headed south, treading as quietly as they could through the snow.

By eleven in the morning they were all queasy with fatigue. Rowan dug up some frozen dandelion roots for them to chew on. The bitter taste was not pleasant but it helped to keep them awake and moving. He called a halt to their slowing march just after noon and told them to gather wood for a fire. In half an hour he had some kind of tea bubbling away inside his cauldron. Breakfast sniffed his portion.

"Not that I don't trust you, but what's in the brew, Mr. Wizard?" he asked.

"Birch and red clover. Improves circulation. It'll give us all a little more body heat and energy," Rowan answered.

They drank their rather unpleasant tea and rested for a few

minutes, but they could all feel that Rowan was anxious to depart and push on before they were fully rested.

"How much farther?" Tristan asked.

"About seven or eight miles," Rowan guessed. "It's harder to gauge pace in the dark, so I'm not completely sure how fast we were going early this morning. I'm still hoping we can get to Providence by nightfall."

He glanced around at the woods, his hair-trigger senses distrustful of everything. They doused the fire and moved out without any more delay. The thought of having to spend one more night in the open was motivation enough to haul them all to their aching feet.

The sun set, and they still hadn't reached the walls of Providence. It wasn't until after eight that they left the woods and came to a large, open field.

"Providence is there," Rowan said, pointing across the huge field to a few lights flickering in the distance. "It's about half a mile away. Come on," Rowan said, turning back to the woods.

Tristan's hand shot out to catch Rowan by the arm. "I thought we were going in. You said we needed shelter," Tristan said, his fatigue wearing his patience thin.

"We're looking for some sign of the underground train that leads into and out of the city," Rowan said. He began pacing around the border of the woods and the field, looking down at the ground.

Breakfast copied him, wandering in the opposite direction from Rowan. "Should we be looking for, like, subway grates or something?"

"Yes." Rowan looked up and pointed to a configuration of lights. "That's the southern gate. A tunnel runs due south out of Providence, so it's got to be somewhere around here. Look for vents melting the snow, or anything metal or man-made. But keep an eye out for Woven while you look. They tend to be even more concentrated around the cities."

That struck Lily as strange. "Why?" she asked. "Most animals stay away from populated areas. They avoid people, in fact."

Rowan looked up at her and shrugged. "Woven aren't animals, Lily. Not natural ones, anyway. They come toward people. And the more people, the more Woven."

Lily frowned to herself. She knew the Woven weren't like other animals, but they had still been made *from* animals. It didn't make sense to Lily that their behavior would be so alien.

"It's like they have a vendetta against people or something, which is impossible. That's human behavior," Lily argued.

"Well, there's a legend that they are part human," Rowan said, still searching the ground.

"But you don't believe it," Tristan guessed.

Rowan didn't answer right away. "When I was a kid one of the girls in my tribe captured a wild Woven just a few days after it had hatched. It looked like a tiny cat with iridescent butterfly wings. It was beautiful." He kicked at the snow, ostensibly to uncover the bare ground, but with more force than necessary. "She fed it, cared for it, tried to teach it tricks like one of the tame Woven that they breed in the cities for rich people. She had that thing for years."

"What happened?" Una asked, like she could sense that there wasn't a happy ending to this story.

"It ate her." Rowan continued to kick the snow aside angrily. "She loved that thing and it ate her while she slept. Not because it was hungry—no. Ahanu would go without food sometimes to feed it. It ate her because that's what wild Woven do. I don't care what the legends say. Anything that's even part human wouldn't eat a little girl who loved it."

Lily stopped arguing for Rowan's sake, but she still couldn't let it go. There was no animal she could think of that behaved like that. Not even insects killed unless they were hungry or threatened. People were the only creatures on earth that killed for spite. Lily searched the ground like the rest of her coven, but her mind wasn't fully on her task. The Woven were a riddle to her, and maybe it was because of Lillian's memories and how important getting rid of the Woven had been to her at one time, but Lily was starting to feel as if the Woven were the riddle she was meant to solve.

They all blundered around in the dark without speaking for twenty minutes before Una called to the group.

"Here!" she said. "I think this is definitely something." They gathered around a raised patch on the ground. It was about five feet wide and five feet long, forming a perfect square. "Not a lot of right angles in nature," she said.

"Everyone take a side and start digging," Rowan said excitedly.

They worked feverishly and had the frozen sod up in half an hour. A large metal plate, flaky with rust, was embedded in the ground.

"Light a fire," Rowan ordered. "Lily? We'll need your strength to lift this," he said. She nodded quickly, giving her assent.

They got a fire going and Lily fed her mechanics enough energy to pull the huge metal plate up from its bed. Beneath the plate was an iron grate that was welded over the top of a duct. Rowan bent back some of the bars of the grate, leaving enough space for them to climb through. He put his head down the hole, his willstone brightly shining with magelight.

"There's no ladder," he said, frowning. He brushed some dirt from his hands. "This duct has been out of use for a while. It may not even meet up with the main line."

"I don't think we have much of a choice but to follow it," Tristan said. He stuck his head down next to Rowan's and let his magelight add more brightness. "At least there are plenty of handholds," he said.

Rowan nodded in agreement. "Una, you go first, then Breakfast, me and Lily, then Tristan. Tristan, close up the hole behind us, and I'll carry Lily," he said. "Everyone take as much energy as you can from Lily now."

Lily stood close to the fire and rose up into the air on her witch wind. She fed their willstones until Rowan told her the fire was nearly out. She let go of the power loop, dropping out of the air and into his outstretched arms. He gathered her close, stamped out the last of the embers, and swung down the hole after Breakfast.

Rowan. I hate being underground. It's like being back in the oubliette.

No it isn't, because I'm here. You're safe, Lily. No one's going to hurt you while I'm around.

Rowan held her shaking body tightly to his as Tristan heaved the large metal plate back over the hole, blotting out the moon and the stars.

CHAPTER
10

Lily turned her face into Rowan's chest and squeezed her eyes tightly shut. The smell of earth and rust wrapped around her and sank so deeply into her skin she could taste it on the back of her tongue.

She tried to focus on the sway of Rowan's body as he climbed down. She listened to the beat of his heart. Steady and strong. The enchanting hue of his magelight lit the other side of her eyelids reassuringly. She tried to imagine his magelight as a candle burning in front of her, although she could feel no heat and could gather no power from it. Magelight could not fuel her. Lily touched her willstones with the tips of her fingers, feeling their soft, solid shapes. She told herself that no one was going to take them away from her this time, or ever again.

"What's wrong with Lily?" Tristan asked anxiously. He could feel her fear. They all could.

"Witches don't like to be underground," Rowan answered. "They're cut off from the light of the sun and moon. It drains them."

"Witches can get energy from the moon?" Breakfast asked, surprised.

"Of course," Rowan replied. Lily could hear the smile in his voice. "Didn't you ever hear of witches dancing naked in the light of the full moon? Why else do you think they'd do that?"

"'Cause it's wicked fun?" Una offered.

"Well, okay. So there are two reasons," Rowan admitted.

"Hey, Lily. Just imagine you're buck naked and shakin' it on a cloudy night," Breakfast said cheerfully.

"I'll try, Breakfast," Lily said, her voice only wavering a little. "Are we there yet?"

"Almost," Una answered. "I can see the bottom."

"What's down there?" Tristan asked.

"A concrete thingamajig," Una said uncertainly. "It could be a platform."

Lily could feel it getting warmer as they descended. The smell of earth was replaced by the smell of steam and grease, peppered with bursts of ozone and recycled air. Not too far off, Lily could hear the unmistakable double-tap thud of a train moving down the tracks and the muffled squeal of metal on metal. She felt Rowan finally let go of some of the tension he'd been carrying for days. He was still on guard, but no longer on edge like a hunted animal. As Rowan relaxed, so did Lily.

"Una and Breakfast—go down and scout around. Don't go far, though," Rowan warned. "And try to avoid being seen. Your clothes are mostly cotton, which is a very expensive material here."

"No way," Una said disbelievingly.

"Cotton needs a lot of land to grow. And with the Woven, land is a precious thing. So keep your heads down, okay? There are some desperate people down in the train tunnels, and I don't want you to get robbed."

Lily calmed herself enough to peel her face away from Rowan's chest and watched as Una and Breakfast reached the bottom and went off in separate directions. It was only a few minutes before she heard Una's voice in her head, although barely. The concrete walls of the subway didn't block her connection to her claimed as profoundly as granite did, but the soil here contained enough quartz to interfere.

It looks like a deserted platform. It's safe to come down.

"Una says it's safe," Lily repeated.

Rowan, Lily, and Tristan descended the rest of the way and came to what appeared to be a service tunnel. They climbed through a knocked-out hole in the wall and found themselves next to Breakfast and Una on what looked like a deserted subway stop. The walls were tiled with an intricate pattern in a style akin to art deco. The name of the stop, rendered in black-and-white inlay, was RANCH FOUR.

"I saw something like this once," Una said. "There was a show about the New York City subway system, and they had pictures of stops on the line that never opened or that had closed years ago. It was so cool. It was like looking back in time."

"Ranch Four?" Tristan said. "What's that?"

"They have animal ranches outside the cities in this world. They raise luxury meats for rich people on them," Lily said distastefully.

"Before this ranch was even built it was overrun by Woven. That was decades ago, though," Rowan said in a faraway voice. He looked at Lily, his brow furrowed. "How did you know about the ranches?"

Lily thought fast. "Tristan told me about them. The other Tristan," she answered, looking away. It wasn't totally a lie, either. "He said the ranches were work camps for criminals and poor people."

"The Covens round up homeless citizens a few times a year to give them jobs," he said, adding heavy sarcasm to the second half of his sentence. "The ranches are one of the places they send them."

"Sounds like slave labor," Breakfast said.

"The Covens can't take away a person's citizenship and banish them to the Outlands unless they've committed a serious crime, and the cities are only so big. Housing is expensive in walled cities that only have so much space. The poor have nowhere to go. A lot of them come to the underground train tunnels to hide from the guards." Rowan ran his hand across a bit of graffiti that had been painted near the hole they'd climbed through to get from the service tunnel into the station. "This station belongs to a gang."

"Where are they?" Tristan said. He looked around. There were no sleeping bags or piles of personal items—no sign that anyone lived down here. Tristan's face suddenly froze. "Woven?" he whispered.

Rowan shook his head, perplexed and looking around like Tristan. "No. Woven don't come into the train tunnels."

"Why?" Lily blurted out.

"I don't know, Lily. They just don't."

"Okay, that's ridiculous," she said, exasperated. "Hasn't anyone in this world thought that maybe it was a tad *weird* that Woven don't go down in the tunnels? What? Are they superstitious or something?"

Rowan shrugged. "The Woven do what they do, and I don't know anyone who's ever stopped to ask them why they do it. We're usually too busy trying to kill them."

Lily leaned back, struck by a thought. "That's the problem," she said musingly. She waved a hand in the air dismissively. "Forget it," she said, and changed the subject before Rowan could pick up on what she was thinking and get agitated. "So where'd the gang go?"

"Well, it looks like they move through here a lot," Breakfast said, looking down. "Look—there's no dust on the ground, but there is on that bench over there."

"You're right, Breakfast. Good eye," Rowan said. "The trail leads down the tracks."

"Do we stay or try to find them?" Una asked. "I could really use some food."

Rowan bit his lower lip and frowned in thought, looking at Tristan. "What do you say?"

Tristan glanced at Lily, worried. His eyes darted down to the three willstones that hung around her neck. "If they see her, will they know who she is?"

"I can hide two of my stones and use a glamour," Lily said, already removing her largest and smallest willstones and tucking them into her bra.

"Something less pretty than your normal face," Rowan suggested. "You want to blend in."

"Got it." Lily altered her face until it bordered on plain. "You should change your face, too," she told Rowan.

"Why?" Una asked. "Would he be recognized, too?"

Lily grinned. "Rowan is known as Lord Fall here," she said. "He's totally famous."

"Really?" Una quipped impishly, looking Rowan over.

"I *was* Lord Fall, now I'm just an Outlander. But I should still use a glamour," Rowan said, changing the way the dim light hit his face until Lily barely recognized him. "Our clothes are still a problem, though."

"We stole them, and we're looking to trade with them. You said they were valuable," Breakfast said, brewing up a plan. "Come on, guys. We're badass thieves, on the run from the city guard. Act the part."

"I don't know," Rowan said, looking Lily over. She snatched a thought from the front of his mind. Nothing in the world could make someone as refined and fragile-looking as Lily appear like a badass.

Even with her glamour-altered face, there was still something inherently graceful about the way she moved that she could never wholly hide.

Lily could feel her mechanics' empty bellies rumbling, and their hunger upset her in a way her own hunger wouldn't. Her coven was her responsibility and she felt an inexplicable need to provide for them. "If we want to catch a train south, we're going to have to go to a station that's still in use," she said equitably, trying to win Rowan over with sugar rather than spice. "We're bound to run into other people when we do that anyway."

I'll be fine, Rowan, she added reassuringly in mindspeak.

He finally relented, and they set off down the tracks. They still had some of Lily's strength in them, and Rowan wanted to encounter whatever awaited them before it completely wore off.

They followed the tracks until they could see more signs of habitation and came to an abrupt halt when they spotted the first tunnel denizen, standing next to a barrel fire. The scruffy kid, who was twelve or thirteen tops, saw them and froze like a deer in headlights. Before anyone in Lily's group could call out to him, the kid took off down the tracks.

"A lookout," Rowan said, dismayed.

"Don't worry, Ro. We're just here to trade," Breakfast reminded him calmly. He rubbed his hands together in delighted anticipation as they followed the lookout at a cautious pace. He was enjoying this.

They went around a bend in the track and saw the lookout talking to a tight huddle of grubby-looking preteens. Breakfast took the lead.

"Okay, you three just hang back, stick close to Lily, and look scary." Breakfast glanced back at Rowan, Tristan, and Una. "Like you normally do. Let me handle this."

"Maybe I should be the one—" Rowan began.

"No, let Breakfast go talk to them," Una interrupted, her eyes narrowed into a slyer-than-usual position.

Rowan looked to Tristan. "He's got this," Tristan said confidently. "There's a reason we always send Breakfast to buy the weed before a party." Rowan looked confused and Tristan smiled reassuringly. "Breakfast is clutch at dealing with people like this. He hardly ever gets his ass kicked."

The "hardly ever" part of Tristan's sentence made Rowan even more nervous than before, but it was too late. Breakfast was already talking with the cluster of tunnel teens. They saw him gesture casually back to the group, and Lily took note of how the tunnel kids zeroed in on her and Rowan. Their posture stiffened as they regarded Rowan's gigantic willstone, which was still roiling with Lily's energy.

Breakfast worked on them with his innocuous goofiness and mildly irritating charm, and persuaded the kids to bring Lily's group to trade with the elders. They got plenty of stares as they made their way through the tent city that had sprung up in the abandoned branches of the subway tunnels.

The people down here weren't Outlanders—they were more European-looking. Lily had been expecting a blend of races, but as she considered it, it made sense. These were the castoffs of the cities who didn't have the skills to survive outside the walls. They wouldn't be accepted into an Outlander tribe, and without a tribe, a person outside the walls was as good as dead. That's why they hid in the tunnels. They had no other place to go, except into indentured servitude at one of the ranches. Most of the faces that looked fearfully at Rowan's giant smoke stone were young kids—dirty, pale little things who looked desperately malnourished.

So many women and children, Rowan. There are no grown men here.

The men usually have to turn themselves in. They go to work on the ranches, and the city guard turns a blind eye to the fact that their families are hiding down here. The ranches get the strongest and cheapest labor, and the cities only have to deal with the nonviolent women and children.

Lily looked around her. They'd been brought down the tracks to another abandoned station —but this one was full of people. She wondered briefly why this station was occupied when the other one wasn't, but kept her questions to herself.

It's like they're hostages. Why doesn't the city do something about this?

Because they all make money off it, Lily. Ranching is extremely lucrative. Ranchers donate money to the Council's election campaigns, and the city conveniently ignores the people who live down here.

What about the Covens? Didn't Lillian try to do something about this?

She could feel Rowan cringe inwardly. Just the mention of Lillian's name made something inside him recoil.

Yes, she did. The Covens used to have limited power. Remember, the Covens aren't elected—witches are born with their power, like aristocracy, but the Council is elected. They used to be the only branch of government that could write laws, but Lillian said that the Council was corrupted by the need to raise election funds, and she campaigned to make it possible for witches to write laws, too. At first she used that power to help the tunnel people and the Outlanders. But later, when she changed, she used it to draft legislation that allowed her to hang scientists.

Lily didn't ask any more questions. Somehow, the answers she got from Rowan always seemed to lead back to Lillian and her hangings. Her curiosity flared again. How could anyone go so quickly from being a hero of the people to a tyrant?

Lily heard Breakfast's voice take on a particularly jovial tone and picked up her head. He had begun conversing with three middle-aged women, and from the way the rest of the tunnel denizens seemed to defer to them, Lily supposed they were the leaders of this underground gang. The exchange had started out amicably enough, but their voices began to rise. A pale, blond woman with a stout body and thick, meaty hands stepped away from the group and marched toward Lily and Rowan.

"These two," the woman said angrily, glancing back at Breakfast. "You can't tell me they're not Coven. No one with a willstone that active would have been left untrained. And her? The little witch? She even *smells* like magic. The whole lot of you are her claimed or I've never seen a coven in my life."

"I don't belong to any of the Thirteen Covens, but I am a witch," Lily snarled back at her. She felt Rowan put a hand on her upper arm, but she shook it off. Lily didn't like this woman, and being underground where she felt cut off and endangered, she didn't feel like playing nice. Something told her being nice wouldn't help anyway—not with this woman. "Now, who are you?"

"Queen of the Fairies," the woman said sarcastically. "What do you want?"

"To trade and to get the hell out of here," Lily replied.

The woman actually smiled. "That's all I wanted to hear, witch." She looked Rowan up and down, her eyes rounding with worry when they regarded his willstone. Her own willstone was small and vaguely pinkish in hue, although Lily had noticed that people with little or no magic tended to have nearly colorless willstones that resembled white quartz or dull opals.

The woman spun on her heel and stormed away, shouting orders as she went. "Outfit them fairly, and show them where to jump a train out of town. Then make *damn* sure they get on it."

"Hey!" Lily shouted after her. The woman stopped and turned, her lips pinched thin, showing she was at the end of her patience. "We'll get out and stay out on one condition," Lily said.

"I'm listening," the woman replied.

"If you tell anyone we were here, I'll come back for *you*."

"Never laid eyes on you in my life," the woman said, and then disappeared down the curving tracks.

Lily's coven was taken to what appeared to be one of the larger barrel fires. Some of the older teen lookouts brought food, and then they laid out an array of trade goods. Rowan sorted through the wearhyde clothes, blades, and bundles of wovensbane—an herb that smelled like citronella when burned that sometimes managed to repel the Woven.

"Some of these jackets look warm enough," Tristan said, trying to make the best of it. "And I've noticed that even though everyone here wears leather pants and jackets, they still wear some sort of cotton or linen tops. We can use our own shirts at least."

"It's not leather, it's wearhyde," Lily corrected. "It's grown from a culture, not skinned from an animal, and I think it's even nicer than leather."

"You would, Your Vegan-ness," Una said, smiling.

"These are probably the best-quality supplies they have," Rowan whispered to Breakfast. "I wouldn't haggle too much."

"I wasn't going to haggle at all," Breakfast said. He ran a frustrated hand through his hair. "In fact, I think they need our help more than they need to trade." Breakfast waved one of the older teens closer. The grubby kid balked for a moment. He didn't want to come anywhere near Rowan.

"It's alright, Riley," Una said, rolling her eyes. "He's not going to bite you. Tell him what you told us."

"Are you really a witch?" Riley asked Lily cautiously.

"She is," Rowan answered for her. Lily could tell his answering for her was a reflex. No one was allowed to speak directly to the witch unless she addressed them first, and now that Lily and Rowan were back in his world, some of his old habits with Lillian were seeping back into his behavior.

"Tell them about the babies being born strange," said a high, piping voice from the shadows. A little boy, no older than five, stepped forward.

"Quiet, Pip." Riley reached out and put his hand on the little boy's head and then turned back to Rowan. "It's not just the babies. A lot of women have fallen sick and the witches in the city say they can't help them."

"They're lying to you," Rowan snapped angrily. "There isn't much a witch can't cure. What are the symptoms and how did the sickness start?"

Riley and Pip shared a look, and then Riley finally decided to continue. "It started about two years back. A professor from Salem asked some of the tunnel women to smuggle metal containers filled with what looked like ordinary dust out of each of the cities. But when the women came back they had burns on their hands and faces, like sunburns only much worse. Then they started getting sick. A lot of them died, and those that didn't had babies that——" Riley suddenly broke off and grimaced like his stomach was turning. "Every woman who helped in the smuggling in every city ended up sick, dead, or with a baby that just wasn't right."

"Where did the smugglers bring the dust?" Rowan asked.

"Outland." Riley suddenly looked sheepishly at his feet to avoid Rowan's eyes. "The Salem professor who organized the whole thing was an Outlander."

A chill rattled down Lily's spine. "Did you get a name?"

Riley nodded. "She was important, so I remembered her name. Professor Chenoa. And there were two others. They weren't real professors, but they were still awfully smart. Hawk and Kiwi? No, that's not right, but it's close."

"Let me see the sick," Lily ordered hollowly. "And I want to see the babies."

Lily glanced at Rowan as she followed Riley down a dark passageway that led away from the main group of tunnel people.

Lily. You know Chenoa, don't you?

I know of her. She and the other two—Hakan and Keme—were the scientists that Lillian wanted. They were the scientists we fought Lillian to protect, Rowan.

Lily saw Rowan's brow furrow in thought. He didn't ask any more questions, not even to find out how Lily knew that. Before she could formulate a question for Rowan that didn't implicate her, the group arrived at a satellite camp for the sick.

"Holy shit," Tristan cursed under his breath.

Rowan staggered forward, wading out into the huddled groups of skeletal woman and twisted, deformed children. Even though he was wearing a glamour, they could tell from his skin tone and from the beaded leather work of his pack that he was an Outlander. They scowled at him as he passed, their hatred palpable. Right or wrong, they apparently blamed him and all Outlanders for what Chenoa had done to them.

"No," Rowan said in disbelief, ignoring their glares. "This isn't natural."

Lily came forward and focused on one of the woman. She was balding and had ulcerous sores around her mouth—like the people in the cinder world. Lily crouched down and looked the woman in the eye. She could see the chromosomal damage in the woman's cells. The woman's liver, kidneys, and immune system were all shutting down, unable to repair themselves.

"Why don't you take a step back, Rowan," Tristan said. As Rowan moved away, Tristan crouched next to Lily and introduced himself to the woman kindly. Tristan remembered her humanity, even if Lily was too stunned to be polite.

It's her DNA. I can't find any cells in her that have undamaged genetic material, Lily. Can you?

No, Tristan. She's past saving.

What did this?

Lily heard Breakfast and then Una in her head.

Their cells can't repair themselves. It's horrible.

What is this? Can you see the air around them? It's filled with little specks of almost nothing that are whizzing around like crazy.

Lily reached out to all of her mechanics, sharing mindspeak with them.

They're radioactive, you guys. We can't stay with them for long. Rowan, do you have any idea how to help these people?

Those that haven't passed the tipping point? Yes. But the ritual will be very difficult for you, Lily. Tell the others to spread out and try to find people who still have some healthy life-helix material.

It took Lily a moment to understand, but when Rowan passed an image of what he needed to her, she instantly understood.

We call that DNA, Rowan.

Try to find healthy DNA. I'm afraid I'll have to stay here while you go scan them. These people don't want me near them. They hate Outlanders.

I'm sorry about that.

I've dealt with prejudice my whole life, Lily, but at least these people have a reason. An Outlander betrayed them and exposed them to some contaminant that did this to them, although I can't think of what it was.

Lily could guess what it was—enriched uranium, which had been made in the laboratories of Lillian's college. Chenoa used the tunnel women to pass the uranium from city to city and then into the Outlands where she and her two acolytes, Hakan and Keme, put it into the thirteen bombs. And she never told the women how dangerous it could be. All this time Lily had sided with Outlanders, wanting to believe that they were pure victims who were blameless and noble. There were no good guys anymore.

Lily felt Rowan put his hand on her arm, startling her out of her thoughts. She smiled at him warmly. At least Rowan was still pure and good. He had no idea about what Chenoa and Alaric had done to these women.

I know this is hard, but you have to be strong, Lily. They need help.

It's okay. I can handle it.

Lily passed on Rowan's instructions and then started approaching the contaminated women, trying to find even a scrap of undamaged DNA. She couldn't help but think of Lillian and she didn't want Rowan to know. Lillian had used the same words Rowan had. She'd said "tipping point" when she talked about her strange illness with Captain Leto, and now Lily knew for certain what that illness was—radiation poisoning. This was how Lillian was dying. Slowly. Painfully.

Lily and her mechanics walked through the medical camp, but very few of the women could be saved. The children were even worse. All of them were under the age of two, and all of them suffered from heart-wrenching birth defects. Lily tried to be respectful, but more than once she had to turn her face away or she knew she'd start crying.

"I can't think of a worse way to die," Una said quietly when they had regrouped.

"I think I'm going to have nightmares for the rest of my life," Breakfast said, agreeing with her.

"Did you find anyone with healthy cells?" Rowan asked. His expression was stormy with anger, but Lily knew it wasn't because these people rejected him. He needed to be angry. Rowan couldn't allow himself to be paralyzed by sadness right now or to get insulted by the prejudice that surrounded him. He had to stay focused and find a way to save these people.

"I got two, maybe three," Breakfast said.

"Three," Una said.

"One," Lily said, looking down.

"I only saw one, too," Tristan said, looking at Lily.

"I got two," Rowan said. "Were any of them children?" Everyone shook his or her head. "I didn't think so. We need to collect clean tissue samples—no contamination or it will be a disaster," Rowan said.

Tristan looked around at the filthy conditions of the med camp. "That's not going to be easy."

Rowan turned to Breakfast. "See what you can get from Riley. We need nine, maybe ten, sterile metal rods that are slightly sharpened on one end and about that big." Rowan held up his forefinger and thumb to indicate about two and a half inches. "Breakfast and Una are going to swipe the inside of their cheeks and collect some cells from the people who might be saved. Don't collect cells from an ulcer. If you have any problems finding undamaged skin inside their mouths, let me know and we'll take blood instead."

"Got it," Una said. Breakfast and Una left them to get what they needed from Riley.

"Tristan, you're with me," Rowan said. "We'll set up for the ritual."

"What do I do?" Lily asked.

"Gather your strength," Rowan replied. He led her to one of the barrel fires and sat her down on a small stool beside it. He met her eyes and let his glamour drop for just a moment so she could see his true face. He looked worried. "You're going to need it."

Lily sat next to the fire, staring at the women, who were staring back at her. She could feel their distrust and awe. They hated witches, but at the same time they had spent their whole lives ruled by them. Old habits like respect and fear die hard. Their stares made Lily uncomfortable, but it didn't take too long for Tristan to come back for her.

"We have a tent set up," Tristan said. He handed Lily a white silk slip that was a little dingy and slightly frayed at the hem. "Rowan said to put this on and we're to meet him there."

"You want me to strip right here?" Lily said, looking around. There wasn't much light down in the tunnels, but Lily was still exposed.

"This ain't Nordstrom's. I doubt they have fitting rooms," Tristan replied, shrugging. Lily glared at him and he started looking around. "Wait," he said. He picked a filthy tarp off the ground and held it up, blocking Lily against a wall.

"I don't believe this," Lily grumbled, and then stripped as quickly as she could behind the meager screen Tristan had created.

Tristan carried her clothes while Lily shoved her bare feet back into her unlaced boots. She clomped along behind him, her arms crossed over her nearly naked frame as they went to the tent.

It was already sweltering inside the small space. A fire blazed and a pot full of water rested on top of the glowing embers. Rowan's shirt was off, and he was stirring something inside the pot. He used tongs to pull a now-sterilized sheet of metal out of the boiling water and laid it to dry by the fire.

"Get the tissue samples from Breakfast and Una," Rowan told Tristan, who left Lily and Rowan in the tent alone together. Rowan was silent as he placed a single knife on a square of black silk in front of him. He looked at Lily.

"This is blood ritual," he said quietly.

Lily swallowed and nodded. "What do I need to do?"

"Bleed," he replied. His eyes rounded for a moment in apology before relaxing and sliding half shut into a calm that bordered on trance.

Rowan turned back and started pulling small glass jars out of the pot, laying them on top of the sterile metal sheet to cool. There were ten in all. Rowan moved the metal plate and glasses away from the fire and placed it between him and Lily.

Tristan and Una returned with ten metal rods, holding them carefully so the tips that had the tissue samples didn't touch. Rowan placed each rod upright in the ten glass jars.

"Thank you, Una," he said, dismissing her. She left the tent and Rowan turned to Tristan. "Take off your shirt. Sit behind Lily and support her. She'll probably faint at some point," he said in a deep and calm voice.

Lily felt Tristan sit cross-legged behind her, his arms at the ready in case she tipped to either side. Lily took a breath to calm herself, focusing on the slow and steady thump of Tristan's heart as he matched Rowan's trance-like energy.

Rowan carefully picked up the first metal rod and showed her the tissue-laden tip. "Look at the cells. Find the life-helix. Do you see it?"

Lily concentrated on the cells, her awareness sinking into them on a smaller and smaller level until she found a perfect, coiled strand of DNA. Every single biological fact about this woman was stored in that one strand. Her whole life on a string. "I see it," Lily said.

"That is pure. Store the pattern in your willstone," he said. Rowan put the rod, tip down, into the sterile glass cup and took Lily's wrist in one hand and his silver dagger in the other. "Let your blood be the creator of that pattern." He slit her wrist and let her bleed into the cup.

Lily watched her blood pool in the cup and mix with the cells in the sample, and she knew instinctively what she needed to do. Her rose-colored willstone flashed and sparkled with power as Lily drew heat and strength from the fire. Her blood cells changed into something more basic and less differentiated and took on the pattern of that particular woman's DNA. As it did so, her blood changed from red to golden.

"Stem cells," she heard Tristan whisper.

"Look at this. It is pure," Rowan said, holding up the next metal rod and flipping it over in the glass. "Let your blood be the creator of that pattern."

He moved her wrist over and let her bleed over the next skin sample. Again, Lily changed her blood as it flowed, creating a stem-cell serum specifically designed for that woman's DNA. They moved on to the next and the next, each time repeating the ritual. By the sixth sample, Lily felt herself swooning to the side as her blood pumped freely from her slit wrist. Tristan was there to hold her up, and Rowan's eyes were there to focus her on the last four samples.

She heard Rowan end the ritual and call out to Breakfast, who was waiting outside the tent, and then she tasted something salty on her lips. Her eyes popped open as the salt revived her and she saw Tristan feeding her pieces of a cracker. She sat up, rubbing her wrist. She still felt a dull ache, but the wound was completely gone. Not even a red seam marked her pale skin.

"Eat," Tristan urged. "Rowan said we aren't done yet."

"Where is he?" Lily croaked.

"Instructing the woman on how to inject the serum." Tristan smiled and shook his head disbelievingly. "He said that they'll be cured. One injection and in a few days it'll be as if they never got sick."

"But only those ten," Lily whispered solemnly. "The rest will die."

"It's still beyond anything we can do back home, Lily," he replied. "It's incredible. A miracle."

Lily smiled at Tristan. "It's your dream come true, isn't it? You're curing sick people."

"Yeah," he said softly. "Even without an Ivy League degree."

"Well, I'm glad I didn't completely ruin your life."

"Oh, you still ruined it," he said, breaking into a huge grin. "I mean, I'm in a tent in a hole in the ground. Not exactly a step up."

They shared a good laugh while Lily finished off her crackers. "Any more?" she asked, still feeling drained.

"This was all we could find for now," he said, his brow drawn with worry. "Are you okay?"

Lily shrugged. "I'll make it."

Rowan came back in the tent, his expression stormy. "I asked about salt again," he said to Tristan. "Breakfast and Riley said they were on it."

"What's next?" Lily asked.

"They need a water purifier badly," Rowan said. "I know how much you hate kitchen magic, but without safe drinking water, making serum for those ten women won't matter much."

"It's okay. Let's do it," Lily said, bracing herself.

Rowan and Tristan exchanged a speaking look and Lily got the sense that they were mindspeaking. They must have become stone kin before the ritual.

Tristan cracked the tent flap and called softly outside to Breakfast and Una. "Tell them we need more wood for the fire," he said to Una.

"And a cauldron of their dirtiest water," Rowan added.

Both were brought, and in a moment the fire was high again. The water purification ritual only took a few minutes. Rowan laid out herbs and minerals in front of Lily, and all she had to do was blow on them to give them the power to make polluted water clean again. This time, it was Lily's golden stone that twinkled in response to her summons. One soft exhale and Lily felt all her energy drain out of her, leaving her limbs heavy and her head swimming with exhaustion.

She felt Rowan catch her wilting torso and lay her gently on her side. His hand stroked her back soothingly while he gave instructions for the cauldron of cleansing water.

"Make sure they know the ratio is thirty thousand to one, Tristan," Rowan said. "Thirty thousand cauldrons of water can be cleaned by this *one cauldron*—be very clear when you tell them because they won't believe it." Rowan's voice dropped to a rumble. "Even I don't believe it."

"What are we dealing with here, Rowan?" Tristan asked fearfully.

"I think she's even stronger than Lillian, but I have no idea how that's possible."

Lily cupped her willstones in her hand reassuringly. Something clicked in her head and the words spilled out of her, uncensored and childlike. "Pink is for medicine magic, gold is for kitchen magic, and smoke is for warrior magic. Each can do its own job better than making one stone do everything, but it's harder to look after three of them. Harder to swallow if they catch me. I'm stronger but I'm less safe." Her eyes flew open in panic—an echo from Lillian although she didn't know exactly what it was that she feared. "They're coming! Don't let them put me in the barn!"

"Shh. Sleep, Lily." Rowan's hand stroked her hair until her eyes drooped shut again. "You're always safe with me," he said.

"But what if you want to leave me again?" Lily asked. She didn't hear his answer and frowned as she drifted off on her raft and strayed into the Mist. Lillian was waiting for her there to show Lily the source of her panic and dread.

. . . They use the noose poles to push me into the barn, and they slide the doors shut behind me. I scramble to my feet and rush the door frantically, banging on it with my fists, but I know it's no use. I hear the chain jingling and the padlock click. I'm trapped.

I hear the sound of people behind me. Moaning. Hacking coughs. Rheumy lungfuls of air bubbling inside half-rotted chests. I turn and face them slowly. It's so dark in here it takes time for my eyes to adjust, but I can already smell what I can't quite see. Blood. Blood everywhere. In the brick of the walls, and the concrete of the floor.

This used to be the slaughterhouse, back when this ranch raised lambs. Back when there were lambs left to eat. I know there are no animals on this ranch anymore. They were all eaten a long time ago. But I smell fresh blood, and as my eyes adjust I see why.

The fearful pack of skinny, sickly people limp toward me. They all have something in common. They are each missing a limb— whether it's a leg, an arm, or both. In the far back, lying on filthy pallets or just sprawled on the excrement-caked ground there are people who have been reduced to bloody stumps. They are the source of the endless moaning. There's a chopping block near the limbless ones. Everyone else avoids it, but they can't drag themselves away. It takes a while for me to understand what I'm looking at. And then I wish I couldn't see and that I never came to understand what really happens inside this barn.

This is a slaughterhouse still, but my captors don't kill their prey outright. No. That would be wasteful. There would be feasting after each slaughter but famine until the next. If they tried to store anything without refrigeration, the meat might spoil. Certainly, many still died of shock or blood loss during the amputation and those that didn't make it were eaten outright, but there were only so many people left in the world. The savages had to make their final food source last.

I look at the maimed bodies huddled in front of me, my mind

shying away from the horror of it. They are the new lambs in this broken, backward society. I was wrong. There *are* animals left in this world. Here, the animals rule, and they eat the people one piece at a time . . .

Lillian, enough. I understand you now, but please stop. I can't take any more. The filth. The suffering. Oh God, I just can't.

I haven't shown you what I owe yet, Lily. If you want to know what really drives me, you have to understand my shame. Soon, when you're calm, I'll show you the worst of it. I'll show you the secret that you and I must carry to our graves.

Lily had trouble opening her eyes. Her head was stuffed up, and her lashes were stuck together with dried tears. She peeled her swollen lids apart. She was alone in the tent. A small fire was banked low, throwing barely enough light to see by.

Lily sat up and pulled her knees to her chest, trying and failing to wipe the inside of her mind clean. She knew that even if she could erase the smells and the sounds of the barn, knowing it had existed had changed her. Lillian hadn't shown her some made-up cautionary tale about the potential horrors of nuclear war to scare her. She'd shown Lily what had truly happened to a version of the world that was very similar to Lillian's. Something that could still happen now in the world that Lily was in. The world Rowan refused to abandon. Alaric and Chenoa still had thirteen bombs for thirteen cities.

Lily now understood why Chenoa and her two acolytes, Hakan and Keme, had been so important to Lillian, and why Lillian had sent out her army to get those three scientists back. They were the ones who knew how to build the bombs. They might have also known where they were hidden, too.

And it was Lily's fault they got away. If Lily had just stayed out of it, Lillian could have found the bombs, gotten rid of them, and ended the conflict between the cities and the Outlanders.

Thousands of braves wouldn't have died in that battle, and the war would have been over months ago.

"Lily?" She twisted around to see Tristan half in and half out of the tent. "Are you okay?"

"Just tired," she lied, smiling up at him. "What's up?"

Tristan glanced behind him nervously before entering the tent and perching on his knees next to Lily. "We have to go kinda soon," he said. "That Mary woman was furious when she found out you were still here. Rowan's still trying to calm her down." He reached out and touched her shoulder gently, his eyes soft with worry. "Are you really okay? You look pale."

Lily patted his hand and went to stand. She lost her balance and tipped into his arms. "Ah—no, I guess not," she mumbled, her depth perception telescoping in and out. She felt Tristan's arms tighten around her, and a rush of tenderness coming from him. He wanted to kiss her.

"Tristan? We need to move," Rowan said as he entered the tent. He saw Lily in Tristan's arms and froze.

I'm having trouble with my balance, Rowan, and Tristan caught me. Nothing happened.

Lily could easily read what Rowan was feeling. He was broadcasting it to her loud and clear. He wasn't jealous—not exactly. He knew that Lily couldn't lie to him in mindspeak and that he didn't have a reason to be jealous. Nothing had happened between her and Tristan. He just *really* didn't like seeing Lily in Tristan's arms. It bothered him on a gut level that no amount of rational explanation could ease.

"Change out of that slip," Rowan said curtly as he dropped a pair of boots and a bundle of wearhyde clothes at Lily's feet. "And remember to recast a face glamour when you leave the tent."

Rowan spun and left them. Lily rubbed her aching head and

sighed. "Great. The only thing worse than having a pissed-off boyfriend is having a *telepathic* pissed-off boyfriend—'cause you know just how pissed off he is."

"Sorry," Tristan said, but Lily could tell he wasn't sorry at all. He was grinning from ear to ear. "Do you need help changing?"

"No," Lily said emphatically.

"You're still shaky, and it's not like I haven't seen you naked," Tristan said with a flirty smile.

"Out," Lily said, turning him by the shoulders and pushing him through the tent flap. She couldn't help but laugh with him. It had been a long time since he'd acted so playfully with her. He hadn't been his lighthearted self since Lily had come back, and she wondered what had revived his old spirit.

Once Tristan was gone, Lily managed to get into her bartered clothes even though her hands were shaking. She needed salt badly, and as she left the tent glamour intact—she immediately sought out Rowan. When she touched his mind she felt tension, but it had nothing to do with Tristan or her. There was a fight brewing. Lily heard raised voices and tried to run in their direction, but all she could manage was a stiff jog at best. Everything ached and her head pounded with every step.

Lily rounded the bend in the tracks and came upon the main group at just the wrong time. Mary turned on her.

"Who are you, really?" she asked, her voice low and dangerous. She pointed to the cauldron of water-purifying potion. "Your mechanics tell us that this one cauldron could clean enough water for an entire year of use. Do you expect us to believe you're more powerful than the Salem Witch herself?"

Lily's eyes sought out her coven desperately. Each of them was surrounded by the largest and strongest boys and girls the tunnel had to offer. Two of the teen boys had grabbed Una by the arms. Lily could feel how much her friend loathed being touched without permission, and a protective instinct kicked up inside her. How dare they touch her mechanics?

"If I'm so powerful, then maybe you should think twice before you threaten my coven," she replied through gritted teeth. Mary recoiled, and Lily felt her smoke willstone flare with agitation. It wanted to be used, and it started sucking heat from every nearby torch and barrel fire in anticipation. A witch wind stirred, moaning down the tunnels, hot and dry, and Lily wondered briefly if her willstones were alive in their own right. She heard Rowan's voice in her head, cutting through her anger and her throbbing headache.

Lily. We don't want to hurt these people. They're frightened, and that's why they're hostile. Please, calm down.

Lily met Rowan's eyes and nodded. She took a deep breath and the witch wind died. Mary stared at her, jaw dropped and eyes so wide they looked nearly all white.

"Let my mechanics go. We don't want a fight and neither do you," Lily said, loud enough for everyone to hear.

Mary looked over her shoulder and nodded once. Una yanked her arms free and shoved the kids who'd held her. Rowan, Tristan, Breakfast, and Una joined Lily, standing behind her in a semicircle. Lily felt calm now that they were near. She looked at Mary and sighed, planting her hands on her hips.

"I gave you serum and water purifier to help you," Lily said.

"Just to help us out of the goodness of your heart?" Mary repeated doubtfully. "You don't want anything in return from us or from our men on the ranches? No riots? No votes for your favorite councilman?"

"Take our gifts, use them—or be a fool and throw them all away," Lily said tiredly, not entirely understanding the complicated politics of how the poor were exploited in this world. "As long as you keep your mouth shut about where you got them, I don't care what you do."

Lily saw something in Mary's eyes change. She realized Lily was only trying to help, and she hated her all the more for it. "Get out," Mary said hollowly.

"Just show us the way," Lily retorted.

Riley separated himself from the crowd quickly and led Lily's coven away, closely followed by his munchkin entourage. From the look on his face as he hurried them down the tracks, he seemed as relieved to get out of that situation as Lily's coven did.

"She's thankful, really, even if she didn't say it, sir," Riley said nervously to Rowan. "Mary's just got this way about her, you know? Not so helpful when dealing with a lady witch, but it's dead useful when we're bargaining with other groups."

"It's alright, Riley, I understand," Rowan replied. "Charity from witches isn't something my people trust, either. It usually ends up costing more than it's worth."

"I *thought* you were an Outlander. It's the way you stand," Riley said, narrowing his eyes and trying to peer through Rowan's glamour. Rowan smiled, confident that Riley couldn't pierce his glamour unless he allowed it. Riley gave up and turned to Breakfast. "You're an Outlander, too, aren't you? What tribe are you from?"

Breakfast looked momentarily baffled and changed the subject. Lily felt Rowan's fingers brush her wrist in that gentle mechanic's touch.

You need salt badly, Lily. And you haven't eaten anything substantial in days.

I know. I've got a raging headache.

"Stop," Rowan called to the group, even though they hadn't traveled more than a few hundred feet from the main group.

He swung his pack off his back and pulled out the jar of olives. Lily sat down on the tracks, too tired to care how dirty they were. She ate the last of the olives and drank the brine while her coven watched anxiously. It helped, but it was still a long way from satisfying her.

Got any more, Rowan?

Rowan turned to Breakfast, and Lily could tell they were conversing in mindspeak. Lily looked hazily at her coven and realized that at some point they'd all earned one another's trust enough to become stone kin. Her claimed had claimed each other.

"I love you guys," she blurted out. She sounded drunk.

"Is she going to be okay?" Riley asked, backing away fearfully. "She's not going to blow up, is she? 'Cause I've heard the strongest witches do that when they croak."

"Of course I'm not going to blow up," Lily said, laughing. She leaned back too far, lost her balance, and slid off the rail and onto the gravel of the track.

Rowan helped her back up and lifted one of Lily's wrists to his mouth. He licked her damp skin, tasting her. A muscle in his jaw jumped and he looked at Tristan, sharing mindspeak. They looked worried.

The group heard a shout coming down the tunnel and picked up their heads. A cluster of lookout teens were running down the tracks, waving their arms overhead.

"City guards," the lookouts shouted. "It's a raid!"

"They're rounding up the older boys to ship out to the ranches. We've got to hide," Riley said. Rowan picked Lily up in his arms and they all started running down the tracks, back toward the main group. "Whatever you do," Riley added anxiously, "don't *kill* anyone. We'll all lose our citizenship if a guard dies in the tunnels, and outside the walls we're as good as Woven chow."

They darted through the people scrambling in the tent city and jumped over a small barricade, ducking down behind it to hide. Riley doused the torches around them and told everyone to stay still.

Rowan passed Lily to Tristan and made a move to jump back out into the panicked crowd.

"No, they'll catch you!" Riley said, grabbing him.

"I have to get Lily salt," Rowan said, easing his arm out of Riley's grip. "As soon as you see your chance to run, you take it, you hear me? I'll find you."

"How?" Una asked. "What if we get blocked by all this?" She gestured to the fact that they were underground, and with enough soil between them it would be impossible to mindspeak.

"I can track anything. Especially my witch," he said, and launched himself over the barricade. Lily made a small noise of protest as she watched him go and peered over the barricade, but in moments he was lost in the swirl of running bodies.

The rest of the group kept their heads down until most of the commotion had passed, and after minutes that seemed to drag on like hours, Riley finally decided it was time to move. Lily reached out for Rowan, but she was too weak and he was too far away for her to feel anything more than the energy of his willstone. She could tell he was still alive and uninjured, but mindspeak was already impossible. Lily leaned against Tristan as they crouched low, ducking behind what little cover they could find, and headed back toward the tunnel that led them away from the main group. They were no more than a few paces away when Riley stiffened and stopped.

Guards were marching down the tunnel, escorting captured boys to their new life on one of the ranches. Lily caught a glimpse of the captured boys' desperate expressions and shuddered. A memory of the barn with its smell of blood and filth loomed up in her mind, hellish and overpowering.

"In here," Riley whispered. He ran to the wall and started prying at what seemed to be nothing. On closer inspection, Lily could make out the bare outline of a service door. "Let me in," he said, kicking at the blocked door.

It opened long enough to allow Lily's group to get inside, and then slammed shut behind them. Among the few pale ovals of scared faces that peered out of the near dark, Lily could just make out Pip and Mary.

"How many did they get?" Riley asked Mary.

"I saw seven taken," she answered. Mary looked at Lily, a hint of compassion softening her eyes. "One of them was your man. Rowan."

Lily pushed herself up and stood straight, sheer panic giving her the strength. "Which way did they go?" she asked.

"You can't help him now," Mary said sadly. "He'll be shipped out to a ranch like the rest of our boys."

"Over my dead body," Lily said, turning and pulling on the door.

Images of the filthy barn and the bestial men who ran it clamored in her head and the thought of Rowan being among them was unbearable. She wouldn't let it happen. She'd send fire roaring down the tunnels, charring every guard to cinders if she had to, but there was no way she was going to allow Rowan to set foot in one of those death camps. Hands reached out and tried to pull her back, but Lily wrenched free of them.

"You can't! Lady Witch, please," Riley begged. "You'll get us all thrown out of the city. We'll die out there with the Woven."

Lily stopped struggling to pull away and looked back at the pleading faces behind her. She couldn't kill the guards and doom these people.

"The Woven," she said, stumbling across a thought. "Everyone's afraid of the Woven." She turned to her coven and saw perplexed expressions, and then widened her regard to include everyone. "Don't worry. I won't kill anyone, but will you all help me? Maybe I can get our boys back. Did anyone see which way they went?"

"I did," Mary said, stepping forward. "This plan of yours better be good."

Little Pip ran point as they crept out of their hiding place. "S'all clear," he lisped around his missing two front baby teeth.

They followed Mary through the maze of branching tunnels while Lily tried to think how she was going to do this. They neared the Ranch Four stop on the subway and Mary called a halt. They could all hear voices and marching boots ahead.

"It's right up there," Mary told them. "The next stop is the staging place for most of the city guards' raids."

Lily nodded, finally understanding why the tunnel people didn't use it. She felt Breakfast brushing up against her mind.

So, what's the plan, boss?

I'm trying to think, Breakfast.

You don't have a plan?

Lily shot him a frown and he looked at Una. They seemed to share a few exchanges in mindspeak that ended in Una giving Breakfast a nasty look and Lily an encouraging one.

Rowan? Are you there?

Yes, Lily. I'm sorry I got captured, but I had to stop short of killing anyone to get away. The guards are trying to goad me into it, though. They want a fight. They're actually hoping that one of them will get killed so they can "clean out" this whole tunnel.

Rowan transmitted a memory flash of one of the guards getting in his face, acting tough and bullying Rowan and the biggest of the captured teens. Lily felt Rowan getting punched in the gut and cringed.

I'm coming, Rowan.

"I need fire, but not too much," Lily told Riley as they passed a torch. "It can't be too bright. Everyone needs to keep out of direct light, okay?"

Riley grabbed the torch and Lily could see her coven starting to understand.

"Can you cast a glamour that big?" Tristan asked. He switched to mindspeak. *Are you strong enough?*

I'd better be.

"I want you to run down the tunnel toward the guards. I'm going to make you all look like Woven, okay?" she told them. They looked back at her, frightened. "I need you to be brave," she told them.

Pip stood up straighter. "I'm brave," he said defiantly.

"Woven never go below ground," Mary said, shaking her head.

"So this should really scare the hell out of them, shouldn't it?" Lily said, hoping she sounded more sure than she felt.

Mary looked uncertain, but nodded her assent anyway. "If the guards don't go for it, you all scramble," she told her people.

Lily turned away and shut her eyes, concentrating on gathering energy from the torch. She was so depleted she didn't know if she'd be able to transmute the heat. Luckily glamours required little energy, or Lily knew she wouldn't be able to do this at all. She concentrated on making each individual in the group look like a different kind of Woven. Her imagination failed her, so she delved into her nightmares instead. They never seemed to run out of strange concoctions of tentacles and pincers, armor and scales.

Lily heard a gasp of surprise coming from Mary and knew that her trick was working. At least for now. When Lily opened her eyes she had to look away. Staring at her nightmares-made-real was too unsettling.

"We've got to really sell this, or it won't work," Breakfast said, turning to Riley.

Riley looked down at the younger kids and gave them an order. "You three pretend you're monkey Woven. I want you to make a lot of noise." The kids were silent and staring, too shaken from the reality of Lily's glamour to move. "Snap out of it!" Riley commanded. "Keep it together, you lot, or we're sunk."

Lily felt a wave of nausea. "I can't hold this forever," she told them.

"We're going," Tristan said.

"Everybody start making noises," Una said encouragingly, and then started moaning like a zombie. The kids followed her cue and started hooting like monkeys.

Rowan. It's a glamour. We're trying to scare off the guards.

I'll try to keep the captured boys from running, but I don't know if I can.

Lily stayed next to the torch while the rest of them started running down the tunnel, clanging on pipes as they went and shrieking at the top of their lungs. She heard a huge commotion of screams and scrambling footfalls. Tristan's mind brushed up against hers.

It's working! They're running away! Wait . . .

Lily heard gunshots.

"No!" she shouted.

She ran down the tunnel, abandoning the torch. When she rounded the bend, she saw the captured tunnel boys fleeing in every direction. Most of the guards had taken off in the opposite direction down the tracks, but a few had remained and they were firing wildly at what they believed to be Woven.

Lily dropped the glamour and the gunfire ceased. Shocked faces peered back at her in the dark.

"Get behind me," she told the children. The guards raised their weapons again and Lily raised her hand. Rowan slid into her head eagerly.

Gift me, Lily.

An earsplitting crack and a blinding flash of light erupted toward her. Lily inhaled the hot rush of power and an unnatural silence bubbled up around the vacuum of absorbed heat, motion, and light. Bullets halted in their progress, their momentum stolen, and then dropped from the air with the sound of scattering stones. A witch wind howled down the tunnel, knocking everyone toward Lily in a wave.

"Witch!" a guard screamed.

Lily unlocked Rowan's willstone and gifted it with a huge burst of energy. They both embraced the sensation with joy and awe. Lily was inside Rowan and their shared body became a blur of motion and strength as they flowed toward their enemies. Guards fell around them, but Lily felt held back. She wanted them dead at her feet, but Rowan was stopping her.

We must not kill, Lily.

Lily ached to take him over completely, to possess him and wear his body around hers. She would kill all the guards for daring to open fire on her mechanics. She would punish them for taking Rowan away from her, for striking him, for not getting down on their knees and begging her for their lives.

Let me keep myself, Lily. Please don't do this.

Lily pulled back and released Rowan. Fatigue fell on her instantly and she stumbled under its weight. The iron taste of bloodlust was in her mouth.

"Catch her!" Una ordered, and Lily felt something break her fall.

"Got her," Pip replied in a squeaky voice. She'd fallen on top of him and nearly squished him. "You alright, Lady Witch?" he asked.

"My head," Lily moaned.

She rolled off Pip and propped herself up on her hands and knees, still shaken by the depth of the rage she'd felt along with the Gift. Lily looked around blearily. She saw Tristan and Rowan bending down and pressing their fingertips to each of the fallen guards' necks.

"They're all alive," Breakfast told Riley.

Mary let out a sigh. "Any of your people hurt?" she asked.

"No," Breakfast replied. "Yours?"

"Two got hit with bullets, but not fatally," she said, waving it off. "A few more got banged up in the fight." Mary looked down at Lily. "Are you okay?" she asked.

Lily shook her head and used Pip as a prop to haul herself up to her feet. "Will there be more guards?" she asked, staggering where she stood.

"Yes," Rowan answered, stepping forward to hold Lily up against his side. He turned to Riley. "We need to get on a train and get out of here. Fast."

Riley looked at Lily uncertainly. "Are you sure—" he began, but Rowan cut him off.

"In about half an hour every guard in Providence is going to be looking for a witch and her mechanics," he said with certainty. "We have to get out of the city now."

"Show them the way to the southbound train," Mary told Riley. She gave Lily a begrudging smile. "And good luck," she said as she left them to go gather up her wounded people.

"She needs salt," Rowan told Riley.

Riley nodded and turned to a small girl. She took off like a shot. Riley smiled at Breakfast. "She's my fastest," he said.

Riley led Lily and her coven down the branching subway tunnels. Lily limped along, propped up between Rowan and Tristan, but she refused to let them carry her the whole way.

Lily, you're being impossible.

I know, Tristan. But you and Rowan are tired, too. I can make it.

They went deeper into the subway line, and the walls shrank around them.

"We can't stay on these tracks," Una said, looking askance at the close walls. They could hear trains on other tracks now, rumbling down other tunnels, and there was no place for them to duck into if a train came.

"Don't worry. I know the train schedule better 'an my own mum's birthday," Riley said confidently, and then continued on his way.

Rowan picked up Lily and followed. She was going to complain, but realized that would be ridiculous. She couldn't stand if she tried.

Rowan? What was all that about me blowing up?

It's not going to happen. You're not dangerously overheated yet. Don't worry.

Something about the way Rowan phrased that didn't put her at ease.

"I'll take her if you get tired," Tristan offered. Rowan nodded, but Lily could tell by the way his arms tightened around her that there was no way he was going to pass her off to Tristan.

Rowan carried her up the rungs of a metal ladder to another one of the smaller service tunnels above the track, and Lily could tell they were almost there. Every step brought them closer to the sound of people, milling around nearby platforms. Lily could even hear music being played, probably by street musicians hoping for tips. It wasn't all that different from the T in her Boston. She heard the sound of a train squealing on the tracks as it slowed and went around a long bend. Beneath them, a hole had been dug right through the concrete.

The runner had not caught up with them. Lily had no salt, and she felt too weak to even consider the acrobatics it would take to jump that train. She couldn't fuel her mechanics to make up for her weakness, either—that would require even more salt that her system didn't have.

"We can't go," Rowan said, shouting over the sound of the train speeding under them.

"This is the last train. It's your only chance for the rest of the night," Riley said.

"Can't we wait until tomorrow?" Breakfast asked.

Riley shrugged. "We're out of my gang's territory. I can't promise you'll be safe."

Lily could sense her mechanics communicating rapidly in mindspeak, but they didn't want her to hear what they were discussing. A decision was made.

"How do we jump this train?" Una asked Riley, her tone determined.

"Drop through this hole while it slows to go 'round the bend, and you should be able to keep your footing," Riley answered. "Try not to make too much noise when you land or they'll set the conductor on you. Hurry, or you're going to run out of cars."

Breakfast clasped hands with Riley, and then kissed Una quickly before saying, "Here goes," and disappearing down the hole. Una went next, silent and graceful as a cat, and then Tristan.

Rowan and Lily went last. They held hands going through the hole and landed at the same time, but as soon as Lily's feet touched down her wobbly legs gave out. She lost Rowan's hand and rolled away from him with a desperate cry.

Rowan scrambled on his knees after her, his hands reaching out to grab hers as she grasped frantically for anything. Her legs swung off the side of the car, caught in the draft, and she slid over the edge.

Her free fall stopped short with a joint-popping jerk. Rowan had managed to get a hold of her wrist, and she dangled painfully off the side of the train from her right arm. The train picked up speed as it cleared the bend, and Rowan strained with all his might just to hold on to Lily while the drag of the wind pulled on her hanging body. Lily heard Tristan shout and then she saw his face as he leaned over the side next to Rowan.

"Give me your hand," Tristan pleaded as he reached frantically for her.

Lily swung her body from her burning shoulder, biting her lip to keep herself from screaming. On the third try she managed to haul herself up enough to reach Tristan's outstretched hand.

Rowan and Tristan pulled her up on top of the train, both of them holding her in a tight huddle. Una and Breakfast had started running down the length of the train when they saw Lily fall and finally reached them, their faces panicked.

"Her shoulder's dislocated," Rowan snarled over the sound of the wind. "I should have insisted we waited until she was strong enough."

"We had no choice," Una replied, trying to calm Rowan down. "Can't we heal her?"

"Without a fire? Not completely," Rowan said. "We'll either have to break into one of the private cars to do it, or wait until the train stops."

"I'll make it," Lily said, gritting her teeth. She felt her mechanics exchange another rapid conversation in mindspeak. Being left out, coupled with the pain of her shoulder and her still aching head, annoyed her. "It's too risky," she snapped. "We're lucky there isn't a conductor up here as it is. We'll have to wait until the train stops."

Rowan tilted Lily's face up to his. "I still have to put it back," he said grimly. "Your shoulder. We can't leave it dislocated all night or it will set like that."

Lily swallowed hard and met his eyes. "Just do it."

Without another word, Rowan pushed Lily onto her back and pressed his knee into her sternum. With both hands he took her injured arm and held it in front of her, bent at the elbow. He then pushed it down in an L shape next to her head. Lily kept her lips pressed together and screamed behind her teeth while Rowan pulled her arm swiftly up alongside her ear. She heard a grinding pop, and the pain was so intense she felt nauseous with it.

Rowan eased off her chest and she saw his willstone flare with light. The pain slackened, and Lily rolled onto her uninjured side, moaning quietly to herself through tight breaths. She saw Tristan's stone glow, and the pain lessened some more. She heard Rowan giving her mechanics instructions in mindspeak.

Encourage the fluid to circulate. Keep the blood moving to help heal the site of injury. Repress the pain signals from the nerves. Easy. We don't want her to go numb, we just want to block the pain. Use your own stores of energy and take nothing from our witch. It will make you tired, but not as tired as she is.

Lily took a deep breath and sighed it out, tears tracing a hot path into her hairline.

"Damn," she heard Una murmur. "Are you okay?"

Lily laughed unevenly, catching her breath. Her shoulder was still a mess, but at least she couldn't feel it anymore. "I've been through worse."

CHAPTER
11

ARRICK FOLLOWED THEIR TRAIL THROUGH THE WOODS. At one of their camps he found blood in the snow. He tasted it just to make sure, and spit it out when he confirmed it was Woven's blood. They'd made good time on their journey. His little brother had pushed the pace, almost as if he knew they were being followed. Maybe Rowan did know, somehow. As Carrick came upon the end of the forest and the edge of Providence's Killing Fields he imagined his brother running in front of him. Hounded.

Carrick licked his lips and looked out across the Killing Fields of Providence, thinking of the glory days when the Killing Fields had earned their name. Every one of the Thirteen Cities was surrounded by a huge meadow where many had died. Witches loved nothing more than fighting a bloody battle right in front of their cities. In the Age of Strife, when witches regularly sent out their armies to slaughter each other, the Killing Fields were soaked with so much blood that the buildup of salt from that blood left the soil sterile for decades. Even now, trees would not grow.

Rowan's trail led Carrick to an exhumed metal plate at the edge of the forest. His little brother had gone into the train tunnels for shelter. Carrick knew that if he followed, the tons of earth might cut him off from his witch, giving his quarry the advantage.

Lillian. I have to go underground to continue following Lily and her coven.

Go, Carrick. Stay close to them, but don't be discovered.

As you wish, My Lady.

Lily slept very little that night. Her mechanics tried to help, but they had to use their own faltering stores of energy to do it. Until she was healed and the injury dealt with, her mechanics could only mask her pain—and they couldn't keep that up for long. They were all tired, cold, and hungry.

After only an hour Lily demanded that they stop, and she gutted it out alone for the rest of the night. Every bump on the tracks brought pain, jarring her out of whatever doze she managed to fall into and the night turned into one long half sleep that was more torturous than it would have been if she'd simply stayed awake. Her mechanics tried to give her comfort by smoothing her hair and holding her hand, but as Lily had already learned, pain builds a barrier between the hurt and the whole. It leaves the sufferer isolated, with nothing but an ocean of time to cross.

Lily could feel herself rising up on her raft, and she could hear Lillian calling to her from the Mist. Lily didn't want to go back to the barn. She fought it, but Lillian was better at directing the currents in the spirit world, and like it or not Lily felt her raft being drawn into Lillian's memory.

. . . I stay in a huddle all night. I back myself into a corner, knees drawn into to my chest, watching the lambs watch me. They keep their distance—too beaten down to approach me. Or maybe I just make them sad. Seeing me, they're probably all reminded of their own first night in the barn.

I hear the sounds of the Woven outside. The chittering noises they make in the dark. My skin crawls. Dawn comes and light seeps through the cracks in the roof, illuminating shafts of dusty air. The feeble sun is not enough to warm anyone in this never-ending winter. I am so low on energy that even I'm shivering.

One of the lambs creeps forward—a little boy no older than seven or eight. He holds out the edge of his shawl, offering to share half. I know it's awful of me, but before I accept I check him for bloody stumps.

"It's okay," the boy says, understanding my hesitation. "The doctor hasn't caught me yet."

I look down, ashamed of myself. The boy is sweet and I smile, gratefully accepting his company. "The doctor?" I ask.

"He takes our arms and legs in a way that doesn't kill us," he whispers. His eyes are blank with terror and he presses against me, trying to warm his emaciated body. "He's the most scary of them all."

"How often does he come?" I ask, my own fear feeding off his.

"Every day when the sun goes down," he says with haunted reverence.

We spend the morning clinging to each other. We don't talk. When a canteen of water is passed around at noon I refuse, allowing the boy to drink my share. He thinks I'm being kind, but really I'm only doing it to protect myself. I doubt anyone who gets put in the barn gets fed, but the less food or drink I allow into my body, the longer it will take for me to pass my willstones. The extra dose of water gives the boy a burst of energy—enough to speak anyway.

"Are you a witch?" he asks, half holding his breath in excitement.

I nod and mime swallowing my willstone. He smiles at me brightly, and then his face falls. "They took mine and smashed it. They smashed all our willstones to make us quiet."

That's why they're all so docile. And why our captors had no qualms about throwing me in the barn with them, no matter how strong a witch I might be. If the lambs don't have willstones, I can't claim them and fill them with power so we can fight our way out. The boy nestled against me has talent, too. He senses I'm a witch and he feels the need to be close to me. He could have been a mechanic.

"You look like the Lady of Salem," he whispers.

I smile at him, but I don't answer. I don't know if admitting it would get me killed faster or not.

"You still have your willstone," he presses. "Could you help us?"

I look around at the squalor and despair surrounding me. There's nothing to burn and no source of energy. "Right now I can't even help myself," I say. The boy goes quiet, his last ray of hope snuffed out.

I look at the lambs. There are well over fifty people here, crammed close to share their body heat. A dark thought occurs to me. They're all dying anyway. I push the thought away, clinging to my humanity for as long as I can.

The day drags by, marked only by the change in position of the shafts of dusty light piercing through the darkness. As the light lengthens, the lambs grow restless. Panicky. The doctor is on his way.

At sunset, the doors burst open and the lambs start screaming. They push to the back, stepping over one another in a desperate bid to get away. I stand where I am, hiding the boy behind me. Let them try and take him away from me.

Armed men push into the room, laughing. Enjoying the chaos and fear of a riot. They avoid me, shouting for everyone to steer clear of me. I notice that they are guarding one lean shape in the middle of their group. His long, silky black hair is braided with vulture feathers.

"That's him!" the boy squeals, hiding his face in my skirts. "That's the doctor."

I know him. The shape of his sensitive mouth, the way he walks, even the curve of his broad shoulders is as familiar to me as the moon in the sky because he gave these features to someone I love more than I love anything. I stagger forward, thinking that if I come closer to him his face will somehow change. That he won't be who I know he is.

"River Fall!" I shout, hoping beyond hope that he doesn't respond. But he turns to me. Tears burn my eyes and grip at my throat.

"Lillian," he says. No emotion. There's nothing inside of him. He comes toward me and his guards move swiftly to pin me down with their noose poles. I'm too stunned to fight. They capture me by the neck and push me against the wall, choking me. The boy lets go of my skirts and rushes forward, attacking my assailants with his little fists, and gets himself captured.

"No," I beg. Not River. He's the gentlest, kindest man I'd ever met. "It can't be you."

"Where is my son, Lillian?" he asks, his deep voice rumbling.

"I don't—" I stop and reach out for Rowan. I can't feel him at all in this world. There's simply no vibration where his huge and powerful presence should be. "He's dead, River."

River's eyes blaze and he comes toward me, snarling. "He's alive! He's alive and he will set all this right again," River says. He makes a wide gesture with his arms, taking in not just the horror inside the barn, but the broken world outside the barn's doors. "My son was taken by another ranch and they hold him hostage. I send them food"—he points at the lambs, spit flying from his mouth—"and they keep him alive. But he'll be back. Rowan will be back and he'll fix everything. My son is the most powerful mechanic ever. He'll fix all of this."

His grief has made him mad. River grabs the boy by his hair, and pulls. I try to scream, but the noose poles cut off my air. I strain and grab, pressing against the rope, but the boy is out of reach. River drags him by his hair to the back of the barn, where the chopping block lies. The boy is screaming and begging, and in a moment I hear him scream even louder.

Inhuman sounds. Almost like a hawk. I wonder if River is taking his arm or his leg . . .

Lily didn't struggle or try to end the memory, but Lillian spared her and stopped. She knew Lily had seen enough anyway.

Do you understand now, Lily? Do you understand why I couldn't explain what I had learned to anyone? Why I pushed Rowan away and wouldn't let him see my memories of the cinder world—not even to make him understand why I had to stop Alaric and his scientists?

Yes, Lillian. You didn't trust yourself enough to only show part of the cinder-world memory. You were afraid Rowan would keep digging until he found his father. He's relentless when he wants to see a memory—like when he wanted to know what Carrick had done to me in the oubliette.

When I first came back I was so weak and sick my mind would have been an open book to him. No one must ever know, Lily. No one but us.

Caleb told me that River was the first person you hanged. You did that in case you failed and the bombs went off, didn't you? You killed River first to make sure he never became that thing in the barn.

If Rowan ever knew, it would change him. I broke his heart, but seeing his father like that would break something much deeper in him. Something much more precious. Have you ever seen Rowan's core?

Yes, Lillian. It's like a diamond—pure and strong.

His father gave him that. Rowan makes all of his moral decisions based on what he thinks his father would do. Seeing River in the barn would take that compass away from him. Do you know what love is, Lily? Real love?

I'm not sure anymore.

Love is being willing to become the villain so that the one you love can stay a hero.

Lily awoke with her head in Una's lap. Her sore arm was bound tightly to her chest.

"The train's beginning to slow," Una said. "We think we're pulling into a station."

"Are we in Richmond?" Lily asked.

"Not yet, but we're getting off anyway to heal you," she answered. "I think we're in Baltimore, so we're not too far." Una looked down at Lily. "That was some dream you had—if it *was* a dream. Felt more like a memory to me."

Lily kept her voice low and her face calm even though she was anything but. "How much did you see?"

"One or two images," Una whispered. She swallowed hard around a lump in her throat. "That wasn't you in the barn. It was Lillian, wasn't it?"

"Yes." Lily sat up and looked Una in the eye.

"Who was the *doctor?*" The way Una said the word it was obvious she meant "butcher."

Lily turned her head and looked pointedly at Rowan, who was caught up in a heated discussion with Breakfast and Tristan. Then she looked back at Una, her eyes begging. "Please, Una. He loved his father. He can never find out."

"I know a thing or two about secrets," Una replied. "About keeping secrets no matter how much they hurt, although lately I'm starting to think that maybe it's better when you don't."

"Please," Lily whispered again.

I won't tell Rowan, but maybe you should. I don't understand what was going on in Lillian's memory, but I could feel an emotion in you that I recognize too well. Shame. That never ends well, Lily. Trust me. The only way to end shame is to bring it out of the dark and into the light.

Lily and Una stared at each other. *Thank you, Una.*

On top of the next train car Rowan, Tristan, and Breakfast were busy discussing what food to get at the station and how best to get it. Rowan was trying to explain to them that stealing wasn't the smartest thing to do in a world cloaked in wards, even though Rowan could break just about anyone's ward of protection if he chose.

"I traded for some money with Riley," Breakfast said reluctantly. "But I wanted to hold on to it in case we needed something to pay the Outlanders."

Rowan shook his head and smiled. "They're my tribe, Breakfast. We don't need to pay them. Just get Lily some salty food, but don't ask to buy salt directly. It'll look suspicious."

As he spoke of her, Rowan glanced over at Lily and saw that she was sitting up. His eyes softened when they met hers and her heart hurt just looking at him. Luckily, he misinterpreted the source of her emotion.

You're still in a lot of pain.

I'll live.

The train stopped. Una and Rowan helped Lily down off the top of the train and brought her above ground while Breakfast and Tristan stayed and went shopping around the station.

"We have to get you out of the city quickly. Cast a glamour before anyone recognizes you," Rowan said urgently. Lily did as he said and they melted into the foot traffic lining the city streets.

Lily noticed that Una was staring up at the soaring architecture. It was the first time she'd seen a city in this world, and the scale was overwhelming.

Baltimore wasn't quite as big as Salem, but it was still New York City tall and compact. Yet it didn't look or feel like any city in Una and Lily's world. Vegetation spilled off every rooftop and terrace, and greenhouses dotted every block. Huge spiraling lattices, called greentowers, soared up into the sky, dwarfing even the tallest skyscrapers.

Rowan quickly explained to Una that vertical farming had become a necessity inside the Thirteen Cities after the Woven took over all the arable land outside the walls. All the structures needed to support vegetation or the people would starve to death inside their walls. The architecture made sense, maybe more sense than the way cities were constructed in Lily's world, but it was still strange to Una's eyes.

And then there were the tame Woven, called guardians, which were chained to the bottom of the greentowers to guard the precious food they supported. Una stared at the guardians, as unsettled as Lily had been when she first saw them. They looked like a combination of dog, bear, and tiger, but Lily thought that the eyes were different. They seemed intelligent—almost human. Lily looked at one of the guardians, and she could have sworn it was looking back at her like it was thinking.

As they hurried through the crowded streets, Una kept catching herself staring at everything like a hick. Lily could see her struggling to act casually.

"Yeah, those are weird-looking cars," Una said under her breath as one of the sleek, futuristic automobiles hummed past.

"They call them elepods. They're electric cars, basically," Lily said.

"Okay. I can deal with that," Una said, keeping it together. "But what the hell is *that*?"

She pointed up into the sky where a winged creature darted and spun. Lily had seen a few of them in Salem, but they seemed more popular here in Baltimore. They looked like tiny dragons, and Lily knew only rich people could afford them.

"That's a pet drake," Rowan said in an offhand way. "The big drakes are grown by the Covens to defend the air space over the Thirteen Cities from flying Woven. They're useful. But the little ones are just pains in the asses for everyone except their owners. Nasty little biters."

"Then why do people get them?" Una asked. "Apart from the fact that they're gorgeous."

Rowan shrugged. "To prove they can afford to pay for the license the Covens require to own one. Even tame Woven are taken very seriously, and every one is meticulously documented."

"That makes sense," Una said, her eyes still glued to the little drakes.

"In Salem they're considered too flashy by most," Rowan added distastefully. Lily could tell he didn't like them. Rowan didn't trust any of the Woven, not even the supposedly tame ones.

"Where do they grow them?" Una asked, staring at the jewel-like creatures with open envy.

"They're grown in the Stacks, like all of the bio-assets the Covens provide the cities," Rowan replied. He suddenly frowned, ending the conversation. They were coming to the city gates, which were surrounded by guards. "Lily. Hide two of your willstones," he whispered.

Lily did as he said and saw his eyes unfocus in the telltale sign of mindspeak. Lily looked up at the colossal wall surrounding Baltimore, and understood. Once they went through those gates, they wouldn't be able to contact Tristan and Breakfast.

"They ran into some trouble. Some idiot mistook Breakfast for an Outlander and picked a fight. Of course Tristan jumped right in," Rowan said, looking very much like he wanted to strangle the both of them.

"They better hurry," Una said under her breath, picking up on the situation as quickly as Lily did.

They were swept up into the line leaving the city. Unfortunately, it was a short line, and they found themselves facing the guards before Tristan and Breakfast had joined them.

Tristan. Breakfast. It'd be great if you showed up about now.

"That's some willstone you got there, Outlander."

One of the guards had singled out Rowan. His eyes flicked over to Lily and Una, inspecting their stones. Una had a medium-size smoke stone. It wasn't huge, but it was almost black in color. She was obviously strong.

"You." Another guard approached Lily, looking quizzically at her rose stone. It was medium size like Una's, but rich in color and complexity. "I've never seen a stone like that."

"I'm weird," Lily retorted.

"What happened to your shoulder?" Both the guards were flanking Lily now, drawn to her.

Lily reminded herself that these were soldiers. They'd probably felt the Gift from their witch, most likely the Lady of Baltimore, and they could sense that Lily was even stronger than she was. Their eyes were hungry and their faces hopeful. They were craving the Gift. Lily felt unsafe.

"We ran into some Woven last night. Came into town to buy med supplies for our tribe," Rowan answered for her. His tone was quiet and he was positioning himself between Lily and the guards. So was Una. Lily could feel too many eyes resting on her. "Our tribe is waiting for us," Rowan said evenly.

The guards couldn't keep noncitizens inside the walls. The city guards had plenty of rules about which Outlanders they let in, but they were generally more concerned about getting all the Outlanders out. City law required that all noncitizens be outside the wall by nightfall. They didn't like it, but unless the guards had a reason to arrest them, they had to let Lily's group pass.

As soon as they were through the gates, Una let out a gusty breath. "I thought we were going to have to fight our way out," she said.

"Another minute or two and we might have had to," Rowan replied.

"What did they want from Lily?"

"Power," Rowan replied simply. "Think about it, Una. Since Lily claimed you, how often have you craved her strength?"

Una's gaze dropped and she frowned, troubled.

"It's okay," Rowan continued. "You learn to recognize it for what it is and control it, like any other kind of desire. Only people with weak character allow it to control them, like those guards."

Rowan suddenly stopped and put a hand on Una's shoulder. It was the first time Lily had ever seen Rowan touch Una outside of their sparring sessions, and for a split second Lily was worried that Una might push his hand off, but she didn't. She trusted Rowan.

"Remember, Una," he said, "we receive the Gift to defend our witch, not for our own pleasure. It's a privilege, and it should be a rare one. You have enough character to control yourself—I have no doubt about that. Or about you."

Una smiled up at Rowan gratefully, and Lily couldn't help but be moved by how much love and respect had grown between them. Rowan was like a brother to Una now. He'd earned that right. As Lily watched this touching exchange between a mentor and his student, she couldn't help but adore Rowan even more. Nor could she help but remember with a pang that he had probably learned the skill of compassionate leadership from his father.

As they moved across the large field that separated the walls of Baltimore from the surrounding forest, Rowan and Una grew silent and tense. Woven could be anywhere. They found a small clearing, and Rowan instructed Una to build a fire.

"We'll wait here for Tristan and Breakfast to catch up while you and I heal Lily," he explained as he opened his pack and began taking out his cauldron and herbs.

Lily sank gratefully to her knees. Her shoulder was still throbbing. "I'm going to try to find Caleb and your Tristan," Lily told him.

Rowan nodded while he worked, his nimble hands laying out the tools he would need. His lips softened in a small smile. He loved being a mechanic. Lily had to force herself to concentrate; she could have stared at him the rest of the day.

She reached out and felt for the particular energies that were Caleb and Tristan. She could feel their relief and their happiness at hearing from her. "They're close," Lily said. "Can you reach them, Rowan?"

His eyes stared at nothing for a moment. "Not yet."

Lily sent Caleb and Tristan an image of exactly where they were. *We're outside of Baltimore*, she told them.

We're only a few miles away from you. We'll be there soon.

Lily relayed their message to Rowan, and he smiled with her before becoming serious again. Rowan set the cauldron onto the fire and turned to Una.

"I'm going to teach you how to heal a dislocated joint," he told her, and the lesson began.

The ritual was over quickly, and it was a bit different from when Rowan and Tristan had healed Lily's broken ankle all those months ago. The mineral-and-herb brew that bubbled in the cauldron was similar, but this time Rowan had Una use the power in her own willstone to direct the heat of the brew into Lily's shoulder instead of having Lily do it as he had with her ankle.

Una willed the heat to form microscopic fingers of energy, which utilized the elements in the brew to rebuild the damage in Lily's shoulder. Not even witches could create something out of nothing, and having the iron, calcium, and collagen in the brew was essential to create new cells and heal an injury. Energy alone wouldn't do it.

Una understood the principles easily enough, but she had some trouble following through. Her true skill was fighting, not healing, but she managed to pull it off. As they worked, Lily noticed that Rowan's smoke stone took on a slightly reddish hue while Una's nearly black stone could not. Rowan's stone was more flexible than Una's. Lily made a mental note to mark which of her mechanics' stones could change color to fit the different tasks of magic. This was supposed to have been a lesson for Una, but Lily found that she was still learning as well.

"Good job, Una," Rowan said as they packed up their silver knives and their hunks of ore. "You'll—"

Rowan suddenly broke off and stood, his eyes flying to the trees and he unsheathed his long knife.

Lily. Give us strength.

The Woven were on Una and Rowan before Lily could even draw the heat of the fire into her body. Coyote-like shapes burst out of the underbrush and launched themselves at Lily's mechanics. They had impossibly long tails, and when Rowan grabbed one of the Woven by the throat, the snarling creature used that tail like a whip, lashing its tail overhead, and whipping Rowan across the shoulder and back. His wearhyde jacket was slashed open, and blood slicked down his back.

Lily's witch wind turned the breeze into a moaning storm. She was tossed six feet into the air and immediately sent power exploding into Una's and Rowan's willstones. But she didn't stay airborne long.

Lily felt a distinct *presence* react to her display of magic. It was not unlike the fear and awe that she could sense when she heard people scream the word "witch," and then she felt a tearing pain in her left forearm as she was pulled to the ground. A huge white coyote Woven, the largest in the group, pinned her to the forest floor and loomed over her.

No! They have Lily! Caleb, Tristan—help me, brothers! Rowan called desperately in mindspeak.

Lily had no weapon and no idea how to defend herself, so she did as Rowan had done and grabbed the Woven by the throat to keep it from biting her. As she dug her fingers into the creature's neck she felt something hard buried under its skin. Lily pinched the lump between her fingers and felt that odd presence again. She decided that the presence wasn't a mind, but a collective of minds—*inhuman* minds that had no language. The eyes of the pale Woven above her widened, and the idea of distinct smells lit up a quiet, long-forgotten section of Lily's brain. Lily recognized each scent as a being, and each being belonged to this pale Woven.

For half a second, images blurred through Lily's thoughts. She saw Una hanging above her from a tree branch, slashing down at her with a knife. Then she saw Rowan straddling her and pushing a knife into her heart. Then she saw Caleb running her down on horseback. Lily only recognized the dizzying sensation for what it was because she'd felt it once before—when Rowan had taught her how to make a mind mosaic.

Lily suddenly felt an urge to jump to her feet and head toward the place where the sun sets. The pale Woven broke eye contact and wrenched herself away from Lily desperately. She sent out a howl, and her pack retreated into the trees to the west.

Still reeling from having her mind splintered into multiple perspectives, Lily blinked her eyes and tried to steady herself. She placed her palm down hard on what she thought was a wall and heard a thumping sound. When her eyes came back into focus, Lily realized that she was smacking Caleb's meaty chest. He'd picked her up and he was moving her closer to the fire.

"Caleb," she said, smiling through the pain in her left arm. He smiled back, his white teeth gleaming brightly against his dark skin. "It's really good to see you," she said, resting her forehead against his.

"Sorry we're late," he said, hugging her carefully.

Tristan was already bent over Rowan, helping him remove his blood-soaked clothes. He looked up at Lily and smiled warmly. "Hi," Tristan said simply.

"It's good to see you, too," she told him. "Even though I've been seeing you," she added with a grimace. The other Tristan gave her a strange look, but Rowan interjected.

"You'll see in a second, Tristan," Rowan said through a groan as he peeled off what was left of his shredded shirt.

"Who's that?" Caleb asked, pointing to Una. Before she could answer, Breakfast and Lily's Tristan caught up with them, already apologizing before they had even reached the clearing. They had a couple of bruises and some scraped knuckles, but they didn't look anywhere near as banged up as Rowan did. He scowled at the two of them, and probably added a few choice words in mindspeak that Lily wasn't privy to.

Introductions and explanations were made while Una and Caleb put salve on Lily's and Rowan's cuts. Although Lily's bite wounds and the lashing that Rowan had taken cut deep, they were still only flesh wounds. With no broken bones, severed nerves, or torn ligaments to mend, the salve did its job quickly. It wasn't nearly enough time for the two Tristans to absorb the fact that they had just met themselves.

The two Tristans sat across the fire from each other, both of them looking like they'd just seen a ghost. They were mirrors of each other, except that Rowan's Tristan had streaks of red and black paint on his face, indicating that he had become one of Alaric's elite fighters, like Caleb.

Lily knew how disoriented both Tristans must be feeling, but she didn't want to bring up right then what she'd felt when she met Lillian. She was still too emotional about what she saw in Lillian's last memory and she knew that if she focused on it now, Rowan would be able to pluck the thought out of her mind easily. Instead, she thought about the pale Woven.

"Do you guys think Woven can mindspeak?" Lily asked, seemingly out of the blue. Everyone stared at her. "You know, with their relatives if they're pack animals. I'm wondering because that pack of Woven seemed really, like, *together*. Mentally, I mean." The more she talked, the more worried everyone looked.

Caleb finally spoke up. "A good pack animal is part of a whole. He follows his alpha without question. I guess that could look like they're reading one another's minds."

"Well, has anyone ever tried to mindspeak with a Woven?" she asked.

Rowan, Caleb, and the Tristan from this world all shuddered simultaneously like the thought disgusted them.

"No, Lily," Rowan said, his lips tight as if he'd tasted something sour. "The tame Woven in the cities are trained to respond to very subtle cues from their masters. But they don't mindspeak. They can't *speak*, Lily."

"I know that, but mindspeak isn't always speech, is it? Sometimes it's more like a sensation or an emotion that you convey. Or a scent?" She said the last word hesitantly, still trying to describe—even for herself—what she'd experienced. "That's crazy, right?"

Everyone nodded and looked at the fire, relieved that Lily could at least recognize how far out on a limb she'd climbed.

"You've lost a lot of blood," Caleb said sensibly. "And it's normal to wonder if animals can think when they've just outsmarted you with an ambush. Sometimes with the wolf-like Woven packs out west it can seem like what they're doing is planned, but they're only acting on instinct, Lily. They're not thinking or feeling anything."

But Lily *had* felt emotion coming from the pale Woven—fear and awe, even determination. She held her tongue. She didn't know what point she was trying to prove about the Woven, she just felt like there was more to them, some layer that hadn't been peeled back yet. She looked at Rowan, sitting to her right. He hated the Woven and hated it even more when Lily talked about them as being anything but the mindless killers he understood them to be. She decided to let it go for now. Again.

"Lunchtime," Breakfast said cheerfully. He pulled out his pack and started distributing the food he and Tristan had bought before they got into some trouble with the locals. There was some heavy discrimination toward the Outlanders here in Baltimore. Lily supposed there had been discrimination in Salem, too. She just hadn't seen much of it because people there didn't show it when Rowan was around. They were too scared of him.

"Why do people keep thinking I'm an Outlander?" Breakfast asked as he chewed pensively on a sandwich.

Caleb gave Breakfast a complicated look. "It was years ago—I can't be sure. Tristan?" he said, turning to his stone kin for input.

"Yeah?" both Tristans responded. They looked at each other and shared a laugh. The other Tristan spoke first.

"I think that's for me," he said. "What, Caleb?"

"Forget it," Caleb said, still shaken by weirdness of the two-Tristan situation. Caleb turned back to Breakfast. "You look like an Outlander I met once," he said. "But he was a kid back then."

"So some Outlanders are white?" Lily's Tristan asked his other self.

"Sure. Technically, I'm an Outlander now. I gave up my citizenship and joined a tribe," Tristan replied, pointing to his painted cheek.

"Rowan's mom was white," Caleb replied. He smiled to himself. "She had red hair like Lily."

"You remember her," Lily said, surprised. Caleb was four years older than Rowan, and they were from the same tribe. It made sense that Caleb remembered Rowan's mom, even if Rowan couldn't.

"A little. Of course I remember River much better," Caleb said, his face growing sad. "But he fixed my dad's leg once. Hell, he patched together everyone in our tribe at one point or another. He was a great man. Remember my twisted knee that time?" Caleb turned to Rowan, who laughed under his breath.

"The infamous gully incident," Rowan said, smiling in a bittersweet way.

Lily stared into the fire while Rowan and Caleb reminisced over one of their childhood escapades. Una's mind brushed against hers, asking for entry.

Rowan's dad—that crazy man in the barn—was considered a great man?

Everyone loved River Fall, Una. The barn and that sequence of events happened in a different version of this world. There was a huge disaster there that hasn't happened here. Yet.

Una's eyes found Lily's over the campfire.

What are you talking about, Lily?

We're talking about nuclear war, Una. I still haven't decided what I'm going to do about it. And you shouldn't know any of this, anyway.

I can keep a secret. Just please don't tell me I left my world to come to one that's about to turn into the "barn world," okay? I'd rather go back home and do time.

I swear that that won't happen here—not while I'm alive. Now hush. I need to think.

Lily broke contact with Una, sat up straight, and shook herself as if someone had poured ice water down her back.

"What is it?" Rowan asked, looking around for danger.

"Nothing," Lily said, passing a hand over her eyes. "I'm just worn out, I guess."

They finished their lunch and struck camp. Breakfast approached his horse distrustfully. While everyone else climbed on their mounts, Breakfast agonized. He couldn't even bring himself to take the reins.

"What's wrong with him?" Rowan's Tristan asked Lily's Tristan.

"He doesn't like horses," he replied, smiling.

"It's not that I don't like them," Breakfast insisted. "I like them just fine in movies."

"You can ride behind me," Una said, shaking her head.

Breakfast couldn't even figure out how to use the stirrup, and after performing several rather acrobatic near-splits, Caleb finally took pity on Breakfast and boosted him up into the saddle behind Una.

"You've never ridden a horse?" Caleb asked Breakfast, an eyebrow cocked in disbelief.

"I try to avoid any mammal bigger than me. Most of them have really sharp teeth," Breakfast replied.

Caleb got back on his horse, shaking his head. He looked at Lily.

Where'd you get that guy?

I grew up with him.

He has the survival skills of a napkin.

Napkins can be useful.

Great. I can blow my nose on him.

Lily chuckled with Caleb as they rode out. She was no horse-woman either, but at least she knew how to keep her seat. Poor Breakfast nearly slid out of the saddle every ten paces.

"How far to Alaric's camp?" Rowan asked his Tristan.

"At this rate?" Tristan asked, looking back at Breakfast, who was clutching frantically at Una even though they were only going at a walking pace. "We'll get there sometime tomorrow, I guess."

"So soon?" Rowan asked, his mood brightening noticeably. "I thought you made camp outside of Richmond. We're still hundreds of miles away."

"Alaric had the whole tribe start moving north to intercept our group as soon as Lily contacted Tristan and me," Caleb said.

"The sachem wanted Lily safely surrounded by all his braves as soon as possible," Tristan said.

Rowan looked pleased, but Lily hesitated. Alaric was eager to have her back, and Lily was pretty sure it wasn't because he missed her.

There was also a part of her that was insulted. Tristan had called them Alaric's braves, but nearly all of them were Lily's claimed. As she thought of them, she could feel them. Her army. They raced to join her, impatient to be near their witch again. She smiled to herself. They didn't belong to Alaric. They belonged to *her*.

"Juliet's excited to see you," Tristan added. "She wanted to come with Caleb and me, but Alaric thought it would be safer for her to stay with him."

Lily looked at Tristan sharply. Before the battle with Lillian, Lily had asked Alaric to watch over her sister. He'd kept his word, but for some reason Lily wasn't grateful that he had. The word "hostage" kept echoing through Lily's head.

"Lily?" Rowan asked, concerned.

Alaric wasn't her enemy, but she didn't want to make the mistake of assuming he would always be her ally. Especially not if she asked him to dismantle the thirteen bombs. Lily looked at Caleb and Tristan. They both wore Alaric's war paint. Too many of the people she loved were tied to him. She wanted Juliet away from Alaric, just in case.

"I wish she'd come," was all Lily would say.

"You'll see her tomorrow," Rowan said with an indulgent smile. He didn't even suspect that something else was troubling her. Lily was getting better at hiding her true feelings from Rowan. The thought made her sad.

They rode deep into the forest for the rest of the day, always on the alert for Woven, and Lily was exhausted by the time they made camp. She'd spent the night before in agony with a dislocated shoulder, and then she'd lost a lot of blood that morning to the pale Woven. Rowan wasn't in good shape, either. The two of them ate quickly and fell asleep together by the fire while the comforting sounds of their friends' voices lulled them into a dreamless sleep.

CHAPTER
12

THE NEXT DAY THEY STARTED AT THE CRACK OF DAWN. Lily's only comfort was that Breakfast looked even more miserable than she did.

"I wasn't cut out for the cowboy life," he said, rubbing his sore bottom. "But now I know why John Wayne walked like he was holding a grape between his butt cheeks."

They all mounted up, some more stiffly than others, and started cutting a quick and quiet trail through the trees. As they moved south, the temperature rose a little. It wasn't spring yet, but in the area that Lily knew of as Virginia, winter was loosening its grip a little.

Lily kept seeing flashes of an animal with light-colored fur between the thick brush. She couldn't see it clearly enough to know what it was, but she could sense it out there in the trees—keeping close, but not attacking. Lily got the feeling they were being followed by the pale coyote Woven, but she didn't bring it up. She didn't want to get into another argument with Rowan about it. She knew he'd probably say that if Woven were following them, they would have attacked already.

They reached Alaric's camp just after nightfall. As they rode in, Lily could feel a giant weight lifting off Rowan's shoulders. He no longer had to be on guard every second, and he dismounted eagerly to greet old friends and fellow braves. Lily got off her horse slowly. She felt the awareness of her presence rippling through her claimed. They stared at her with a reverence that made her uncomfortable. The first to come forward was a young woman, barely out of her teens.

"You saved my husband's life by making him strong in battle," she whispered. "Thank you, Lady."

"And mine," another woman said. She rubbed her pregnant belly. "And my child's life." The woman said something that sounded to Lily like "meegwetch." Lily didn't need to be told it was a word of thanks.

She smiled and nodded at the women, and dozens suddenly streamed forward, all of them speaking in Sioux or Iroquois or some blend. Lily even thought she heard some French, and an amalgam of languages that she couldn't even begin to fathom washed over her. They offered her things—clothes, beads, salt, and herbs. Overwhelmed and speechless, Lily looked around frantically for Rowan, and finally found him in the gathering crowd.

Please tell them it was nothing, and that right now all I want is a nap.

Let them give you their thanks. What you did by claiming them and climbing on that pyre saved all of their lives. No witch has ever fought with them before.

Yeah, well, I don't deserve to be worshipped for that.

Ah, the price of greatness. Smile and wave, Lily.

Lily wanted to throw something at Rowan's head. He grinned and abandoned her there with Breakfast, Una, and her Tristan to help her accept gifts. In between polite smiles and gracious nods, she watched Rowan as he made his way to Alaric. They embraced each other like brothers and immediately left with the other Tristan and Caleb to talk privately in Alaric's carriage. Lily frowned, feeling like she should be the one to talk to Alaric.

"Lily!" Juliet called as she zigzagged her way through the crowd.

Lily gestured for her sister to join her. "Juliet! I'm dying over here."

Juliet laughed as she hugged Lily. "I'm glad you're back." She pulled away and scanned Lily from head to toe. "You look like hell."

"Save me?"

"Can't. You have to stay here and take it like a big girl. We'll talk later," Juliet said, still grinning from ear to ear. She looked good. Her dress wasn't fancy, and the turquoise beads around her wrists were a far cry from the sapphires she used to wear, but her cheeks were rosy and her eyes shone. Juliet hugged Lily one last time and then negotiated her way through the crowd toward Alaric's carriage. Lily noticed that the guards flanking the entrance let Juliet enter without a second thought.

After an hour of accepting presents, two older women came forward and coaxed Lily and Una away from the crowd. The woman brought them to a steamy tent that had two large tubs of heated water in the middle. The old women started peeling Una's and Lily's dirty clothes off them.

"How do you say *I can undress myself* in Native American?" Una asked, blushing furiously.

"No idea," Lily replied. "I think we're just supposed to go with it."

The woman gathered up the dirty and torn clothes and left Lily and Una to bathe. The soapy water was fragrant with dried flowers, and Una and Lily gladly scrubbed every inch of their filthy bodies before settling in for a long soak.

When they were dried and wrapped in clean robes, the women led Una one way and Lily another. Lily was taken to one of the larger armored wagons, rather than a tent. She noticed that flowers and fruit had been laid on the steps up to the door. It didn't seem right to just step over it all. As she was shuttling the gifts one bunch at a time into the carriage she heard Rowan's voice behind her.

"You can just leave it," he told her. "We'll do that in the morning."

"Good! I'm so tired," Lily replied gratefully. She noticed that Rowan's clothes were different and his hair was wet from a bath. He looked calm and relaxed. His gaze slid up one of her bare legs, still pink and dewy from her long soak.

"Not too tired, I hope," he said quietly. Lily started up the steps, suddenly shy, and he followed her into the carriage, watching the way her body moved under her loose robe. He closed the iron-studded door and came toward her slowly.

Lily looked down at the heap of melons in her arms and back up at him, feeling ridiculous. "My last armload was all flowers, which would have made me look wildly sexy. But of course you show up when I'm carrying cantaloupes."

He dropped his head and his shoulders shook with quiet laughter. "My funny Lily," he said, looking up and smiling warmly at her. He started removing the fruit from her arms one piece at a time.

There was something in his eyes that Lily had never seen before. Lily felt a flood of familiarity from him and understood. This carriage—its furnishings, smells, and its small proportions—were second nature to him. Rowan's apartment in the city was slick and luxurious. It showcased his impeccable taste and appreciation for beauty, but it wasn't where his heart resided, and Lily's world had been foreign to him in every way. Rowan had known since he first arrived there that he didn't belong. But this little carriage with its homespun quilts and worn cushions was his home. He was surrounded by people he trusted and languages he had spoken as a child. He was safe, and it was okay for him to be his most vulnerable self.

Lily's arms were finally empty. Nothing stood between them. Rowan's hands shook a little as he slid them under her robe.

"This is the first time I've felt like I'm not going to lose you," he said, barely touching her as he moved his hands over her body. "I don't have to let you go."

"No," Lily whispered.

He kissed her like they were starting all over again. He didn't assume he knew what she liked, or allow himself to get caught up in the moment and rush to the finish. He listened to the little sounds she made and paid attention to the pressure of her body against his, and when he did finally pick her up and carry her to the narrow bed, it was because she couldn't stand on her shaky legs anymore.

The time it took him to get undressed was just long enough for Lily to get nervous. Rowan lay down next to her, gently holding her against his bare skin, waiting for her to be ready for him.

She met his eyes, her cheeks hot, and a fluttering laugh escaped with her words. "I could be terrible at this," she said.

"Impossible," he replied.

"I've never done it before."

"Well, I've never done it in a bed this small before," he said, sharing a laugh with her. "It's okay. I'm nervous, too."

He took her hand and wrapped it around his willstone with complete trust. Lily could feel what Rowan felt as he climbed on top of her. He was fighting his need so he didn't hurt her, but he knew no matter how careful he was, he was going to hurt her a little anyway.

Lily was present inside both of their sensations. She felt the contrast of their bodies—his drawn tighter than a bowstring, and hers softening under him. There was so much sensation she had to give it back to him. Her willstones had swung around and were lying on the pillow under her head. Lily guided one of Rowan's arms under her back until he cupped her willstones in his hand.

She saw his eyes widen with surprise as they shared their union completely with each other.

They slept and woke and loved each other again, giddy and shaking and filled with a happiness that felt like crying. The cantaloupe came in handy around dawn when both of them were so thirsty and depleted Rowan couldn't wait to find his knife, and broke one open with his hands. He scooped pieces into Lily's mouth with his fingers and they kissed in between bites, melon juice running everywhere until both of them were a sticky-sweet mess.

They talked, each of them laid bare and needing to share more of themselves until they'd given everything. Rowan talked mostly about his father. Everything here reminded Rowan of River, and Lily was hungry for any part of Rowan that he wanted to give her. Lily lay on her side, her head propped up on her hand, looking down on him.

"What did you call him when you were a boy?" she asked. "Dad or Papa or something else?"

Rowan lay on his back, one of his hands reaching up into her hair. He spread the strands between his fingers, watching the copper highlights catch the early morning sunlight. He smiled softly to himself.

"O doe da," he answered. His voice dropped to a whisper. "Da."

Lily's eyes filled with tears. Rowan sat up against the pillows and pulled Lily down on top of him. "I'm sorry. I should stop talking about fathers," he said. "You just lost yours."

"It's not that. I know it *should* be that, but it isn't," she admitted.

"Then what is it?"

"You loved your father. You miss him because he meant the world to you and now he's gone. I've always missed my father because he was never there. Him being dead doesn't feel that much different." Lily looked up at Rowan. "Your loss hurts more, but it's so beautiful. You know that, right?"

Rowan nodded, brushing her cheek. "I'm lucky. He made me who I am and because of that I'll always have him with me."

Carrick slipped into camp while everyone was still throwing gifts at Lily's head. It was easy, actually. This used to be his tribe, and even though Carrick had to alter his face slightly with a glamour so no one recognized him, he still knew how to speak and act like he was one of them. He even saw some familiar faces as he made his way through the tents. That could be useful. In the turmoil of Lily's return, Carrick walked right in.

Carrick knew that going after Alaric was pointless. Even with a glamour he wouldn't be able to get close to the sachem without possessing the right password, but Alaric wasn't Carrick's target, anyway. There was someone at this camp who Lillian wanted even more than Alaric.

Hakan, the builder.

Lillian had no idea where Chenoa and Keme were hidden, but she knew that Hakan had to be traveling with Alaric. The bombs were touchy contraptions, and someone who understood how they worked needed to be there to tend to them. Hakan was one of the few who were qualified, and Lillian knew he'd been traveling with Alaric for two months now. It was finding Alaric that had been the problem.

The sachem had a lot of experience eluding Lillian, who could scour the minds of even the most loyal Outlanders for any scrap of information if she managed to claim them. To protect himself, and the personnel that came with him, Alaric had divided his tribe into thirteen factions. Each faction stayed close to a city and came equipped with a body double who looked like Alaric. No faction, except for the one he traveled with, knew where Alaric really was. But Lillian knew Rowan. She knew he would take Lily directly to Alaric, leading Carrick to his target. They intended to get a lot of information out of Hakan, and Carrick had Lillian's permission to use his unique skill set in order to do just that.

Carrick *wanted* to go after Alaric. His bitterness toward his old sachem ran deep, and it stretched back to when Carrick and his father had been thrown out of the tribe and left to wander on their own. There had never been any proof that Carrick and his father had killed that little girl, but Alaric didn't wait for proof. He knew who'd done it. When Alaric seized power ten years ago, he'd thrown Carrick and his father out of the tribe with only a mock trial. Alaric had left them at the mercy of the Woven—and he'd left Carrick at the mercy of his father. They'd settle that score someday. But tonight, it was Hakan's turn.

It took Carrick a few hours of wandering around the camp to find a carriage that looked heavier than the others. Lillian had told him that the carriage with the bomb would be completely lined with lead in order to contain the poison inside. Carrick checked the wheels, looking for the ones that sunk the deepest. When he found the right carriage, he blended into the shadows to wait.

Lillian had laid eyes on Hakan herself. She'd given Carrick the memory of what Hakan looked like, and when Carrick saw him approaching the carriage just before noon the next day, he simply walked up behind him and hit him on the head.

He'd take Hakan elsewhere to begin the questioning.

Lily and Rowan didn't even try to leave their snug nest until noon, when hunger for something more substantial than fruit drove them out of bed. Rowan helped lace Lily into a soft suede-like wearhyde dress with a fringe-hemmed skirt, and then braided a swan feather into her hair while she wrapped her feet and calves in a lovely pair of beaded moccasin boots. When they finally did emerge and made their way to the inner campfire to eat, Lily couldn't bear to be more than a step away from Rowan. She knew she was underfoot, but she couldn't help it. He'd just have to learn how to cook with her arms around his waist.

"You're alive," Caleb said, grinning at Rowan and Lily as he joined them around the fire. "We thought we were going to have to send in a rescue party."

Rowan smiled while he worked, his face tilted down to hide what might have been a blush, but he didn't take Caleb's bait. The two Tristans had come with Caleb, followed closely by Breakfast and Una, and Lily noticed that her Tristan looked sullen and withdrawn. Rowan noticed, too.

I love having you close, Lily, but maybe for Tristan's sake you should go sit down.

Lily nodded and reluctantly left him to join Breakfast and Una at the table. "What'd we miss?" she asked, tearing off a piece of bread.

"Well, three people came up to me and started talking in Iroquois like they knew me," Breakfast said. "So that was interesting."

Caleb turned to Tristan. "Who *was* that guy who looks just like Breakfast?" Caleb asked, frustrated that he couldn't remember.

"I never met him," Tristan replied.

Caleb let it go, but Lily got the sense that he was saying something in mindspeak, and Lily hoped it had something to do with cheering up. Caleb turned to Lily and changed the subject. "The sachem wants to see you when you're ready."

"Yeah," Lily replied, suddenly frowning. "Whenever he's free is fine, I guess."

"I'll see if he's free now," Caleb replied. He stood and left before Lily could come up with a reason to stop him.

Lily had no idea what she was going to say to Alaric. She stared at the ground, desperately trying to come up with a plan. She felt Rowan brush her shoulder and looked up, startled. He was holding a bowl.

"What's the matter?" he asked.

She shook her head and smiled at him. Lily took the bowl and stared at something that looked a lot like vegan chili, but her appetite was suddenly gone. She couldn't bring herself to say anything. Rowan sat next to her and she leaned against him, not caring if Tristan was uncomfortable with it. A nameless anxiety was building in Lily, and she needed to be close to Rowan to reassure herself that he was real and that he was still with her.

"Lily! It's good to see you again," Alaric said. Lily turned and saw the sachem striding toward her in his halting gait. Juliet was by his side. There was something about the way the two of them leaned toward each other, a slight but ever-present favoring of any place in which the other stood, that gave it away.

Juliet and Alaric were a couple—a happy couple, very much in love. It only made what she had to do more painful, but Lily was past the point of tallying up future suffering. Everyone was about to get hurt.

Lily stood. Nerves fluttered in her stomach. "Can we talk in private?" she asked. She immediately heard seven voices all asking her the same question in mindspeak.

Why?

She held up her hands, blocking everyone out and keeping them out. "I want to speak with the sachem alone," she said.

"Anything you say to me is going to get repeated," Alaric replied, stunned. "I have no secrets from Juliet or from my trusted braves."

"You mean *my* sister and *my* claimed," Lily said, a rueful smile tugging at her lips.

The sachem smiled back in kind. "That's the problem with us, isn't it? Who leads this army?"

"That's not our only problem." Lily stared at Alaric, her breath tight in her chest. She could feel Rowan pressing against her mind. He was confused. She couldn't look at him. She had to shut him out or she'd never do what she needed to.

"The other?" Alaric asked. He crossed his arms over his chest, sizing Lily up.

There was no more hiding from this. The time had come for Lily to take a stand or step back and allow the unthinkable to happen.

Lily faced Alaric. "Has Chenoa finished the bombs yet?"

Alaric's face froze. He couldn't have looked more surprised if Lily had spat in his face.

"Lily?" Rowan asked, taking her by the elbow. "What are you talking about?"

"Do they even know about the bombs that you had Chenoa build at Lillian's college?" Lily asked Alaric, making her voice loud so it was sure to carry. "The bombs that you plan to use to annihilate the Thirteen Cities?"

"What bombs?" Juliet asked, turning to Alaric.

Alaric ignored her, as Lily ignored Rowan, and both of them kept their eyes locked with the other. "How do you know about those?" Alaric asked Lily.

"They don't know, do they?" Lily asked Alaric.

"No. So my question is, how do *you*?" he asked. Everyone else quieted down. "I was very careful when I selected braves for you to claim. None of them know," Alaric said. He had her cornered and he knew it. It was too late to back out now.

Lily looked at Rowan. He was confused and he desperately wanted her to say the right thing so he could go on trusting her and loving her as he had for one perfect night. But Lily couldn't say what he wanted to hear. She smiled at Rowan, allowing herself to love him as deeply as she could for one final second before she destroyed him.

"It's okay, Rowan. I'll be the villain so you can stay a hero," she whispered.

Rowan's face blanched. "Lillian said that to me the day she arrested my father," he said.

Lily nodded. "I know." She faced Alaric. "I know because Lillian and I have been in contact since I went back to my world. She showed me everything that she knows, and she knew about the bombs. Where are they?"

Alaric shook his head. "And put myself completely at the mercy of a witch?" Alaric looked at Lily as if she were crazy. "My people are trapped between the Covens and the Woven. We can't survive against both. One of them has to go."

"You're absolutely right," Lily said. "The *Woven* have to go. They're the true enemy of your people. Lillian only became your enemy when she found out about the bombs." Lily turned to Rowan, hoping that she could still convince him. "The shaman told Lillian about the bombs, and that's why she went after scientists. She was just trying to stop Alaric from blowing up the entire eastern seaboard."

"Then why did she hang my father?" Rowan asked. "He was a doctor, not a scientist." Rowan turned to Alaric. "Did my father know anything about the bombs? Anything at all?"

"Not a thing," Alaric said, meeting Rowan's eyes to show that he wasn't lying.

Rowan turned to Lily, waiting for her to explain. She couldn't. She couldn't tell him why Lillian had killed River first.

"Please. You don't understand what these bombs are capable of," she said. "You saw what happened to the tunnel women—how every cell was destroyed. That was just because they carried the material that makes the bombs. Imagine what will happen if Alaric detonates them. They won't just destroy the cities, they'll destroy your woods, too. We call it nuclear winter, and it will poison this entire world. Please bring the fight to the Woven, not the cities. I'll fight with you." Rowan looked down, shaking his head. Lily turned desperately to Caleb, Tristan, and Juliet. She was grasping at straws. "I'll fuel the braves, but we need to get away from the cities. We need to go west. There's a mystery behind the Woven, something that we don't understand, and we can use it to stop them. The answer is west of the Missouri River—the *Pekistanoui*—I can feel it."

"West?" Alaric exclaimed. Lily had never seen fear in his eyes before, not even on the night they went into battle, but she saw fear now. "You have no idea what lies west of that river. I do." It was Alaric's turn to look to the bystanders for support. And he got it from Rowan.

"The *Misi-Ziibi* is Pack territory, and past the *Pekistanoui* is the Hive," Rowan said, his voice low. "With a witch, we could survive the Pack. But even with a witch's army, the Hive would tear us apart. It's impossible, Lily."

"Has anyone tried?" she asked, refusing to give up. "Rowan, you told me yourself that no one knows that much about the Hive. Has a witch ever fueled an army of Outlander braves to fight them?"

Alaric shook his head. "You're asking my people to fight to the last man, Lily. We are too few to risk that."

"Please try," Lily begged, tears in her eyes. "I'll fight and die with you if I have to, but don't attack the cities, Alaric. Please."

"Lillian swore to find a way to get rid of Woven, and I waited, hoping that she would, because I don't want to use those bombs. I'm not a madman," he said tiredly, and Lily knew he was speaking the truth. Alaric was tormented by this decision, but it was a decision he had already made. "I just want my people to survive. We are on the brink of extinction, and the only way to avoid that now is to attack our other enemy. The cities."

"I won't let you," Lily said, swallowing her tears. She faced him, hating that she had to pit herself against this man, but like him, her decision was already made. "I'll stop you, Alaric Windrider, no matter what I have to do."

"Lillian said the same thing to me once." Alaric looked at Rowan, regret etching deep lines into his face. "I guess this is the day Lillian comes back to haunt both of us."

Rowan took Lily by the shoulders and pulled her away from Alaric. He looked her in the eye, pleading with her. "Remember when I told you that Lillian was a master at controlling minds? That she had years of practice and she could do things that you never dreamed of? She's *using* you. She's twisting your mind so that you'll take up her psychotic cause. But you're just as strong as she is, Lily. You can fight her. You can stop this—"

Lily cut him off. "She's not controlling me, Rowan. She showed me her memories. That's it. I know what she knows, and that's how she convinced me that what she's doing is to protect this world—your world."

"Then show me," he said, his face lifting with hope. "Show me what she showed you and maybe it will convince me, too. We can find a solution. Lillian shut me out, but we can figure this out together. You and me, Lily. Please don't shut me out like she did."

Lily almost did it. She almost opened up her mind to Rowan and let him see everything. But the sound of the boy screaming when River dragged him by his hair to the chopping block filled her ears, and she knew she wouldn't be capable of keeping that from Rowan. No matter how hard she tried to hide it from him, he'd keep digging, searching for why his father had to die, because that's what he really needed to understand. It wasn't about the bombs for him. Lily could easily show Rowan the cinder world and that would explain her opposition to Alaric and his weapon, but it still wouldn't explain why Lillian had killed his father. A half-truth wouldn't work. It was all or nothing.

"I have to shut you out because I love you, Rowan," she said. "But I'm begging you—have faith in me. Trust that I'm doing this for a good reason. For the *best* reason."

His eyes unfocused and he looked through her, like he was remembering something. "And then she started hanging people," he whispered.

There was no warning. His face didn't change. He didn't even really look at her while he did it. Rowan reached out and ripped Lily's willstones off her neck.

Lily couldn't move.

But it didn't hurt. There was no feeling of invasion or violation as there had been when Gideon and Carrick had taken her stones. Rowan was too much a part of her for her willstones to revolt against his touch. She simply couldn't move a muscle, not even to close her eyes. Her will had been separated from her physical body, leaving her as limp as a darted grizzly. She was aware that it was something Rowan was doing to her stones that made her like that. His will was suppressing hers somehow, and he was so powerful she couldn't even blink.

It was difficult to focus on what was happening around her. People started yelling. Juliet was frantic. The Tristans went for Rowan, calling him a traitor and worse. Rowan pulled out his knife and stood over Lily. Caleb put himself in the middle. He was trying to make sense of it all. Alaric defended Rowan, saying that if Rowan had done this to Lillian to begin with, no one would have died. Alaric's painted warriors appeared out of nowhere and the Tristans were dragged away. Juliet cried. Lily hated seeing her sister cry.

Lily felt herself being lifted and carried. Rowan had her, but she couldn't see him because her head had fallen to the side. All she could see was the ground and people's legs as they went past. He put her in a cage and locked it.

He didn't look back.

The farther Rowan took her willstones away from her body, the hazier everything became. It was night and then it was day again. Someone tried to pour water between her lips, but Lily's jaw was clamped shut. Night came, and Lily could have sworn she saw *two* Breakfasts standing in the group that came to stare at her and argue. One Breakfast had the same short hair she'd always seen him with, and the other had long hair that was braided with beads and feathers like an Outlander's. The longhaired Breakfast was pleading with the group. He kept saying that the technology for the bombs had been stolen from another world and that they would create a cinder world like the ones he had seen in his spirit walks. Lily wondered when Breakfast had learned to spirit walk. More arguing followed.

Everyone went away.

The stars were so bright they dazzled Lily's eyes. A shadow suddenly blocked them out. Its hunched shoulders and cocked head reminded her of Carrick. He stood outside her bars, staring at her. He told her not to worry, that he would take care of the bombs. Remove just *one part* and they couldn't explode, he said. The shadow crouched down close to her, holding up a little metal piece. He said a man had died over it. There was blood on his hands. He reached through the bars and touched her cheek, telling her that they were on the same side now. He said that everything had turned. He was her true champion and Rowan had become her torturer. He stroked her cheek. He said that she would learn to love him, that he wasn't so different from his brother after all.

The shadow went away.

Dawn came and turmoil came with it. Arguments thundered over her like a storm cloud. Alaric came to her cage, opened it, and shook her limp body. He was demanding she tell them where the missing thing had gone. He leaned close to her. There was rage in his eyes and he said he wanted her dead before she got to the other bombs. Rowan pulled him away. He said Lily couldn't be responsible. Look at her, he shouted. Alaric calmed down and said that it didn't matter anyway. They'd make another copy of the missing piece as soon as they found Hakan. Rowan looked at Lily for a long time after Alaric went away. His face suddenly changed and he rubbed something off her cheek. Blood, he whispered. He looked around, frightened, and then locked her back in her cage.

Lily's eyes grew dim.

She felt arms lifting her, carrying her away. Everything was dark. Maybe she was dying. She felt a deep, dull pain as if someone were moving the bones around in her body, and then she recognized the warmth of her willstones against her skin. She had her willstones back again. She drew in a gasping breath. She saw Tristan's face. Her Tristan, and everything came back into focus. Tristan attached her willstones around her neck for her.

"She's alive," he said, his hushed voice breaking with relief. She felt water in her mouth and swallowed it, but it wasn't enough. She gulped the water down frantically, tasting a hint of herbs that eased the pounding in her head. She heard another voice whisper to Tristan, and the canteen was taken away. Her eyes slid shut.

Lily realized Tristan was carrying her. Una's and Juliet's faces appeared nearby. They were running through the camp. It was dark out, but Lily could still see some guards watching them pass as they stole away from camp. No one raised the alarm.

Far off, on the other side of the camp, Lily could hear the sounds of a skirmish. Terrified, she listened for the howls and screeches of Woven, but all she heard were human voices fighting with one another. She could feel some of her claimed dying, and clutched at her chest with each heartbreaking loss.

When they got to the edge of camp, Lily saw Caleb, Breakfast, and the other Tristan already mounted and holding the reins of five fresh horses. A handful of braves were with them, speaking in hushed tones. They left as soon as Lily arrived, each of the braves pausing a moment to touch a hand to their chest in a gesture of respect as they passed her.

Her Tristan passed Lily up into Caleb's arms. Caleb's face was bruised and swollen. So was the other Tristan's. They'd both been in a terrible fight. She tried to ask what had happened.

"Later," Caleb whispered, holding her in front of him on his horse. "We've got to get you out of here."

Her mouth was so dry. She looked around. "Where are we going?" she croaked.

Everyone exchanged frightened looks. Lily noticed Juliet's eyes were red and swollen with crying. "West, like you wanted," Juliet replied.

CHAPTER
13

THEY RODE ALL NIGHT. NO ONE SPOKE FOR FEAR OF THE Woven. Lily clung to Caleb, wishing she were back in the cage without her willstones. At least then she wouldn't have to feel anything. Now that she was no longer numb she had to face what had happened.

When she'd made her choice and told everyone that she had been in contact with Lillian, she'd known it might mean she would lose Rowan. Deep inside, Lily had always wondered how he could look at her and not think of Lillian anyway, and when she'd openly admitted that she agreed with Lillian, Lily knew she would be giving him up. She might even have to fight him.

But what he did was worse than fight her. At least in a fight, you have to hear each other's argument. Rowan took away her willstones. He took away her *voice*.

Lily wasn't sad yet. She felt embarrassed and off balance, like someone who'd put her foot down hard, expecting there to be one more step on the stairway, only to stumble in front of everyone. She couldn't stop thinking of the night they'd spent together, and what a fool she'd been to give herself to him. It hit her in waves, alternating between the heat of shame and the chill of disbelief. He knew what had happened to her in the oubliette, and he still did the same thing to her that Gideon and Carrick had done. He'd robbed her of her will.

In the early morning hours, Caleb decided that they'd gone far enough and called a halt to rest the horses and eat. Everyone chewed mechanically, like they had no appetite. It wasn't just fear of what they faced in the west that stole everyone's spirit. They had all lost someone they'd loved. Lily wasn't the only one Rowan and Alaric had turned against.

And poor Juliet—Lily stared at her sister's swollen face and shaking hands. Juliet looked as wrecked as Lily felt, but Lily couldn't cry like her sister. Not yet. Maybe not ever. It had been Lily's decision to listen to Lillian in the first place, and then her decision to take Lillian's side. She had walked into this with open eyes, and she had to keep them open or they could all die out here in the Woven Woods. Crying was a luxury, a release she couldn't afford.

After they'd eaten, Lily felt strong enough to talk. "What happened?" she asked.

"I'll tell her," Breakfast said with a tired sigh. "Well, for starters, I finally found out why everyone kept mistaking me for an Outlander. It's because there's another *me* here."

"He's the young shaman in training that we were trying to locate for you when you were first here," Tristan said.

"He was on a vision quest on the Ocean of Grass," Lily recalled.

"He came back. And I met myself." Breakfast's tone was even, but his expression was still one of shock. "And myself said that he had spirit walked into these places called cinder worlds." Breakfast shook his head to clear it. "Anyway, so Red Leaf—that's his name—came out against the bombs. He said that he'd seen this mistake made on other worlds, and that Alaric would wipe out the Outlanders along with the cities."

"How did the tribe take it?" Lily asked.

"A lot of braves were angry that Alaric hadn't told them about the bombs and that he'd planned on using them without consulting the rest of us," Caleb said. He threw something into the fire in agitation, showing that he was one of the angry ones.

"So that *did* happen," Lily said.

She shivered, realizing that if she hadn't hallucinated seeing two Breakfasts, she hadn't hallucinated seeing Carrick. She rubbed her cheek repeatedly, trying to scrape away any trace of the blood he'd marked her with—as if they'd both been responsible for shedding it.

"Were you conscious while you were in the cage?" Una asked. "Your eyes were open, but Rowan said—" She suddenly broke off, stumbling painfully over Rowan's name. She'd trusted him, too. Una had learned to love Rowan like a brother. It was an honor she'd never given anyone before, and the loss of him had hurt her deeply.

"I wouldn't say I was conscious, but a few things managed to sink in," Lily said quietly. "Keep going."

"So the tribe started to divide," Breakfast said. "One side agreed with the sachem and the other with the shaman. But that's not all."

"Let me guess. Someone disarmed the bomb that Alaric had been concealing at camp and no one knows who did it, right?" Lily said. She nodded, already knowing she was right. "It was Carrick. He came to my cage." Everyone stiffened and Lily raised a hand. "He didn't hurt me, and I'm sure he's long gone. He's Lillian's henchman now, and her main objective for everything—the trials, the hangings, all of it— has been to get rid the bombs and the people who know how to make them. She'll send Carrick after the other twelve bombs before Alaric has a chance to use them."

"Thank God," Una said. It earned her a few sharp looks. "Look, Carrick is a psycho, but he's doing this world a huge service. You three didn't grow up seeing movies about nuclear war like we did," Una continued defensively, aiming her comments at Juliet, Caleb, and the other Tristan. "You have no idea what nuclear fallout is. It'll kill *all* of you, slowly and painfully. Lily. Show them what happened to the tunnel women just for carrying the bomb parts."

Lily did as Una asked, and then waited for Una, Breakfast, and her Tristan to finish answering all of the disbelieving questions before bringing the conversation back to what she needed to know. "You said the tribe started to divide," she said, prompting the other Tristan.

"Caleb and I didn't think it was right to kill everyone in the cities without at least trying to fight the Woven now that we have a witch who's with us," he answered. "Plenty of braves sided with you and your idea to go west and fight the Woven, Lily."

She vaguely recalled Rowan standing up for her against Alaric at one point during the foggy time she spent in the cage. "Did Rowan?" she asked. Her voice was small and pathetically hopeful.

Juliet's forehead pinched with sadness. "No," she answered. "He and Alaric said that the only braves who wanted to go west were the ones who'd never seen the Hive."

Lily sat back, deflated. This wasn't about her broken heart, she reminded herself. She had to focus and think like a leader. Like Alaric would. "How many braves are with me, Caleb?"

Caleb and his Tristan shared a look. "About thirty from Alaric's group. They'll follow us when they can," Caleb replied. "More may come from the other twelve factions once they hear you're back. A lot of them are your claimed, and they all hate the Woven. They may want to join us in fighting them." Caleb's words were optimistic but his tone wasn't.

"What happened while we were leaving camp?" Lily asked. "There was something going on. People were dying."

"Caleb, your Tristan, and I took on Rowan to get your willstones back," the other Tristan said quietly. "We had to fight our way out."

Lily studied their faces. Even under their warpaint, she could see that the other Tristan and Caleb had gotten the worst of it, and her Tristan didn't have a mark on him. She wondered what had happened, but she didn't want to bring it up in case she said something to embarrass her Tristan.

"A lot of Outlanders were angry that Alaric was letting you starve in that cage," Juliet added. "They feel like they owe you their lives so they helped us get away. Even most of the braves that sided with Alaric thought he should let you live."

Lily gave a mirthless laugh, smiling so she didn't start crying. "But not Alaric or Rowan."

"No. Not them," Juliet replied.

Tristan looked up at Lily, like he wanted to say something, but after a moment he looked away.

The conversation was over and everyone went back to finishing supper. Lily crossed her arms over her chest, holding everything inside as best as she could. It was worse than she thought. Rowan would have let her die. A bitter voice in her head said he was just being smart. It was probably easier for him to let her die than to smash his willstone again.

"You should eat," her Tristan said softly.

Lily looked up at him and realized that everyone else was asleep around the fire. She'd lost track of how long she'd been sitting there.

"Really. Finish your food," Tristan urged. He sat down next to her.

She picked up her bowl and swallowed what was in front of her without bothering to taste it.

"I'll keep watch," Lily told him when she had finished.

"You need to sleep," he replied.

She tilted her lips into a bitter smile. "I won't be sleeping for a long time so I may as well make myself useful. I'll wake you if something comes."

Tristan lay down next to her. He stared up at her, worried. "I'm sorry about Rowan," he said. He reached out and laid a hand on her wrist, trying to comfort her. "I'm so sorry he hurt you."

"Go to sleep," Lily replied, her eyes scanning the trees.

Eventually, Tristan fell asleep and Lily was finally alone. She needed answers, and there was only one person who could give them to her.

You used me, Lillian. You had Carrick follow us from my world. Was it because you knew Rowan would take me right to Alaric?

I wanted a man Alaric never lets out of his sight. Hakan, the builder. He knows how to disarm the bombs, and he knows where most of them are. Carrick gave me Hakan, and now I know what Hakan knows.

I can't believe it. I didn't have to say anything to Rowan. I lost him for nothing.

I didn't tell you to tell him, Lily. In fact, I was very careful to never disturb you with my memories when Rowan was near. I didn't want him to accidentally pick up on my presence. I didn't want you to lose him.

Then why have me come back here at all, Lillian, if not to argue your side? You said that was the whole point of showing me your memories!

Yes, I need you on my side, and that's why I showed you my memories. But I never wanted you to tell anyone. In fact, I told you not to.

If you don't want me to argue for you, then why do you need me, Lillian? Why did you kill my father to get me to come back here?

Have you been paying attention to anything I showed you? The shaman told me that no one knows where all the bombs are—I don't even think Alaric knows. But you claimed an army of Outlanders, Lily. Some combination of all those minds must know something. I forced you to come back to this world first to lead me to Hakan, who is one of the three people who knows how to disarm them, and now I need you in this world so you can go into the minds of your claimed and find the bombs that Hakan can't locate.

Alaric said that he was careful about who he allowed me to claim. He said none of my braves even know about the bombs.

It doesn't matter what they think they know. Use your claimed to make a mind mosaic. Someone has seen something, even if they don't know what that something is. Find all the suspicious carriages and tell me where they are. Your claimed don't even have to know you're in their minds.

I just have to violate the privacy of thousands of people who trust me. That's despicable, Lillian.

But it will end the war. Do you want to be the good guy, or do you want to save lives?

I think I hate you more now than ever.

Think of how much you'll hate yourself if even one of those bombs goes off. Think of all the people who are going to die because you're too squeamish to do something you find despicable. Haven't you learned yet? Someone has to be the villain so everyone else can stay alive. Think of the one thing you would never do—that's what you'll have to do in order to end this war. It's what I had to do.

Lily cut off contact with Lillian and stared at the fire, bitterness gnawing at her. Lillian's version of the future was a dictatorship, while Alaric's version was a smoking wasteland. Neither of those worlds were acceptable to Lily.

She saw something dart through the underbrush and instantly stiffened, adrenaline pumping through her veins. Lily opened her mouth to cry out and wake the others, but stopped. The thing in the underbrush was running away. She saw only a long, pale tail as it retreated.

Lily sat back, not completely sure why she had let the pale

coyote Woven go, and saw Juliet's big eyes staring up at her from where she lay. Her sister knew her better than anyone. She also knew Lillian better than anyone.

"How do I do this, Juliet? How do I stop this war?" Lily whispered. "Lillian's still using me. I'm her pawn. She's always two steps ahead."

"That's because you're in her world, where she's in control, and you're still thinking like her," Juliet whispered back. "Don't."

Lily looked at the pale Woven's trail. The underbrush was still moving slightly where it had run away. "Did Lillian ever think to go west?" she asked.

Juliet propped herself up on her elbow and looked at Lily. "Never."

Lily looked back at her sister, and they shared a determined smile. "Good."

Lily stared at a map of what she still thought of as North America, except in this version of the world, North America ended just a little bit past the Mississippi River. Everything west of that was filled in with nondescript cross-hatching, as if to say, *Here, There Be Dragons.* Which, Lily supposed, was entirely possible.

"Okay, so all we have to do is follow this trail we're on and we get to a ferry that will take us across this river?" Lily asked.

Caleb and Tristan exchanged looks.

"Maybe," Tristan replied. "It was there two months ago. According to some."

"My cousin said he saw it still functional three months ago," Dana said. "If the Woven haven't attacked it, it should be fine."

"That's comforting," Una said sarcastically.

They had been riding west for over a week. About forty braves had joined them, making things both easier and harder. There were more eyes on the lookout for Woven, but there were also more mouths to feed.

Dana was one of the people Lily had found in Lillian's dungeon. Lily had freed her, and during the battle with Lillian that had followed shortly after, Dana proved herself to be a good general. As soon as she found out that Lily was back, Dana had joined her with fifteen other braves, but not even she could promise that she would go all the way west. Mostly, she and her braves wanted to be on the other side of the mountains if Alaric proved crazy enough to detonate his bombs.

Dana had been a leader among one of the other twelve factions in Alaric's tribe, and every time Lily regarded Dana for too long, she wondered what would happen if she slipped into her mind. Would she find some bit of information she could pass on to Lillian about the bombs? Lily made herself look away. She'd possessed Dana once to free her sister from the dungeon and had promised never to do it again to anyone. Lily didn't doubt that Dana would try to make good on her promise to kill Lily if she caught her sifting through her mind without permission.

"Why are you guys talking about crossing a river that's miles away? What about *those*?" Breakfast pointed to the Appalachian Mountains looming above them. "We've got to get through those first."

"There are trails and trading posts all through there," Caleb said, shrugging like it wasn't a big deal. "And spring's here. We'll be able to find food." He suddenly wrinkled his brow in worry. "The rivers coming down the mountains might be all swollen with melt water, though. That could be a problem."

"But aren't mountains, like, *high*?" Breakfast asked timorously.

Dana clapped Breakfast on the shoulder. "You'll be alright, little shaman," she said seductively. "I'll catch you if you fall."

Una's lips tightened, and she glared at Dana. Breakfast had become quite the catch since it was discovered that he was the "other Red Leaf." All the people in this world wanted partners with magical talents so their children might inherit those abilities. Dana had made it clear she thought Una had enough power of her own to pass on to a child, and that she should share the wealth where Breakfast was concerned. As for Breakfast, he was not accustomed to his new status as man-candy, and he blushed and dropped his head, deathly afraid of Una's wrath.

The two Tristans could barely contain their laughter. For once, neither of them was the cause of a jealous fight. Mechanics like them were desirable, yes, but spirit walkers like Breakfast were so rare as to be nearly extinct. Goofy little Breakfast had suddenly become a stud. All Lily had to do was train him to spirit walk, and he'd probably have a harem.

Don't rub it in, Tristan, Lily said to her Tristan in mindspeak. *Una's having a rough time with it.*

I know how she feels. It sucks to see someone hanging all over the person you love.

Lily glanced up at him, and he smiled at her in a way that used to make her forget her own name. She quickly went back to frowning down at the map.

"I know this trail," she said. "You only have a part of it here, but in my world it was called the Trail of Tears. This particular route out of the mountains and along this river is the one the Cherokee followed when they were thrown off their land. We—I spent some time looking at it." Lily's voice thickened and she cleared her throat.

Keep it together, girl, Una said soothingly in mindspeak.

Lily took a breath and pointed at some of the *Here, There Be Dragons* cross-hatching. "I know every step west through here and along the Missouri River."

"So you know the way," the other Tristan said. "The geography of our worlds is the same, right?"

"Mostly," Tristan told his other self. "Our world did a lot of dam building for hydroelectric power out west, but not before the Trail of Tears."

Lily nodded to confirm what Tristan was saying. "It's the same. And there's more water along the northern route than the southern."

The Outlanders watched Lily trace her finger across the unknown lands in silence. She could feel their fear.

"It's far, and it will be dangerous, but we need to get here," Lily said. She brought her finger all the way over, past the cross-hatching, to where there was nothing on their map but blank paper. Lily picked up a pencil and drew the western coastline in for them. None of the native Outlanders had any idea their continent was so big. She went back and started filling in some of the major details from her willstone-enhanced photographic memory. "These are the Rocky Mountains. They're even higher than the Appalachians. This here is all desert. We call this spot Death Valley. It's one of the hottest, driest places in the world."

Lily. Quit while you're ahead, Tristan whispered in her head. *They're all backing out.*

I know, Tristan. But it's better they know the truth.

"I never said this was going to be easy, but at least I know what's out there," Lily said. "I know where the rivers are, the lakes, and the mountains. I know how other people from my world have gotten across the West." She looked around, meeting everyone's eyes. "We can do this."

Lily left out the most glaring difficulty they faced. In her world, the great explorers didn't have to fight off the Woven all the way to California, but at this point the Woven went without saying.

The meeting ended and the sky darkened. While the rest of the group went off to get something hot to eat, Lily went to the perimeter to stand watch. She pulled a jar of pickles out of her pack and munched on them as she looked out into the gathering dark.

"Guard duty has become your new favorite thing, hasn't it?" Tristan asked.

Lily turned to see him coming toward her and smiled up at him. She could still tell the difference between him and his double, although Tristan dressed like an Outlander now. He wore dark wearhyde from head to toe and his hair was getting longer, but there was still something about the way that he looked at her—a familiarity that only they shared—that set him apart from the other Tristan.

"Beats the hell out of lying on the ground, not sleeping," she said.

"At least let yourself *lean* against something, Lil. You don't have to punish yourself forever, you know," he said.

"I'm not—" Lily started to argue, and stopped.

He was right. She had been punishing herself. She'd lied to Rowan for weeks by hiding the truth about Lillian, and although she had no idea how she could have handled the situation differently, she still felt guilty. She'd broken his heart, and it was the look he'd had on his face while she'd done it that kept her up at night.

"Okay. So I'm punishing myself," Lily admitted.

Tristan could tell she didn't want to talk about it and led her over to a large tree. He tugged on her hand until she sat down next to him and they rested their backs against the tree trunk, their shoulders touching.

"You ran that meeting well," Tristan said after a long silence. "You're a good leader."

Lily let out a doubtful laugh. "I think I just lost half the group with that little speech."

Tristan nodded. "Maybe that's a good thing."

"Yeah. Less blood on my hands."

"Don't say that. I only meant that you're being honest, and that you'll weed out the less committed that way." Tristan turned to her, his face serious. "You're the best chance these people have ever had for survival, and they know it. Whether they go across country, or stay huddled up against the cities, the chances are that most of them are going to die young because of the Woven anyway. At least with you they can take a few hundred down with them." He suddenly smiled, his blue eyes glinting. "And fighting with a witch inside you is *definitely* more fun."

Lily laughed and shook her head. "You're enjoying this too much—running around the woods, killing things."

"It has its perks," he whispered, staring at her mouth.

Lily looked away, and cast around for something else to focus on. Tristan leaned back and let the moment pass so effortlessly that Lily wondered if she'd imagined a tension that wasn't there. She felt him stiffen and followed his intense gaze out into the brush. Lily saw movement and a streak of pale fur. Tristan leaned forward to stand, but Lily put a hand out to stop him.

"She's not going to attack," Lily said quickly.

"*She?*" Tristan said, every muscle in his body still clenched for action. "You know that Woven?"

"She's not a threat." Lily sighed and ran a frustrated hand through her hair. "She led the coyote Woven pack that ambushed us outside of Baltimore, and she's been following us since then. The thing is, every time she's had a chance to kill me, she hasn't. I can't explain it, but there's something different about her. She's a leader somehow, an alpha. I haven't figured it out yet, but there's more to the Woven than just mindless killing. At least with a select few."

Tristan's eyes widened like he was worried about her. "A select few? Like certain breeds, or certain Woven?"

"I don't know, Tristan. The more I watch the Woven, the more

I think this world has been dealing with them the wrong way. Maybe we shouldn't be out to destroy them all." Lily leaned back and purposely clunked her head against the tree trunk. "But I have over thirty braves who are following me because I promised I was heading west to do just that. Do you think I've lost my mind?"

"Yeah," he said casually. "But that pale Woven isn't attacking. If she doesn't attack us, why should we attack her?"

Lily grinned. "Don't let Caleb hear you say that."

"Right?" Tristan said, smiling back at her. "The Outlanders hate the Woven on, like, an irrational level."

"Irrational—unless you've grown up watching them kill people you love, I guess," Lily added quietly.

"Maybe it's a good thing we didn't grow up here," he said, struck by an idea. "Maybe it's time someone with fresh eyes looked at the Woven problem. Studied their behavior."

Lily crossed her arms and leaned back. "Like a science experiment."

"Why not? Someone should be studying them instead of just killing and burning them," Tristan said, leaning back against the tree like Lily. "They're treated like vampires that'll rise from the dead if you don't utterly destroy them. It's bananas."

"You're right. We need to start thinking about them scientifically, not superstitiously," Lily decided. "We shouldn't be slaughtering every one we see. It's a waste of energy, anyway. I'm going to tell everyone to only fight the Woven that attack us, and the next time anyone kills one, I'll have the carcass brought to us so we can study it."

Tristan sat back up. "Are we finally getting you to dissect?" he teased. "I thought your vegan sensibilities were too refined for that."

"I was *not* going to dissect a cat, Tristan," Lily huffed, angry that he'd bring up a debate she'd had with her physiology teacher nearly two years ago. "And by the way, I did just as well as you on that anatomy exam *without* dissecting. So there. And this is different, anyway. These are Woven, not cats."

"Mr. Carn would freaking *love* this," Tristan said, still chuckling to himself as he leaned back against Lily's shoulder.

"It's good to have you on my side," Lily said, thinking about Rowan and how he'd fought her on every question she'd posed about the Woven.

"I'm always on your side," Tristan said as if it were obvious.

And it was. He'd always stuck up for her, always defended her. He was here when she was taking the biggest risk in her life by dragging a bunch of people across a continent to follow a hunch. Rowan wasn't.

"Well, thanks," Lily said, swallowing the lump in her throat.

Tristan smiled to himself, staring at the trees. He didn't need to answer her.

They reached the trail through the Appalachians with five fewer braves than they'd started with. One had been picked off in the night by the Woven, and the other four had turned back. Lily wasn't angry. Climbing the mountains wasn't going to be easy with a large group; and the fewer she had to fuel, the easier it would be on her. As it was, Lily found it hard to resist any of their faint whispers for strength. She *wanted* to fuel them, maybe a little too much, but it was still energy spent. Her tribe was making great time because of Lily's strength, but it left her tired all the time. Just looking up at the mountains they had yet to cross was enough to make her want to cry.

She felt Tristan come up behind her as she stared at the looming peaks, which were turning from a golden pink to lavender as dusk descended.

"'Purple mountain majesties,'" she mumbled, finally understanding the true meaning of that line from "America the Beautiful."

"They do look a bit purple," Tristan answered. "And you don't have to carry us up them, you know."

Lily turned and saw the painted streaks on his cheeks, identifying him as the *other* Tristan. He was holding out a bowl of some kind of salty, grain-based concoction that she'd been having for dinner while on the trail. She took the bowl and smiled up at him, struck by the thought that she hadn't had much time alone with this Tristan. In fact, Lily almost felt as if he'd been avoiding her. He turned to leave her to eat her salty porridge alone, but she put out a hand and stopped him.

"Sit with me," she said, offering him the patch of dirt to her right. He joined her, but was careful to leave a respectful gap between them. He was keeping his distance, and she couldn't figure out why. "How have things been for you since . . . well, you know." Lily tipped her chin at her Tristan, who was busy brushing down his horse.

"You mean since I met myself?" He gave a shaky laugh, and then furrowed his brow. "It's the strangest thing that's ever happened to me. It's almost like my shadow came to life and started talking to me."

"But it can't be all bad. You two are spending a lot of time together," Lily said. "It seems like you're always together now." She watched his face change with every racing thought and found that she was smiling to herself, enjoying how vulnerable his mobile features made him. It was something that both the Tristans shared. They both wore their hearts on their sleeves.

"It feels natural to be around him. Like I finally have someone who totally understands me." Tristan looked Lily in the eye. "Rowan and Caleb were closer to each other than they were to me because they're both Outlanders, and they've known each other longer. I've never had anyone. Until now."

"My experience of meeting myself has been a little different," Lily said, grimacing. "Do you two share memories with each other?"

"All the time," he said, nodding slowly. "We didn't decide to start doing it — it just happened that way. It's easier, I guess. We don't have to explain anything to each other. We just show it."

"It must be strange to see his memories and see the world that he and I come from."

"Yes and no," he said, studying Lily's face. "One thing is consistent, though. You're everywhere in both of our versions of the world." Lily felt her cheeks heat up and looked down at her porridge. He laughed playfully. "For me, it was more a worship situation. But not for him. He's always loved you, you know. Even when he messed up."

"I know," Lily whispered. "Is that why you're keeping your distance? Because of him?"

"Because I'm used to keeping my distance from you," he said, his smile a little sad. "You've always been off-limits for me, but this time I don't resent that. He loves you more."

The way he said *more* made Lily think he meant more than anyone—including Rowan. Before she could ask him to clarify, the other Tristan got up and left her to stare at the mountains that were turning midnight blue in the gathering dark.

Two days later they began their ascent. Caleb assured Lily that the trail they were taking wouldn't require them to be roped up, but he was already making allotments for lost pack animals and supplies. There was no doubt that the terrain was going to get steep and rough.

"And the Woven are different in the mountains," Dana added as they dismounted and started their ascent. "More raptors. Remember to look up every now and again."

Lily tilted her head back and scanned the skies. She'd never seen a raptor Woven, and she hoped she never did.

"I wouldn't try to study raptor behavior yet," the other Tristan said with raised eyebrows. "I'd just duck for now."

Since their talk under the tree, Lily and her Tristan had spent every guard duty taking notes on what they observed about the Woven, and they had dissected three of them together, but so far they hadn't found a pattern in either the Woven's behavior or their biology. Lily hadn't given up hope yet that she would find something. She and Tristan had to work much too fast when they dissected, and a lot got missed. Woven organs were so full of toxins that they seemed to dissolve from the inside out as soon as the creatures were dead, and Lily still believed that she would find something if only she got a fresh-enough sample to work with, which was proving difficult. The fourth Woven carcass that was brought to them was so far gone there was no point in putting on gloves to take a look.

"It's useless. You have to start dissecting it immediately in order to find anything that hasn't been corroded," her Tristan said in frustration.

"It's like they've got a self-destruct button," Lily added, her brow knitted together.

"And what doesn't dissolve gets eaten by other Woven. One dead Woven brings dozens, like they're their favorite food or something."

Lily turned to Tristan, shaking her head. "That doesn't happen in the natural world."

Since then, Lily had told her braves not to bother bringing her any Woven that had been dead longer than a few minutes. Secretly she knew that if she really wanted to see what made the Woven tick she'd either have to dissect one still alive or kill one herself, which no one would allow. If she got hurt, they were all vulnerable.

The first day up the mountain her tribe made record time, but by the time twilight was falling, Lily was dead on her feet. Juliet came alongside her as they toiled up a steep hill to the campsite.

"You shouldn't keep giving them extra energy," Juliet said. "Save your strength for yourself."

Lily smiled at her sister and shook her head. "If I lie down without being completely exhausted, I think about *him*. And then I don't sleep at all."

Juliet looked away, her face in shadow. "Isn't it odd? They hurt us, but now that they're gone, we beat ourselves up even more. Why do we do that?"

"I don't know," Lily admitted. "Maybe we think we deserve it." They both let the conversation drop. Neither of them were ready to talk deeply about Rowan and Alaric yet, and they each got back to work. Work was good—it kept them both glued together.

The days passed, and the higher Lily's party climbed, the colder it got, taxing the tribe even more. Icy, rotten snow still clung to the edges of the trail, but fresh green shoots and bright blossoms grew between the patches of snow. It gave the ponies something tender to eat, though they rarely dared to duck their heads. The mountain slopes were eerily quiet, setting both the humans and the horses on edge. Occasionally, Lily saw a normal deer, or a normal hawk, its wings spread wide as it hung on an updraft, but there were fewer normal wild animals in this world than she would have thought. The ones that she did see were the furry burrowing kind, although once she did catch a glimpse of puma far away on another slope.

"Where are the regular animals?" she asked Dana after spending a morning searching fruitlessly. "The non-Woven kind?"

"They're around, but they steer clear of Woven," Dana whispered back. "Which means there are Woven nearby right now, so lower your voice."

As she watched her footing in the treacherous slurry of rock, ice, mud, and water, Lily saw a great shadow blanket the ground. At first she thought it must be a storm front rolling in, and then she felt her Tristan tackle her from behind and cover her body with his.

"Raptor," he whispered, his lips brushing the edge of her ear.

She heard the horses whinny and paw at the earth, ready to bolt. Lily turned under Tristan until she could see up and caught her breath. Circling above them, still hundreds of feet in the air, was something the size of a small aircraft. She saw the wings beat once lazily and it climbed up onto a higher updraft and flew away, as if it sensed it had been spotted.

"It's enormous," Lily said, still unable to completely grasp what she was looking at

Caleb crouched down next to Lily and Tristan and shaded his eyes to look up. "They can carry a full-grown man away in their talons," he said. "They just swoop down, and all you hear is a shout that fades away, like someone jumping off a cliff."

"How many times have you crossed the mountains, Caleb?" Breakfast asked.

Lily repositioned herself and saw Breakfast pinned under Una the same way she was pinned under Tristan and she gave him a weak smile in camaraderie.

"Only twice before, to get to the buffalo-hunting grounds. I'm not much of a buffalo hunter. Rowan and his dad used to go every—" Caleb suddenly broke off and looked down, his brow furrowed.

Lily knew she was holding her breath and forced herself to let it out. Every time she heard Rowan's name it knocked the wind out of her—out of all of them. It was like he was still with them, riding on the currents above them and casting a shadow upon the whole group.

Over the next few days as they crossed the mountains, Lily's neck got sore from constantly scanning the sky. She wasn't even aware that she was doing it half the time. Fear would slink in every few paces, and she'd have to glance up. The raptor stayed with them, biding its time, and waiting for the moment when they got careless. It got close enough once that Lily could make out its bald head and scaly talons. The greasy black color of its feathers reminded her of a giant buzzard. Caleb had told her that the hooked beaks had teeth. After that, Lily pictured a feathered pterodactyl when she thought of it. The one consolation was that raptors couldn't hunt at night. But that was when the lion Woven came out, and Lily's tribe traded an aerial terror for a terrestrial one.

The raptor got one of the pack ponies on the fifth day in the mountains. They all felt a pounding rush of wings, saw a flash of greasy black feathers, and the pony, the extra tents, and the grain it was carrying disappeared in one swoop.

It was the lions that got one of the braves. He was picked off so quickly, he didn't even have a chance to scream.

Lily noticed that there was a kind of begrudging respect that the Outlanders reserved for the Pride, the Pack, and the Hive that went hand in hand with a deeper kind of hatred. It was a personal hatred they felt, one that outstripped the disgust and loathing they seemed to feel for the insect, simian, or reptilian type of Woven. Of course, Lily wanted to ask either Caleb or Dana why that was, but the time couldn't have been worse for questions—not when the loss of one of her claimed was still so near.

At first the group didn't dare go out into the brush to try to fight the Pride for the body. It was too dark to risk it, and the brave was already dead anyway. But as the night wore on and the tribe had to listen to the lions snarling and snapping at the other as they fought over the feast, it wore away their morale, and at Lily's patience.

"The Pride is too smart to attack us head on. We've got too large a group," Dana told Lily as she huddled miserably inside her jacket. The dead brave had been one of hers. She'd never liked Lily's command that they only kill attacking Woven to begin with, and Lily could feel resentment building in her. Dana's whole point in joining her was to kill the Woven, not study them. "They'll follow us like we're a walking icebox, picking us off one at a time," Dana grumbled.

Caleb grunted his assent and threw another log on the fire, trying to drown out the sound of a human being eaten. "We need to get out of the mountains," he said. "With a raptor above and the Pride all around us, we're sitting ducks."

Lily could feel the hatred her tribe harbored for the Woven building with every growl from the Pride. She felt her tribe's anger seeping into her. She didn't want to be merciful and fight off only the ones that attacked anymore. She wanted them all to die. Lily pulled the heat of the fire into her skin. A witch wind moaned, silencing the lions.

"Kill them," she ordered.

Enflamed with Lily's strength and anger, Caleb, the Tristans, Una, and Dana stood up from around the fire and rolled into the darkness like a cloud of deadly smoke.

Leave one alive, Lily whispered in her Tristan's mind. *Dana said the lions were smart.*

What are you going to do with it?

I'm going to run a little experiment.

Lily could hear sounds of a skirmish, but it was over quickly and none of her braves were injured. It wasn't a fair fight with a witch fueling one side, and Lily repressed a twinge of regret before thinking of the brave she'd lost. Then she didn't regret a thing. A few hisses, a few shouts, and then she heard her Tristan's voice in her head again.

It's a female. She's badly injured.

Lily released the loop of power and her witch wind died,

allowing her to drop to the ground and go to Tristan. Caleb and Una had joined him, and they were looking from Tristan to the injured Woven, confused.

"Just finish her off," Una said. "She's suffering."

"No. Hold her down," Lily countermanded as she strode through the brush.

She got close enough to clearly see the massive, leathery body of the mountain lion Woven. She was twice the size of a regular lion and she had the rounded shoulders and sloped back of a saber-toothed tiger, but her hide was not covered in pretty striped or golden fur. It was bare, thick, and nearly armored, like a rhino. Her eyes were different, too—rounded instead of almond-shaped. Lily leaned in, looking the Woven in her all-too-human eyes.

"Don't get that close!" Caleb chided, pulling her back. "Tristan, kill that thing."

"No," Lily insisted. "Hold it steady."

The Woven struggled under Tristan's and Una's hands, but it couldn't move. Her back was broken and she could barely raise her head. Lily grabbed her neck and felt the skin along her throat. She could hear Dana and Caleb protesting, but tuned them out. Her fingers found a lump at the notch in the Woven's collarbone. She pinched the lump through the skin with the tips of her fingers and looked the Woven in the eye.

Lily felt a mind there, shying away from hers. She delved deeper and reached through the Woven until she found the suggestion of other minds attached to this one, the way a shadow is attached to a body. Those minds weren't there anymore, but the shape of them was. Lily realized the shadow minds were the dead of her Pride.

As the Woven heaved her last breath, Lily felt a surge of emotion directed at her, coming from the Woven. It wasn't anger or animal terror. It was a complicated emotion she could only describe as defiance.

"Give me your knife," Lily said, holding her hand out to Una. Una gave her knife over, and she cut around the lump.

"Your hands!" Dana warned as stinging fluid landed on Lily's fingers. "Woven turn acidic after death," she added needlessly.

Lily ignored the sting that quickly turned to an itch and then a burn, and dug around inside the pocket she had cut until she extracted the root of the lump.

"Water, quick!" Caleb said, and started rinsing the acid off Lily's hands.

When all the acid was gone, Lily rushed to the campfire to see what she had extracted. It was a crystal, only slightly corroded around the edges. Everyone gasped.

"I got it out in time," Lily said. "The acid their organs release when they die didn't have a chance to destroy it."

"That's a willstone," Tristan said. A long silence followed his statement.

"What does this mean?" Breakfast asked quietly.

"I have no idea," Lily replied.

After another week, they made it to the foothills on the other side of the Appalachians. The Woven had kept their distance after the incident with the lions, and with no attacks to fight, Lily's tribe traveled swiftly.

Although the respite was welcomed by most, it frustrated Lily. She desperately wanted to study the Woven and get some answers to her questions. Debate over the Woven raged among the braves. They could accept that the pack hunters—especially the wolf Woven out west—used willstones to communicate in some basic way, but they all swore up and down that no one had ever seen a Woven do any kind of magic.

"They're not that intelligent," Dana argued. "And they're scared of fire. If they had crucibles and witches among them, wouldn't they be attracted to it?"

Lily couldn't argue with that, but still, the notion that the Woven had willstones inside their bodies disturbed her. It seemed as if the willstone had grown inside the lion Woven as if it were a part of her, like another organ. Not even humans were *that* bonded to their willstones. Lily needed to know what the Woven used their willstones for, if they used them at all.

Lily spent more time on guard duty desperate for a glimpse of them. Occasionally, she would catch a flash of pale fur in the distance and she would be tempted to rush out and chase it, but something always held her back. Lily had a sense that the apparent cease-fire between their two species was more than just coincidence, and she didn't want to make the mistake of thinking these creatures were her friends. Just because the pale Woven hadn't attacked the main group didn't rule out the possibility that she would pick off strays that wandered too far from the campfire.

They followed a cold, fast-flowing stream of melt water out of the mountains for another week. The small streams fed larger and larger tributaries until they reached what Lily knew of as the Ohio River.

"I've never been to Ohio," Breakfast said, staring out at the sunset gracing the vast tracts of open land that lay before them.

"I don't think it looks like this in our world," Una said, smiling.

"Yeah, pretty sure it doesn't," Breakfast agreed. "Probably a freeway right here. Or a mall."

"Right? And it'd be one of those nonsensical malls that had a tire shop right next to a nail salon." Una's face fell. "I'd kill for a mani-pedi," she said mournfully.

Lily and her Tristan shared a smile. He threw an arm over her shoulder. "This is the weirdest road trip ever," he said. "Not what I imagined I'd be doing this spring."

"We'd be graduating right about now," Lily said, struck by the idea.

"Yeah," he said, his eyes drifting across the view. "The whole senior class would be signing yearbooks and saying good-bye. Well, most of us would be, that is."

Lily thought about Scot for the first time since she'd left her world, and her homesickness intensified. She couldn't go home. None of them could. They were all remembering that—and the people they'd left behind.

"Who knew Ohio was so gorgeous?" Breakfast said cheerfully. He never let the group wallow for too long.

Una shook her head at him, a tender smile on her face. "My bighearted boy," she said, and gave him one of her rare public kisses.

Lily became intensely aware of the weight of Tristan's arm across her shoulders and the warmth of his body against hers. She stole a glance at him. His hair was longer, and his skin was tanned from wind and sunshine. He was leaner now, but just as strong as he ever was. He looked rougher, and she realized that somewhere along the way, her Tristan had stopped appearing and behaving like a charming but irresponsible boy. He'd stopped being the guy who'd cheated on her, and had become a man. The change suited him.

Tristan caught Lily staring at him and glanced down shyly. "Come on. Let's give them some time alone," he said, and led Lily back to the campfire and the chatter of friends. Over the next few nights, Tristan caught Lily staring at him over the flames, and he wasn't the only one.

Una became particularly interested in the thickening atmosphere between Tristan and Lily, and brought it up one afternoon when they were alone and stuck with dish duty by the river.

"So, what's up with you and Tristan?" Una asked.

Lily scrubbed a crusty pot with a little more force than necessary. "Nothing. I'm just looking," she replied.

"He is easy to look at," Una said with a grin. "You know, no one would blame you if they saw him coming out of your tent in the morning."

"That's not going to happen, Una."

"I'm just saying." Una raised her soapy hands in surrender.

Lily paused in her work and looked up at Una. "It's nice to be wanted, but I'm not ready. Would you be ready to move on to another guy if Breakfast hurt you?"

"Immediately," Una said quickly. "I find another guy and get him into my tent right away. But I'd never move on."

Lily smiled in understanding. "I can't do that, Una."

They left the mountains behind and were able to travel much faster. As they rode west, they ran into other small tribes, some heading to the Ocean of Grass to hunt buffalo and others hunting for minerals and ores that trickled down with the mountain streams.

"Most of the rivers have been picked clean," Caleb said as they parted company with a hungry tribe that was little more than four or five family groups clinging to one another. Juliet had given them a small pot of healing salve for basically nothing, as they had nothing to trade. "But no one wants to go into the mines," he said, shifting in his saddle and stifling his compassion. "I don't think they're going to have much of a choice, though."

"Where are the mines?" Lily asked.

"Back in the hills," the other Tristan said. "They mine coal, iron, zinc, and other minerals that the cities need and that Outlanders generally don't. Only the most desperate go down into them."

"Are there Woven down in them?" Lily asked.

"Woven don't go underground," Juliet said. She looked at her and held up a hand in surrender before Lily could comment. "No one knows why, exactly. But I'm sure you'll figure it out."

"The mines are dangerous in other ways, I'm guessing. Are there a lot of cave-ins?" she asked.

Rowan had mentioned the mines once before and how the cities exploited the Outlanders by paying them a pittance for the ores they sold after all the hazardous work they did. The way Rowan had talked about the mines made it seem like most Outlanders would do anything to avoid them. Lily didn't bring Rowan into the conversation. It had been over a month since she'd last seen him, but it didn't matter. She still felt like he was near.

Caleb sat tight-lipped and shifted uncomfortably again in his saddle. "Yes, there are a lot of cave-ins, bad air, you name it. It's hell down in the mines. I spent a season in them after I dropped out of training as a mechanic at the Citadel," he said quietly.

Lily looked at Caleb, surprised he'd mentioned the Citadel. He rarely spoke about his training as a mechanic. He'd left everything but warrior magic to Lily's other mechanics, and avoided assisting her in the rituals to make clean water, cleansers, or medicine for the group. Lily sensed a dark memory behind his dislike for the rituals, and she wished he'd talk about it. She got the terrible feeling that the witch or crucible who trained him had mistreated him in some way.

Lily saw Una staring at Caleb with wide, sad eyes and wondered if the two of them had more in common than she was privy to. She didn't pry. Keeping the peace between so many telepathically connected individuals meant that they all had to give one another space and know when to back off a subject. Lily's inner circle of Juliet, the Tristans, Una, Breakfast, and Caleb would sometimes go days without speaking and purposely put a lot of physical distance between themselves on the trail. Not because they were arguing, but because they needed a break from always having someone so close to them, brushing up against their minds.

The rest of the braves needed their space as well. While they craved Lily's strength and her presence, it was the first time any of them had spent so much time around a witch. Many of them found it hard to adjust to having her in their minds and none of them were accustomed to sharing their headspace with someone who could potentially possess them. It set them on edge. Tempers ran high and the trail seemed to get longer every day.

Lily started to understand why witches lived in citadels, separated from the rest of their claimed for most of the day. She had become a sounding board for everyone's emotions, and more often than not, even non-stone kin were affected by one another's moods because they were connected through her. Lily needed a buffer, but there was no way to seclude herself while they all rode on horseback across the ever-flattening terrain.

CHAPTER
14

CARRICK BARTERED HIS LAST BEAVER PELT FOR A SACK OF grain. It was a small sack, but he'd have to make do. There were still two bombs left for him to locate and disarm. Hakan, the builder, didn't have any idea where to start looking for them and Carrick had to make his supplies last for as long as his search took. The money and first-class train passes Lillian had given him had made his trip between the cities downright enjoyable, but Carrick was in the wild now. City money wouldn't get him grain or beans out here.

At least the winter hadn't been too harsh and some of the smaller family groups Carrick encountered still had stores of food they could trade. Some didn't, of course. Being an Outlander often meant you went hungry, no matter what the winters were like.

Now, if only Lillian had given him some witch's medicine, then he could have bartered for more than just one sack of grain. He could have even gotten some dried peaches or a jug of maple syrup. Witch's medicine was just about the most valuable thing there was in the Outlands. Carrick would ask her for it next time he was back in Salem, which probably wouldn't be for a while yet.

With Lillian's help, he'd beaten all of Alaric's messengers to the bombs, but he still had two to go and Lillian had made it clear that even one bomb was too many. She'd shared a brief glimpse of a cinder world with Carrick to motivate him, but he didn't care much one way or the other. Cinder world, not cinder world, what was the difference? People had always killed each other, and Carrick couldn't see that he'd be worse off if one of the bombs detonated, as long as it detonated far away from him. He might even do better, he figured. Cinder worlds were where men like Carrick—men who weren't squeamish and knew how to take what they wanted—could run the whole place. One thing kept him motivated, though. He'd grown to crave the power with which his witch supplied him, and in the cinder worlds witches were done in first. Lillian wanted the bombs defused, and as long as he did what she said, he knew that she'd keep sending him those heady rushes of invincibility.

For as long as she lived, that is. The last time he'd seen her she looked worse. Her skin had a green tinge to it, and her eyes burned with fever. Carrick didn't think she'd last longer than a few more months—maybe a year at best—but he took comfort in knowing that there was still Lily. She was fresh and healthy. Carrick spent many hours thinking of her and her three willstones. Lily had been his first taste of real power and it had been the sweetest. Someday, he promised himself. First, he had to deal with his half brother.

Carrick got swiftly back on Rowan's trail after making his trade. Again, Rowan was moving away from the cities. The mountains would cause problems with his connection to his witch. Lillian was special, Carrick knew that, and she could keep the connection with her claimed over vast distances, but granite was granite, and not even she could penetrate that if there was enough of it. He didn't like the thought of losing Lillian's strength. He told Lillian in mindspeak that he didn't think Rowan was leading him to the two unsecured bombs anymore, but she'd still wanted Rowan followed and Alaric's plans for him discovered.

Carrick didn't know what Alaric was using Rowan for anymore now that Lily was gone. If anything, with Lily's possible control over his mind and body, Rowan was a security threat to the sachem. After watching them for over a week, he'd realized that Alaric and Rowan were stone kin, and as such their private discussions were beyond even his most cunning attempts at eavesdropping. That had come as a surprise. It was rumored that Alaric had no stone kin. Lillian had wondered how long that had been going on, and she doubted if anyone knew about it. Not even Lily.

Something had happened between Rowan and Alaric—maybe it had been a fight, or maybe it had been an order—and then Rowan had left Alaric's tribe unimpeded and in the middle of the day. Lillian sent out other spies to find either Chenoa, Keme, or the bombs, and she sent out Carrick to follow his half brother. Carrick was the only one of her spies suited for that task. He could still feel his brother, even though Rowan had buried their connection so deep even Carrick couldn't sense it anymore. That didn't matter. Their blood bond wasn't what Carrick followed now.

Carrick knew everything there was to know about suffering. It was his one true gift. After a childhood spent sending off wounded animals to drag themselves panting and whimpering with pain into the darkness, he even knew how to *track* suffering.

Rowan had no idea he left a trail of sorrow behind him as bright and clear as painted stones.

Lily dropped her bedroll on the ground next to her sister's and looked around. She didn't see Juliet anywhere. The sun was setting, and by this time her sister would usually have some kind of meal waiting for the two of them. Lily laughed at her own annoyance. She was starting to think like some fifties' husband who expected his wife to have dinner on the table as soon as he got home from work.

She reached out to Juliet and followed the connection between them to the perimeter of camp. Her sister sat atop a small rise that was covered in shin-high grass and dotted with vibrant spring wildflowers. Lily joined her, sitting down next to her in the fragrant grass. They looked out over a vast plain that was so mind-bogglingly large that it seemed to stretch on past the edge of the gathering evening, through the night, and straight on to the next morning. Lily fancied she could see all the way to tomorrow's dawn rising behind this setting sun.

"Look at them run," Juliet said.

An uncountable number of buffalo undulated across the plain like a dark tide of muscle and blood washing over the Ocean of Grass. The pounding of their hooves thrummed through the earth and felt like a heartbeat under Lily's hand.

"Alaric told me about this," Juliet continued quietly. "He said seeing it would open me up so wide that all the hurt inside would just spill out."

Lily realized her sister was crying. She wished she could join her, but her hurt was more complicated than her sister's. It wasn't clean. When Lily did an autopsy on her love for Rowan she saw that most of the evidence pointed at her. And Lily had never been good at feeling one emotion at a time, like pure sadness or utter joy. Her sister had that talent, but not her. Everything Lily felt was tainted with other feelings, and sometimes she wondered if all the complications she put on her emotions kept her from ever really feeling anything. Except once. There was one night when all she had felt was love. Having that single taste just made it worse.

"Thank you for choosing me over Alaric," Lily said. It was the first time they'd talked about it—the first time Lily acknowledged what Juliet had sacrificed for her.

"I couldn't let you die," Juliet replied, wiping at her face.

"Actually, you could have. I'm not your real sister."

Laughter bubbled up through Juliet's tears. "Yeah you are. Only my real sister would drag me all the way out here."

Lily dropped her head and let her shoulder shake with laughter. At least they could still share a laugh, even if Lily couldn't cry.

"Where the heck are we, anyway?" Juliet said, looking around with a puzzled frown.

"Missouri, almost to Kansas," Lily answered, even though that meant nothing to this Juliet.

"It's flat."

"Yeah."

"I mean *really* flat." Juliet shaded her eyes and peered into the tricky twilight. "What's going on down there?"

Lily followed her sister's pointing finger and saw a cluster of buffalo suddenly turn against the tide of their fellows. From between the parting buffalo came a pale, loping figure trotting across the plain.

"That's the pale Woven," Lily said, grabbing her sister's hand and stiffening. She hadn't seen the pale coyote in weeks, and Lily had thought she'd stopped following them.

"What's *that*?" Juliet asked in a shaking whisper.

The pale coyote stopped and came to rest, and a hulking shape that Lily had never seen before came out from between the now-scattering buffalo. It was twice the size of the already large coyote Woven. Its snout was elongated and its ears pointed like a wolf's, but the dark Woven's long forearms ended in what Lily could see were clawed, but still human-like hands. The wolf Woven had a stooped back and slightly shorter hind legs, like a hyena's, and it ran toward the pale coyote on all fours with a strange, rocking canter.

The first word that popped into Lily's mind was *werewolf*.

"I think that's a member of the Pack," Lily whispered in response.

The wolf Woven came to face the coyote Woven and sat back on its hind legs, looking for all the world like they were engaged in a conversation. They didn't sniff each other or circle around, like two normal canines would, but rather they sat very still, neither of them so much as twitching. After what seemed like forever to Lily, but was probably only a minute or two, the pale coyote stood up and went back the way it came. The wolf watched the coyote leave and then trotted casually through the herd of buffalo like it owned them.

Lily looked over at her sister. Juliet's mouth was parted and her eyes unblinking. "What did we just see?" Juliet asked fearfully.

"We need to tell the rest of the tribe," Lily said.

"Were they *mindspeaking*?" Juliet said incredulously.

"I don't know," Lily said, clenching her jaw in anger. "But we're definitely in Pack territory now, and they definitely have more human in them than anyone's been willing to admit."

Lily stormed back to camp, calling in mindspeak for her inner circle to gather around the fire. By the time she got there, she had already relayed what she and Juliet had witnessed.

"I want to know why everyone seemed to leave out the fact that the Pack is half human," Lily demanded.

"They *aren't human*," Dana snapped. "It doesn't matter what they look like."

"Does it matter that a coyote and a wolf just sat down across from each other like they were having a human conversation?" Lily sputtered. "See, that's something that would matter where I come from."

Caleb and Dana shared a tight-lipped look.

"Just say it out loud, you guys," Lily said tiredly.

"Our people have always given human attributes to animals,"

Caleb said in a rare burst of anger. "We don't think of animals the way you do, Lily. We know they're not dumb. They cooperate, they communicate—they do lots of things that humans do. The thing that separates them from us is that we don't eat our dead. We bury them and we mourn them. They don't love their families like we do, or honor their ancestors, and it's an insult to *us* for you to keep saying that they're human."

Lily sighed and ran a hand through her hair, feeling like she'd just stepped into a cultural minefield. "And what about mindspeak? What about using willstones? Regular animals don't do that, only Woven do. Come on, you guys. I know this is a big deal to you, but let's stop with the whole 'they're so different from us' thing, because it isn't helping anymore. The Woven are more like us than they are like animals, whether you like it or not."

"Even the insect Woven? The ones that eat their own offspring?" Dana asked angrily. "No. I won't believe that. And when you see the Hive, you won't believe it either. The Hive's Warrior Sisters look more human than even the Pack does, but the *things* they do—" Dana suddenly broke off with a shiver.

"You've *seen* the Hive with your own eyes?" Lily asked. As far as she could tell, Dana was the only person apart from Rowan and Alaric who had claimed to have actually encountered the Hive.

"Yes," Dana replied. "When I was a child, before I had a willstone. The Workers just look like bees, but the Warrior Sisters—they look almost human. All females. All identical twin sisters. I only saw them once, and I don't know if what I remember is real or if it's a nightmare or I'd show you what we're about to face. I'm hoping it's just a nightmare."

Lily could feel herself losing the sympathy of more and more braves, and she knew that by morning her tribe would be smaller. She saw the two Tristans looking at each other, and then heard her Tristan's voice in her head.

Leave it, Lily. The Hive is off-limits to Outlanders.

I've noticed. These Warrior Sisters have reached mythical proportions in their minds, even though only two or three people claim to have ever even seen them. I don't believe in the bogeyman, Tristan.

But they do. Let it go.

"Why don't we focus on the Pack right now, and fight the Hive when we meet them," her Tristan said calmly.

"No one *fights* the Hive, Tristan," Caleb said. "You just run."

"Well, the Hive isn't here. And we can still prepare for the Pack," the other Tristan said. "They hunt at night just as well as they do during the day. We need to get ready."

Lily stood by the fire, hands on her hips, while everyone else split up and prepared for a fight. Howls rode on the wind as the last bit of light heaved itself over the edge of the horizon.

"Lily?" her Tristan said. She turned and noticed that he was still with her. "Do you want me to stay and guard you while we fight, or do you want Breakfast?" he asked.

"You. No, him," Lily replied, quickly changing her mind. She grinned. "Una would kill me if I sent Breakfast out there to fight something he's never seen before."

"He tends to lock up when he sees a new Woven," he agreed sheepishly. "Only for a second, though. He's getting much better."

"He's had to," Lily said, frowning at the fire. "Do you think I'm wrong about the Woven?"

Tristan thought for a second before replying. "I think you're asking the Outlanders to change what they believe about the Woven, and more importantly, what they believe about themselves. That's a lot. Some of them will do it, some of them won't."

"I'm just trying to find a way to stop the Woven from killing the Outlanders. Trying to eradicate the Woven doesn't work. Lillian taught me that," Lily said, looking down and shaking her head at the irony of it. "But if the Woven and the Outlanders can coexist somehow, Alaric doesn't have to destroy the cities. He told me that the only reason he was thinking of blowing up the cities was because he couldn't fight both them and the Woven. If the Woven stop killing the Outlanders, then Alaric has no reason to attack the cities. The Outlanders wouldn't be trapped." She spread her arms wide to include the huge tracts of land that now lay in darkness. "They could come out here and they would have all this." Lily gave him a wan smile. "Piece of cake, right?"

"If it was easy someone else would have already done it," he said

"And no one has," Lily replied, her brow pinching with dread. "Not on any of the thousands of worlds I've seen. Thousands of other Lilys have tried to solve this same problem and none of them have done it."

"All it takes is one." Tristan touched Lily's shoulder, and she turned to face him. He stood close to her, and his level gaze was full of faith. "It'll be you," he whispered, and tilted his head, kissing her swiftly before leaving to find Breakfast.

Lily stared after him, stuck in the moment. Of course she knew how he felt about her. He was in love with her. The trouble was, she didn't know how she felt about him anymore. There was a hole in her, and what amazed Lily was how big it had gotten. It had started where her heart used to be, and somewhere along the way the hole had eaten her through and through. And now, when she looked inside herself, she saw nothing. Not a good trade for Tristan—all his love and devotion for her big, giant nothing.

Lily shook her head to clear it and sat down next to the fire, reminding herself that she needed to focus. She reached out to her tribe, connecting their minds to one another as if they were spokes on a giant wheel. There were thirty-one braves out there beyond the sphere of firelight, and they needed her strength.

She felt Breakfast take a seat next to her and together they waited through the long night, listening to the mournful howls of the Pack circling just beyond the edge of vision. But the attack never came, and Lily never gave the order for her braves to find the Pack and kill them.

One by one, Lily could feel her braves deciding to leave her. While they sat crouched in the dark, aching to seek out the Pack and slay them, they lashed out at her and accused her of not doing as she said she would. They'd come west to kill Woven, and Lily was denying them that.

A part of her understood. A larger part of her felt betrayed. Knowing that all but a few braves outside of her inner circle of mechanics were going to leave her made Lily ache for someone—anyone—who could understand her. Someone who knew what it was to lead against the majority rule. There was only one person who truly understood what Lily faced. Herself.

Lillian. They all want to leave me, even though what I'm doing is for their own good. Killing the Woven one by one won't solve the problem.

No. It won't, Lily. The Woven reproduce too quickly.

My braves think I'm betraying them, but I'm trying to save them. I feel abandoned. Is that how you feel?

Yes. I understand what you're going through. I know what it is to do something for the good of the many, only to be hated for it. I even know what it is to hate yourself for doing it. I did what I had to in order to get out of the barn because I knew that I couldn't save their world, but I could still save mine. And I did it for people who despise me now.

What did you do, Lillian? How did you get out of the barn?

It is my most shameful moment. It's when I did the one thing I thought I would never do.

. . . I cradle the boy in my lap and use what energy I have left to ease his suffering. It's no use. I'm so weak I can barely hold his emaciated body in my arms, let alone calm his severed and screaming nerves.

River took his arm. The boy howls, screaming that his missing limb burns. I know what it is to burn. I wish I could do it for him. I wish I could do it for all of them. I grit my teeth in frustration and count the clothes on all the bodies around me. If I were to get them to give me all their clothes to burn, would that be enough to fuel me?

Fuel me for what? I can't claim these willstone-less people. I can't make an army out of lambs. I drop my face into my hands and scream along with the boy in my lap. They're all going to die, mutilated and starving in the dark. There's nothing I can do to save any of them.

But they can save me.

I must say good-bye to the person I thought I was, and give up the self-serving image of myself as *good*. Good people die with a smile, allowing the world to disintegrate around them, just so they can protect their precious understanding of themselves. But I will not allow myself to die in this barn just so I can have a hero's ending. I will give up myself in order to save my world—to save Rowan's world.

I make my choice.

"Everyone! Listen to me," I say. "The doctor will be coming back soon, but I have a plan." A few of the more lucid ones turn their eyes to me. I place the boy on the ground and stand. "I'm a witch and I know a way to get out of here."

"If you're a witch, then where is your willstone?" asks one of them.

"I swallowed my stone when they took me. We don't have a lot of time left," I reply.

"I recognize you," another says. "You're the Salem Witch. They said you died in the blast."

"There's no time to explain," I say. "I'm alive because I can do something that no one knows I can I do." I smother the last bit of my humanity. "I can take us all out of here—to another world."

Some of the lambs move away, but most move closer. They don't believe me, but they *want* to, and that might be enough. "Look at me," I say, holding out my bare arms so they can see smooth skin. "Look how unblemished I am. That's because I wasn't here when the blast happened. I was on another world, and I can get you all out of here. I can take you back where I came from."

They shuffle closer, confused. They trust no one, but they also have nothing to lose. I feel the boy touch my ankle and I look down at him. Before River took his arm I told him I couldn't help him—I couldn't even save myself. He looks up at me now, wondering which was the lie. I know I will think of that look on his face for as long as I live. And I must live. I must go back to my world or the same thing that happened here will happen there. I look back up at the lambs and smile brightly, selling my big lie.

"It's easy," I say. "I just need for everyone to join hands and stand around me in a tight group."

They take some encouraging, but all that is required of them is to huddle and they are lambs. They huddle naturally.

"Bare hands, everyone," I say, stripping the makeshift mittens off the ones around me. Some don't have hands, and I amend my order. "I need you all to be touching one another's bare skin in some way. We need to create a circuit of people. Anyone who is left out of the circuit will be left behind."

They understand and obey. I stand in the middle of them, smelling their rank bodies and their rotten breath. They are dead already, I remind myself. At least this way they will only suffer for a few seconds longer.

I've never drained this many, and I have no idea if the energy in their weakened state will be enough to fuel my worldjump, but desperation has a way of silencing doubt. The last person I touch is the boy. His eyes round with disappointment and he tries to shake me off. I don't let him. If I am to eat this sin, I must clean the plate.

"Thank you," I whisper, and then drain the very life from their bodies.

And I reach through the darkness between the worlds, back to my home. The home I must save in order to pay this grisly debt . . .

The sun rose, and Lily found that more than half of her braves had saddled their horses and were preparing to leave her.

"We joined her to fight the Woven, not stand there and stare at them while they circle us," Dana snapped at Caleb while she cinched her saddle around her horse.

"You're a coward. You're afraid of the Hive," he spat back at her.

"As you should be," she countered unabashedly. "Even one sting from a Worker can kill—but they don't always kill you. No. Sometimes they just sting you so you can't move. That's when the Sisters come to carry you off, still alive."

"That's just something grown-ups tell little children to frighten them," Caleb scoffed.

"Is it? You know for sure?" Dana asked. "I've heard that they do. And we don't know what they do with the ones they take, because no one that's been taken by the Hive is ever heard from again."

"Oh, come on! What's next, Dana, a ghost story?" Caleb's face twisted with disgust. "You know, maybe Lily's right. Maybe the Woven aren't as bad as I thought. At least they can count on one another to work as a team."

Dana wheeled her horse to charge at Caleb, and Lily stepped in between, forcing Dana to pull her horse up short.

"Enough. Let them go, Caleb," Lily said, looking over every one of the braves who were about to leave her. They couldn't meet her eyes. They hadn't sworn themselves to Lily, and she couldn't accuse them of oath breaking, but they all knew that's what it was.

"Stop them, Lily," Caleb said in an urgent and low tone. "We can't make it with just a handful of us."

"Listen, Caleb," she said, placing a hand on his wide bicep to calm him. "What I'm trying to do can't be done if I'm surrounded by people who don't believe in me. Let them go."

The rest of Dana's braves mounted up and started to ride off. None of them stopped, and only Dana looked back.

I'm sorry, Lily. I can't go any farther, Dana said in mindspeak.

She was waiting for some kind of absolution. Lily didn't give it because she couldn't lie in mindspeak.

"Don't let the Workers sting you," Dana shouted. "I hear that they don't always decide to kill, but when they do, I know for a fact that they only have to sting you once." She looked directly at Caleb. "*That* I've seen for myself."

Dana turned back around and focused on the road ahead of her.

Caleb heaved a breath. "This will leave only fifteen of us," he said. "Fifteen to get all the way to your California."

"One of those fifteen is Lily," her Tristan said defiantly. He raised his voice. "You think you can make it back to the cities without a witch?" He raised his voice even louder so that those already riding away could hear. "You'll all be dead in a week without her!"

"Tristan," Lily said, reaching out to take him by the arm. He shook her off and stormed away.

"That went well," she muttered to herself, rolling her eyes.

"Give him some time," Caleb said.

"What else can I do? He's pretty much the only one left who believes in me. Even you don't believe in what I'm trying to do," Lily said.

She wasn't accusing Caleb, just stating a fact. Caleb had made it clear that he didn't agree with Lily about the Woven. As far as he was concerned, they were worse than animals and there was no way they'd ever be able to coexist with the Outlanders.

"I don't need to believe you in order to follow you," Caleb replied.

Lily gave him a baffled look as she turned his words over in her head. "Nope, that actually makes no sense, Caleb."

He laughed and looked down at his hands, thinking of a better way to put it. "You could have made those braves stay. You could have *forced* them by taking control of their minds and bodies, but you didn't even think of doing that, did you?"

"Of course not," Lily whispered, remembering how it felt to be paralyzed and thrown in a cage—and remembering that there were still things she wasn't willing to do. "It's wrong."

"The witch I had before I left the Citadel? She used to possess me for *fun*. Just to prove she had power over me," Caleb said. "Alaric has power in those bombs, and he hid them from us so he could use them without putting it to a vote. You're the best leader I've ever had." He paused before adding one more thing. "And you're nothing like Lillian."

Some door that had been shut tight unlocked in Lily, and she leaned her forehead against Caleb's chest. "Why can't Rowan see that?" Lily replied, a sob escaping from her mid-sentence.

Caleb took it in his stride. He let her lean into him, crying tears that seemed to scrape her raw as they came out. He said soothing things that didn't impart any wisdom or change what Lily felt, but that comforted her nonetheless. He talked about how much he missed Elias, and Lily only cried harder. So many had been lost in this war, and she knew the dying wasn't done yet. When Lily finally heaved her last sigh, Caleb looked at her and frowned in thought.

"Not that I'm trying to bring up Rowan and get you crying again," he began cautiously, "but something's always bothered me about how we left things with him."

"Me too," Lily said ironically as she dabbed at her leaky eyes.

"No, what I mean is *how* we got away with you." Caleb picked up a stick and started drawing in the dirt around the fire. "So it was me, Tristan, and *your* Tristan who went to Rowan's tent to get your willstones back. Rowan's tent was in the middle of camp." He drew an X in the middle of a circle. "We woke Rowan up trying to get your willstones from around his neck and he knocked my Tristan unconscious before he was even out of bed. I jumped in and we went at it. Then Rowan knocked me out."

"Yeah. I remember seeing your face," Lily said apologetically.

"We'll get to that in a second," he replied. "I wake up ten minutes later next to my Tristan, who wakes up just after me. The thing is, we're *here* with horses tied up right next to us." Caleb made another X on the outside of the circle of Alaric's camp. "Even if your Tristan had beaten Rowan in two or three punches, how the hell could he have carried us out here by himself in ten minutes? You were unconscious. You couldn't have fueled him, so he would have had to pick me up, carry me, then go back for the other Tristan and carry him."

"Can someone do that in ten minutes?" Lily asked.

"Not alone," Caleb said. "And another thing? Your Tristan didn't have a scratch on him."

"Yeah, I figured he didn't fight at all," Lily said, grimacing. "He obviously doesn't want to say what happened, so I didn't want to ask him in case it's embarrassing."

Caleb frowned and leaned back. "Maybe you're right." He swiped his foot across his crude drawing, erasing it. "Maybe it's best if we just let it go. He got you out. I guess it doesn't matter how."

Caleb left Lily sitting next to the fire. She still felt shaky and strangely elated from crying.

"Hey, Lily? Sorry I blew up like that," her Tristan said, coming up behind her. Lily turned to face him, still wiping her nose, and he saw her tear-streaked face. "What happened?" he asked, his expression darkening. "What did Caleb say to you?"

"Nothing upsetting. I had a good cry, not a bad one," Lily said, giving him a teary smile. She took Tristan's hand and pulled herself up by it. "There were some things I needed to let go of."

He kept her hand in his. "What? What did you let go of?" he asked hopefully.

"That I'm not like Lillian," she said. "I may agree with her, but I'm not going to do things the way she did."

"Good," Tristan said quietly. He looked disappointed, and Lily knew why. He was hoping she'd let go of Rowan.

Lily stretched up on her tiptoes to kiss him on the cheek. The smell of him was so familiar and comforting. His hands on the small of her back eased her closer until she could feel the solid shape of him on the other side of her clothes. For the first time in months she remembered what it was like to kiss him, and how once, long ago and a universe away, it had felt when he'd moved against her and said her name. Lily let her lips rest against his skin longer than a friend would, and then spun around and left him.

But Lily didn't get the chance to decide how she felt about him. Just days later, her tribe left Pack territory and encountered the Hive.

CHAPTER
15

L ILY HEARD THE HIVE LONG BEFORE SHE SAW THEM.
It started as an anxious static in the air. The remaining braves slowed their horses and shared puzzled looks. Although still faint, the vastness of the sound was almost like a waterfall in the distance— low, steady, and enormously powerful. Then the sound grew until the buzzing shook the little bones in Lily's head. The horses shied and stamped their feet as Lily and her braves craned their necks in all directions across the rippling grass of the plains, trying to find the source of the buzz. It seemed to come from everywhere.

"Look!" Caleb shouted, pointing at a smudge of pewter-colored fog on the horizon.

"That can't be," Una mumbled. She tugged on her spooked horse's reins and squinted. The darkness grew, creeping across the blue dome of the wide sky in a line. No lightning touched down. No funnel cloud announced a tornado. The unnatural fog flew against the wind. "It *is* the Hive," she breathed, awe and fear immobilizing her face.

Lily felt hands around her waist, snatching her off her horse. "Fire," her Tristan said in her ear as he placed her numb body on the ground. "You need to build a fire."

There was nowhere to run, nowhere to hide. The gentle breeze sighed through the grass, turning it over and flashing the light side of the blades against the dark in teasing ripples. Its placid beauty taunted them. There wasn't a tree, a rock, or a river in sight. The open plain left them as exposed as if they were in a raft on a becalmed ocean.

"What do I burn? There's no wood," Lily said, holding her hands out uselessly.

"Burn the grass," Caleb ordered as he dismounted. "Light it all on fire if you have to." He turned to the remaining braves and addressed them. "Everyone get off your horses and set them loose. They'll only slow you down in this fight, and they'll probably just die under you anyway."

Juliet steadied Lily's hands while she struck at her flint. "Calm down."

Lily looked up at her sister, and her voice came out wispy and weak. "I think I've killed us all."

"We're not dead yet. Breakfast! Hurry and help," she said, yanking up what hunks of yellowing grass the sea of green around them offered, and laying them in a pile in front of Lily.

Breakfast unsheathed his dagger and started hacking his way through bundles of grass. "Here," he said, handing Juliet an extra knife. His face was grim and his mouth set in a line.

"We'll keep gathering as much fuel as we can, and you keep giving us strength, okay?" Juliet said. Her big brown eyes were level and bracing. Lily nodded, focusing her panic into purpose.

"Stay upwind of the fire. I don't have any way to contain it," she said, and then turned her attention to the blaze already building at her feet.

Lily connected herself to the fourteen willstones awaiting her power. She drew in a breath, and the wind followed. The buzzing of the nearing Hive was drowned out by Lily's shrieking witch wind. Licks of fire caught in the underbrush and the blaze spread out astonishingly fast. She gathered the heat—taking it, changing it, and then feeding it into the unlocked willstones of her braves.

A column of witch wind threw her into the air with a clap of thunder. Lily felt the physical sensations of all her braves as they raced toward the Hive ahead of the wildfire, but brightest and clearest among them was her Tristan. She let her mind nudge against his and he welcomed her in, opening himself to her so she could share his body. She felt his muscle and skin wrap around her. His hands flexed, and Lily felt the grip of his knives in them. They both reveled in the Gift, sharing the thrill with each other as Lily beat back the temptation to take him over completely. She wilted under the urge that ran through her like lust, and for just a moment she felt Tristan shy away from her with fear.

Please, Lily. Don't.

I swear, I won't.

Lily calmed herself and waited for the craving to pass. The only other person she'd shared this depth of sensation with had been Rowan, and Lily realized that by choosing Tristan to shelter her consciousness during the battle she had made him her new head mechanic. He seized the honor by pulling ahead of the other braves and leading the charge against the Hive.

They entered the swarm at a dead run. Sheer speed killed the first line of Workers on impact, but the Hive adjusted quickly and soon Lily felt the brush of furry bodies and the flutter of delicate wings against Tristan's cheek. She suddenly felt a sharp stab on one of her brave's throats. Pain and adrenaline shot through him. His heart pumped three times and stopped.

Lily felt his death and screamed. She sent a gust of searing-hot witch wind into the swarm—scalding her own warriors, but more importantly, singeing the edges of the Workers' wings. They looked just like normal bees and their delicate wings were just as vulnerable to fire. Workers dropped out of the air by the thousands. Behind the front line of falling Worker bees, Lily saw larger shapes alighting on the battlefield and moving toward her braves. They were too far away from her Tristan for Lily to see them clearly yet, but she could make out the way they moved. The Warrior Sisters ran up to the front lines with a hopping, gliding motion that reminded Lily vaguely of an ostrich.

The Hive regrouped quickly against Lily's scorching witch wind and sent the Workers out in thick clumps. The Workers on the outside of the tight balls of bee-bodies still fell from the air in droves, but the ones on the inside were able to land. The braves swatted at them, killing many, but in moments every inch of their skin was crawling with Workers. Lily sent energy coursing into her warriors. She thickened their skin to make them nearly impervious to the little stingers of the Workers. The Workers couldn't penetrate deep enough to inject their toxin into the braves' bloodstream. But sting after sting kept coming and finally the venom left on the surface of the skin started to eat its way in through the protection Lily supplied. Two more braves died as the Workers finally managed to sink their stingers in.

Lily needed to give her braves more strength—she needed to find a way to keep the Workers from stinging at all. She had to burn. She heard Breakfast's voice in her head.

But there's no stake. There will be nothing to hold you down in the fire.

I'll hold myself down, Breakfast.

Lily positioned herself over the raging brush fire and dove down into the flames. Her skin began to burn, and she shrieked angrily at her own pain. She dug her fingers into the charred earth, gripping the ground to keep herself anchored there despite what her reflexes were urging her to do, and sucked heat into her smoke-colored willstone.

A moment of silence halted all motion on the battlefield, and for a heartbeat everything was still. Then a boom resounded across the burning prairie as a beam of light shot out of Lily and into the wheel of hurricane clouds above. Power pulsed across the blazing grass and the Worker bees were swept back. Her braves paused for a moment in ecstasy, drawing in a deep draft of pure power, and launched themselves at the Warrior Sisters as they entered the fray.

Through her Tristan's eyes, Lily saw her first Warrior Sister head-on.

Her upper body was shaped like a woman's and she had unnervingly human hands, but her legs were too long and they tapered at the bottom into insect barbs instead of feet. She had thick thighs and her knees were on the back, like those of an ostrich or a grasshopper, explaining her strange gait and breathtaking speed. The Sister's skin was vaguely yellow and covered in plates of shiny black armor. As the Sister neared, Lily could see that the armor was a part of her, and it grew out of her skin in an exoskeleton.

Her head was the most disturbing part of her. She had a long stalk for a neck and her skull was ovoid, hairless, and topped with huge, multifaceted eyes. Her mouth was a jumble of tubes that was framed with a pair of shortened legs that brushed her face and constantly cleaned ash off her iridescent, alien eyes. Her head twitched and swiveled on her stalk-neck in blindingly fast and jerky motions. Lily got the sense that the Sister could see in a complete circle around her. She had no blind spot—not below or behind or above.

The Sister was over ten feet tall and she strode toward Lily's Tristan, her enormous black-veined wings vibrating irritably as she tucked them behind her. Those human hands of hers unwound something she had wrapped around her narrow waist. It was a whip that was tipped in barbs. She unfurled the whip in one hand as she neared and ran her other hand across the small of her back, which came back covered in vaguely golden ichor. She transferred the ichor to the barbs at the end of the whip.

She milked herself for venom, Lily.

I saw, Tristan. Everyone, listen—don't let the Sisters catch you with the ends of their whips! Cut them off if you can!

As Lily sent out her warning to all her braves the Sister spun her whip over her head and cracked it at Tristan. He dove to the side, narrowly escaping the stinging cat-o'-nine-tails she wielded. She reversed the direction of the whip and sent it back at him, but he wove his way inside the arc of her lash and stuck his blade between the plates of her exoskeleton.

The Sister twitched as she died. Three more Sisters dropped from the sky and a swarm of Workers zeroed in to attack Tristan in concert. Lily heard no spoken commands from the Sisters or the Workers, but they fought as one.

They are all connected. The Hive has one mind and it fights as an organism.

Lily didn't know if the thought was hers, one of the Tristans', Una's, or everyone's, but she sent it out to all her braves. If the Hive fought as one, so must they. She pulled her single consciousness out of her Tristan and instead imagined herself as plural, like a tapestry of many threads. Lily let go of her sense of *I*, of being one person, and became *They.*

They moved into a circle and focused first on becoming fire. They allowed the fire to engulf them, but fire would not kill them—it could only fuel them. The Workers died in droves, falling off their skin as husks of blackened carbon, and the Sisters cringed for a moment before diving back into the flames with Lily's They.

They cut through the Sisters—charred bodies falling around

them and piling up, but more came. Always more. They lost one, two, then three threads. They howled and wept with every loss of Themselves. The whips cracked and the Workers flew into the fire to die without hesitation. Wave after wave. Sting after sting. The wildfire moved on, but They were pinned down by the bodies of Workers and Warrior Sisters everywhere—thousands of bodies.

They lost one more thread—an absence unlike any other—and Lily pulled herself out of the tapestry.

Tristan!

No answer.

"Tristan!" Lily screamed, but only a thin wail came out of her.

She heard a whip crack and felt the lash across her back. Hot and numb, the venom seeped into her blood. Lily could see Sisters swooping down to pick up her loved ones and fly off with them. She saw Juliet, Breakfast, Una, Caleb, and the other Tristan getting hauled up into the air.

Her Tristan, her best friend, was not among them.

She felt nothing—not hands holding her nor the temperature changing nor the wind rushing past—but she saw the ground get smaller and farther away as she was lifted off her stomach and flown upward. The black battlefield below still smoked. Everything went dark.

Carrick saw the smoke from miles away. Then he felt the thunder in the ground. A prairie fire was stampeding the buffalo.

Carrick didn't feel fear often, but he felt it now. There was no high ground to climb, no river to put between him and tide of hooves and horns, and he'd lost his connection with Lillian when he followed Rowan over the mountains. Strength from his witch would not avail him, anyway. Neither would cleverness or high ground or any river but one of the great ones, for that matter. Surviving a stampede came down to luck. Either the buffalo came your way or they didn't.

Carrick could guess who had set the fire. Lily and her tribe must have needed to fight something. Something huge.

Rowan was ahead of him—out of direct sight—but not so far away that Carrick couldn't clearly distinguish his brother's track lying directly over Lily's. After maintaining a nearly inhuman pace, Rowan had caught up with her. He'd pushed himself over the mountains and across the plains with what seemed to Carrick to be a suicidal single-mindedness and now Rowan was only a few hours behind Lily and her tribe. Carrick was only a few hours behind Rowan and his endurance was at its limits.

Carrick stood in his stirrups, trying to see what enemy could be dire enough that Lily's tribe would risk a prairie fire to stop it. All he could see was smoke rimming the horizon, and the air rippling like water over the grass.

He saw a figure detach itself from the heat-haze. It wasn't the front line of the stampeding herd yet, although that was sure to be coming soon. It was Rowan, riding like hell, and heading straight for him. Carrick pulled up on the reins and wheeled his horse around. The horse was smart enough to not need any whipping, and reached a flat-out run in a matter of seconds.

Glancing over his shoulder wouldn't help, Carrick knew that, but he couldn't stop himself. Rowan was gaining him, but the stampede was gaining on Rowan. The ground shook as if to break. The pounding filled the air like a solid wall of noise—something felt as much as heard. Carrick's insides rattled against his bones, and his teeth clacked in his head as the horse under him galloped in panic. The pounding in the ground was joined by a strange buzzing in the air. Carrick glanced back again and nearly lost his seat. He eased back on the reins and tried to control his frenzied mount.

There were *things* in the air above Rowan. Flying things that

Carrick had never seen before, but he could guess what they were from the stories his father had told him.

The Hive.

Rowan slashed at the air with one arm and clung to his horse's reins with the other, trying to fight off the Warrior Sisters who harried him from above. Carrick turned to face forward in his saddle and let the reins go with a terror that bordered on blindness.

First he felt the buzzing of the Workers' wings on the back of his neck, and then two pairs of impossibly strong hands grabbed his arms and tore him from his horse's back. Carrick didn't know if he screamed or not as the Sisters hauled him up into the air. The ground shrank away from him, his neck wrenching painfully as he was jerked into the sky. He tried to right himself, but the force of the Sisters' ascent was too much to fight.

Staring down as the ground rushed away from him, Carrick saw the green grass beneath him turn into a sea of ruddy brown bodies as the herd of buffalo swept across the plain. Dust rose up in great plumes bearing the smell of churned earth, blood, and musky hide. Smoke from the fire joined the dust to blot out the sun. The Sisters flew him west through the murky air. The thunder of the stampede was drowned out by the buzzing of the Hive all around him as they flew.

Out of the corner of Carrick's eye he saw Rowan's body dangling between two Sisters. Rowan's eyes were shut and his body was limp. Carrick couldn't tell if he was alive or dead.

The smell of flowers was all around her.

Lily opened her eyes and saw green stems and bright blossoms waving gently in the breeze. Her raw skin was smeared with ash and her clothes were singed tatters, clinging to the dried scabs on her body. She wondered how long she had been unconscious. She saw that her burns were already healing somewhat. Had it been a whole day? Two days?

Lily licked her lips and realized that someone must have poured water in her mouth because it was cleaned of ash and it felt damp. She concentrated on the last vestiges of venom in her veins and realized that it had not only knocked her out and kept her immobile, it had eased her pain and kept her injury from festering. A chemical cocktail that complicated had to have been engineered.

She heard groaning, and pushed herself up onto her elbows. Just next to her was Juliet. Lily sat up and found Una, already sitting upright with a blank and devastated look on her face. Caleb was just pulling himself up to standing and Tristan was beside him, still clutching a dagger. Lily looked frantically to her other side and found the source of the groaning. It was Breakfast. He flopped onto his back and grabbed his head.

"Lily," the other Tristan said, coming toward her. He staggered to Lily and helped her sit all the way up.

"He's dead. My Tristan is dead," she whispered, clutching at the other Tristan's hand.

He nodded and dropped his head. Lily looked around her in a daze, too numb to feel anything just yet. They were in the middle of a field of flowers. The sun was bright and the sky was as blue as a robin's egg. Lily could taste the ocean on the air. She lifted her face into the salty breeze. It was coming from the west. The ocean was to the *west*.

The other Tristan—now the only Tristan—and Lily helped each other stand, and then bent down to help Juliet up to her feet. Lily saw Caleb, Breakfast, and Una already standing and facing west.

The sun was just tipping down into a late afternoon and it hung over the walls of an immense city. Flowers were every-where—pouring over the sides of the walls and carpeting the tops of every building that soared up behind the colossal wall.

"This is no city I've ever been to," Caleb said.

"That's because you've never been this far west," Una said.

"No one has ever been this far west," Juliet said.

"Are you sure Lillian didn't know about this?" Tristan asked.

"Of course I'm sure!" Juliet looked scared.

"Lillian didn't know," Lily said, holding up a hand before an argument could break out. "If she did, she would have sent an army out here to conquer it. She's not the kind of person who likes having anything beyond her control."

Everyone heard the logic in what Lily said and dropped that possibility. The truth was, if either Lillian or Alaric knew that there was another city all the way across the continent, they would have tried to get here long ago.

"But how could this have been kept a secret?" Breakfast asked skeptically.

"I don't know," Lily mumbled. "But I bet it wasn't easy."

She staggered forward, staring at what shouldn't be there. The perfume of the flowers being crushed beneath her soot-blackened feet sweetened the soft breeze. The sky was the exact shade of blue that Rowan imagined in his dreams of California, and the sun shone with the same sparkling golden light.

"That's the Pacific Ocean," Lily said. "That's impossible. We hadn't even made it through Kansas." She heard her voice catch, and realized that she was crying.

"The Hive must have flown us over half the country to get us here," Una said.

Lily couldn't start mourning Tristan now or she knew she'd fall apart. She didn't really believe it yet, anyway. A part of her kept whispering that it was impossible. Tristan couldn't be dead because she couldn't imagine a world without him. Lily swiped angrily at the tears streaming down her face and read what was written over the main gate of this impossibly beautiful Shangri-la.

WELCOME TO BOWER CITY.

CAST OF CHARACTERS

Ahanu: Outlander girl who tried to tame a Woven

Alaric Windrider: known as the Sachem, he became the leader of the Outlanders after his wife and baby daughter froze outside the Citadel

Anukit Carrick's abusive father who worked as bait man for his tribe

Caleb Crow an Outlander who is friends and stone kin with Rowan, one of Lily's claimed; Elias was his partner

Carrick: an Outlander who once kidnapped and tortured Lily; formerly Gideon's right-hand man, now working for Lillian; Rowan's half brother

Chenoa Longshadow: An Outlander scientist Lillian is desperate to put on trial; she was a professor at Lillian's school, and the driving force behind developing the nuclear bombs

Councilman Bainbridge: one of the ruling council of Salem

Councilman Roberts: the longest-serving Salem councilman

Councilman Thomas Danforth: leader of the Salem Council, father of Gideon

Councilman Wake: a member of the ruling council of Salem

Dana: an Outlander elder who Lily claimed while freeing her from Lillian's prison; she is a tanner and has a young son

Dr. Rosenthal: superintendent of Lily's school system in Salem, Massachusetts

Esmeralda: ran a safe house for Outlanders in Salem; betrayed Lily to Gideon out of jealousy

Gavin: a young page and possible mechanic who works for Lillian

Gideon Danforth: Lillian's head mechanic after Rowan left and a commander in her army; Lillian sent him to his death after he kidnapped Lily and allowed her to be tortured

Hakan: Outlander scientist involved in Chenoa's nuclear bomb project

Hans Krebs: scientist who determined the citric acid cycle

James Proctor: Lily's absent father, who lives in Richmond

Juliet Proctor: Lily's and Lillian's sister; Lily's Juliet is a registered EMT who attends Boston University; and Lillian's Juliet turned away from her sister after Lillian went too far in her quest to stamp out Chenoa and her friends in the scientist trials

Keme: Outlander scientist involved in Chenoa's nuclear bomb project

Lillian: the Salem Witch, also known as the Lady of Salem; she is the tyrannical ruler of Salem who, after falling victim to a deadly illness, pulled Lily into her universe to take her place

Lily Proctor: a seventeen-year-old from Salem, Massachusetts; after Lillian pulls her through to an alternate universe, she discovers that her crippling allergies are actually signs that she is a powerful Crucible and Witch

Mary: Rowan and Carrick's mother; now deceased, this beautiful Outlander was originally married to Anoki, and then left him to marry River Fall

Michael Snowshower: an Outlander doctor and scientist who gave Chenoa and her team medicine for dying Outlander children; Lillian's breaking this deal drove Juliet away

Miranda Clark: a sophomore girl from Lily's high school who Tristan hooked up with, breaking Lily's heart

Mr. Carnello: also called Mr. Carn; Lily's senior-year physics teacher

Red Leaf: Breakfast's alternate, who is studying to be the new shaman

Riley: a teen boy who lives in an underground subway outside of Richmond

River Fall: an Outlander doctor and Rowan's father; he was the first person hanged by Lillian

Rowan Fall: also known as Lord Fall, this Outlander was originally Lillian's true love and head mechanic; after Lillian killed his father, he ran away to join Alaric and eventually fell in love with and was claimed by Lily

Scot: a teen boy from Lily's high school who almost killed her in an attempt to take advantage of her at a party

Special Agent Simms: the FBI agent in charge of Lily's case

Stuart "Breakfast" Doyle: Tristan's friend and Una's boyfriend, he becomes one of Lily's claimed

Tristan Corey: Lily's best friend and first love, Rowan's best friend and stone kin; although Tristan was never claimed by Lillian, Lily has befriended and claimed both versions of him

Una Stone: a teen girl in Lily's poetry class; she is Tristan's friend and Breakfast's girlfriend, and becomes one of Lily's claimed

ACKNOWLEDGMENTS

I'd like to thank Jean Feiwel at Feiwel and Friends for her faith in this series, my coeditor Holly West for her keen eye and diligence, and Mollie Glick, my long-suffering agent. Mollie and I were both pregnant while I was writing this book, which made for some pretty interesting pregnancy-brain conversations that mostly centered around one of us forgetting what we were going to say. Big kisses for my family back home. For Kelly Gryncel Davis—you fought the Big C like a goddess, and you will be sorely missed. For my husband and baby girl—one of you was a huge help, and the other made me have to take about a million bathroom breaks. I'm not pointing any fingers, but you know who you are. I love you both with all my heart.

LOOK OUT FOR THE
BREATHTAKING FINALE OF
THE WORLDWALKER TRILOGY

COMING SOON!

THE STORY BEGINS IN

TRIAL BY FIRE

JOSEPHINE ANGELINI